PRAISE FOR *MIDNIGHT SUN* AND AMANDA HARTE

"Ms. Harte's beautiful story of life in 1909 Alaska will bring you hours of reading pleasure. . . . She gives you three stories in one in this SPLENDID book. Don't miss this rising star! 4 1/2 BELLS!"

—*Bell, Book and Candle*

"Amanda Harte is a new star on the horizon!"

—Elaine Barbieri

"Amanda Harte has taken on the rip-roaring 1909 Alaskan frontier in high style in *Midnight Sun*. Doctor Amelia Sheldon has her hands full at her new post in Gold Landing . . . but she handles all with courage and grace. Banish the dark of a long Alaskan winter with a season of miracles. Enjoy *Midnight Sun*!"

—Eileen Charbonneau, RITA Award–winning author
of *Rachel Lemoyne*

WHITE-HOT KISS

"This is so much more than one building. It's what I worked for during all those years of school." As her eyes met his, the warmth that he had kindled earlier began to grow. "I owe it to you."

He dropped her hand but did not move away. "If you mean it, how about a real thank you?" And he pulled her into his arms, drawing her close to him. For a second they stood there, their arms entwined, their eyes saying what their lips dared not. Then William lowered his mouth to hers.

This was not the gentle, exploratory kiss he had given her after the Fourth of July celebration. While that one had been warm and comforting, this one was white-hot, a flame burning out of control. Wild and passionate, the kiss was the culmination of all the looks she and William had shared throughout the day. And, oh, how wonderful it felt!

MIDNIGHT SUN

AMANDA HARTE

LEISURE BOOKS NEW YORK CITY

*For Lois Buhrmaster Seyse, whose tales of Alaska introduced me to the midnight sun. If I were writing a dictionary, one entry would be easy: **friend** see Lois.*

A LEISURE BOOK®

April 1999

Published by

Dorchester Publishing Co., Inc.
276 Fifth Avenue
New York, NY 10001

ISBN 0-8439-4503-6

MIDNIGHT SUN

Chapter One

April 1909

There were two things on earth that William Gunning hated, and rain was one of them. It wasn't the precipitation he minded, although at this time of the year it was little more than liquid ice. What he hated was the effect it had on his men. It was still a mystery to him how men who spent their daylight hours deep within the earth were aware of the weather on the surface, but there was no denying the evidence. When the rain persisted, the amount of ore they mined decreased. And this spring neither he nor they could afford that.

William frowned as he stared at the papers in front of him. It didn't take a fancy accountant or an overpriced lawyer like Abe Ferguson to tell him he would be in trouble if the rain didn't stop soon. He had taken a chance by sinking the first shaft deep into the frozen earth, defying the conventional wisdom that the only gold in Alaska was in the streams, but what choice had there been? The river gold was gone. If he hadn't financed the mine, Gold Landing would have died the swift death of a hundred other gold-rush towns, taking men's dreams and, in all too many cases, their lives, along with the last of the sparkling nuggets.

As the rain beat against the windowpane and a gust of wind set it to rattling, William looked up. There had been a time when he had found the sound of rain comforting, but that was years and miles ago. Now rain meant trouble.

The men who worked his mine traded the promise of instant riches for lesser wages, but at least they had steady pay. This spring, with production dwindling almost daily, even that was in jeopardy. The vein they were mining would take another month—maybe two—to exhaust. And then? If the exploratory drilling didn't uncover another gold-laden vein soon, he would be forced to close the mine.

Damn it all! He couldn't let that happen.

The sound of the front door opening was as unwelcome as the rain.

"Did you hear about the new doctor?" Alex Fielding stripped off his sodden parka, then flopped into the chair nearest the cast-iron stove.

William glared at the intruder. People told him that he and Alex resembled each other enough to be brothers rather than cousins. He disagreed. Oh, they might both have brown hair and gray eyes and be six feet tall, but the similarities ended there. For one thing, Alex wore a full beard like most Alaskan men, while William battled with a razor each morning. For another, Alex was stretched out in that chair as if he didn't have a care in the world. He would never spend his days—or his nights—worrying about keeping a town alive. Alex lived for the moment, and judging by the grin that threatened to split his face, at this particular moment he'd found something to tickle his fancy.

William frowned at the production reports. If Alex thought he needed a distraction, he was wrong. What William needed was another strike.

"Well, did you? Did you hear the news?" His cousin was nothing if not persistent, a trait that William had had cause to rue on more than one occasion. This, it appeared, was going to be one of those occasions.

William waited a moment longer before he answered. "I heard Ben's assistant came on the boat, but it was raining so hard no one could see what she looked like."

The arrival of a newcomer was a major social event in Gold Landing, as in most Alaskan towns. For weeks in advance there would be speculation, occasionally even fierce debates, over the future resident's age, appearance, religion and political views, not to mention, if both the newcomer and the speculator were female, the size and state of her wardrobe. When the boat arrived, the majority of the town's 350 residents would just happen to be somewhere in the vicinity of the landing, ostensibly performing some highly important task, but in reality hoping to be the first to catch a glimpse of the object of their speculation.

Unfortunately, this time Mother Nature had deprived Gold Landing's citizens of one of their favorite pastimes. The rain had been so heavy that when the new doctor had disembarked, Ella Roberts, the schoolteacher who had agreed to let her share her home, had whisked her into her buggy without so much as an introduction. Moreover, or so William had heard, the doctor had worn a hooded cloak and had kept her head down. Privately William suspected that the demure posture owed less to the rain than to the woman's need to hide her face. Undoubtedly the reason she had become a doctor was that she was as homely as a moose, and no one in Philadelphia was desperate enough to marry her.

"You mean you haven't heard?" Alex's voice rose a few notes in surprise, reminding William it was unusual for him to be unaware of a newcomer to Gold Landing, especially when that newcomer was a single woman. The truth was, if he hadn't been preoccupied with the mine and that damnable rain, William would have been at the levee, welcoming the town's newest resident. One of the few faults he could find with Alaska was the overwhelming shortage of women. There were times when a man craved feminine companionship, and not just the type Gloria's doves provided.

"Go ahead. Spit it out, Alex. I can see you're bursting to tell me about the good doctor." William shoved the papers aside as he moved from behind his desk to reach for the coffeepot. Maybe an infusion of the hot liquid would help clear his mind. "It would be a damned shame if you had an apoplectic fit and turned into her first patient."

"That's just it." Alex waved his hand in an expansive gesture. "I wouldn't be her first patient. It's all anyone can talk about ever since Emil Johnson came in, telling everybody how she saved Martha's life, and the baby's, too." Alex's face grew sober as he retold the story. "They were both dying. The baby had even stopped breathing." When William did no more than drain the last of his coffee, Alex continued, "Emil said he's never seen anything like it. It was a miracle.''

A miracle. Gold Landing could use one of those, but not in the form of a doctor. If the Lord was doling out miracles, a nice, big gold strike was what the town needed.

William reached for the coffeepot a second time. "What does Ben say about it?" he asked, one brow raised quizzically. "Was it a miracle or just good luck?"

Alex shrugged his shoulders. "Who knows? Ben was drunk again, and the new doc had to go alone."

"So that's why Ben didn't join the poker game last night. I wondered." Ben's periodic drinking sprees were no secret. Though not frequent, they happened often enough that they no longer qualified as news, and William suspected he was one of the few people in Gold Landing who still wondered what precipitated them.

He refilled his cup and poured one for Alex. Placing the mugs on the desk, he smiled at his cousin, his gray eyes no longer resembling the Tanana River on a cold October day. "Is there more news about the miracle-working midwife?"

He didn't really care. Doctors had never been an important part of William's life. When he was a child, his family could not have paid the fee, and now that money was no longer a concern, he had no need of medical care, for his health was the envy of Gold Landing. His men, it was true, called Dr. Ben for the inevitable accidents that befell miners—pinched fingers, gouges from an ax—but, thank God, there had been no real emergencies. Still, it was obvious that Alex had a need to tell his story, and the sooner he was finished, the sooner he'd leave William alone.

"Sure is. Emil says she's one good-looking gal."

William hooted. "A lot Emil knows. That wife of his has no meat on her bones."

"Not everyone shares your taste in females." Alex spat out the last word, turning it into an epithet. "Now, do you want to hear about her or not?"

The wind howled again. Perhaps it was only his imagination, but William thought it sounded less ferocious.

"Do I have a choice?"

The younger man seemed oblivious to William's sarcasm, for he continued, "She's a real lady. Nice, not snooty. Emil says you'd never know she was a rich Easterner." Alex swallowed his coffee, then continued. "Why, she even cooked dinner for him. A swell meal, too, not pork and beans."

"I think someone's been pulling your leg." William leaned back in his chair. "Ben told us about her last week. He says she's a Philadelphia socialite who came to Alaska as a lark. Just what we need!" William snorted in disgust. "Ben should have known better."

When Alex started to protest, William silenced him with a glare. "The man was definitely soused the day he decided to hire a female. But it won't be a problem for long. I give her less than a month before she turns tail and heads back."

As Alex stifled a yawn, William pulled out his watch, his fingers lingering for an extra moment on the large nugget that he wore as a fob. It was later than he'd thought.

"Emil says she's not like that," Alex protested. "Why, if Karen wouldn't be spitting mad, I'd go to Dr. Ben's office today to see her."

William's chair creaked as he leaned farther back. "Karen's got you wrapped around her little finger, and she knows it. Why else would you be working at night? Just so you can spend the days building her the cabin she wants. Women!" William shook his head as though dismissing the fairer sex. "It's still a mystery to me how you've escaped so far, my friend, but your time is coming as surely as the sun sets in December."

It was a familiar refrain. Ever since he had become engaged, Alex had urged his cousin toward matrimony, pointing out that no woman in her right mind would object to being Mrs. William Gunning, when the title brought not just the state of wedded bliss but a more than ample share of worldly goods with which to be endowed. Yet, despite the subtle and not so subtle ploys of the handful of eligible women of Gold Landing, William had remained single.

"Your time is coming," Alex repeated.

William just laughed. But the laughter ended when Alex

13

left and he returned to his ledgers. Two cups of coffee hadn't changed the figures or provided any inspiration. An hour later, when every attempt to concentrate on his paperwork had proved futile, William shook his head in disgust. Quickly changing into overalls, he headed for the mine. A few hours of hard labor would clear his brain, and then he would find the other relief he needed in June Woods's arms.

As he left the office, William smiled. The sun had come out, and that god-awful rain had stopped. Maybe now the mine's production would increase. Maybe there really would be a miracle. Maybe he would find what they all needed: a new lode.

He strode briskly down River Street. When the town had been laid out, there'd been only two streets: Main and River. The town's primary institutions, its church, hotel and store, had been erected on Main, where the wealthier residents had quickly snatched up the higher-priced lots, leaving River Street for newcomers and commercial properties. As for the other side of the river, that was reserved for the ne'er-do-wells and the Athapaskans, the formerly nomadic Indian tribe that had discovered the advantage of permanent settlements.

Although most people preferred Main Street, William liked River, and had built the mine office there next to Sam Baranov's sawmill. The whine of the saws and the smell of freshly cut wood might annoy the people who lived farther down the street in the half dozen small log cabins and the two-story boardinghouse, but to William they were a sign of all that was good about Gold Landing. They were proof that the town was alive and growing.

He turned left onto Second Street, heading toward the river and his mine. William descended into the shaft that he knew as well as the rooms of his house, ducking his head as the tunnel grew progressively lower. Though many men hated being deep within the earth, William was not one of them. He had a healthy respect for the earth, but he also viewed mining as a challenge, pitting his skills against the inexorable forces of Mother Nature, wresting her treasures from her. And as with every other challenge he had ever faced, he was determined that he would emerge the victor.

When he reached the end of the tunnel, he heard the rhythmic thud of picks hitting rock and dirt. He also heard men's voices.

"I say we owe Dr. Ben a drink," Jake Bolton announced.

Chet Wing chuckled. "Damned right. We sure as hell don't need no lady doctor, but if she's as purty as Emil says, she's gonna make some man here a mighty fine wife."

Her again. William wondered how long it would be before the new doctor ceased to be the town's primary topic of conversation.

"Hell. If we put it about that we had a midwife here, maybe we could get other women to come to Gold Landing." Jake sounded serious as he made the suggestion.

"Brides for all of us."

"I could raise a glass to that."

Brides. A nice thought. But first they needed gold.

It wasn't the first mistake Amelia Sheldon had ever made, but it just might be the worst. Amelia pummeled her pillow, trying to find a comfortable position. By all rights, she ought to be exhausted. The journey to Alaska had drained what little energy had remained after final exams, and her first full day in Gold Landing had been a long one, ending only as the sun began to rise. Yet now when she had the opportunity, sleep eluded her, driven away by her anger.

She might as well dress and do something useful. Amelia pulled a clean white shirtwaist and her navy skirt from the wardrobe.

The unfortunate part was, she had no one to blame but herself. Her family and friends had all warned her, telling her Alaska was no place for a woman. It was a frozen piece of ground inhabited by little more than moose and mosquitoes, or so Lydia Sheldon had told her daughter. It was most certainly not an appropriate home for the gently reared second daughter of one of Philadelphia's most illustrious families.

But Amelia had not listened. From the time she first saw

them in print, those three words had seduced her, promising her heart's desire. And so she had come. "Physician seeks assistant." There had been more, the lure of a junior partnership at the end of a year, the possibility of a full partnership a year later. That was why she had endured the interminable classes, the dreary labs and the frequently frustrating nights in the wards. That was why she had undertaken the almost endless train journey across the continent and the weeks in that pitching boat as she traveled north to Alaska. That was why she was living in a town where dogs outnumbered humans, a town so primitive her mother would have swooned from horror. It would all be worth it, for she would be a doctor, a real doctor, albeit an assistant.

An assistant. *Ha!* Amelia gave her petticoat ties an angry tug. The man might have advertised for an assistant, but what he wanted was a midwife. That had been apparent from the moment she had met Benjamin J. Taylor, the drunk and slovenly creature who was Gold Landing's only excuse for a physician. Oh, he had magnanimously told her she could treat all the female ailments, but he left no doubt that the "real" work—from bandaging a sprained ankle to investigating the causes of lung diseases—was his domain. When she had protested, he told her that men—true Alaskan men—didn't want a woman treating them.

A midwife! Amelia shuddered as she fastened the back of her shirtwaist to the skirt hooks. If she had known that was his intention, she would have saved herself a long and exceedingly tedious journey. She could have remained in Philadelphia, for there was no shortage of openings for midwives there, if that was what she wanted to do.

But Dr. Ben—as she had learned the townspeople called him—had advertised for an assistant. When he had responded positively to her application, she had been so blinded by excitement that she forgot her cardinal rule to consider all possibilities. And so she could blame no one but herself for her folly.

She wielded her brush with more energy than normal as she arranged her dark brown hair into its customary pompadour,

16

frowning at her reflection all the while. For the first time in many, many years, sensible, levelheaded Amelia Sheldon had failed to think before acting. She had let her emotions sway her, and look where that had brought her. Instead of curing mankind's ailments, she would have the opportunity to do no more than deliver babies in a soggy Alaskan town, working for a man who appeared to be drunk more often than not. It would be hell on earth, a constant reminder of dreams that would never come true and of the single greatest failure of her life.

"Miss Sheldon! Miss Sheldon!" A woman pounded on the door, her voice harsh with fear as she shouted. "We need you!"

Amelia ran downstairs to open the door.

"Come quick!" The woman was three or four inches shorter than Amelia's own five and a half feet, with light blue eyes and hair a shade of blond rarely seen in nature. Though it was difficult to tell through the thick makeup, Amelia guessed she was close to her own age of twenty-five. Whereas Amelia was slender, this woman's body was generously curved, a fact that her bright blue velvet gown emphasized. Her painted face and the dress's low-cut, tightly fitting bodice and scandalously short skirt told Amelia the woman lived on what was euphemistically called the "other side" of town.

Amelia shook her head slowly. "You'll have to see Dr. Ben." She had cared for her one and only case in Gold Landing. Though there was no denying the satisfaction she had felt at stopping Martha Johnson's hemorrhage, that simply wasn't enough. Tomorrow she would resign her position as Dr. Ben's assistant and book passage on the first boat home.

"We need *you*," the woman insisted. "You was the one who saved Martha Johnson and her baby." A tear leaked out of the woman's eye, cutting a furrow in her thick makeup. "Please," she implored.

And so for the second time in twenty-four hours, Amelia Sheldon stood at the bedside of a hemorrhaging woman. This time, instead of being in a log cabin with simple furnishings and immaculate sheets, she found herself in a room whose

17

walls were covered with red flocked paper, while the ceiling was painted blue. Her patient lay on a huge bed with a gilded headboard and sheets so badly stained Amelia doubted they'd ever been white.

This time there was no sense of anticipation and no anxious husband pacing the floor, for this time the bleeding was not the result of what Amelia's mother was wont to call a blessed event. Far from it.

Amelia held the unconscious woman's wrist, feeling the thready pulse, seeing the bluish tinge that colored her lips, and her heart began to thud. Even at the worst moment, Martha Johnson had not been this close to death.

"What happened?" she demanded as she began her examination. Though she had little doubt of the answer, Amelia wanted one of the two women who stood by her side to confirm her diagnosis. Her patient was a young woman, perhaps no more than twenty, still wearing remnants of the heavy makeup that seemed characteristic of the inhabitants of this particular establishment.

"Claudia didn't want the baby no more," explained the blonde, who had introduced herself as June Woods. It had been June who had begged Amelia to come with her.

As she examined the damage Claudia's self-induced abortion had caused, Amelia tried to hide her fears. The hemorrhaging was far worse than Martha Johnson's had been. While no arteries had been cut, the bleeding was substantial, and judging by the woman's pallor and faint pulse, it had been of longer duration. God only knew how long Claudia had lain in her own blood before June had found her.

"What a fool!" The third woman shook her head, her lips pursed in disapproval. "I thought Claudia was smarter than that." When Amelia had followed June through the front door of the gaudily decorated building whose sign proclaimed it to be Gloria's, a tall, statuesque woman with auburn hair greeted Amelia and indicated that she was the proprietor of the establishment. Unlike June, Gloria wore sedate clothing and could have passed for a Philadelphia society matron.

"He said he wanted to marry her," June said tearfully to

explain why Claudia had taken no precautions against pregnancy.

Gloria hooted. "And she believed him? I've told you girls a million times, that's the oldest line in the world. You're just deluding yourselves if you think one of them will marry you."

Amelia reached for another bandage. Though Gloria's words were sharp, she was adept as a physician's aide, seeming to know when Amelia needed bandages and fresh water. And her acidic tone, Amelia suspected, was designed to keep June from bursting into tears.

As Claudia's breathing became shallower, Amelia's anger increased. She was doing everything she could—everything any physician could—and it wasn't enough.

Amelia was no stranger to death. Normally it saddened her to lose a battle with the ultimate enemy. But today she felt nothing except anger: anger that a young woman's life was being cut short so needlessly, anger that another life had ended before it had seen a single sunrise.

"Will she be all right, Miss Sheldon?" Gloria's voice was softer now, as though she recognized the seriousness of Claudia's condition.

It had been less than a day since Emil Johnson had asked the same question. Then Amelia had been concerned. Now she was afraid it would take a miracle to save Claudia.

There were no miracles. An hour later, Amelia drew the sheet over the young woman's face and turned to Gloria. "I'm sorry." The words were inadequate, but there was no way to tell her how much it hurt, how damnably much it hurt, to lose a patient.

The redhead put a hand on Amelia's shoulder. "You did what you could. That's all Claudia or I could ask of you."

June Woods sobbed.

Amelia followed Gloria into the small room she used as an office. Trying not to think of the woman who lay so still upstairs, Amelia looked around her. The room was far different from Claudia's bedchamber, far different from Amelia's expectations. The walls bore an ivory paper with a delicate green pattern, and the table and chairs appeared to be Chippendale, while the rug that covered part of the highly polished floor could only be an Aubusson. Amelia had not expected such elegance in Alaska, and certainly not in a whorehouse.

Gloria closed the door, then pulled a bottle of whiskey and two glasses from a small cabinet. "You need it," she said in response to Amelia's raised eyebrows.

Though the strong liquid burned her throat, Amelia nodded as she felt herself begin to relax. Was this why Dr. Ben drank—to ease the pain of losing a patient?

"I'm glad you came to Gold Landing, Miss Sheldon." Gloria refilled her glass.

Amelia stared at the other woman for a long time. "I'm surprised you would say that. I wasn't much good to Claudia." It hurt just pronouncing the words and thinking of the young woman who would never again laugh or cry, and the baby that would never be born.

"I meant what I said. You did all you could. Maybe next time it'll be different." As Gloria closed her eyes, the brief spasm of pain that crossed her face told Amelia how much Claudia's death had affected her. "Life's not easy for my girls, and Lord knows Dr. Ben doesn't help. It seems like whenever we need him, he has something more important to do."

Gloria opened her eyes and looked at Amelia. "From what I hear, it's not just my girls, either. Seems like he goes on a bender whenever it's time to deliver a baby. Don't know what it is with him and women." Gloria took a long swallow of her whiskey. "Oh, Ben makes professional visits here, but not the kind he should. He comes as a customer, not a doctor."

Amelia shook her head slowly. She had thought that life would be different in Alaska, that women would be treated as equals. She had thought she would be able to rise above the stereotype of women as midwives and prove that she could handle the full range of medicine. She had thought she could put her own sorrow behind her.

She was wrong.

It was no different here. She might as well go home. At least there the streets were paved and dogs were pets, not vicious-looking creatures bred to pull a sled.

She would leave on the next boat.

"I imagine Ella Roberts is glad you're here."

Gloria's words interrupted Amelia's thoughts. In the few hours she'd spent with the woman who'd so generously opened her home to her, Amelia had discovered they had many common interests. Ella, she knew instinctively, would be a friend. And Ella had told her how badly Gold Landing needed her.

"Dr. Ben's a fine doctor when he's sober," Ella had said, "but I'm always scared he'll be drunk when I need him. So far there's never been an emergency at the school, and now that you're here, I won't have to worry anymore."

She could leave. She should leave. And yet . . . At home she'd be one doctor among many. Here there would be days when she was the only one. People's lives would depend on her, and maybe—just maybe—she could make a difference. Maybe—just maybe—she could prevent another young woman from suffering Claudia's fate.

"I want to schedule monthly exams for your girls," Amelia said firmly.

The redheaded woman smiled and raised her glass in a toast. "Welcome to Gold Landing, Doctor."

"The man is impossible!" Ella Roberts pounded her fist on the desk in front of the schoolroom. Her dark brown eyes flashed, and the black braids she'd coiled around her head threatened to break loose. "Someone's got to stop him!"

"Aw, honey, what's the matter with Dr. Ben now? Was he too drunk to pull a sliver out of one of the boys' fingers?" Larry Wilson dipped a rag in the pail of water and began to clean the blackboard while Ella arranged schoolbooks in a neat row along the front of her desk. She had dismissed the children half an hour before. Though normally they helped tidy the room, they had been so excited by the sun's appearance after days of cold rain that Ella had let them leave early. Now Larry was helping her.

"You should have called me," he said. "I could have done it, and I wouldn't have charged much. Just a kiss or two."

Amanda Harte

Larry was a good-looking man with brown hair and eyes and a luxuriant mustache that framed his lips, lips that were now smiling at her in the strangest way. As the blood rushed to her face, Ella ducked her head, not wanting her fiancé to see the embarrassment his words had caused. He didn't mean to upset her; she was sure of that. It was just that sometimes Larry was a little too . . . eager.

"Ben was worse than you can imagine," she said when her cheeks had cooled. "He's been downright insulting to Amelia. You know what he said when she returned from the Johnsons', after she'd just saved Martha and the baby?" Without giving Larry a chance to reply, Ella continued, "He asked her which one had died."

Larry dipped the rag back into the pail. "So? She lost the next patient, didn't she?"

Ella gathered her notebooks. "You don't understand. Dr. Ben's making Amelia's life so miserable, I'm afraid she's going to leave."

"So?" Larry put his arm around Ella's shoulders.

Moving impatiently out of his embrace, Ella said, "I don't want her to leave. I like Amelia. This is the first time I've had a housemate I thought could be a friend, and I don't want to lose her."

"But honey, you wouldn't need a housemate if you'd just set the wedding date. I'll be your housemate and a whole lot more."

Ella opened the schoolhouse door. Ignoring Larry's last words, she said, "Amelia needs to meet more people. When she sees how nice everyone else in Gold Landing is, maybe she'll stay." Ella smiled. "A party. That's it. I'll have a party for her."

22

Chapter Two

"A party welcoming Amelia Sheldon! How'd I get invited to that?"

William gave Ben Taylor a long look. Tonight his friend looked every one of his forty-three years. Gray hairs seemed to outnumber the brown, and there was a new weariness in the dark, bespectacled eyes. William dealt another hand before he said lightly, "Probably by hiring her. Don't they call it poetic justice? After all, you're the reason she came to Gold Landing."

The two men who had joined William and Dr. Ben for their weekly poker game snickered until the doctor's forbidding expression quelled their mirth. The truth was, and all four of them knew it, that no one in Gold Landing turned down an invitation to a party. Especially now when winter had finally ended and the lengthening days seemed to encourage celebrations for the slightest of reasons. Not that the arrival of a young, unmarried female could be considered anything other than a major cause for celebration.

Ben ran his fingers through his hair, then continued his complaint. "And it would have to be at Ella's house. You know that old prude won't have a drop of liquor around."

"She's not that old," Alex Fielding pointed out.

"Of course, she *is* a prude." Frank Stratton stroked his full beard and leaned back in the chair, his considerable girth causing it to creak. William smiled. Frank had never been known for his charitable words.

As if in preparation for the party, William took a swallow of his drink, then fixed his gray eyes on Ben. Since the new doctor had arrived, Ben's drinking had moderated. Though he complained constantly about his assistant, he apparently did not find the situation bad enough to seek oblivion in a bottle.

"A night of abstinence wouldn't hurt you," William told

his friend. "Besides, you've gotta come. No way will I suffer alone." He sniffed, trying to identify the unusual odor. Ben's kitchen had never smelled like this before. "If the midwife is as bad as you say, you and I can slip outside for a quick nip. I'll even bring the flask."

"Sure wish I was invited." Alex had complained ever since he'd heard about the party and realized he and Karen had not been invited.

"Why should you get an invitation?" Frank groused good-naturedly. "You've already got yourself a woman."

Their weekly poker games had started three years earlier when Alex had joined his cousin in Gold Landing. Now that Alex was engaged and working the night shift, the others threatened to give his spot to Sam Baranov.

"You figure that's what Ella has in mind—marrying off Amelia?" Ben looked hopeful.

William sniffed again. He ought to recognize the smell. It seemed vaguely familiar.

Alex nodded. "That's how women are—always thinking about marriage."

William snorted, remembering the number of times Alex had extolled the virtues of matrimony since his own engagement.

"Can't imagine who'd want to marry her." Ben looked around the table, then rose to refill the men's glasses. The games alternated between William's house and the big room behind Ben's office that served as his kitchen, dining room and parlor. By unspoken consent, no one had suggested meeting in Frank's cabin. Since his mother had come to Gold Landing to keep house for her son, Frank's cabin had not been a place where men felt welcome.

"C'mon, Ben. The new doctor can't be that bad." William had to admit he was intrigued, as much by Ben's caustic comments as by Alex's praise. He figured she had come to Alaska to find a husband, but if she was as pretty as the men claimed, he didn't understand why she had left Philadelphia. Surely there were eligible men there.

Ben shrugged. "All she does is harangue me. 'Clean up the

office.' 'Stop drinking.' 'Build a clinic.' Nag, nag, nag. And she does it with her nose in the air. Little Miss Philadelphia Society Belle.''

Clean. That was what the smell was. Some sort of soap. William bit back a smile at the thought of Ben scrubbing the kitchen. As he studied the cards in his hand, he said mildly, ''Serves you right, Ben. You knew she was a woman when you hired her. That should have been your clue that you were gonna have a problem.''

''What's wrong with women?'' Ben took another long swig of his whiskey, then stared at William. ''I don't notice you disdaining female companionship.''

''No, I don't. The female sex—or at least one of them—plays a role in my life, and someday I'll probably marry one. I won't deny that.''

As Alex grinned, William glared. He was not about to admit to anyone just how often his thoughts turned to marriage. It was time he found a wife and started a family. The problem was, though the single women he had met obviously viewed him as a likely candidate, he could not envision spending the rest of his life with any of them. He knew what he wanted and would not settle for less.

William glanced at his cards, planned his next move, then said, ''You don't catch me hiring a woman, do you? No, sirree! And if I did make that kind of mistake, you can be sure I'd let her know who's boss.''

''You don't know Amelia Sheldon. Wait until you meet her.'' It was Ben's turn to laugh. ''She's uppity and impudent and thinks she's too good for Gold Landing. Just wait. You'll see.''

By the time Amelia came down the stairs, the other guests had arrived. She had protested, telling Ella she wanted to help with the last-minute arrangements, but Ella had been adamant. ''You're the guest of honor. I want you to make an entrance.'' And so Amelia lingered in her room, putting the final touches on her hair.

She wore a sapphire gown, one of the new princess styles

that even her sister admitted flattered Amelia. The artful seams emphasized her slender waist, while the high neckline and demitrain gave the illusion of greater-than-average height. Though Belinda claimed the dress was plain, Amelia found the lack of furbelows a pleasant change from the ruffled styles of previous years. Indeed, the only ruffles were those that cuffed the long, fitted sleeves.

"Seductive," Belinda had announced when Amelia modeled the gown. That comment had almost convinced Amelia to leave the dress home. After all, she was going to Gold Landing to be a physician, not to find a husband, despite her mother's admonitions. But vanity triumphed. It was a gown only a few women could resist, and Amelia Sheldon was not one of those few. Though she left other dresses in Philadelphia, the shimmering silk was carefully packed in her trunk.

Amelia walked down the stairs, pausing at the door to Ella's parlor. Tonight the furniture had been pushed against the walls to make room for the guests. It was to be a small party, only ten others besides Ella and Amelia. "That way you'll have a chance to get to know them," Ella had explained.

Someone had cranked the gramophone, filling the room with music. The guests stood in small groups, glasses of punch in their hands, speaking softly, while Ella moved from group to group.

It had taken hours of coaxing, but Amelia had finally convinced Ella to unbraid her hair. Though she had refused to wear a pompadour, she had gathered it in a loose chignon, and the softer style flattered her. Ella was, Amelia realized, an attractive woman, though she seemed to do her best to hide her beauty.

As Amelia entered the room, all conversation stopped.

"Ladies and gentlemen." Ella rushed to the doorway and placed her hand on Amelia's. "Let me introduce Amelia Sheldon."

Amelia looked around the room. She had an impression of colorful gowns, dark suits and white shirts; of smiling faces and curious glances. Her eyes moved from face to face, smiling back, until she reached him.

The man dominated the room. Taller than the other men, he had broader shoulders, and rugged features that looked as though they might have been chiseled from bedrock. Unlike some big men who slouched so their size would be less obvious, he held his head high, his shoulders squared. It was not an arrogant stance, merely the pose of a man who was supremely comfortable with himself.

Though he wore a suit and tie like every other man in the room, and his thick brown hair was styled like several others', with the newly fashionable side part, there was nothing ordinary about this man. His confidence ensured that he would stand out in any crowd, even if he were short and thin. As it was, Amelia had the feeling she was seeing Alaska personified: rugged, grand and unforgettable.

Her mother had taught her it was rude to stare; this man's mother had evidently neglected that particular lesson, for he was staring directly at her. Though she knew better, Amelia couldn't help it. She stared back, mesmerized, her eyes cataloging details like the faint shadows under his eyes, the crescent-shaped scar on his left cheek and the huge gold nugget on his watch chain.

"Amelia, I'd like you to meet Abe Ferguson."

With an effort Amelia pulled her gaze from the big man and looked at the one whom Ella led toward her, the man whose name figured so often in Ella's conversation that she had accused her of matchmaking.

"I'm not looking for a husband," she had assured Ella, to no avail.

"But when I marry Larry, you'll need somewhere to live," Ella had protested. "Besides, I think you and Abe will have a lot in common."

What Ella had not told Amelia was how handsome he was and how unlike the other men in Gold Landing, as far different from the big man as Amelia could imagine. Abe was of medium height, perhaps four inches taller than Amelia herself, with a slender build and aristocratic features that seemed out of place in this land where men earned their living by physical labor. The spectacles he wore did nothing to hide the intelligence in his blue eyes, and when he smiled, the cleft in his chin deepened. He looked like a scholar, a man who would choose to live in Cambridge or Princeton, not on the frontier.

Abe's clothing was impeccably tailored, and as he bowed his blond head in acknowledgment of the introduction, Amelia had the fleeting thought that he was going to kiss her hand. Instead, he took it in his, holding it perhaps an instant longer than mere courtesy demanded.

"The pleasure is mine," he said in a well-modulated voice whose accent left no doubt that he was not a native Alaskan.

"Ella told me you're from Boston," Amelia said. From the corner of her eyes, she saw the big man turn his back.

"Guilty as charged." As Abe smiled, the tiny lines that radiated from his blue eyes made Amelia revise her estimate. He was not as young as she had first thought. Though she had believed him to be in his mid-twenties, now he appeared at least thirty.

"Tell me, what's a Boston attorney doing in Gold Landing, Alaska?"

"Probably the same thing as a Philadelphia physician: practicing his—or should I say her?—trade."

While Abe spoke, Amelia found herself listening more to his voice than his words. The clear voice with its distinctive accent reminded her vividly of home, and she couldn't help contrasting her mother's dinner parties with this one. At home there were fine carpets underfoot, and crystal chandeliers reflected the light of dozens of candles, for although the house had electricity, Lydia Sheldon insisted that candlelight was more flattering to her guests.

Ella's parlor boasted none of the amenities that made the Sheldon house one of Philadelphia's most elegant homes. The floor was rough-hewn pine, not the finest oak, and there were no chandeliers, crystal or otherwise. Light came from plain electric fixtures. And yet Amelia could not ignore the vitality that filled the room, a sense of liveliness and purpose that she had never experienced in her parents' beautifully appointed home. Most of the men and women who were Ella's guests were Alaskans by choice, not by an accident of birth, and they were obviously proud of the fact.

"How long have you been here?"

Abe shrugged as he handed Amelia a glass of punch. "Five years. A lifetime. Some days I can't tell the difference."

Amelia sipped the punch, savoring the tart flavor of what Ella had assured her were native Alaskan cranberries.

"Do you miss your home?"

The question appeared to surprise Abe. "This is home," he said. "Oh, there are times when I miss the opera and the symphony, but Alaska gets into your blood. Once you've seen the midnight sun and the northern lights, you won't want to leave."

Amelia had seen neither, but she sensed the truth in Abe's words. Already Alaska had begun to weave its magic. When the rain had stopped, she had climbed the hill outside of town. Evergreen forests punctuated the snow-covered fields, and in the distance mountains rose, taller and more magnificent than anything she had ever seen. Above it all was a sky so blue it made her want to cry for sheer joy. No wonder the natives called it the great land.

"Abe, simply because you're a glib talker doesn't mean you get to monopolize our guest of honor." The man who interrupted was of medium height, with hair that was more gray than its original brown. "Clara wants to meet you," he told Amelia, introducing himself as Ray Francis, the town's banker. "She said she's tired of just hearing about the new doctor. She wants to talk to you yourself."

As Amelia walked to the back of the room with Ray Francis, she looked briefly at the other guests. Ben Taylor she knew. The dowdy woman who gazed adoringly at him had to be Vera Kane. According to Ella, the widow Kane was definitely interested in Dr. Ben.

The tall man with the clerical collar was obviously Reverend Langdon, and the pale woman whose hand rested lightly on his arm was probably his wife. What was her name? Bertha. The attractive younger woman with the same pale coloring must be their daughter, Charlotte.

29

By process of elimination, she determined that the big man must be William Gunning, Gold Landing's sterling citizen, or so Ella claimed, for, besides founding the town, he had donated much of the money to build the school.

Clara Francis was talking; Amelia was certain of that, and yet she had no idea what the older woman had asked. For just as Clara phrased her question, he turned, and once again her eyes met his.

He was not handsome. Feature for feature, Abe Ferguson was the more handsome man. Yet William Gunning, with his decidedly rugged build and his roughly chiseled nose and chin, exuded power, a raw magnetism that made physical beauty irrelevant. Even the scar seemed to add to his appeal.

Amelia stared at the man, her blue eyes meeting his gray ones. The man smiled. Amelia could not, for her heart was beating as though she had run a race. Indeed, she could barely breathe, much less form a smile. She heard nothing but the blood pounding in her head and the throbbing of her heart.

It was absurd. Belinda had described the sensation a dozen times, telling Amelia that eventually she would meet a man who would turn her insides to jelly and her brain to mush. Amelia had scoffed, certain her sister had exaggerated. But Belinda had not exaggerated. If anything, she had failed to describe the strange sensation adequately.

It was lust. Amelia knew that. She also knew that it was something she had to avoid, since it could lead nowhere. She had no future with this or any other man. Since there was no inoculation, her only hope was quarantine.

With difficulty, she turned to Clara Francis. As the conversation continued, Amelia was careful to keep her attention focused on Clara and Ray. She turned slightly so that William Gunning was not in her line of sight. But even as she spoke to the banker, she was aware that the big man stood only a few feet away. Though she could not ignore him all night, somehow she had to get her emotions under control before she spoke to him. Gratefully accepting another cup of punch from Ella's fiancé Larry, Amelia continued to talk to Clara Francis.

"You can call her a doctor if you like, but the truth is, she's a midwife and a *cheechako* to boot.'' The big man was speaking. His words carried clearly, telling Amelia he had deliberately moved in her direction just as she had deliberately turned away from him.

Clara gasped, then began to babble, but Amelia shook her head, silencing the older woman. Since she was the only female doctor and the only *cheechako,* the term Alaskans gave to first-year residents, there was no doubt William Gunning was talking about her, and even less doubt that he wanted her to know it. What she didn't know was why he was being confrontational. Had he felt the strange current that was almost like an electric shock? Was this his way of dealing with it? In school she had learned about the fight-or-flight reaction. She had chosen flight, trying to place a safe distance between herself and William. Had he decided to fight?

The man continued to speak. Though his voice was not as cultured as Abe's, it was compelling, underscoring the way he dominated the party. Without raising it above normal speaking levels, he had captured the attention of every person in the room. Grandpa had told her some men were like that. Born leaders, he had called them when he recounted his experiences as a doctor during the Civil War. Born leader? More likely a born bully.

''That's not to discount midwives,'' William conceded, ''for Lord knows they have their place. Few of us would be here without them.'' The men who stood near him chuckled. ''My point is, women aren't real doctors. They don't have what it takes.''

Amelia gasped. Though his tone was conversational, there was no doubt of his sincerity.

''Mr. Gunning, please.'' Ella rushed to stand next to her. ''You don't mean that.''

''Yes, ma'am, I do.''

A bully. That was what he was, and there was only one way to deal with bullies. Brushing off Ella's restraining hand, she faced him, her sapphire eyes glittering dangerously.

''Are you brave enough to say that to my face?''

''Sure.'' William Gunning tipped his head down as though

31

to remind her of his physical superiority. "You can claim you're a doctor, but we all know why you're here. Dr. Ben hired a midwife."

He had tossed the gauntlet. She had no choice but to accept it.

"Just how did you determine that?" Amelia's words were clipped as she strove to keep from shouting at him. Had she thought the man was attractive? So were the most dangerous snakes. He was a natural predator, ready to attack what he thought were weaker creatures. There was one vital difference, though. She was not helpless prey. If William Gunning thought she was weak, he had much to learn.

William shrugged his shoulders, releasing a faint woodsy scent. "It's no secret. We know what your job is. We know why you were hired."

"I beg your pardon," Amelia said, her voice cold with anger, an anger that went beyond his attack on her credentials and was directed at herself for that moment of madness when she had been mesmerized by his smile.

"Is that the royal 'we,' or are you speaking for all of Gold Landing?" she demanded. She took a deep breath, regretting it a second later when her senses were tantalized by the pine fragrance that clung to the big man.

"William, please. This is not the place for an argument." Reverend Langdon approached.

William raised one brow as though disdaining a reply, his apparent nonchalance only fueling Amelia's anger. Just because William Gunning owned the gold mine did not mean he owned Gold Landing's inhabitants, too.

The gramophone wound down, but no one seemed to notice. The guests had moved to the center of the room, closer to Amelia and William, as if unwilling to miss a word either one uttered.

"I didn't realize you were privy to my correspondence or that Dr. Ben took you into his confidence," Amelia said in a voice that somehow did not betray the turmoil raging within her. "But since you obviously believe you know everything about my reasons for coming to Gold Landing, you must be aware that Dr. Taylor hired an assistant. That is clearly stated in the contract between us. An assistant,'' she repeated.

Ben, who had moved to William's left side, nodded.

''Since you're so well informed, I'm sure you also know that the word 'midwife' does not appear anywhere in that contract.'' Amelia's expression, perfected from years of watching her mother snub social climbers, left no doubt that she considered William Gunning a member of an inferior species.

The man appeared to be oblivious to her implied insult. ''Ben might call you an assistant,'' he replied with maddening calm, ''but you're only a midwife.'' The lights flickered, and for a second everyone's attention turned to the three bulbs on the wall. When they once again burned steadily, William said, ''Midwifery is all women can handle.''

''That's enough, William. For God's sake, this is a party.'' Amelia heard Abe's voice and realized he'd moved to stand behind her.

''Stay out of this, Abe. This is between the doctor''—somehow he managed to make the word into an insult—''and me.''

William's words had touched a still-raw nerve. It was all too true that Dr. Ben saw her as a midwife. On the other hand, it was not true that that was the limit of her capabilities, and this man had no cause to think it was.

It appeared that William Gunning was one of the men Ben had described, ''real'' men who believed women couldn't be physicians. While she knew their opinions were based on prejudice rather than facts, Amelia had little patience for prejudice and the ignorance that fueled it. How alarming it was to learn that the man Ella called Gold Landing's sterling citizen was tarnished by prejudice.

''It appears you must have made a mistake when you came to Alaska,'' Amelia said. ''From everything I've read, this is a place where women are equal to men. Women can do everything a man can. Why, I hear we'll soon be able to vote.''

Though Bertha Langdon's punch glass clinked loudly when she set it on the table, no one turned in her direction.

''If there are mistakes, they are yours, Doctor.'' Again, he used her title as a way of demeaning her. ''First of all, I was

33

born here, so I reckon I know a bit more about Alaska than a *cheechako* like you does. And second, don't believe everything you read.'' His eyes moved boldly down her body. ''There are still some things only a man can do.''

The insolence of him! Of course he would think that way. Crude, ignorant, overbearing. He was like the nightshade: attractive on the surface but poisonous if one came too close. She had no intention of coming any closer.

''For that matter, there are some things that only a woman can do.'' Amelia used her haughtiest tone as she flung his words back at him. ''Medicine may be a male-dominated profession, but it is not reserved exclusively for men.''

William raised a brow, and if she hadn't known better, Amelia would have said that she saw amusement in his gray eyes. It couldn't be, for there was nothing even remotely amusing about their discussion. ''Did you hear those big words?'' he asked, turning to the other guests, who now stood silently watching the verbal duel.

It appeared that Gold Landing's etiquette had no rules for dealing with a situation like this. While her mother looked vaguely disapproving, Charlotte Langdon gazed adoringly at William.

As if encouraged, William resumed his attack. ''She talks like our lawyer friend, doesn't she? 'Male-dominated.' 'Reserved exclusively.' Well, then, for your information, Miss Sheldon, my mine is both male-dominated and reserved exclusively for men.''

The man's expression was supercilious, yet more evidence of the way he dominated Gold Landing—financially, physically and now philosophically. He obviously expected everyone to agree with him.

''Why am I not surprised?'' Amelia's question was rhetorical. ''I can guess what role women play in your life.''

A low chuckle from one of the men told Amelia she was correct in her assumption of where William spent many of his nights.

Ella gasped, while Vera Kane drew a fan from somewhere and began to wield it furiously.

"The women in my life are not doctors, that's for sure. If I needed to see a doctor—which, thank God, I don't—I'd like to be sure I survived the experience."

It was a low blow, yet no more than she should have expected. Still, it hurt—oh, how it hurt!—to be reminded of Claudia. Like every bully, William Gunning was trying to keep her off balance and defensive. No longer.

"May I ask just how you determined that women are unable to be doctors?" Amelia raised her head imperiously. "Is there something you know that I'm perhaps unaware of? Some basic flaw in our natures?" Her tone was sarcastic, designed to flay the skin of his sensibilities. Unfortunately the man's hide was probably as thick as the muscles in his arms. His lips quivered slightly, and again Amelia had the impression that he was somehow enjoying her anger. How dare he!

"You want to know the problem?" His tone was condescending, as though explaining an elementary concept to a not-very-bright child. "Women are weak; you're afraid of blood; you don't have the minds for doctoring."

One of the women gasped; someone snickered; Amelia fumed. This was one battle he would not win.

She straightened her spine and stared into those cold gray eyes. "But we make good midwives? Is that correct?" she demanded.

"Yeah." William grinned, and this time there was no doubt he was enjoying her anger. The bully obviously thought he had won. He was wrong.

"Thank you." Amelia turned to the other guests. "I want to be sure I answer this man's arguments completely." She turned back to William. "Have you ever seen a baby being born, Mr. Gunning?" she demanded.

"Amelia!" Ella's face turned white, then red. "I beg you."

"I'm sorry, Ella, but I need to finish this." She faced William. "Have you?" William shook his head. "Then you are speaking from a position of ignorance. If you knew anything about childbirth, you'd know just how misguided your statements are."

Amelia gestured with her right hand, and her sleeve rustled

softly. "Women are weak, are we? I ask any doctor, male or female, to deny the strength needed to deliver a breech baby. Not just brute strength, which almost anyone . . ." She paused momentarily and looked at the other guests to give her words more impact. "Almost anyone, even a miner, could provide strength. But skill? That's a far rarer commodity."

To Amelia's satisfaction, her barb seemed to meet its target, for a muscle twitched at the corner of William's mouth as he clenched his jaw, and the hint of amusement disappeared from his eyes.

"What was next?" The question was rhetorical, and before William could reply, Amelia continued, "Fear of blood, I think. If women were afraid of blood, childbirth would hardly be the place to get started. They'd try something less messy, like lung diseases."

Charlotte Langdon's mouth dropped open. When she started to speak, her mother silenced her. William shifted his weight, and Amelia had the impression of a fighter moving into battle stance.

She smiled sweetly, then said, "As far as minds go, a woman physician has to pass the same exams as a man. If that doesn't prove that she's equal, then you might consider the fact that women normally have to have higher scores than men just to be accepted to medical school, thanks to the antiquated attitudes of the males who run those same schools."

She drew a breath, then continued in a deceptively soft voice, "I'm afraid I don't understand your logic, Mr. Gunning. You've said that women make good midwives but lack the qualities to be good doctors. Yet it seems that the requirements you've established for being a doctor are clearly met by mid-wifery."

Amelia ignored the chuckle that came from behind her, keeping her attention focused on the man who looked as if he wanted to strangle her. Though he said nothing, his eyes met hers with an unmistakable challenge.

"If that's true," Amelia said, "and I think I've proven that it is, surely it follows that women are not only capable, but eminently well qualified, to be doctors.'' She inclined her head in a regal gesture. ''I rest my case.''

There was a moment of stunned silence as the guests looked from William to Amelia, unsure what to do say or do. Then Abe Ferguson stepped between William and Amelia and laughed. ''I certainly hope Dr. Sheldon never decides to be a lawyer, or I'll be out of business.''

Abe bowed with a flourish and took Amelia's hand in his. ''Would you consider a partnership?''

Chapter Three

It was one of the first clear nights of spring. A crescent moon shone in the cloudless sky, its silver gleam reflecting on the surface of the water. It was a night when lovers, no longer confined inside by the harsh weather, strolled along the riverbanks, oblivious to the cold that radiated from the still-frozen earth. But William Gunning was not strolling, and his mood was far from loverlike.

"Damn the woman! How dare she humiliate me like that?" William unbuttoned his jacket as he increased his pace. It wasn't fair. How could such a beautiful woman have the tongue of a viper?

He had been aware of her from the moment she had entered Ella's parlor. For once his men had not exaggerated. She *was* beautiful. Her face reminded him of the princess in the one picture book Polly had had. Its covers were worn from constant handling, but none of the pages was stained, for Polly had insisted that the children wash their hands before they touched it. Yes, Amelia had looked like a princess, and that dark cloud of hair was like a crown. He had never seen eyes that deep shade of blue. As for her body . . .

William clenched his teeth. He should have listened to Ben. After all, the man worked with her every day. Ben knew what she was like, and he had warned William. He should have known better, but instead of using his head, he had reacted with another part of his anatomy.

When she had walked into the room, it had taken all of his strength to remain where he was and not rush to her side. Damn it! He was William Gunning, not some lovesick boy. He was not going to stand around sniffing her like a dog in heat, and he most definitely was not going to become the next subject for Gold Landing's gossip. He would approach her discreetly, treat her the same as every other lady in the room.

Only after the party would he invite her to walk along the river.

It sure as hell hadn't worked out the way he had planned. While he stayed talking to Charlotte Langdon, Abe Ferguson monopolized the guest of honor. It was Abe who made her smile and who brought a blush to those already rosy cheeks. Abe, that East Coast dandy who wasn't even man enough to wear a gun.

But she had liked him; that much was obvious. She had smiled at him, those big blue eyes promising the world to Abe Ferguson, those luscious lips curving upward with pleasure over something that useless lawyer said, while he, William Gunning, was reduced to exchanging pleasantries with Charlotte Langdon.

He strode quickly, his footsteps ringing on the boardwalk. When he reached the mine office, his dogs began to yip, alerted by either the sound of his steps or his smell.

"Good boy, Nugget." He patted the lead dog, then ruffled the others' fur. At least the huskies knew a real man when they saw him.

It was probably foolish, antagonizing Amelia the way he had. Polly would have tanned his hide for treating a lady that way. But it sure had riled him, watching Amelia fawn all over Abe just because the man owned more books than the Fairbanks library.

Besides, who would have guessed that Amelia would be such a spitfire? He had thought he would get her attention with his remarks, find out why she thought she wanted to be a doctor. For the life of him, he couldn't figure out why a woman would want to do a man's job when there were much more rewarding things only she could do—like raise children.

His plan sure had gone awry. Little did he know Amelia would blister him with her sarcasm. And the way she had looked at him, as if he were some sort of loathsome creature that slithered out from under a rock.

Ben was right. She was an uppity broad.

He had plenty of other things to think about—important things like how he was going to keep the mine open if production continued to dwindle. The people of Gold Landing depended on him, and that was important—far more important than the fact that one spoiled East Coast society belle preferred Abe Ferguson to him.

She wasn't his kind of woman, anyway. She might have the face of a princess and a body that set a man's blood to boiling, but she wasn't the woman for him. *No, sirree.* If Abe Ferguson was the kind of man she found attractive, if his highfalutin words were what charmed her, then she was one of those women Polly had warned him about: shallow females who thought that what mattered was a pretty face and a fancy education, not what a man had done with his life.

"Don't be fooled by the surface," Polly used to tell him. "Test what's underneath." She was referring to the river, warning him that even when the surface was frozen, it might not be thick enough to support his weight, but William figured her advice applied to people, too.

He turned the corner, his feet moving mechanically while his mind raced. It was only when he saw the light shining in the window that he realized where his feet had led him. A smile crossed his face. To hell with Amelia Sheldon! She wasn't the only woman in the world. What he needed right now was a real woman. What he needed was June.

A bell tinkled softly, announcing his arrival as William opened the door. The room inside was warm and welcoming, carefully designed to soothe the spirit and titillate the senses. A thick rug covered the floor, while overstuffed couches beckoned a man to sit and relax with a companion at his side. Everything was soft and comforting. Even the lighting was subdued, deliberately chosen to flatter the girls who spent their evenings entertaining Gold Landing's men.

Gloria had overlooked no detail when she had had the house built. She had designed it to be the premier establishment of its type, and it was. It was she who had insisted on two stoves in the parlor, noting that men liked to warm themselves during the long Alaskan winters. And it was Gloria who had chosen a heavy curtain rather than a door to block the entrance to the long hallway. There would be no creaking or slamming door to announce a couple's departure from the parlor. Gloria's patrons could be discreet.

"Good evening, William." Gloria's voice welcomed a man as well as her stoves did. "A beautiful night, isn't it?"

But William was not in the mood to discuss the weather. "Is June here?" His eyes scanned the room quickly, lighting on the petite figure sitting in one corner, her small hands gracefully plying needle and thread.

When she saw William, June Woods rose from her chair and moved quickly to his side. A smile lit her face, and her blue eyes sparkled with pleasure. "Hello, William," she said softly, tipping her head up to look at him.

Though June stood no taller than a child, her head barely reaching William's shoulder, no one would mistake her body for a child's. Her breasts and hips were curved and voluptuous, a fact that the clothes Gloria selected for her emphasized. Her face was round and her features regular; June Woods was not beautiful. Yet, despite the heavy makeup and tinted hair, she retained an air of innocence that made men feel protective toward her.

"Hello, June." William returned her smile. This woman, at least, was predictable. Though he might pay for her favors, he knew she would never turn on him. Her tongue was sweet, not venomous, and the look she gave him was adoring, not disdainful.

"I've almost finished another shirt." She gestured to the pile of sewing she had left in the corner.

"I'm a lucky man," William said as he held the heavy curtain aside for her. He meant it. But when they reached her room, William found himself wondering how Amelia Sheldon would feel in his arms.

Abe Ferguson closed the book in disgust. It was no use. Not even Charles Dickens, whose words normally banished the day's cares, could hold his attention. Tonight he had only one thought.

He was reading *A Tale of Two Cities*, not one of his favorite stories. But tonight it no longer seemed foolishly sentimental.

Instead, as he turned the pages, Lucie Manette's golden hair suddenly became shimmering brown, and he found himself wondering whether he was playing the role of Charles Darnay or Sydney Carton.

Tonight even his well-appointed study did nothing to soothe him. Though Gold Landing's residents might scoff at the shipment of books that came with each mail delivery, Abe didn't care. Reading had always brought him pleasure. In fact, until tonight he would have said that reading provided more joy than anything else.

Until tonight.

He strode to the window, his hands thrust deep in his pockets. God, she was beautiful! His eyes stared sightlessly at the empty yard. When he had heard that Ben Taylor had hired an assistant, he had never expected someone like Amelia Sheldon. The assistant, he had thought, would be plain and sensible, not a gorgeous creature like Amelia.

And it wasn't just that she was beautiful. Abe had met plenty of beautiful women. There was more to Amelia than beauty. She was intelligent and sensitive and brave. Yes, brave. Who else would have dared to defy that bully William Gunning the way she did? With a smile of satisfaction Abe remembered the expression on William's face when Amelia finished her summation. Served him right!

Abe's smile softened as he thought of dinner and Amelia at his side. It had been years since he had met a woman with a mind as quick as hers, and he couldn't remember when he had enjoyed an evening more. They shared the same interests, had read the same books, even liked the same music.

He had teased Amelia with the prospect of a partnership, but what a partnership theirs would be! The conversations they would have. The books they would share. And then the nights. Ah, yes, the nights. One thing was certain. It would not be boring with Amelia Sheldon in Gold Landing.

"It was a nice evening, wasn't it?" Ella asked. Her parlor was back to normal, with only the lingering scents of perfume and tobacco as reminders of the party. Even the fire was almost gone, leaving nothing more than glowing embers.

"Sure was," Larry Wilson agreed, fingering his mustache. "But our wedding reception will be even better." He moved closer to her on the horsehair settee.

Ella smiled shyly. "That will be nice, won't it?" She heard the clank of dishes in the kitchen. Although Ella had protested, Amelia had insisted on washing them. And since Amelia was in the next room, a suitable chaperone, Ella had not refused when Larry had asked to stay for a few minutes after the rest of the guests had left.

He shifted his weight, moving slightly closer to Ella. "Let's set a date," he said, and slid his arm along the back of the settee. "Let's get married."

As one of the embers crackled, Ella started. Larry let his arm drop onto her shoulder and pressed it encouragingly, murmuring soothing words. "You know I love you, honey," he said, drawing her body closer to his. "Let's get married soon."

"But I have school," she protested. Her heart started to beat as if she'd climbed the stairs too quickly.

"School's almost over. Let's have the wedding this summer."

This summer? What was Larry thinking? He didn't understand.

"I could never be ready that soon." Ella shook her head. "Oh, Larry, there are so many things to do for a wedding."

"If you really loved me, you'd marry me." He turned so that he was facing her, his dark eyes sober. "Let's elope."

"What would people think?" Ella blurted out the words, scandalized as she thought of the couples who eloped. In a town that loved parties as much as Gold Landing did, there was only one reason for an elopement: the first blessed event would occur less than nine months after the wedding. Would the people of Gold Landing think that she and Larry . . . ? Unable to continue the thought, she shook her head vigorously. "We can't elope," she said firmly.

"Ella, honey, I don't know how much longer I can wait." Larry moved closer until his lips touched hers.

It was a gentle kiss, the barest touching of lips, but Ella broke away as though she were burned. "No, Larry! Not until we're married!" She jumped to her feet.

With a resigned sigh, Larry walked to the front door.

Ben Taylor reached for the whiskey bottle, then stopped. Not tonight. Tonight he didn't need whiskey.

With a chuckle, he walked to his bedroom. The smallest room in the house, it was simply furnished with a bed and a chest of drawers. When Amelia had glimpsed it the one day he had left the door open, she had chided him, saying the room needed personal touches and suggesting pictures or plants. Utter nonsense. What did a man need with furbelows when all he did was sleep in a room? Plants would die. As for pictures, they were reminders of things best left forgotten.

Meddling females. Still, Ben couldn't remember when he had enjoyed an evening more. He had been right. Ella Roberts hadn't served a drop of liquor, and if William had brought his flask, there had been no sign of it. It hadn't mattered. William had provided stimulation of a different variety.

Who would have thought Amelia Sheldon would stand up to William that way? Ben laughed, remembering William's face when she had made that crack about miners. That had gotten his attention, sure as strawberries grew in June. Served him right, too. After all, he had started the fight.

Strange; if anyone had asked, Ben would have bet that William would have liked Amelia. She was a good-looking woman, even if she did have airs about her. And William had always had an eye for good-looking women. It was odd the way the antagonism had grown.

And then there was Ella. Ben couldn't put his finger on it, but she looked different tonight—softer, somehow. Not that *soft* was a word you'd use to describe that straitlaced schoolteacher. She was about as rigid as they came.

Ben wasn't sure which had been funnier—the sparks that flew between William and Amelia or Ella's reaction to them. She had been horrified by their argument, wanting it to stop at the same time that she had wanted to protect Amelia. As if Amelia needed protection!

Ben laughed again, thinking of the gossip that was bound to result from tonight. If there was anything Gold Landing enjoyed, it was a juicy bit of gossip. And the way Amelia had lit into William certainly qualified as a juicy morsel. Unless Ben was wrong, he would have more patients than he could handle, all suddenly stricken with mysterious ailments just so they could see the new doctor. Maybe hiring Amelia hadn't been a mistake.

As Ben drifted off to sleep, his last thought was surprise that Ella Roberts's party had been such a success.

Amelia polished the glasses with a ferocity out of proportion to the need to make Ella's stemware sparkle. If the glasses had been her own, she might have thrown one against a wall. But since they were Ella's, she vented her anger by polishing each until it was spotless and shone brilliantly.

How infuriating that one man could be so narrow-minded. Imagine thinking women doctors were incompetent! It wasn't as though he had experience with doctors of any kind. She had learned that much during dinner. Bertha Langdon, the minister's wife, had tried to calm her, telling Amelia that, as far as Gold Landing knew, William had never been sick. He saw Dr. Ben often, but only socially. Knowing that the man didn't have the excuse of poor experiences with a doctor, male or female, as a reason for his scathing remarks only proved her assumptions. His attack was caused by blind, baseless prejudice.

It was incomprehensible that a man who was so intelligent, one who had made such a success of his life, could be so blind. How could he dismiss her—and all women—so easily?

Unbidden came the memory of those first moments when she had seen him, when that jolt of awareness, more powerful than an electric current, had flowed between them. It was lust, pure animal attraction. Fortunately, human beings were endowed with brains, and those brains kept them from choosing a mate based solely on physical characteristics.

She was not choosing a mate! That was not the reason she'd come to Alaska. Far from it. If her destiny wasn't to be a wife and mother—and it wasn't—she would find fulfillment in curing others' ailments.

As Amelia's hand tightened on a goblet, once again she resisted the urge to fling it. The truth was, she wanted to throw something hard and sharp at William Gunning, something that would shatter his complacent grin, something that would put another scar on that handsome face of his.

It was absurd, truly absurd, to care what William thought. She didn't, of course. Only a fool would waste her time even thinking about him when it was obvious that he was a huge bundle of prejudices. Whatever else she was, Amelia Sheldon was not a fool.

She slid a stack of plates into the dishwater, then began to scrub them as if the motion would eradicate William's smile and the hint of amusement she had seen in those gray eyes.

William Gunning might be wealthy and Gold Landing's most prominent citizen, but that was only a veneer over a tough, barbaric core. Though he might be attractive on the surface, there was most definitely nothing attractive once one peeled away the outer layer.

He was not like Abe.

Amelia smiled, thinking of the attorney. He had stayed by her side throughout the rest of the evening, and his gentle banter had kept her laughing. Had it not been for Abe, she might have lost her temper, but he had kept her well away from that man. He had talked to her about Philadelphia and had told her about his home in Boston. They had discussed books and concerts and operas, things that would have been foreign to William. Abe had understood why she had come to Gold Landing and—more important—why she had stayed. He was suave, cultured, kind.

Abe had been the perfect companion. He was the friend she needed. Why, then, was it another man's mocking gray eyes and grin that she saw when she closed her eyes?

Chapter Four

"Dr. Sheldon! Dr. Sheldon! Quick!" A man pounded on the door, his big fist threatening to knock it from its frame.

Amelia's eyes flew open, her sleepiness disappearing as quickly as it had when she had been a resident on call at night. Thrusting her arms into a robe, she ran downstairs to the front door. Somehow, though Ella's room was on the first floor, the knocking had not wakened her. "What is it?"

He stood on the porch, a burly, dark-haired man with the full beard so common among Alaskan miners. His dark eyes reflected fear. "There's been an accident at the mine." The man grimaced, as though feeling the pain himself. "Alex Fielding's arm is caught under a beam."

There was no mistaking the urgency in his voice or the silent pleading in his eyes, no need either to ask why Dr. Ben wasn't attending this patient. Without hesitation, Amelia ran back to her room. She flung off her robe, pulled on the first skirt and shirtwaist her hands touched, then grabbed her bag. Seconds later, she was in the man's wagon. "Is Alex conscious?" she asked when the jolting became rhythmic.

"Yep." The man, who had identified himself as John nodded without shifting his gaze from the road. "Unless he got lucky and passed out."

When they reached the deeply rutted continuation of First Street, Amelia grabbed the side of the wagon to steady herself. Though the clock said four A.M., the sun had already begun to rise. It was a dangerous time to be out, for the large animals—caribou and moose—would be grazing, creating the ever-present danger that they would cross the road and spook the mules.

With a grim expression, Amelia tried to recall the classes that dealt with arm injuries. They had concentrated on setting bones, but from John's description, a broken bone was the

47

least of Alex Fielding's problems. There was the brachial artery. If that were damaged . . .

As soon as the wagon halted, Amelia leaped down, heedless of the mud that covered her shoes and spattered her skirt. A group of men were clustered by the gaping hole that led into the mine shaft, their strained expressions confirming the gravity of the situation.

"It's the lady doctor," she heard a man whisper in astonishment.

"You can't go there." Another man tried to block the way. Amelia walked around him, and if annoyance made her grip her bag tighter, only she knew it.

"The mine's no place for a woman."

Spoken like the mine owner himself. Her blue eyes sparkling with anger, Amelia stopped and faced the man. "I'm a doctor," she said, emphasizing the last word. "Now let me through."

Perhaps it was the tone of her voice, perhaps the realization that a man's life was in danger. Though there was a low murmur of protest, the men moved aside, letting Amelia enter the mine.

It was not what she had expected. If she had been asked to describe a mine shaft, she would have said it was a long hallway with no windows. But instead of the reasonably proportioned space she had envisioned, she found a tunnel so small she could not imagine grown men using it. The roof was low, forcing her to bend her head, and the floor that sloped downward at an alarming pitch was rough under her thin shoes. Most of all, it was cold, reminding Amelia that the first step in Alaskan mining was thawing the earth.

Despite her sense of urgency, Amelia was forced to pick her way, following the directions John had given her. Alex, he said, had been working in the farthest tunnel doing exploratory drilling in the hope of finding a new lode. Once she turned off the main shaft, the tunnel seemed to stretch endlessly, lighted only by her lantern. *Hurry!* her heart urged her, while her mind advised caution. She could not fall, not now. Even so, she bumped occasionally against the side walls, stumbling as the adrenaline that coursed through her veins quickened her pace.

As the tunnel widened and veered to the right, a large form loomed in front of her. Amelia gasped, startled by the sight. John had said the mine had been evacuated. No one should have been here.

"Where's Ben?" the form demanded.

At the sound of his voice, Amelia stopped. *Oh, no! Not him!* Since the night he had attempted to humiliate her, she had ruthlessly thrust every thought of William Gunning from her mind. When the memory of his mocking gray eyes and smile had intruded, she had deliberately focused her attention on something else—anything at all—to avoid thinking of him. When patients mentioned his name, her stern gaze made it eminently clear that William Gunning was not a subject to be discussed in her presence. And now here he was, when she needed every ounce of strength to help Alex Fielding.

"Dr. Ben is, shall we say, incapacitated. Now, if you'll move, I must get to my patient." Though the cold had penetrated her shoes, she could feel heat rise to her cheeks.

William Gunning blocked her way. "You're a midwife. What do you know about mining injuries?"

Drawing in a sharp breath, Amelia clenched her fists in an effort to control her fury. She would not let him deliberately goad her to anger, not now, when a man's life was at stake.

"I know enough to assure you that if I don't treat him immediately, he may lose his arm," she responded tartly. "Whether you like it or not, I'm the only doctor available."

The big man turned sideways, his stiff movements making it evident that he was acting under duress. In her haste to pass him, Amelia's gait became uncharacteristically awkward, and her hand brushed against William's thigh. It was only a fleeting touch, but a tingle of excitement rushed from the sensitive pads of her fingertips up her arm as her senses registered the lean, sinewy hardness. Abruptly she drew her hand back.

Moving as quickly as she could, Amelia reached the site of the cave-in. Oh, God! A small cry of dismay escaped her lips. It was worse, much worse, than she had imagined. Half the roof had collapsed, filling the already narrow passage with boulders. No wonder William wasn't with the injured man. The tunnel was too small for someone his size.

Almost reluctantly, Amelia looked at the roof, trying to assess the danger. She knew little about mine construction, but what she saw filled her with terror. The supporting beams had given way and were now precariously balanced in the rubble. Even as she watched, one of them began to slip. A flurry of dust preceded ominous creaking.

Amelia's gaze moved beyond the cave-in. There, in the midst of the rubble and the filth, lay Alex Fielding, so silent and still that she feared she would be too late to help him.

Amelia dropped to her knees and began to crawl. *Please God, let him be alive,* she prayed as she thrust her bag in front of her, then slid to her stomach and inched the last few yards to her patient. Here at least the mine shaft was high enough that she could kneel. She heard him moan. Thank God! She had a chance. All other thoughts fled as she pulled her lantern closer and knelt beside him.

"Hello, Alex. I'm Dr. Sheldon." Although her mind recoiled at the horror before her, she smiled and spoke reassuringly as she began to examine the arm. Brushing aside the dust, she saw less bleeding than she had feared. Her fingers probed the wound, trying to assess the damage. "I'll try not to hurt you."

The beam creaked again, sending dust to the floor. Amelia sneezed, then continued her examination. As she touched the skin above his elbow, Alex made an effort not to wince. "You can't hurt me any more than the beam did." He took a breath, expelling it in small gasps. "Will I lose my arm?"

Amelia did not reply. She strove to keep from frowning as she looked at the mangled arm. Hadn't they taught her in medical school that a good doctor never alarmed a patient? A calm bedside manner was important.

She had practiced her bedside manner in class, and then in Philadelphia's best hospitals. But all the classes in the world could not have prepared her for the reality of this filthy, poorly lit Alaskan gold mine. She had listened, horrified, to her grandfather's tales of surgical conditions during the Civil War, never dreaming that when she herself became a physician she would be practicing in equally poor surroundings.

Instead of replying to Alex's question, she spoke lightly. "How's your fiancée?" Amelia tried to remember the girl's name but failed. "When's the wedding?"

A weak smile flickered across Alex Fielding's face, reminding her of someone, although at the moment she could not remember who. "Two weeks. Karen's sure gonna be mad if I don't make it to the wedding."

"You will." While she had been speaking, trying to distract her patient, her fingers had continued their exploration. She reached for her bag, withdrawing a hypodermic and the morphine. At least she had that. It was more than Grandpa had been able to give the wounded soldiers.

"Right now I'm going to ease the pain," she said, willing her voice to remain calm. "Just relax, and when you wake up, you'll be back in your own bed."

Amelia heard the beam shift but refused to look at it. She kept her fingers on Alex's uninjured wrist, monitoring his pulse as the powerful drug took effect.

"What are you doing to Alex?" a voice behind her demanded.

Amelia twisted her head in surprise. Though William was unable to enter the cave-in site, he lay on the ground, only his head fitting into the low passageway.

"I have to amputate the forearm," she said softly, hating to put words to her decision. When she had first seen the injury, she had known it was inevitable. The beam had fallen on top of the forearm, and although blood seeped from the area above the wound, Alex's hand and lower arm were dangerously white. Her examination showed that they were cold and clammy. Though her brain knew the reason, her heart balked at accepting it.

Amelia's first hope had been to lift the beam and try to save the arm, but a quick assessment had convinced her that that was futile. Two large wooden beams had once supported the roof of the tunnel. The ceiling was now riddled with holes, the result, Amelia assumed, of exploratory drilling. Apparently they had so weakened the roof that it had begun to collapse, dislodging one of the beams and loosening the other.

The one that pinned Alex's arm was now wedged between the floor and the second beam, preventing it from sliding to the ground and allowing the tunnel to collapse completely. Though it creaked and moved, the upright beam seemed to have stabilized, but Amelia knew that if the other were moved to free Alex's arm, the ceiling would be in danger of immediate collapse.

There was no choice.

The wood had crushed the bones, shattering them beyond hope of repair. Even if by some miracle she were able to move the beam and free his arm, Alex would never regain use of it. Amputation was the only answer.

"No!"

Once again Amelia turned to look at William, anger blazing in her blue eyes. Damn him! Did he think she was enjoying this? Couldn't he see that her stomach churned at the thought of having to maim a man? Didn't he realize that she was trying desperately to keep her hands from shaking?

"Would you please leave?" she asked, her voice low but determined. "Every minute that I waste arguing with you endangers this man's life. As his doctor, I can't allow that."

"And as his cousin, I can't allow you to amputate his arm." His cousin. That was why Alex looked familiar. "Think, woman! How will he work with only one arm?"

It was like the night of Ella's party. Seemingly without effort, he managed to find her sensitive spots and irritate them. The beam had smashed Alex's right arm. It didn't require a mine owner to tell her how critical that arm was to a working man. If there were any way—any way at all—to save it, she would. Yet, instead of letting her do her job, William was arguing with her, his arrogant tone abrading her already frayed nerves.

"At least he'll be alive, which is more than I can say if you don't let me proceed." She enunciated each word carefully in an attempt to keep from shouting at him. Cousin or no cousin, she would not let him interfere with her patient.

Amelia turned back to Alex and began to prepare his arm for surgery. This was not like the operating rooms in medical school, where everything was antiseptic. There, she and her fellow students had worried about preventing infection. Here, her only thought was preventing death.

She stared at the arm for a moment, willing her hands to be steady. Then, biting her lip to keep from crying out, she made the first incision. Amelia heard William gasp as the saw rasped through bone, but she forced herself to ignore him. She closed her ears to his groans as she did to the sound of creaking beams and slipping boulders, knowing there was nothing she could do to stop them if they decided to fall.

It took only minutes. Her rational mind knew that, and yet Amelia could have sworn that hours passed before she had stanched the bleeding. And still the beams continued to creak, forming a counterpoint to William's ragged breathing.

"Let's get Alex out," she said at last. "I'll dress his arm when we're safe."

For once William did not protest. He reached forward and grasped Alex's ankles, while Amelia guided his shoulders. When they had pulled the injured man through the narrowest part of the tunnel, William said, "You go first. I don't like the sound of those beams."

As the dust settled, Amelia shook her head. "This is not the place for chivalry, William. As much as I hate to give you the satisfaction of admitting there's something you can do better than me, I can't carry your cousin through the tunnel as easily as you can. Go! I'll be right behind you." Amelia's tone was sharper than she intended, tinged with fear and fatigue. She had been taught in medical school that it was normal to be physically and emotionally exhausted after performing surgery, but there had been no classes on the aftereffects of surgery in a mine shaft that was in imminent danger of collapse.

As William moved forward, his cousin cradled in his arms, Amelia crawled back to the site of the cave-in and gathered her instruments, throwing them haphazardly into her bag. She had to get out! Alex was safe, and with that knowledge came the realization of just how precarious her own situation was. She was alone in a mine that could collapse at any minute.

Once more Amelia scrambled through the narrow passageway, scraping her hands on rocks, ignoring the sharp stinging. All that mattered was getting out of the mine. When at last she cleared the low area, she grabbed her bag and began to run.

Perhaps she had somehow dislodged the beam. Perhaps it was nothing more than gravity. All Amelia knew was that the creaking changed. There was a momentary rumbling followed by the sickening sound of timbers splintering and boulders crashing to the ground. The mine shaft disappeared, replaced by a pile of rubble and a cloud of dust.

Though it was not yet five A.M., it had been a long day for most of Gold Landing. The news of the accident spread quickly, rousing the townspeople hours before normal. The men congregated outside the entrance to the mine. Gone was the jocularity that usually characterized their gatherings, replaced by fear, a fear so intense they could taste it. They stood in small groups, saying little, their drawn faces expressing what their tongues could not. One of them was injured, perhaps dying, and each of them knew he could have been the one lying under that beam.

For them, the mine was more than a livelihood. It was life itself. The men who descended into the bowels of the earth each day knew they were tempting fate, that they could not continue to gouge out Earth's belly with impunity. One day she would exact her revenge.

The women's lot was different. Unlike the men, who felt they had some control over their destinies, the women were forced to wait, powerless to affect the fates their men confronted. But as they sent their husbands, lovers and sons to the mine, they forced smiles onto their faces, trying to camouflage the ever-present fear that this would be their final farewell.

And so, when the news of the collapsed roof came, there

was little surprise, only a sense of inevitability.

"William's down there with Alex and the lady doctor," one of the men said in a hushed voice.

Another nodded. Few mine owners would have gone into a collapsed shaft, but William was not like other owners. He was a demanding yet fair boss, never asking more than the men could give, always ready to help them when he could. Although few of the men could have put words to his feelings, each knew that William was in that mine tunnel because it was his mine and he was responsible for it, not because the injured man was his cousin. He would have gone down that tunnel for any one of them. And so they kept a silent vigil.

"I hear something!"

"John, Jake, someone!" William's voice bellowed from the entrance. "Get a stretcher!"

Seconds later he emerged from the mine, his cousin clasped in his arms. William's face was somber, his lips pursed as if he were in pain. The light breeze that ruffled Alex's hair was the only sign of movement anyone saw, and so the men remained silent, not knowing whether Alex was still alive. But when William placed him on the makeshift stretcher, and Alex groaned, they let out a collective sigh of relief.

"Cover him," William commanded as he turned to reenter the mine. An instant later, the earth rumbled with the sound that turned a miner's dreams into nightmares. The lady doctor was still inside!

When three men ran toward the entrance, William blocked them. "No," he said firmly. "I'll go alone."

"You'll need help." Jake Bolton reached for a pick. Chet Wing grabbed a lantern.

William shook his head again. "It's too dangerous."

They ignored him, but they were too late. As they ducked their heads to enter the tunnel, a dust-covered figure emerged.

The crowd was silent no more. Shouts and cheers filled the air. Whatever doubts the men of Gold Landing might have harbored about the new doctor evaporated like dew in summer sun.

Gold Landing had its first heroine.

Chapter Five

"Ben, we've got to talk." Amelia made her final notes in Alex Fielding's chart, then turned to the other doctor. He was slouched in a chair in their small office, his eyes mere slits in his face. If she had had any doubt about why he had been unable to answer the call to the mine, it had disappeared the moment she had seen him sprawled on the waiting room couch, an empty bottle on the floor beside him. Amelia wasn't sure which had shocked her more: Ben's obvious intoxication or the fact that he had collapsed in a place where one of their patients could observe his state.

"Tomorrow." Groaning, Ben reached for the mug of coffee she had placed in front of him. The rich aroma started to dispel the stench of stale smoke and whiskey.

Amelia shook her head. Though she did not relish the confrontation, she knew her position was stronger today than it would be tomorrow.

Once she had assured herself that Alex's condition was stable, she had returned home, scrubbing her skin until the last of the dust had been washed away. If only it were possible to wash away the memories of that mine shaft, the smell of crumbling rock, the sound of creaking timbers and the taste of fear. Though in time they would fade, she knew they would never disappear completely. It was the memory of the horror she had faced that propelled her toward Ben's office.

"Who was it who said, 'Tomorrow never comes'? Sorry, Ben, but we need to talk today."

Ben took a deep swallow of coffee, then peered at her over the top of his spectacles. "Don't tell me you want to talk about your caseload."

As the small cuckoo clock that was the only personal touch in the room announced the hour, Amelia took a deep breath. "That's precisely what we need to discuss." She had approached Ben several times since her arrival in Gold Landing, asking why he wouldn't grant her full assistant status, why the only cases he assigned to her were obstetrics and gynecology. Each time he had refused to discuss his reasons, merely stating in his most unequivocal manner that the decision was final. Though he had no way of knowing how painful those cases were for her, that every time she held a baby in her arms, her heart felt as though it were being wrenched from her body, he still owed her an explanation.

"You already know my answer. Nothing has changed."

Of course he would say that. Amelia took another deep breath in the hope of controlling her temper. Lack of sleep and the strain of the surgery she had performed had left her nerves badly frayed and her temper ready to erupt.

She looked around the room, focusing on the bare white-washed walls, resolving to hang prints on one, a cheerful wall-paper on another. As her breathing slowed, she turned back to Ben.

"That's where you're wrong," she said. Amazingly her voice sounded calm. "Today changed everything. What happened in the mine this morning proved that I can handle a lot more than midwifery."

Ben kept his eyes focused on the floor as he took another swallow of coffee. It was not a good sign. Normally Ben had no trouble meeting her gaze, and she was certain the painted planks held no interest for him.

"Okay," he agreed. "You've convinced me. You're not confined to pregnancy cases." He agreed! Amelia's pulse began to race with anticipation. But her elation was short-lived, for Ben added, "From today on, you can handle all the female patients. If one of them scalds her hand or breaks a toe, you treat her." His tone left no doubt that he considered his pronouncement to be magnanimous.

Patience, Amelia counseled herself. She drew a deep breath, and the lingering smell of strong soap reminded her that she had made some progress in converting Ben. At least the office was clean. Though the man moved more slowly than a glacier, he wasn't an unyielding obstacle like William Gunning.

"I can do more than that, and you know it. I proved that this morning." Amelia shuddered, remembering the cold, dark tunnel where she had performed her first major surgery. "I can handle any medical emergency, whether the patient's male or female."

The clock continued to mark the seconds while Ben stared at the floor. With apparent reluctance, he let his bloodshot eyes meet hers. "I'm not going to argue with you. Whether or not you're correct, it's irrelevant." He spoke slowly, and Amelia wasn't sure whether to attribute his precise enunciation to his hangover or his belief that she was slow to comprehend. "The men don't need you. They have me."

It was hardly the explanation she had expected. For a moment Amelia remained silent, too shocked to respond. Then, one brow raised as if in disbelief, she asked, "Do they? It's strange, isn't it, but I could have sworn you refused to answer a call this morning."

Ben flinched, and she knew her barb had hit its target. "Damn it, Amelia! Last night was a mistake. I should never have started drinking."

"At least you recognize that."

He glared at her, his face reddening with anger. "You think you're perfect, don't you?" Without letting Amelia reply, he continued, "Let me tell you something, little lady. You're human. You make mistakes like the rest of us."

How dare he try to turn the tables and lay the guilt on her! Amelia could feel her face flush and her pulse begin to race at the injustice of his attack. "That's where you're wrong, Ben. I don't make mistakes like that."

Ben slammed the coffee mug onto the desk. "Don't push me, Amelia. I can always cancel your contract."

"And just who would that hurt?" she demanded as she swept out of the office, her head held high.

"Amelia! Wait for me!"

She was a block from Dr. Ben's office, her anger still unabated, despite the pace she had set for herself. There was simply no way she could go home feeling the way she did, and so she had headed west on Main, planning to walk to the edge of town. Fortunately, this was one of those rare times when the street was empty, or so she had thought until she heard Abe Ferguson's distinctive accent.

"Good afternoon, Dr. Sheldon." Abe tucked her hand into the crook of his arm, then nodded when Herb Ashton came out to unroll his striped awning. Amelia's lips twitched as she remembered Ella's account of the controversy that awning had generated. Apparently Gold Landing's residents had found the black and green stripes too great a contrast for the white store-fronts and had insisted that Herb remove the awning. The fact that it was still there raised the storekeeper a notch in Amelia's esteem. Perhaps in time the townspeople would grow as accustomed to the thought of a woman doctor as they were to a striped awning on Main Street.

She smiled again, feeling the tension begin to drain from her body.

"After this morning's events, I'm not sure whether I should toast you with champagne or put you on a pedestal," Abe said as they continued walking along the boardwalk. "Since I don't have either close at hand, let me just extend my congratulations."

A buggy raced down the street, spraying mud. Though they ducked into the hotel's doorway, they were too late. Amelia's dark skirt was almost as spattered as Abe's trousers.

She started laughing. "If Belinda could see me now, she'd say it served me right for coming to Alaska."

"Belinda?"

"My sister."

"Who apparently didn't approve of your coming here."

Shaking the mud from her skirt, Amelia nodded. "Belinda and my mother warned me I was going to the wilderness. They'd see unpaved streets as proof that they were right."

The distant howling of someone's sled dogs would have confirmed their opinion, as would the moose she had spotted in the distance yesterday. There was no doubt that Alaska was a wilderness, an incredibly beautiful one.

"Surely you don't regret coming—especially not today,

when Gold Landing discovered it has a genuine heroine.''

They reached the end of the boardwalk and, rather than walk through mud, headed back.

''A heroine?'' Amelia laughed at the thought. Though it seemed likely that Abe was exaggerating, she sensed at least a grain of truth in his words. And, oh, how sweet they were! If the townspeople recognized her as a real doctor, she would find a way to convince Ben to let her treat the men.

Where the hell was Ben Taylor when you needed him? William flung on his coat and headed out the front door. If Alex hadn't been sleeping, he might have slammed the door just for the satisfaction of hearing a noise. Since Amelia had left, the house had been deathly silent, the only sound Alex's breathing.

Damn Ben! When the man was sober, he was a good doctor. William's men swore by Ben, claiming he could work miracles. Miracles? Ha! What had happened this morning was no less than criminal. The mine had its first serious accident, and where was Ben? Home, too drunk to stand up, much less save a man's arm. Thanks to Ben's negligence, his criminal negligence, Alex's life had depended on a midwife's skills.

The sun was shining, a light breeze stirred the air, and the first birds to return after the long winter warbled their jubilation at being home. It was a close to perfect day, but William was oblivious to everything except his anger. He didn't care how hungover Ben was. The doctor was going to listen to some simple facts this afternoon, and then there were going to be a few changes in Gold Landing.

William's men were too important to have their health, their very lives, dependent on a drunken doctor and his fresh-from-medical-school midwife assistant. Oh, it was true the men were impressed with those big blue eyes and the face that was prettier than a film star's, and the women droned on for hours about how she'd saved Martha Johnson's life, but William knew the truth. Beauty had nothing to do with skill. Amelia had tried her best, but it wasn't good enough. If Ben had been in that mine shaft, the results would have been different.

William stormed down Main Street, ignoring the two people who called to him, asking about Alex, as he headed for Ben's house. He had no time and even less inclination for conversation now. He was going to give Ben a piece of his mind, and then he was going back to Alex. Lord knew, the man would need a friendly face when he came out of the morphine and realized what had happened.

His arm! Oh, God, Alex's arm!

William's eyes were the color of steel, his expression as unyielding as the rock his men dragged from the earth, as he strode down the street. How was he going to tell Alex what had happened?

Amputation! The very word brought back memories that William had spent half a lifetime trying to banish. At least Alex had been dead to the world. *She* had had to bear the pain. Seemingly without volition, his hand moved to his cheek to touch the scar. Damn it all! He wouldn't think about that day.

His eyes narrowed. A man and a woman were approaching, walking slowly, so engrossed in whatever they were saying that they could have been lovers. William glared at them, willing them to step out of his way. Then he glowered as he recognized them.

How dare Amelia Sheldon show her face on the streets of Gold Landing today! And to make things worse, she was with that useless lawyer again. They were laughing. Damn it! They were laughing. While Alex lay in his bed, a cripple for life, the cause of his misery was smiling at Abe Ferguson as if he were God's gift to Gold Landing. It was bad enough that she was smiling. The fact that it was at Abe, a man who contributed nothing of value to the town, a man who hadn't dirtied his hands once in his worthless life, a man whose only claim to fame was that he had a fancy education, made the crime far worse.

"Good afternoon, Doctor." William infused his words with sarcasm as the distance between them narrowed. "Is our resident legal expert giving you advice about malpractice?"

That got her attention, all right. She turned those blue eyes from Abe's pasty face and stared at him. "Malpractice?" she asked. "Why would we be discussing that?"

William feigned nonchalance as he shrugged. "Isn't it obvious? If I can find a real lawyer"—to make certain that Abe understood the insult, William glared at him for a moment—"he'll probably advise Alex to sue you."

Though the color drained from Amelia's face, the attorney did nothing more than raise an eyebrow. By the fires of Hades, wasn't there anything that angered that man? Of course not. William answered his own question. Abe was too cold-blooded to feel any real emotion.

"A suit on what grounds?"

As Abe posed the question, Amelia laid one of those delicate white hands on his sleeve. It couldn't be deliberate. Even she wouldn't be cruel enough to touch another man's arm simply as a reminder that William's cousin no longer had both of his. It was probably just an instinctive gesture.

William clenched his teeth. "Without his arm, Alex is gonna have trouble working." William directed his words at Amelia. "As I see it, if it hadn't been for you, he'd still have both arms."

Two birds landed on the roof of Ben's house and began to twitter. Amelia glanced at them, as if surprised by the sound. Then she glared at William.

"Just what do you mean by that?" The color rose in her cheeks. Damn! She was pretty when she was mad. Her face flushed like a flower, and those blue eyes sparkled more than the nugget he wore on his watch chain. But Amelia's beauty wasn't the issue. Her skill was. "No one could have saved Alex's arm," she declared hotly.

She was wrong. Totally, absolutely wrong.

"Ben Taylor could have saved it. Any man could have." He heard her gasp at the import of his words. "It's only hysterical women who don't think. They do whatever occurs to them first, and they think later. Because you did that, my cousin is a cripple."

William was goading her now, giving her a little of the pain he had felt ever since he had heard of the mine's collapse. He watched as she breathed deeply, obviously struggling to control her temper. Suddenly William was aware that there was a warm, pliant body under those prim doctor's clothes. Angry at the direction his thoughts were taking, he attacked again. "Think about it. Did you do everything you could have to save Alex's arm?"

Her face blanched under the assault. "You think about it!" she cried. "Who was it who kept me from reaching him? Who questioned my every move? You may be his cousin, but today you were just a man whose ignorance might have cost a life. If I were you, I wouldn't be impugning someone else."

Abe laid his hand on top of hers, as though to comfort her, and the sight inflamed William's already raw nerves. He opened his mouth to speak, then closed it as Amelia continued her tirade.

"You're fortunate Alex is your cousin," Amelia said. Though she kept her voice low, there was no mistaking the anger in it. "If he weren't, he'd probably sue *you* for criminal negligence. Think about why that mine shaft collapsed. If the beam was unsafe, it's your fault. Who ordered new drilling? Who sent Alex into that tunnel?"

William closed his eyes in pain. She had discovered his worst nightmare.

It was early afternoon, hours before visitors were expected. Some of the girls were just now waking; others had taken advantage of the comparative quiet to refurbish their gowns or wash their hair. June Woods, however, sat in a secluded corner of the small yard, plying her needle with a vengeance. It wasn't the sun she sought but the solitude. Today she needed to be alone with her thoughts and her fears.

Like the rest of Gold Landing, June had heard about the accident soon after it occurred. But while the other girls had returned to bed, sleep had eluded her.

William was in danger.

Even the news that he had escaped before the roof had collapsed, that he was not injured, had not quelled her fears. Another accident would happen, and once again William would risk his life for one of his miners. That was William, and nothing she could say or do would stop him.

"Ouch!" June winced as the needle pierced her finger. She shook her hand sharply, and a drop of blood flew onto the ground.

"What's wrong?"

June turned, a smile lighting her face. "William! I didn't expect you."

His hair was still wet, as though he had just bathed, and June noted that his shirt buttons were not aligned. Glancing down, she saw unmatched boots. Though she said nothing, her thoughts raced, trying to understand why he had come in the middle of the afternoon, why his clothing was in disarray. Neither had happened before.

"Is your room ready?"

Wordlessly, June led him into the house. When they reached her room, she stood for a moment, uncertain. But when William's arms closed around her and his lips fastened on hers, her doubts disappeared. For whatever reason, he needed her. That would have to be enough for now.

An hour later he lay beside her, one heavy arm draped across her body. "Oh, God, June," he said, and the despair in his voice seemed an echo of the desperation she had sensed in his lovemaking. "She accused me of being responsible for the accident. She said I pressed too hard for the new drilling, and that was why Alex lost his arm."

There was no question whom he meant. June's lips tightened. How dare that lady doctor insult William? Didn't she know who he was? Not only was he the most important man in Gold Landing, he was the handsomest one in all of Alaska. Today the man had worries enough without some fancy East Coast sawbones making his life miserable.

Though her thoughts were anything but placid, June softened her voice. "Honey, that's not true." She raised her hand to touch William's cheek, her fingertips tracing the harsh planes. "What does she know? She's never been in a mine before." Instinct told June not to mention the woman's name.

"Everyone in Gold Landing knows there's no one in the territory who has a better, safer mine than you."

"But what if she's right?" The words were so soft that June barely heard them. This, then, was the real problem. That bitch had said something that had hurt him.

"She's not." June turned, molding her body to his. One finger moved lightly over his mouth while her lips pressed kisses on his chest.

With a groan, William reached for her, and for a short while she was able to help him obliterate the memory of Alex's accident and a pair of angry blue eyes.

"It's all your fault."

With a herculean effort, Ben Taylor raised his eyelids a fraction of an inch. Peering through the slits, he looked at the woman who stood inside the door. Damn it! Why did she come today? Couldn't she see that his head was throbbing as though one of William's miners were pounding it with his ax? And his eyes! Just the effort of opening them brought a fresh wave of pain.

"Shut those shades!" he barked. Maybe if the room were dark, the pain would subside.

The woman did not budge.

"Shut them yourself."

Wearily Ben forced his eyes open. "What do you want?" She stood there like some sort of avenging angel.

"I want you to admit that it's all your fault."

"What's my fault?" Ben reached toward the lower drawer of his desk. He kept a bottle hidden there for emergencies like this.

"Oh, no, you don't, Ben Taylor." With a movement so swift it made his head throb again, she slammed the drawer closed. "I know what you've got stashed in that drawer, and you're not going to use it. That's what started all this trouble."

Ben clasped his head in his hands, hoping the pressure of his fingers would alleviate the pounding. "Look, woman, just say what you want to say and then get out of here."

She stared at him for a moment, her pursed lips communicating her disapproval more effectively than words. "You're pathetic," she announced. "You call yourself a physician, but what you really are is a drunken old man. Oh, you're fine for the little things when we don't really need a doctor, but whenever there's an emergency, you're not around."

As her words penetrated the haze that surrounded him, Ben's eyes snapped open, and he stared at the woman who stood opposite him as though he were seeing her for the first time. Why was she here? She was the last person in Gold Landing he would have expected in his office.

"She sent you, didn't she?" he demanded.

"Who?"

"Amelia, of course. You wouldn't have enough courage to come here by yourself."

Ella Roberts placed her hand palm down on the desk. "You're a fine one to talk about courage. The only kind you've ever found comes out of a bottle. Some courage that is!"

When the cuckoo clock began to ring, Ella's eyes widened as if in surprise. Amelia had reacted the same way the first time she'd heard it. What was it about women that they found the clock so incongruous? Another day, when he was feeling better, he would find the answer.

"Amelia didn't send me," Ella announced. "She doesn't even know I'm here. I simply realized it was time someone in Gold Landing told you what a despicable character you are."

"Despicable? My, my. The schoolmarm knows some big words, doesn't she?"

Far from silencing her, his sarcasm appeared only to fuel Ella's anger. "Would you like to hear a few more, like 'irresponsible' and 'reprehensible'? Or how about 'culpable'? Because that's what you are. If there's any blame to be attributed in today's accident, it's to you."

She certainly was riled.

"I suppose you think I caused that beam to fall on Alex's arm." Ben laughed, an act he immediately regretted. Was there no way to stop his head from throbbing? "Even though

I should be flattered that you think I'm capable of superhuman feats, I'm afraid I can't take the credit for that. Try again, Ella.''

''Of course I don't think you caused the accident.'' Ella's dark eyes flashed as she regarded him. ''But you should have been there to care for Alex. It wasn't fair to leave Amelia in that situation.'' As she inhaled, Ben saw her breasts rise. Odd. He'd never thought of Ella Roberts as having any feminine parts.

''You told her she's a midwife.'' Though her body might have curves, Ella's voice, while unmistakably female, was anything but feminine. ''You haven't allowed Amelia to assume any other responsibilities. But when it comes to an emergency that would test the skills of a veteran physician, you simply abdicate. A real doctor wouldn't do that, Ben Taylor.''

Ben lowered his eyes, unable to meet her clear gaze. The accusations had found their mark. How did the woman know that he had spent the last hour berating himself for being unable to help Alex? Was she a mind reader, sensing his own frustration and that damnable feeling of impotence? He had taken an oath to alleviate pain, to serve his patients, and yet when one had needed him, he had not been there. He didn't need this woman to remind him of his failure.

Instinctively Ben lashed out. ''You're a fine one to talk about 'real' anything,'' he jeered. ''I'm surprised you think you could recognize a real doctor, because all of Gold Landing knows you have no idea what a real man is like.'' He started to laugh again, then thought the better of it. ''God only knows what you'd do if you found one.'' When she flinched, he continued, ''Ella Roberts, the perfect spinster, the woman who knows the proper way to do everything.'' This time he did laugh, an action he regretted a second later. ''Everything except the important things, that is.''

As she gasped, Ben narrowed his eyes. ''I can't for the life of me figure out why Larry Wilson wants to marry you. You wouldn't know how to warm his bed. Or,'' he asked with a suggestive lift to his eyebrows, ''did you think Larry was interested in a platonic relationship?'' When her face turned white, Ben felt a momentary satisfaction. ''Believe me, Ella, Larry's a real man, and he expects a real wife. Now, what are you going to do about that?''

Chapter Six

Weddings were for the women, or so the people of Gold Landing claimed. Men didn't care for all that tomfoolery, getting gussied up in fancy clothes, listening to Bertha Langdon singing some sentimental tune, watching the other women pull out their handkerchiefs and dab at their eyes. A man didn't go to a wedding by choice, even if they did serve some mighty fine punch afterward.

Today was the exception. Today the mine was closed, and every man in town had slicked down his hair, forced himself into his best clothes and headed for the church. They owed it to Alex. The man was starting married life with enough of a handicap. The least they could do was be there to help him along the way.

William grinned. Truth was, he was looking forward to this wedding. There was nothing he could do to bring back Alex's arm. Ben had convinced him that no one—not even Ben himself—could have saved it, and so William had abandoned his idea of suing Amelia. What mattered was the future, and that was something he could influence. Once the ceremony was over, he planned to tell Alex that he and Karen wouldn't have any financial worries. The way William figured it, that was the second best gift he could give his cousin. He already had what he wanted most, Karen.

But now, in part because of Alex's accident, William had found a new lode, and if he was as good a judge of gold as he thought, it was a rich one. The quartz was so laden with the precious metal that it would take years to exhaust, and that meant that Gold Landing's men would have a steady income. Alex would get his share. Even if he couldn't handle a pick and shovel, William would give him part of the profits. He had earned them.

The day of the accident, when William had finally been able

to sleep, he had been troubled with nightmares. There was the old, familiar, dream, the one that had haunted him for years. But this time there had been a second one. A woman dressed in black stood at the entrance to the mine, pointing a bony finger at him. "Your fault," she cried, over and over again. "Your fault." Though he never saw her face, William awoke certain that the specter was Amelia.

She was wrong. The collapse wasn't his fault. He would prove it.

And so he had gone back into the shaft. When he had reached the low area and found that the rubble was too deep to be moved, he had started tunneling around it. One way or another, he was going to get to the room where Alex had been working. One way or another, he was going to check that ceiling to satisfy himself that there was nothing he could have done to prevent the cave-in.

William didn't believe in miracles, but he sure as summer sun wasn't going to argue with the evidence. His detour was only a few yards long when he found the gold. The lode that he had needed so badly was there, just waiting for his men to tap it. And tap it they would. Starting tomorrow. Today they had a wedding to celebrate.

Amelia reached for a hymnal. Though Ella had told her that weddings were popular social events, she had not expected to see the entire town at Alex and Karen's nuptials. Yet, as far as she could tell, other than Gloria's girls, who had not been invited, no one had missed the event. And, almost without exception, all eyes were fixed on the groom. He stood in front of the altar, a grin of pure happiness on his face as he looked at the woman who was soon to be his wife.

The scent of fresh flowers mingled with perfume and tobacco as Karen walked down the aisle. Normally the bride was the center of attention. Not today. Today she was upstaged by her groom, or more specifically by his right arm. Alex had pinned back his coatsleeve, leaving no doubt that the arm ended just above the elbow. There were a few hushed comments, but mostly the congregation watched and wondered.

"Dearly beloved, we are gathered here . . ." The ceremony began. Though it was only two weeks since the accident and the arm was far from healed, Alex appeared to have accepted his loss. When he smiled at his left hand's awkwardness as he placed the gold band on Karen's finger, it was a mocking smile, apparently devoid of self-pity. If Karen had cried, and Amelia had no doubt she had, she had done it in private. Whenever Amelia had seen Karen with her patient, the young woman had been smiling, looking at Alex as though he were the incarnation of every dream she had ever had.

"You may now kiss the bride."

A hush of anticipation filled the church as Alex put his arm around his wife. Though Karen gazed up at her groom, Amelia's eyes returned again and again to the man at his side. He wasn't handsome. She had told herself that a hundred times, but it was no use. Her gaze was drawn to William as salmon were drawn to the river of their birth, seemingly without conscious thought or volition.

Like Alex, William wore formal clothes, including the boiled shirt that Amelia's father had declared was man's punishment for leaving the Garden of Eden. But while Alex looked uncomfortable in the heavily starched shirt with its high collar, William seemed oblivious to his clothing.

It was ridiculous to be staring at him, but lust, Amelia was discovering, was more powerful than common sense. She had chided her sister Belinda for falling in and out of love so easily and seemingly indiscriminately. Today she felt only sympathy for Belinda.

"You have a beautiful bride," Amelia told Alex as she passed through the receiving line, watching as he extended his left hand to the men as easily as if he had been doing it for years. Now that the ceremony was over, it seemed that everyone spoke at once. Amelia raised her voice to be heard over the conversation and the organist's rendition of Mendelssohn.

Alex grinned in acknowledgment of the compliment while Karen spoke. "It's thanks to you that we even had a wedding," she said, and her eyes darted toward Alex, as though

71

reassuring herself that he was still standing next to her. "Alex wouldn't be alive if it weren't for you."

On the other side of Alex, William Gunning stiffened. Though he said nothing, his rigid posture told Amelia he did not share the new Mrs. Fielding's opinion, and when she greeted him, as common courtesy dictated, his eyes did not meet hers. That was a good sign, Amelia told herself. William, it appeared, was not suffering from the same ailment she was. He had no compulsion to stare at her.

With the ceremony over, guests filed into the community room, standing in small groups as they waited for the bridal party. When the church had been built, the townspeople had realized it would be used for more than religious services, and so they had attached a second building to one side, leaving it as a single large room that could be used for social gatherings and meetings that required only a few seats. Chairs lined two of the walls, while tables laden with food and drink were placed along a third.

Cheers rang out when the bride and groom arrived. Now the fun could begin; now the punch could flow. Amelia stood on the sidelines, watching the people of Gold Landing celebrate. And celebrate they did, thanks to William. He seemed to be making his way around the room, talking to each group of guests. Amelia had no idea what he said, but when he left, the people were invariably smiling.

"He's quite a man, isn't he?" Bertha Langdon smoothed the wrinkles from her kid gloves, then chuckled when they reappeared an instant later. With an exaggerated sigh of dismay, she looked at Amelia. "Gloves are such a bother, aren't they? But we were discussing William. My husband says he's a born leader."

Martha Johnson shifted her daughter to her other arm as she joined the discussion. "Emil says the same thing, but it's surprising, when you think about William's background."

Amelia didn't care about William Gunning. His upbringing, his leadership skills, even his wealth, which was the usual topic of conversation, meant nothing to her, and so she would not encourage the women. But, despite her best resolve, her eyebrow rose in what Martha Johnson chose to interpret as a question.

The noise level rose to a din, yet little Rachel Amelia appeared oblivious to her surroundings. Martha handed her daughter to Amelia, and for a moment Amelia succumbed to the delight of holding the sleeping child. She was perfection, pure and simple, as she slumbered, her tiny mouth open in an *O* as if something had surprised her. It felt good—so very good—to be holding Rachel that for a moment Amelia didn't hear what Martha was saying. If only Rachel were hers!

"Doesn't talk about it very much." Gradually Martha's words penetrated Amelia's absorption. "Heard his childhood was mighty bleak. They say his mother died when he was an infant, and his father disappeared."

Bertha cooed over the baby. "The men say he was a scavenger for a couple years before some woman took him in. No one knows much, but apparently the woman died, and William wound up responsible for half a dozen youngsters," she added. "But, like Martha says, he won't talk about it. Says the past is the past."

Remembering her own privileged childhood in Philadelphia, Amelia shuddered. She had known William had not been raised in the luxury she had taken for granted, but she hadn't realized he had been an orphan. How dreadful!

But today was a day for celebration, not pity, and so Amelia forced her thoughts back to the party. William would not want pity from anyone, especially not her. That much she knew.

As Herb Ashton began to tune his fiddle, feet started to tap, and the noise level rose again. "Ladies and gentlemen, let's clear the floor for the bride and groom." A sudden hush greeted his announcement. Then the guests moved to the sides, leaving Alex and Karen in the center of the room.

There was one awkward moment when Alex tried to put his missing arm around Karen's waist, but he recovered quickly and soon they were dancing as though they had done it a hundred times. Amelia's eyes misted, watching the happy couple. When the dance ended, there was a burst of applause and more than one woman wiped her eyes surreptitiously before the guests sought their partners.

"Would you mind holding the baby for one dance?" Martha Johnson asked, raising her voice to be heard.

With a smile Amelia urged Martha and Emil onto the floor. William, she noted, was dancing with Karen, while Alex partnered Bertha Langdon. Shoes and boots clattered on the polished plank floor as the music turned to a turkey trot.

"You look like a Madonna."

Amelia turned, startled by Abe's arrival. Though she had seen him in the church, this was the first time tonight they had spoken. "A Madonna?" That was one thing she would never be. She shook her head, trying to ignore the stab of pain Abe's words caused. "What you see is an honorary godmother pressed into service." Thankful that her voice sounded normal, Amelia shifted Rachel into her other arm. "Do you want to hold her?"

The normally unflappable Abe Ferguson looked startled by Amelia's suggestion. "I'd probably drop her," he admitted. "They didn't teach baby holding in law school."

When the dance was over and Martha had reclaimed her daughter, Abe turned to Amelia. "May I have the pleasure of the next dance?" He bowed slightly, and for a second Amelia thought she had been transported back to Philadelphia. How many times had the boys in her dancing class bowed in just the same way?

"Of course." She moved into Abe's arms, enjoying the sensation of being on a dance floor again. Today she was wearing a gown of violet satin with three deep skirt ruffles. The full sleeves ended below her elbows and were gathered into wide Irish lace ruffles that matched the lace-trimmed yoke. It was, Belinda had told her, a dress that begged to be danced in. To their mother's dismay, there had been little time for dances in medical school, but now Amelia saw no reason not to indulge in such a pleasant pastime.

"At the risk of being disloyal to the bride, I must confess that you're the most beautiful woman in the room."

Amelia smiled. Abe had definitely attended the same classes

she had, for her partners in Philadelphia had murmured similar compliments. Though she knew they were empty platitudes, Amelia enjoyed them for what they were: part of a ritual.

A portly man whom Amelia recognized as Frank Stratton bumped into her.

"Sorry," he muttered.

"Frank, you're so clumsy," his partner chided him. "How are you gonna catch a nice lady like the doctor if you can't dance?"

Abe's blue eyes twinkled as they met Amelia's. "Mrs. Stratton has a point."

"Then it's fortunate, isn't it, that I'm not in the market for a husband."

Abe feigned dismay. "Tell me it's not my dancing."

"*Au contraire.* You're the finest partner I've ever had."

"Don't you like dancing?" Amelia asked Ella when Abe escorted Bertha Langdon onto the floor and she and Ella sat down. Though Amelia's black kid pumps with grosgrain bows were pretty, they were not designed for long periods of standing. Ella's high-buttoned shoes were far more practical.

"I don't know whether I like dancing." Ella's dark eyes were serious, and frown lines appeared between them. "I've never done it," she explained. "I don't know how."

But as she looked down, Amelia saw that Ella's foot was tapping in time to the music. She smiled. "Dancing is easy," she said. "I'll teach you."

Ella opened her mouth, but before she could speak, a familiar voice asked, "Will you dance with me?"

Dance with William Gunning? She loved to dance. Moreover, the song Herb Ashton had begun to play was one of her favorites. She would love to dance to this particular tune, but not with this man.

"Why?" she asked. William had not exchanged a civil word with her since she had arrived in Alaska, and now he wanted her to dance with him. It made no sense. What made even less sense was the way her body responded to him. Though she could attribute her flushed cheeks to the warm room, there was no excuse for her pulse to have accelerated,

75

no reason other than the truth: animal attraction.

Amelia turned to Ella, but the woman had disappeared, probably because she had no desire to be between Amelia and William when the sparks flew.

"Why should we dance?" As William repeated the question, his eyes sparkled with more than a trace of amusement. "This is a wedding. People are dancing. It seems a reasonable thing to do." When Amelia did not respond, he continued, "If you're worried, I promise I won't sue you if you step on my feet."

A lawsuit. Of course he would think of that. Her name and crime seemed to be linked in his mind.

"I assure you, I won't step on your feet."

As William grinned, Amelia could feel her flush deepen. "I'm glad to hear that. I just polished these shoes."

Without deigning a glance at his feet, she retorted, "Your shoes are safe. I won't step on them or any other part of your anatomy for the simple reason that I'm not going to dance with you."

"Coward!"

She narrowed her eyes at William as she had seen her mother do when snubbing a social upstart. "Courage isn't measured by a dance," she announced.

"Isn't it?" William, it appeared, was oblivious to her intended insult. His smile seemed genuine, and for once she detected no barbs in his words. "Look, Amelia, a lot of people know we've disagreed in the past. Some of them were at Ella's party and heard our argument. You know we've been fodder for the gossips in this town. Today I thought we'd give them something different to talk about."

Put that way, how could she refuse? With a small smile that conceded the battle to him, Amelia placed her hand on his arm and walked into the center of the dance floor. The abrupt silence and then renewed buzz of conversation that followed in their wake told Amelia that William had been right. They were indeed major grist for the rumor mill.

William, it was soon obvious, had never attended the fancy dancing school that Abe had. His movements were less polished, and yet what he lacked in finesse, he made up for in enthusiasm. His steps may not have been perfect, but they were exuberant, leaving no doubt that dancing was a pastime William Gunning enjoyed as much as she did.

"Congratulations. I heard about the gold strike." Amelia smiled at him. If they were playing roles, she would do her part. Besides, if she was smiling, it would be less obvious that her pulse had accelerated to a dangerous pace and that her heart threatened to break through her ribs. Smiling might disguise the fact that her nostrils twitched at the woodsy scent that clung to him, and that her fingertips thrilled to the feel of his firm muscles. For it was vitally important that no one realize just how dangerous William Gunning was to her equilibrium.

An ebullient smile lit his face. "If I was a praying man, I'd say the strike was the answer to my prayers. Simple fact is, we needed that gold."

For a moment his gray eyes were serious, and Amelia sensed that William's worries had been for the whole town, not only his personal wealth. He spoke of the mine as if it were a living thing, making Amelia realize that William saw it as not only a source of employment for his men but also as an extension of himself. No wonder the new strike was so important.

"Mind if I cut in?" Alex tapped William's shoulder when he and Amelia were halfway through their second dance.

William frowned, and for a moment Amelia thought he was going to refuse his cousin. Then he nodded. "Good idea, Alex. Be sure you're real nice to the lady doctor now, because your wife's gonna need her services in about nine months."

Alex flushed. "You got a problem with that?"

"Hell, no. That's why a man gets married, isn't it? To have children."

"There are other reasons," Alex said mildly, holding out his arm to Amelia. "Companionship and—" He broke off, blushing.

William shook his head. "You can pay for the rest. It's the

children that make marriage worthwhile. Without them, there's no point in being shackled.''

Though she smiled at Alex and tried to pretend that nothing was wrong, for Amelia, the day was spoiled. Her mother was right. No one would want her.

It was a hovel. There was no other way to describe it. With walls whose chinks had never seen mud or the moss that many natives used instead of cement and only a small stove for heat, it seemed uninhabitable to Amelia, especially during the long Alaskan winters. Though she had visited one of the Philadelphia poorhouses and had been appalled by its squalor, it was palatial compared to this cabin.

Ella had warned her that Shantytown, as the townspeople referred to the cluster of dwellings on the other side of the river, was no place for a lady, but even that warning had not prepared Amelia for the dire conditions. Filth, crowding and almost incredible poverty marked the tumbledown shacks that housed miners whose claims had never panned out and who had refused William's offer of work.

''Will my baby be all right?'' The pale woman who had introduced herself as Carrie Gould stood next to Amelia, twisting her hands in her tattered skirt as Amelia examined the youngster.

The stench from the pile of rags that served as the family's bed overpowered even the pan of rancid grease. Amelia kept her expression as calm as she could. Two-year-old Paul had a sore throat and a high fever, and his mother confirmed that he had suffered bouts of vomiting and chills. Though those symptoms could be the precursors of several diseases, it was scarlet fever that Amelia feared, for Ben had reported a case only last week.

If Paul had the illness that had claimed so many youngsters' lives, it was likely that his five brothers would also contract it. Amelia sent the boys outside while she examined Paul, but she knew they would soon be back. With eight people living in a room half the size of her own bedroom, isolation was impossible.

"We have to bring the fever down," she told Carrie Gould. "I need buckets of cold water." She would give him quinine, though she doubted its value if this was indeed scarlet fever.

"Anything," the worried mother said. "I'll do anything for him. I love my boys, Dr. Sheldon."

Love was wonderful. Unfortunately, it might not be enough.

Three hours later, her rounds complete, Amelia returned to the office. She poured herself a cup of tea, then sank into the chair she had appropriated for her own. Though she had never considered the medical office opulent, in contrast to the Goulds' cabin, it looked palatial. Amelia was reminded of the tales that William had grown up in poverty. Had it been as dire as Shantytown?

"Ben, I've been thinking."

He looked up from the charts he was reviewing. "We're not going to talk about expanding your cases again, are we?" Ben asked. "Because my answer hasn't changed."

Amelia took a swallow of tea, then shook her head. Somewhat to her surprise, Ben had not objected when she had started treating the people who lived in Shantytown. Though they, like Carrie Gould and her family, were too poor to afford to pay her, Ben had said nothing other than that it was her decision. If she wanted to treat the indigent, she could, and there had been no restrictions. Men, women, children: Amelia could treat any and all of them.

"That's not what I wanted to talk about today." She gestured at the room with its single desk, three chairs and an examining table. It was more cheerful than it had been a month ago, now that she had hung pictures and wallpaper, but it was still small. "We've outgrown this office."

"Why do you say that?" Ben appeared to be genuinely puzzled. "We don't treat very many patients here." He leaned back in his chair, the picture of a man in repose.

As far as Amelia could tell, Ben had not had a drink in over a month. His eyes were clear, and he seemed, if not happy, at least content. Though she had once despaired of their working together, Amelia now found their practice exhilarating. That was, she knew, the result of her work in Shantytown. While the conditions were appalling, she relished the variety of cases she treated. Contentment would turn to happiness if only Ben would agree to her new plan.

"That's the problem," Amelia said. "We can't treat them here because we don't have the room. Some of our patients need isolation, even full quarantine. They can't all get that at home."

Ben peered over his spectacles, his expression skeptical. "So what do you recommend?"

"A clinic." The seed had taken root weeks before, and today's call on the Gould family had brought it to flower. "Gold Landing needs a clinic."

"Gold Landing needs a lot of things," Ben agreed, "but a clinic isn't one of them."

She had been afraid he would react that way. When she had mentioned the idea to Ella, her roommate had warned her that Ben was resistant to change. Amelia would have to find a way to convince him.

"Ben, the town's growing. It has new needs."

"I agree. That's why I hired you. I knew we needed more than one doctor."

That was one solution, but it was no longer enough. Amelia leaned back in her chair.

"With people moving farther out of town, rounds take a long time. If the patients came to us . . ."

Ben stood and walked to the window. A robin had built a nest in the cottonwood next to the window. "No chicks yet," he announced in answer to Amelia's unspoken question. "What makes you think people would come to us? They don't do that very often."

"Some do," Amelia pointed out. Since she wanted Ben's agreement, she forbore from mentioning that more would probably come if they could depend on Ben's being available to treat them.

"Even if I thought it was a good idea, which I don't," Ben was quick to add, "just how would you propose paying for this clinic?"

She had expected this question and had her answer ready. "Ella told me that the whole town contributed to the school fund."

Without turning to look at her, Ben said, "A school's different. Everyone's child needs an education, but not everyone needs a clinic."

Amelia stared at Ben, outraged by his statement. "Ben, you're a physician. How can you say that? Everyone needs medical care at some time."

"Medical care, sure." This time he turned, fixing his eyes on her. "Not necessarily a clinic. There are plenty of people who would never use a clinic. They expect us to come to them, and they're willing to pay for that service."

"But that doesn't mean that a clinic is a bad idea."

Ben shrugged. "I'm simply telling you what the townfolk will say."

If Ben Taylor thought she would give up that easily, he was mistaken. Though the Gould boy's illness had not been scarlet fever, Amelia knew she would not always be so lucky. Gold Landing needed a clinic, and she was going to do everything in her power to ensure that the town had it. She would plan her campaign as carefully as Grandpa told her the army had planned its battles.

"Any mail for me, Mr. Ashton?" The boat had arrived that morning, bringing supplies from outside along with what many residents prized more highly than sugar and flour: the mail.

Herb Ashton shook his head. "Afraid not, Miss Sheldon. But I got a new supply of muslin, if you need any. And there's some nice lace trimmings."

Swallowing her disappointment, Amelia turned in the direction he had indicated. She had hoped this week's boat would bring a letter from Belinda. Though she knew it took weeks—sometimes months—for mail to cross the country, she wanted to hear that her sister was happy. It was too much to hope that their mother had accepted Amelia's decision, but surely Belinda wouldn't refuse to write.

81

Since she could not conjure a letter, Amelia decided to look at the lace. If she added some trim to her white shirtwaist and changed the color of the bow, she could wear it the next time she had dinner with Abe.

Though most items in the store were arranged on open shelves and were visible to everyone, Herb had placed many of the feminine goods at the back of the store with bolts of fabric between them and the front door, thus providing shoppers a measure of privacy.

Amelia headed for the back of the store. The fabric was piled so high that she didn't see him until she rounded the corner. Looking every bit as comfortable holding a ladies' unmentionable in front of him as he did wielding a miner's pick, William Gunning stood in the ladies section. Amelia stopped, startled. She needed to talk to William, but not here, not with him holding a satin corset trimmed with blue ribbons and the most delicate lace Amelia had ever seen.

"Amelia." He nodded his greeting, then carried the garment to the front of the store. His footsteps rang on the wooden floor, and she heard a soft clink as the garters landed on the counter.

"June's gonna like this right well," Amelia heard Herb Ashton say.

"I thought so." There was more than a hint of amusement in William's voice. "Would you wrap it for me? I wouldn't want to scandalize the good folks of Gold Landing, carrying it down the street."

Amelia stared at the bolts of lace, trying to close her ears to the conversation, but she was as unsuccessful at that as she was at ignoring the faint scent that told her William had been here only seconds before.

Herb laughed conspiratorially. "There aren't many who haven't seen one of them."

"Yeah, but no one admits it. Isn't that why they call them 'unmentionables'?" He was still laughing when the door closed behind him.

So what if William bought the most beautiful corset imaginable for a woman named June? He was a grown man; it was his money; he could spend it any way he wanted. It didn't matter in the least. Amelia shook her head, annoyed at the direction her thoughts were going.

Who was June? It was of no importance, she told herself firmly, but a voice in the back of her mind pointed out that there was only one June in Gold Landing. Surely not! Not that she cared. Dropping the lace back onto the table, Amelia walked to the door. She had other business to discuss with William, and this was as good a time as any.

"William." He was halfway down the block. She lengthened her stride to catch up with him.

He turned, raising one eyebrow as though surprised to see her. "Good afternoon, Dr. Sheldon. Nice weather we're having." Since the day was cloudy and damp, with a wind that threatened to knock Amelia's hat off her head, she assumed he was joking.

"May I talk to you for a moment?" she asked. Surely he would agree with her plan. Though the man had no regard for women doctors, he cared about the town. What she was asking was for Gold Landing, not herself. When he nodded, she continued, "Gold Landing is growing."

"Sure is. The mine is prospering, and it's brought new people and business to the town." There was no doubt that William realized and relished his own role in that growth.

"That's true," Amelia agreed. "And those people have needs."

William doffed his hat in greeting as Vera Kane passed them. Amelia smiled, suspecting that the widow was on her way to consult Ben over an imaginary ailment.

"I'm not sure where this conversation is headed," William said. "Sure, we have needs, but they're pretty nearly all satisfied."

Amelia nodded. "True. Except for medical care."

"That's why we have Ben and you."

The wind tugged at the wide brim of Amelia's hat. She clapped her hand onto the brim, pushing her hat pins in more securely.

83

"The town is growing so rapidly that Dr. Ben and I can't be everywhere."

"So have Ben hire another assistant. If business is that good, he shouldn't object."

Amelia shook her head. That wasn't the answer. "What we really need is a clinic. Dr. Ben and I would be able to treat patients there, and we'd have an infirmary for people who needed special care."

Though William had been smiling, when Amelia mentioned the word *clinic* his lips straightened, and his gray eyes grew cold. "It's better for people to be treated at home."

"In many cases, that's true," Amelia agreed. "Still, I'm sure you realize that not everyone has a home like yours. There are people whose dwellings—I won't even dignify them by calling them houses—are totally inappropriate for medical care. There's absolutely no way to maintain proper hygiene."

Vera Kane strode past them without even a nod of greeting. She walked so quickly her skirt swirled around her ankles, revealing a froth of white eyelet. Ben, Amelia surmised from the woman's pursed lips, had not provided the sympathetic ear the widow sought.

William raised one brow, as though he were aware of the reason for Vera's frequent visits to the doctor. When he looked back at Amelia, his expression was once more sober. "Are you talking about the folks in Shantytown?"

Amelia nodded. "Them, and the Athapaskans, too. Some of them want care beyond what their shaman provides."

"The Indians." Though William's voice was toneless, his eyes blazed as he stared at Amelia, and the scar on his cheek seemed more prominent than usual.

As the wind shifted, Amelia could hear dogs barking and the distant whine of Sam Baranov's sawmill. She nodded again. "I'm sure you understand their need. Now—"

"No." It was one word delivered with the force of a lightning bolt.

Amelia's eyes widened. "No, what?"

"No, I don't understand their need." Had she thought his voice flat? Now it simmered with anger. "They made their

84

choice,'' William continued. ''If they want to live near the town, I can't stop them. That's their decision. But don't suggest bringing them where they don't belong.''

Amelia paused, trying to understand William. Could this possibly be the man Ella claimed treated the miners like part of his family?

''The Athapaskans are human beings, just like you and me.''

He shook his head, and a lock of brown hair spilled out from under his hat. ''That's where you're wrong. They're not like you and me. They're little more than animals.''

His voice was virulent, his anger palpable. The night of Ella's party when he had attacked her own credentials, Amelia had believed she was dealing with simple prejudice. Though she had known it would be difficult, she had been confident she could overcome that prejudice. She would show him that she—a woman—was as competent a physician as any man.

This was different. The tone of his voice and the look on his face told Amelia that William's condemnation of the Indians was not caused by prejudice but by hatred, a deeply ingrained loathing.

For a moment Amelia was so shocked she couldn't speak. ''You don't mean that,'' she said, hoping somehow she had misunderstood.

William regarded her with an expression as frigid as a glacier. ''I assure you that I mean every word of it. Do you want me to repeat my statement?''

The wind was cold and damp, penetrating her clothing and chilling her to the bone, but it seemed warm compared to his frown. Amelia stared at him for a long moment. ''No, I do not. Once was more than enough.'' Though her voice was low, she could not hide the tremor that betrayed both anger and sorrow. ''That was the most ignorant, prejudiced thing I've heard since I came to Alaska.''

William shrugged and settled his hat. ''If it's education you want, I suggest you go see that fancy lawyer friend of yours.''

''I may do just that.''

Chapter Seven

"Mr. Gunning. Mr. Gunning." The child had obviously been waiting for him, knowing he would pass this way as he walked to the mine. He stood at the corner of River and Second, only a few hundred yards from Sam Baranov's sawmill. At this time of day the mill was silent, a fact that River Street's residents undoubtedly appreciated.

William bent down and ruffled the boy's sandy hair. "Mornin', Theophile. What are you doing up so early?"

The lad's lower lip trembled, and for a moment William was afraid he would start crying. "You promised you'd call me Theo," he said.

"So I did." Lord, little boys were sensitive. "So, Theo, tell me why you're up so early."

As William emphasized the shorter name, the boy grinned. "It's that dratted sun," he announced, and William guessed he was parroting his mother. "I couldn't sleep." That was a familiar complaint at this time of the year, when the sun set for no more than four hours. "Got something to show you." Theo, who had been standing with one arm behind his back, handed William what appeared to be a tree branch with its bark stripped. Closer examination revealed a series of gouges in the wood.

Slowly, William turned the stick in his hand, examining it from every angle. "Good carving," he said when he had completed his examination. He had no idea what Theo had thought he was creating, but if he was lucky, the boy would tell him. After the slipup with his name, he could not afford another mistake.

As a mule team hauled a wagon loaded with trees toward the sawmill, William motioned Theo to the edge of the road. This part of River Street boasted none of the boardwalks that lined Main.

Theo's thin shoulders straightened. "I held the knife the way you showed me," he said. " 'Course it slipped sometimes."

"It does that to me, too." William turned his left palm up and pointed to two scars. "That's how I got those," he explained. "I wasn't as good as you." There had been no one to teach William the correct way to hold a knife. He had learned to carve the hard way and had the scars to prove it.

"Honest?" The boy's eyes widened.

William traced the carving with his forefinger, then handed the stick back to Theo. "I couldn't have done better myself."

As the wagon lumbered by, Theo grinned and darted a glance down the street. His feet shifted, and William knew he was anxious to get home. This morning it was not his mother's breakfast that beckoned but the chance to tell his older brothers of the accolades he had received.

"Know what it's for?"

This was the question William had been dreading. The boy would be hurt if he guessed incorrectly, but for the life of him, William could not imagine what anyone would do with a two-foot branch, no matter how carefully it had been carved.

"It's a walking stick," Theo announced proudly. Apparently he was in such a hurry to leave that he could not wait for William's reply. "Just like the ones you said the *chee-chakos* bought to cross the Chilkoot Pass."

William nodded sagely. "A man can always use a walking stick."

Theo shook his head. "This ain't for a man. I'm gonna give it to the lady doctor. Ma said she's gonna lose her footing on the tundra someday, so I figured she needed a walking stick."

The lady doctor. Oh, no. William could imagine the disdain on her face when Theo presented her with his crudely carved stick, which was at least two feet too short to be of any use. With one of those barbed comments that she seemed to like so much, she would destroy the little confidence the boy had developed.

"Good thinking," was all William said. "Dr. Sheldon certainly can use a walking stick." The truth was, she probably could. It was just this particular one that was of little value. Somehow he would find the doctor before Theo did, and he would explain how much her approval would mean to the boy. She would probably try to flay his hide the way she always did, but William's hide was tough. Theo's wasn't.

As Theo scampered home, William continued toward the mine. There was a good chance Amelia would not listen to him. It was obvious she had been angry when he had refused to support her plan for a clinic. Imagine wanting to treat Indians along with whites! Everyone in Alaska knew that wasn't done. Why, the Nelson Act even made it official, requiring separate schools, but Amelia was so new to the territory, she didn't know what was right and wrong. She would learn. William only hoped she didn't learn the hard way.

It was the last day of school, and judging from the sounds that filtered out of the small building, Alaskan schoolchildren greeted the start of the summer holidays with the same joy Amelia and her sister had. When she entered the room, Amelia found the smaller children sitting in a circle while the older ones appeared to be helping Ella pack books and clean the blackboard.

The drawings that had papered one of the whitewashed walls were gone, and the potted flowers had been moved from the windowsill to a box on Ella's desk. Now virtually devoid of decoration, the room looked stark, a fact that bothered the children not one whit.

"No, Ed, you can't tie Mabel's braids to the chair." Though she was facing in the opposite direction, Ella appeared to know everything that was occurring in her classroom. "Rebecca, give Helena her doll." Ella smiled a greeting as Amelia laid her black bag on her desk. "Jeremy, I think Dr. Sheldon would help you put the box on the shelf if you asked her."

Ella was in her element, no doubt about that. At home, she was quiet, almost reticent, but here her face glowed with enthusiasm. Today a few strands had escaped from the braids that Ella insisted on wearing, although they had been out of fashion for years. She would probably frown, saying the errant hair was messy, but the loose strands lent softness to her face and, combined with her smile, made her pretty.

"You really enjoy this, don't you?" Amelia asked when the last of the children had left, hugging their teacher and assuring her that they would be good all summer.

Ella nodded, then turned back to the blackboard. Although one of the students had cleaned it, it still bore chalky streaks. "I love teaching. Every moment." She dipped a rag in the pail, then grinned at Amelia. "Well, almost every moment. I can't truthfully say I enjoyed the day Jeremy brought a family of mice in his lunch pail." She wiped the board. "Still, it's so rewarding, working with the children, watching them grow and knowing that I had a part in that."

Though Amelia had assumed that Ella loved both teaching and her students, this was the first time she had expressed her thoughts. "In a couple years you'll have children of your own," Amelia said softly, trying to ignore the anguish that did not seem to diminish, no matter how much time passed. She had thought she would grow to accept her own infertility, but so far she had failed.

"Maybe." Ella wrung out the rag before she continued. "Sometimes I dream about holding my child. I can picture her." She smiled. "I just know it'll be a little girl. In my dream, it feels so good. But Amelia, I'm scared." Ella's eyes darkened for an instant. "How will I bear the pain?"

It was a common fear. "Childbirth is painful," Amelia confirmed. "Luckily, we doctors can help with that."

"It's not that. It's . . ." Ella blushed at the sound of a man's whistling. "Oh, here comes Larry."

The church was almost as full as it had been the day of Alex and Karen's wedding. Ella had told Amelia that virtually every adult in Gold Landing attended the quarterly town meetings, and it appeared that she had not been exaggerating. The citizens took their government seriously. Glen McBride, obviously proud of his role as mayor, stood in front of the group. "Well, folks, I believe we've completed all of our old business. Is there anything new?"

This was the moment she had been waiting for. Amelia took a deep breath to calm her nerves, then rose, placing the carved wooden stick that Theo had given her on her chair. "Your honor." She raised her voice so it would carry to the back of the church, which was still as bright as noon, even though it was late evening. "I'd like to address the town on an issue I believe to be of great importance."

The low murmuring that had characterized the first hour stopped. "Go right ahead, Miss Sheldon." The mayor motioned to Amelia to come to the front.

She looked at the people who had gathered for the meeting and who now stared at her, their curiosity evident. Many were her patients; she knew the others by sight. They were all good people; she was certain of that. The question was, would they agree with her? Would they take her side if William opposed her? For one thing had been eminently clear throughout the meeting: though Glen McBride might be the duly elected mayor of Gold Landing, no decisions were made without consulting William.

Tonight he sat in the last pew, a spot normally occupied by either the tardy or the shy. Since William was neither, Amelia wondered why he had chosen the seat. While most of the citizens wore their workaday clothes, William was attired in a suit, and even from the front of the church, Amelia could see the gold nugget fob on his watch chain. Tonight he looked like a prosperous businessman, not a man who spent at least one day a week wielding a pick and shovel.

Amelia wrenched her gaze from William and addressed the assembly. "As you know, Gold Landing is growing rapidly. We've seen new families come on almost every boat, and the old ones are increasing in size."

A heavyset man in the back of the room chuckled. "We keep you in business, delivering those babies, don't we?"

Amelia smiled. Though she suspected he wanted to remind her she was a midwife, she would not give him the satisfaction of reacting to his words. "Precisely. The town's medical needs continue to increase, and there's certainly no indication that

that trend is going to stop. As a result, Dr. Ben and I have a very full caseload.''

Though Amelia heard a few people shift on their pews, she looked at William, watching for his reaction. By now he must know what she was going to propose, yet his expression remained calm, with no hint of the anger he had displayed when she had asked for his support.

"You ain't complaining about being busy, are you?" another man demanded.

"Indeed not."

The first man rose, and Amelia recognized him as Frank Stratton. "How come you're up there and Dr. Ben isn't?"

As all eyes turned toward Ben, Amelia looked back at William. His lips twitched, as if he were trying to suppress a smile, but his eyes were serious when they met hers. She had heard the man was a good poker player. If tonight was any indication, he had mastered the art of concealing his thoughts.

"As I was saying," Amelia continued without answering Frank's question, "we're busy caring for the sick and injured, but sometimes we can't get to everyone."

"She's right," a woman chimed in, raising her voice to be heard over the low conversation. "It was awfully late when she got to my house last week."

Frank Stratton had no sympathy. He shifted his considerable weight from one foot to another. "Good thing the doctor is practicing here in the land of the midnight sun, isn't it? Sure makes it easier, goin' 'round in the evenings."

Though a few people tittered, the majority kept their gaze on Amelia, watching for her response. The only way she knew to deal with a man like Frank Stratton was to ignore his attempts at humor. "If Gold Landing had a clinic, many of the patients could go there for treatment rather than having to wait for Dr. Ben and me to reach them. They would receive medical care more quickly."

"A clinic, huh? Is that what this is all about?"

Though a cool breeze came through the open door, Amelia felt her palms grow moist. She had not been this nervous even during final exams. It was important, vitally important, that the citizens understand how urgent the need was.

She nodded. "I believe that the time has come for Gold Landing to establish a clinic."

"Just who's gonna come to this clinic?" Frank demanded.

Amelia saw William lean forward ever so slightly, as if this was what he was waiting for. She chose her words carefully. "The clinic would be open to everyone in Gold Landing."

More murmurs.

"Everybody? Does that include the folks in Shantytown?" Martha Johnson asked.

Rather than answer the question directly, Amelia posed one of her own. "Do you think they should be able to use the clinic, even though they won't be able to pay the same fees as you?"

There was a moment of silence, then a number of whispered comments. Martha looked at Emil before she replied. "Reckon sick is sick," she said. "I surely wouldn't want it on my conscience that someone else's baby didn't get the same chance my Rachel did."

The murmurs grew louder as people discussed Martha's answer.

" 'Pears to me we've gotten offtrack." Glen McBride stepped forward and tried to bring the meeting back to order. "The question at hand is whether Gold Landing needs a clinic, not who the doctors are gonna treat. Dr. Sheldon said she thinks we need a clinic."

"Well, I don't agree." A man Amelia recognized as one of the miners rose. "We don't need newfangled notions here. There's nothing wrong with the way we've always operated."

This was an argument she had anticipated, and Amelia was prepared for it. "Times change," she said, smiling to take the sting from her words. "Only a few years ago, everyone panned for gold in the streams. Now you work in a mine shaft." Her eyes darted to William. He was once more leaning back, apparently relaxed, but his expression was one of intense concentration. "If the citizens of Gold Landing hadn't been willing to change the way they operated"—she repeated the miner's words to make her point—"the town would have died as so many other Alaskan gold towns did."

More whispers greeted her statement. Although Amelia couldn't tell whether the soft conversations meant agreement with her, at least the citizens weren't apathetic.

Amelia tried not to frown as Frank Stratton rose again. "Sure, times change, but that doesn't mean we need a clinic. William, we haven't heard your opinion."

The muttering increased as people turned toward the back of the church. William rose. "You're asking the wrong man. If it was a question about mining, I could answer that, but folks, when it comes to medicine, I'm plumb ignorant." He chuckled, then said conspiratorially, "I thank the good Lord every morning that the only time I see Ben is when we're playing poker."

Laughter erupted, defusing some of the tension. Amelia's palms began to dry.

"So, William," Frank Stratton asked, "do you think we need a clinic?"

"I thought I just explained that *I* don't need one, but I can't answer for everyone in Gold Landing. That's a decision each one of you has got to make."

Amelia let out a breath she hadn't realized she had been holding. William may not have supported her, but he also had not scuttled her proposal.

"I still don't agree," Frank said, "but I reckon we should ask our senior doctor what he thinks." He turned to Ben, who had sat silently in his pew throughout Amelia's presentation. "Dr. Ben, what do you think?"

Amelia watched as people shifted on the hard wooden seats so they could see Ben. Without rising, he said, "I defer to my assistant on this matter." Ben had agreed, albeit reluctantly, that he would not oppose her, but it was clear from his manner that he would provide no support, either. William raised an eyebrow, as if surprised by Ben's lack of support.

Frank grinned, celebrating his victory. "Well, folks, it seems Dr. Ben doesn't like the idea any better than we do. I make a motion that we ask the lady doctor to sit down and forget about nonsense like clinics.''

Before anyone could second the motion, Abe Ferguson jumped to his feet. ''You've made an excellent point, Frank,'' he said, nodding to emphasize his words. Amelia noticed that in this light his hair appeared the same shade of blond as her sister's, and for a moment she wished she were back in Philadelphia, where there would be no debate over a clinic.

''Before we vote, I'd like to ask Dr. Ben three questions. As Frank pointed out, he is our senior medical expert. I believe we should be guided by him.''

This time there was no doubt about it. The murmurs signified approval. While Ben appeared angry, an expression of grudging respect crossed William's face.

''Dr. Ben, would you stand for a moment so everyone can hear your responses?'' Abe addressed the doctor as he might have a hostile witness. It was, Amelia suspected, a valid analogy. Ben rose, his reluctance evident.

''We all applaud your having hired an assistant,'' Abe said. ''One question, though. Even with Dr. Sheldon helping, are you able to treat every complaint the day you hear about it?''

For a long moment, Ben did not reply. Then he shook his head.

''I didn't hear that,'' Abe said.

As the wind whistled, someone rose to close the door.

Ben glared. ''No,'' he said, his voice carrying clearly to the last pew.

''Thank you.'' The light reflected off Abe's spectacles as he nodded. ''Now, my second question. If Gold Landing had a clinic, is it likely you'd be able to treat more patients than you and Dr. Sheldon do now?''

Again Ben glared at Abe, obviously not liking the direction the questions were leading. ''Yes,'' he admitted, pushing his own glasses back on his nose.

''Thank you, Doctor. I'll only take your time for a minute longer. My final question is, as a physician, would you agree that it's good medicine to save as many lives as possible?''

''Yes.''

Abe waited until Ben was seated; then he said, "Ladies and gentlemen, I move that we appoint a committee to select the site for Gold Landing's first medical clinic."

To Amelia's surprise, William rose. "I second the motion." It passed.

He might have been wrong. Though she looked like an empty-headed socialite who had come to Alaska on a lark and who had no use for anyone who didn't have the same fancy background she did, she sure wasn't acting that way. William transferred his hat to his left hand and moved out of the pew so the others could leave.

It appeared Polly had been right when she had told him to see what lay below the surface. A man could forget that admonition when the surface was as pretty as Amelia, but it was sage advice. And in Amelia's case, there were many depths to explore.

He nodded as Emil Johnson thanked him for seconding the motion. Now that the meeting was over, people were in a hurry to leave. All except Amelia. She stood up there, talking to the mayor.

Funny, she was a lot tougher than she looked. It took guts to stand up in front of the town and argue for her beliefs, especially when a jackass like Frank Stratton kept heckling her. Lord, that man liked to hear the sound of his own voice. But she hadn't backed down. She stood there and waited until he ran out of steam, then continued with her own speech. Not many men would have done that, and William sure as mosquitoes in the summer didn't know any other woman who would have had that kind of courage.

She had a mind of her own, but she also listened to reason. Why, tonight she hadn't so much as mentioned treating those damned Indians. She had obviously recognized the truth in what he had told her. That made it a whole lot easier to support that clinic that she thought was so important.

Ben clapped him on the back as he left. "Cribbage tonight?"

William shook his head. He had other plans for what was left of the evening.

Amelia was kinder than he had thought at first. He remembered the way she had taken little Theo's stick into the town meeting. It served no earthly purpose, and yet she had carried it in one hand, her black doctor's bag in the other, just as if it were one of her most treasured possessions. William hadn't missed the way she had hung on to it for a second before she started speaking. He would bet Theo's mother had seen that. Even if she didn't tell her son that the lady doctor had used his gift, William would. He would make sure he saw the boy tomorrow before he went into the mine.

Nope, the new doctor sure wasn't what he had expected. He had been hard on her when she had first come, but Lord, she looked like a fragile piece of china, not like a woman who could survive in the north. So far she had proven him wrong, and he owed her an apology. He had been too hard on her after Alex's accident. He had let his own anger and his worries about how Alex was going to deal with the loss of his arm cloud his judgment, and so he had taken out his pain on Amelia. She hadn't deserved that.

William didn't doubt, despite Ben's protests to the contrary, that Dr. Ben could have saved Alex's arm. He was a better physician than Amelia would ever be. Women simply weren't cut out to be doctors. But the simple fact was, Dr. Ben hadn't been there, so it didn't matter just how talented a surgeon he was. If it hadn't been for Amelia, Alex would have died. Those were the facts, plain and simple. Another fact was, he owed her an apology.

As the church emptied, William made his way forward. There was no time like the present. He would tell her he was sorry, and then maybe he would invite her to the Grand for a cup of coffee or sherry or whatever it was she drank.

"Amelia."

But she brushed right past him as if he were smaller than a gnat, her eyes fixed on the back of the church.

"Oh, Abe, thank you!" She tipped her face up to the soft-spoken lawyer and smiled. "I can't tell you how much I appreciate your support."

William felt as if he had been punched. He grimaced, then drew a deep breath, trying to quell the pain. Though his first reaction was to wipe that smirk off Abe's face, he knew that would accomplish little.

What had he expected? Of course Amelia would rather be with Abe than with him. They were the same kind of people. They shared the same things—education, culture, memories of the East, books. Abe was always talking about the books he read. William figured it was a substitute for the life that silly lawyer didn't have. Still, ever since Amelia Sheldon had come to Gold Landing, Abe had had a friend. That was more than William could claim. Oh, he had plenty of friends, but not one was a woman. And tonight that seemed like a damned shame.

He strode out of the church, then turned left. Tonight he would take the long way home rather than risk seeing Amelia with Abe. A man didn't deliberately open himself to pain. He avoided it if he could, and he made sure it didn't happen a second time.

Polly had taught him years ago that even though a man made his own life, he had to be realistic about it. He, William, would probably never be President of the country, but he could be the owner of a mine. And so he had set about building the best gold mine in the territory.

Now he wanted something else. He knew he had to be realistic, but being friends with Amelia Sheldon wasn't like running for President. He didn't have to be born into the right family or know the right people. It might not be easy, but it was something he could do. It was something he *would* do.

William smiled, remembering the times he had spoken to Amelia. Lord knew, they weren't the easiest times of his life. She had a tongue that was sharper than a bear's claw, but one thing was certain: talking to her wasn't boring. She made a man come alive. And that was good.

Before the summer sun set, he was going to make Amelia Sheldon his friend.

"Amelia!" It was two days later when she came out of the Johnsons' cabin. William had spent those two days learning

97

her routine. Afternoons, she did her rounds on the east side of town. He reckoned that if he just happened to be on the path when she headed back to town, she couldn't object if he walked with her. After all, you never could be too careful. Everyone knew there were bears in the brush, especially now that it was summer and they were foraging for food.

Today the sun shone brightly, and there was not a cloud in sight. Even without climbing the hill, he could see the distant mountains, their snowcapped peaks rising majestically above the tree-covered slopes.

Amelia wore the dark skirt and white shirtwaist that seemed to be her work uniform. For the life of him, William couldn't understand how she managed to look so neat, so clean, after a day spent traipsing around the countryside. But her clothing was immaculate, and not a hair escaped her coiffure.

She stopped, evidently surprised to see him. He had expected that. After the disagreements they had had, a man could hardly expect her to welcome him. At least not today. She reminded him of some of the children he had known, a little wary at first. He would have to gain her confidence.

"How's your namesake?" he asked, knowing the reason she had visited the Johnsons was to check on the baby.

Amelia smiled, her happiness evident in those blue eyes that outshone even the Alaskan sky. "She's healthy and growing. Her parents and I couldn't ask for more."

William matched his pace to hers, shortening his stride. How did she keep her balance on the uneven tundra in those frivolous-looking high-buttoned shoes? And then there was her bag. Judging from the way she held it, it was far from light. He would have offered to carry her bag, but he didn't think she would agree.

"It must be a good feeling, knowing Rachel is alive because of you." The way he figured it, the only reason a person would want to be a doctor was to save lives. According to Ben, there wasn't much money in it.

Amelia stopped again, fixing her gaze on him. This time, though her blue eyes sparkled, there was a faint sadness behind the smile. Odd. He wouldn't have expected sorrow. "I didn't do it alone,'' she said softly. ''Martha's a strong woman, and she was determined to have that baby. If she had stopped fighting, there wouldn't have been a single thing I could have done.''

''But she couldn't have done it alone. The way I hear it, both of them would have died if you hadn't been there.''

Though the wide brim of Amelia's hat cast shadows on her face, William saw her lips tremble ever so slightly. She was silent for a moment before she said, ''That's probably true. I think God put me in that cabin to help them and to make sure that Rachel Amelia had a chance at life.'' This time there was no doubt that her voice quavered with emotion.

It was odd. In all the years he had known Ben Taylor, he had never heard him speak that way. Oh, he knew Ben experienced a rush of pleasure when he saved a life, but there had never been anything so . . . *mystical* was the only word William could find to describe Amelia's words.

''You sound as though medicine's a calling for you,'' he said. When he had wondered why Amelia—or any woman—would want a man's job, he had never considered that she might view it the way Reverend Langdon did his work, as something he had to do.

Amelia nodded. ''It's something I've wanted all my life.''

The chasm that separated him from Amelia loomed deeper and wider than before. She had had a purpose from childhood on, while the only constant in William's life had been the desire to survive.

The soft breeze carried the scent of lilacs. William looked around. They were too far from the Johnsons' cabin to smell theirs, and lilacs did not grow wild here. He sniffed again, then saw the spray of purple flowers peeking out of Amelia's bag.

''Is that a new remedy?''

Amelia laughed, a soft tinkle that seemed to banish her momentary sorrow. ''Not in the conventional sense, but my grandfather always said that people respond to pleasant fragrances.''

''Your grandpa was a farmer?'' William could not keep the

surprise from his voice. His view of Amelia Sheldon did not include a farm.

"No, Grandpa was a doctor. He's the reason I chose medicine."

The cold edge of envy stabbed William. What must it have been like to have grown up with a family? He had never known his parents, much less his grandparents. He had known that he and Amelia were different. That was why they disagreed so often. What he had not realized was that they appeared to share nothing other than living in Gold Landing.

Willing his voice to remain even, he said, "Then he was the first Dr. Sheldon."

"Actually, Dr. Bailey. He was my mother's father." Amelia smiled as if she remembered something pleasant. "By the time I was born, he was fairly old, but he was still practicing medicine and trying to convince young men to study it."

"So instead a young woman followed in his footsteps."

"I'm trying," Amelia admitted.

The breeze shifted, bringing the fresh scent of pine needles. William inhaled deeply. He had always loved the smell of pine.

As they walked, Amelia sniffed, then smiled. "Lovely," she said before she continued her tale. "Grandpa used to tell me that we're all born for one reason, and that's to make the earth a better place. He did it by saving soldiers during the Civil War. As for me, I'd like to think Rachel Johnson was my first small step."

Her eyes shone, and her voice reminded him of Reverend Langdon preaching a sermon. Who would have thought the doctor was such an idealist? William frowned, remembering the day she had pleaded the Indians' case. This friendship was going to be more difficult than he had expected. There she was, a shiny-eyed dreamer from a fancy family, and here he was, a man with no illusions about anyone or anything, a man who had seen the rough side of life once too often. What on earth did they have in common?

"Idealism like that's nice," William said as they walked

toward town, "but a man's got to be practical. You've got to live."

She put her hand on his arm and looked up at him, those blue eyes shining with happiness and something that, if he hadn't known better, he would have called admiration. "Exactly," she said. "Isn't that what you've done? When the gold streams were overworked and the town was threatened, you found a way to save it."

The way she talked, you would think he was some kind of hero, like the knight in Polly's book. "Are you talking about my mine?"

"Of course."

He hated to disillusion her, but if they were going to have any sort of friendship, it had to be based in reality, not her starry-eyed dreams. "Amelia, digging that mine was a business decision, pure and simple. I made a hell of a lot of money doing that."

She nodded as those rosy lips curved into the sweetest smile he had ever seen. "Making money is no crime. The important thing is, you saved the town at the same time. That's what I mean about making things better."

She didn't understand. He had said it as plainly as he could, but she didn't seem to hear. "Don't try to make me into something I'm not. I'm no saint."

Her laughter bubbled like a mountain stream. "Oh, William, I never said you were!"

But he was the most fascinating man she had ever met. At first glance, he seemed so simple: a rough, uneducated miner with more than his share of prejudices. But the more time she spent with him, the more facets she discovered. He might be rough, but he was also kind and honest and honorable.

William Gunning, it seemed, was a bit like the nuggets he wrested from the earth. Surrounded by dirt and rock, the gold wasn't easy to find, but it was there, waiting for the careful miner.

They were worlds apart, separated by far more than their backgrounds, and yet that shouldn't keep them from being friends, should it?

Chapter Eight

"I heard you convinced the townspeople they needed a clinic." Gloria leaned back in the chair, resting her vividly colored hair against its high back. "Good work. I won't say it's overdue, but it's certainly time."

Amelia shook her head, wondering, not for the first time, what her mother would say if she could see her. Lydia would undoubtedly be scandalized by the fact that her daughter not only treated Gold Landing's prostitutes, but actually enjoyed her conversations with the madam. "I wish I could take credit for the clinic," she said, "but I'm afraid if it had been left to me, the motion would have died. Abe Ferguson turned the tide." Amelia smiled, remembering his skillful questioning. "It's no wonder he's a lawyer, the way he can persuade people."

"That's what I've heard." Gloria offered Amelia a second cup of coffee, then refilled her own. The china bore a delicate Limoges pattern, as elegant as the rest of the room. "I probably shouldn't tell you this, but Abe's one of the two men in Gold Landing who's never been here." Gloria smiled. "My girls have been trying to decide just what they'd have to do to entice him through these doors. Of course, they don't dare speculate about the other man, since he's the minister."

Gloria's words unleashed a barrage of emotions in Amelia, and she set her cup on the table, lest Gloria hear it rattle against the saucer. Pleasure that Abe had as much integrity as she had thought warred with the strangely disturbing reminder that William frequented Gloria's establishment. It didn't matter, of course. It was not as though they were courting. William was simply a friend, although it did seem that she met him more and more often on her afternoon rounds. So what if the conversations they shared were as exhilarating as the icy water in the stream and if she found herself looking for him when she left the distant cabins? The fact that he visited Gloria's girls did not change a thing.

"I only wish we had been able to convince the town to use brick," Amelia said, deliberately forcing herself to think of something other than William. Her voice quavered ever so slightly, a fact she was sure Gloria would realize was caused by her concern over possible fires and had nothing whatsoever to do with how William Gunning might or might not spend his evenings. "After the great Fairbanks fire, I thought the townspeople would agree to brick."

"Be happy with what you're getting," Gloria advised. "And don't forget that when they rebuilt Fairbanks, they used timber. This isn't Philadelphia, Amelia. Brick's expensive."

Amelia nodded, thankful that the older woman hadn't noticed her momentary discomfort. "Even after the clinic's built, I'm planning to continue my monthly visits. I'll do the routine checkups here, but if you or your girls need emergency care, come to the clinic."

Gloria stared at Amelia for a long moment, waiting until the delicate ormolu clock stopped chiming before she spoke. "We can't go there." Her voice was as matter-of-fact as if they were discussing the weather.

"Why not?"

"Oh, Amelia, don't be naive. You didn't see us at the town meeting, did you? And we won't be at the Fourth of July celebrations, either."

Neither of those statements surprised Amelia. Whether they were called soiled doves or working girls, the women who practiced what was commonly considered to be the world's oldest profession were not part of any town's society. That had been true in Philadelphia, and even though the social classes were less distinct here in Alaska, there were still lines that could not be crossed. But social events were one thing; medical care was different.

"You have needs, too," Amelia protested.

Gloria's lips curved into a wry smile. "Not according to the town. We're here to satisfy some rather specific needs, but we're not allowed to have any of our own."

103

"That's not fair."

"Amelia, my dear, haven't you learned that life isn't fair?"

"Foolishness, that's what it is."

William glanced up from the cribbage board after he planned his next move. "What now?" he asked. It wasn't unusual for Ben to complain about something; the only question was what had provoked his ire this time. William suspected it was not the fact that both Frank and Alex had backed out of their weekly poker game tonight, leaving William and Ben to play cribbage.

At least they were in his kitchen rather than Ben's rather cramped quarters. When he had built the house, William had insisted on spacious rooms and high ceilings. There would be no physical reminders of the tiny cabin where he had spent his childhood. But memories, he discovered, were not so easily left behind.

"What's wrong? That Independence Day nonsense, that's what." Ben snorted, then pushed his spectacles back on his nose.

"I thought you liked the parade and fireworks." William knew he did. Fourth of July in Alaska was a cause for celebration, not just of the country's independence but of the long summer days, that brief time known as the midnight sun. Although other holidays involved gala celebrations, nothing compared to July Fourth.

"They're okay." Ben shuffled the cards. "What I hate is that picnic basket folderol."

He had a valid point. William laughed, remembering some of his experiences. Like many towns, Gold Landing had an annual picnic basket auction, where each of the women prepared a special supper, placing it in a carefully decorated basket. The auctioneer was in his glory, convincing the men to outbid each other for both the basket and the privilege of eating supper with the woman who had prepared it. And since men greatly outnumbered women in Gold Landing, competition could be fierce. No man wanted to join the chow line that night and eat with other men when he could have a homemade meal and feminine companionship.

"What's the matter, Ben? I thought you'd be happy this year. After all, the money is going for the clinic."

The roast that he had put in the oven an hour before was starting to fill the kitchen with its aroma. Though William did not enjoy cooking, he knew enough that he did not starve.

Ben sniffed appreciatively. "That supposes I thought the clinic was a good idea."

"C'mon, Ben. You know you like the idea; it's just the fact that Amelia thought of it that rankles." William had heard Ben's complaints but had finally gotten him to admit that maybe, perhaps, possibly Gold Landing might benefit from a clinic.

"Could be," Ben agreed. "But that still doesn't make me like the picnic supper."

"So don't bid on any of the baskets."

Ben peered over the top of his spectacles, aghast. "And eat with the men? No, thanks!"

"Then what's the problem?" Though William knew the answer, he enjoyed baiting his friend.

"I never can figure out whose basket I'm getting."

"I'm sure Vera Kane will give you a hint about which one is hers." Although no one, even the auctioneer, was supposed to know who had prepared which basket, it was generally accepted that women provided little clues. One might tie a favorite color ribbon on her basket. Another might paint a special design.

"I imagine Vera would, if I wanted her basket."

William raised a brow. "I thought you were seeing her." It was no secret that Ben had paid more than professional calls to the widow Kane's cabin, and her frequent visits to Ben's office were common knowledge.

Ben shrugged, then reached for his glass. "It's simple," he said. "She wants to get married. I don't."

William was surprised. He thought everyone wanted to marry . . . eventually. "Now, Ben, I can understand your reluctance to enter into the state of wedded bliss. Only a crazy man would take that step without a lot of careful thought. But there are some compensations. Like children."

Ben's expression remained shuttered.

From the corner of his eye William caught a glimpse of motion in the backyard. He turned his head and saw a cow moose browsing on the flowers Alex's Karen had planted only a week ago. Karen would be angry as all get-out when she learned that her geraniums had turned into moose fodder. Though he had protested that he didn't need them, William had to admit that the bright flowers had been pretty while they lasted.

"You don't want children?"

"No." Ben dropped his gaze to the table and took a long swallow of whiskey.

"No little Ben Taylors to cure the next generation's ailments?"

Ben looked up. The shutters had fallen, revealing brown eyes filled with pain. "I said no."

"Why not?" Though William had the vague notion that Ben might have been married before he came to Gold Landing, his friend had been remarkably closedmouthed about his past. Even when he drank too much, he did not reveal details of his life before Alaska. But the expression in his eyes told William that whatever had happened, it still haunted him. "Can I help?" William knew all about pain and being haunted.

"It's none of your business." Ben emptied his glass. "Now, are we playing cribbage or not?"

Amelia managed a smile for the anxious young woman. "Well, Mrs. Fielding, I'd say that your suspicions are correct. You're going to have a baby." Her voice was surprisingly calm, as though the words were not among the most painful in the English language for her. It hurt so damnably much, confirming another woman's pregnancy.

Amelia chided herself. She was happy for Karen and Alex. Truly, she was. And yet the knowledge that she would never be in Karen's situation, enjoying the wonder of her first pregnancy, was a wound that never healed. Gloria was right: life was not always fair.

Karen stretched her hand across the small table where the doctor had joined her for a cup of coffee and touched Amelia's hand. "I'm so glad you're here, Dr. Sheldon. I just wouldn't feel as comfortable with Dr. Ben. A woman understands what another woman is going through."

But I don't, Amelia wanted to protest. *I only wish I did.* She managed another smile and said, "Dr. Ben agrees with you. That's why he hired me—to help the women." The thought no longer rankled, now that she had her practice in Shantytown. But the pain of watching other women with their children was constant.

"You know, you're really lucky, Dr. Sheldon. After all your schooling and experience helping us, you'll know just what to expect when you have your own babies."

Lucky was not the way Amelia would have described herself.

"I know it's probably unpatriotic," Ella said later that day while she and Amelia were washing the dinner dishes, "but I hate the picnic supper. I get myself into such a tizzy, worrying about who's going to bid for my basket."

Amelia swirled the last glass in the soapy water. "Won't Larry buy it?"

"How would he know which one was mine?"

Amelia handed her the glass to dry. "I thought you'd hint. Tell him what decorations you were going to use."

Ella stopped, the towel hanging limp in her hands. "But that would be cheating."

Amelia smiled. She should have known that Ella, with her firm ideas of right and wrong, would feel that way. "Was it cheating when I asked you to fry enough chicken for my basket, too?" she asked.

Ella shook her head. "That's what friends are for."

Two days later, Amelia walked toward the open field where the main festivities would be held. Though it was still an hour before the parade would start, Main Street bustled with activity. Men were driving stakes into the ground and stringing rope between them to keep spectators safely cordoned from the street. It was, Amelia knew, a necessary precaution, for in the excitement of the celebration, people might venture into the parade path. That was one of Ella's primary worries, for this year the schoolchildren had asked to participate.

Ella had spent hours each afternoon teaching them to march in time to music, and more time each evening sewing bunting for them to wear. Today Amelia—and the rest of Gold Landing—would see the results of their efforts.

As Amelia walked down Main Street, she waved at the people who had decided to watch the parade in the center of town. Every building on Main was draped with red, white and blue bunting, and, perhaps in deference to his customers' sensibilities, Herb Ashton had completely covered his awning with the nation's colors. Flags hung from the light poles and festooned front porches. Even in Philadelphia, the birthplace of independence, Amelia had never seen such an outpouring of patriotism.

At the far end of town she joined Martha Johnson and several of her other patients from outlying cabins, spreading her blanket next to theirs. While some towns erected viewing stands, Ella had told Amelia that Gold Landing preferred a more casual celebration.

"Isn't it wonderful?" Amelia cried, rising and waving a small flag as the band approached.

Gold Landing's marching band consisted of half a dozen men whose enthusiasm exceeded their talent. Their instruments were a little out of tune; they played wrong notes as often as the right ones, yet no one seemed to notice. The onlookers sang along, and those who did not know the words joined in by clapping. The children, led by Ella, marched behind the band, and if some of the flags they waved had obviously been dropped in the dust, no one paid any heed. They were too busy singing and clapping along with the students.

Amelia wasn't certain who was proudest of the schoolchildren's parade: Ella, the parents or the children themselves. All she knew was that watching those children place their hands over their hearts and recite the Pledge of Allegiance was one of the most stirring moments of her life.

The mayor's speech was not. Amelia listened at first as he reminded them of the sacrifices the country's founding fathers had made, but when his voice continued to drone louder and more monotonously than the mosquitoes, she found her attention wandering. She looked at the others, wondering if they were as bored as she. Martha Johnson had Rachel to keep her occupied. Ella, who had joined Amelia after the parade, was smiling, probably at the memory of the children's success. She couldn't find the mayor's speech pleasing.

Amelia had assumed that Ella would sit with Larry, but she had learned that no one except married couples sat together during the parade and speeches. It was only when the games began—the footraces, tugs-of-war and relays—that courting couples would pair off.

Amelia's gaze moved on, searching the crowd. She wasn't looking for anyone in particular, of course. She simply wanted to see who had come to the celebration.

Abe sat with Herb Ashton, his straw hat perched at a jaunty angle. Amelia kept looking. As if by chance, her gaze lighted on William, who sat on the opposite side of the field with Ben and Frank Stratton. Of course the poker buddies would stick together. Ben looked totally bored. As for William, his expression was blank. He wore a blue chambray shirt that accented his broad shoulders, and like several of the other men, his straw hat sported a red-white-and-blue-striped ribbon. Though he lounged, leaning back on his elbows, no one would mistake his position for indolence. Instead, he reminded Amelia of the tigers she had seen at the zoo, apparently at ease but actually poised to leap.

The analogy was apt, for William exuded both the power and the grace of the big cats. She suspected he could be as ferocious as a tiger, and yet there was another side to the man who ran Gold Landing's mine. The William who joined her at the end of her rounds was strong and opinionated, but he also listened. And when his gray eyes met hers and he smiled

109

that smile that could melt the thickest glacier, there were times when she forgot that they had no future, that they could never be anything other than friends.

They had come a long way from that first disastrous encounter in Ella's parlor. Though Amelia suspected that William still doubted she or any woman could be a good doctor, he no longer berated her for her choice of professions. For her part, Amelia had learned that he was a man who cared deeply about people. She thought of the way he worried about little Theo.

As Rachel began to fuss, Amelia gathered her into her arms and began to croon. It was as foolish as picking the scab off a cut, and yet she could not help herself. The baby was so sweet.

Amelia forced her gaze back to the mayor. Surely he would finish soon. When he did, the burst of applause was so generous that he opened his mouth as if to give an encore. Amelia stifled a groan. But before he could begin, the minister climbed onto the speakers' platform.

"All right, gentlemen. If you're like me, watching the parade and listening to the mayor's fine speech has worked up a powerful appetite. The time has come to satisfy that appetite and raise some money for our new clinic." Reverend Langdon had agreed to be this year's auctioneer. "Yes, folks, we've gotten to the event many of you tell me is more exciting than the fireworks. It's time for the picnic basket auction."

The crowd, which had grown restless during the mayor's speech, settled back with a collective sigh. As the minister pulled out the first basket, Ella gasped, then turned to Amelia, apprehension filling her dark eyes. "Not first," she murmured.

The minister held up the basket, showing off its red gingham ribbon, telling the audience that he smelled fried chicken. "How much am I bid for this beautiful, bounteous basket brimming with biscuits and . . ." He chuckled. "Will someone start the bidding so I can stop thinking of words that start with a *b*?"

Larry jumped to his feet. "I bid two bits."

The crowd roared its appreciation of Larry's wit. Though

two other men joined the bidding, in the end it was Larry who prevailed, much to Ella's obvious relief.

"Did you have anything to do with this?" she asked Amelia as she rose to collect her basket and take her place at Larry's side.

Amelia smiled and repeated Ella's own words: "That's what friends are for."

On the other side of the field, William exhaled. "At least I don't have to worry about getting stuck with Ella's basket," he told Ben. "I can't imagine eating a meal with her. She wouldn't say two words the whole time."

Ben relit his pipe. "You might be surprised. The last time I saw her, she had a tongue like a viper."

"Ella Roberts? Are we talking about the same woman?"

"Yeah. She sounded like she'd swallowed a dictionary and was spitting out all the bad words. 'Course," Ben admitted, "I might have deserved a few of them." He pointed to the basket the auctioneer was holding aloft. "That looks like it could be Amelia's. Do you reckon Abe will bid on it?"

"Sure as bears eat honey."

A puffy white cloud scudded across the sky, then stopped, apparently snagged by one of the distant mountain peaks. William stared at the cloud for a long moment before he allowed his gaze to return to Amelia.

Was it her basket? She was watching the bidding with interest, but William could not say that this basket held her attention more than any of the preceding ones. Still, there was no denying the fact that the navy ribbon on its handle matched the trim on her shirtwaist. Not that he had been studying her, of course. A man just noticed some things.

Abe Ferguson obviously thought the basket was hers, because he opened the bidding at a dollar.

William would not bid on it. Definitely not. Oh, there was no doubt that he would rather eat supper with Amelia Sheldon than any of the other women in Gold Landing. She had the prettiest smile of all of them, and that soft white shirtwaist didn't do much to camouflage curves that would fit a man's hand so well. He doubted she could cook, so the food inside the basket was probably close to inedible, but at least she would talk to him, and that would be ample compensation for a mediocre meal. Most of the other ladies kept their eyes on the ground and would not venture an opinion on anything more significant than tomorrow's weather.

Amelia was different, which was why he would not bid on her basket. He wasn't about to subject her to the kind of gossip that would result if they had supper together. Lord knew, he heard in excruciating detail every time she and that useless lawyer shared dinner in the Grand Hotel.

Sure, he wanted to sit next to Amelia. She was probably wearing some of that flowery perfume that made a man want to see if she tasted as good as she smelled. And William didn't doubt for a minute that she would tickle his funny bone with some comment about the mayor's speech. But it wasn't worth the gossip. He would rather meet her outside of town, where they weren't the object of constant speculation.

Ben rose to his feet. "I bid six bits," he announced, gesturing with his pipe.

"Are you crazy?" William demanded when the doctor was once more seated. "Why did you bid for Amelia's basket? You surely don't want to spend the evening with her." Even though William did.

Ben laughed. "I'm not that dumb. Watch what happens." Abe jumped to his feet and increased the bid. "See? As you took great pains to tell me, the money is for a good cause. Besides, I like watching Abe cough up more money. It serves him right for making me look like a fool at that town meeting."

Though two other men joined the bidding, each time Abe increased the amount until he was the final bidder, promising the princely sum of ten dollars.

"Sold to our very own lawyer," Reverend Langdon announced, his face beaming. "And now, who's the lucky lady whose basket has earned so much money for our clinic?"

Everyone turned toward Amelia. William tried not to look. Why torture himself with the knowledge that that smile was for the one man in Gold Landing he truly despised? But his eyes had a will of their own. To his surprise, she remained seated and seemed to be looking around, as if searching for someone. Then she smiled. Heads turned in the direction of Amelia's gaze, and there was a collective gasp as Vera Kane rose.

"Who said there was no justice?" William demanded when he had stopped laughing. It served Abe right.

The next basket, a plain round wicker one with no ribbons or embellishments, did not provoke much competition. "I might as well bid on this one," Frank Stratton said when the bidding remained low. William chuckled, knowing that Frank hated to part with a dime and only participated in the auction at his mother's insistence.

Reverend Langdon asked for another bid, then nodded. "Okay, Frank. Come claim your supper and see which of Gold Landing's fair ladies will join you."

This time William darted a glance at Amelia, and for the second time he was surprised, for she rose gracefully to her feet. As Amelia walked toward the platform, Ben started laughing. "Talk about justice!"

William groaned. "It's not over yet. We don't know whose we'll get." When he won Charlotte Langdon's basket and Ben was paired with Martha Johnson, William knew that Fate had a wry sense of humor.

Though the sun was still high in the sky, the day was almost over. The mayor pulled out his pocket watch and announced that in ten minutes it would be eleven o'clock and time to start the final event of the celebration: the fireworks.

Ella looked around. Where was Amelia? She hadn't seen her since the picnic supper. Poor Amelia, getting stuck with Frank Stratton. Larry said it served Frank right for making such a fuss at the town meeting, but all Ella could think was how bad it must have been for Amelia.

Ella searched the crowd, nervous that she had lost sight of Amelia. Where was she? The fireworks had started. Surely she would not want to miss them.

Whoosh! Bang! Sizzle! The explosions continued, each

113

bringing brightly colored stars to the sky, and with each detonation the crowd roared its pleasure. A portly woman whom Ella recognized as Mrs. Stratton jostled Ella, knocking her into Larry. As he wrapped his arms around her, Ella's palms began to sweat. *No!*

"I've got to find Amelia," she told Larry in a shaky voice. Breaking loose from his grasp, she ran pell-mell through the crowd, murmuring apologies as she stepped on feet and bumped elbows. She had to get away.

Bang! The noise came from behind her. Ella turned, her pulse accelerating as she realized something was wrong. Terribly wrong. All the fireworks were supposed to be lighted in the center of the field. Why had this explosion come from the other direction? A child screamed in pain. Ella pivoted toward the cry. There in the bright twilight she saw a small form crouched at the edge of the field, yards away from everyone, howling in agony. For a second, Ella stood still, paralyzed by fear. Then she started to run.

"Jeremy!" she cried when she reached the boy. The practical joker from her classroom lay huddled on the ground, holding his hand in front of him. *Dear Lord, no. Let it all be a dream.* But it was no dream. Ella knelt next to the child and took his hand in hers.

"What happened?" she asked, reaching for her handkerchief. The wound was bleeding so profusely that she could not see what was wrong. She could feel the bile rising in her throat. *Not now,* she told herself. *Jeremy needs you.* She would bind the wound as best she could. Then they would find Amelia. Amelia would know what to do.

"I wanted to help with the fireworks," the child said, sobbing. His body trembled from shock and fear. Without a thought for her skirts, Ella sat on the ground, drawing Jeremy into her arms.

"There, there," she said, keeping her voice low and calm. Her own panic began to subside as she realized that the child would live. "You'll be all right."

"They said I was too little to help," Jeremy told her.

"So you took a firecracker and tried to light it yourself."

114

It was not hard to imagine what the boy had done. Mischievous Jeremy was learning a lesson the hard way, and oh, how it hurt to see that. A child should not have to know such anguish. Unbidden, the memories of an almost unbearable pain swept through her, and she shuddered.

"We've got to find the doctor," she announced, trying to regain her composure. She could not let Jeremy sense her fears.

She stood and looked for Amelia, but there was no sign of her friend. Then she saw him. He was standing on the edge of the crowd, his pipe in one hand. "Ben. Dr. Ben!" she shouted. "We need you."

He covered the distance in seconds. "What have we here?" He undid Ella's makeshift bandage.

"Is it bad, Doctor?" the boy asked, his voice as shaky as Ella's had been earlier. He leaned back against her, seeking comfort.

"I won't lie to you, son," Ben said, his face grave. "This is a serious laceration. I'm going to have to stitch it."

As Ella felt Jeremy tremble, she drew him closer.

"What's a lass . . . a lasso . . . whatever you said?"

"Laceration," Ben repeated as he put a reassuring hand on Jeremy's shoulder. "That's a fancy way of saying a cut. Now, let's get you to my office and fix it."

The boy clung to her. "I want you, Miss Roberts. Stay with me. Please."

The fireworks continued, brilliant bursts of color against the still-bright sky. It was no longer a beautiful sight for Jeremy. As each one exploded, he cringed.

Ella looked at the doctor. "Ben?" she asked.

"Good idea." He nodded, then scooped the boy into his arms.

Another explosion. Another soft whimper.

"I'm not a baby," Jeremy protested. "I can walk."

"Of course you can," Ella agreed. "The doctor knows that. He just wants to get us to his office as fast as he can so he can get back to the fireworks. Isn't that right, Dr. Ben?"

"Miss Roberts is correct. We don't want to miss the finale,

do we?'' Each year at the conclusion of the fireworks, the band reassembled and played the national anthem. Ella doubted they would be back by then, but if the thought distracted Jeremy and made his pain easier to bear, she would not argue with Ben.

She gathered her skirts in both hands as she ran down Main Street, trying to keep pace with Ben. For the first time, Ella wished she had listened to Amelia and shortened her skirts. She raced up the stairs and flung open the door to Ben's office. When Jeremy was lying on the examining table and Ben began to cleanse his wound, the boy looked at Ella. ''Will you tell me a story, Miss Roberts?''

And so, while Ben sutured the finger, Ella invented a tale of a boy whose finger was eaten by an evil dragon, and the only way he could get it back was to visit a magician. Using nothing more than a needle and thread, the magician would weave a new finger for the boy.

''All done,'' the doctor said a few minutes later, his eyes twinkling as they met Ella's.

''And that's the way the boy regained his finger,'' Ella concluded her story.

They walked back to the fireworks, Jeremy skipping between the two adults, a wide grin on his face. ''Dr. Ben is a magician,'' he announced. ''It didn't hurt when he sewed my finger back on. Wait till the guys hear that.''

It was not much of an exaggeration, Ella thought. The man was definitely a skilled doctor. Who else would have treated not just Jeremy's wound but the boy himself? Another doctor might have talked down to Jeremy, refusing to tell him the truth because he was only eight years old. Ben seemed to realize that by acting as if Jeremy were an adult, he had a better patient.

And then there was the way he touched the child. He was so gentle with Jeremy that Ella doubted even the boy's father could have been more loving. Ella's eyes widened at the thought. Ben appeared to love children. Why didn't he have any of his own?

Who would have dreamed it? Ben thought as he left Jeremy

with his parents. Ella Roberts, the woman most of Gold Landing's adults considered to be made of ice, was a warm, caring person . . . at least with her students.

That had been a masterful stroke, telling him a story to keep his mind off the stitches. And the way she had held him had been positively maternal. It didn't make sense. If the woman loved children as much as it seemed, why did she keep postponing her marriage?

At last that endless supper was over and he could take Charlotte Langdon back to her parents. Oh, William had to admit that her supper had been delicious, some sort of fancy ham thing with potato salad and the best blueberry pie he had ever eaten. But even the most mouthwatering meal couldn't compensate for the pain of spending two hours with Charlotte I-can't-think-of-a-thing-to-say Langdon. He needed a change. He needed to spend some time with a woman who had opinions. He needed Amelia.

She had been sitting with Frank Stratton on the other side of the field. Now, that would have been a conversation worth overhearing. William could just imagine how those two had gotten along. But Frank was back with the other single men waiting for the fireworks to start, and there was no sign of Amelia.

Or was there? William caught a glimpse of someone moving near the river. There was no mistaking her graceful but purposeful walk. It looked as though the doctor wanted a few minutes of solitude. Or maybe she just wanted a few minutes away from Frank. William quickened his pace.

"I'll leave if you'd rather be alone," William said when he reached her side.

As Amelia turned, the smile she gave him warmed his blood. A man could get ideas—dangerous ideas—when a woman smiled like that.

"Don't go," she said, her voice raising his temperature another degree. "I just needed to get away from the crowds for a bit."

He could understand that. Even though he had promised

himself he would not single Amelia out today, the temptation
had been too great. After being surrounded by people all day,
he longed for a quiet moment with only one person.

He looked at the river. Anything to cool his blood, although
if Amelia kept smiling that way, he doubted even a swim in
its frigid depths would have much effect.

"Was it the crowds, or a specific person you were escap-
ing?" William asked. "I wondered if you'd had a little too
much Frank for dinner."

She laughed, her smile brighter than the first of the
fireworks that rent the sky. "How did you guess? As a physician, I shouldn't wish illness on anyone, but I have to admit
that I was trying to figure out how to induce laryngitis."

William tucked her hand into the crook of his arm. Lord, it
felt good being with Amelia. She could make him laugh. He
felt her hand on his arm, warmer than the summer sun. And
her scent! It was even sweeter than he remembered, teasing
his senses and making him want to draw her closer.

He couldn't, of course. This was too public a place. And so
he spoke. "I had the opposite problem," he confessed. "Charlotte can't put three consecutive words together."

This was the quiet part of the river before it bent southward
into Gold Landing. Normally few people came this far outside
town. Though on a normal night William would not have worried about being seen, tonight was anything but normal. Just
a few hundred yards away, the majority of Gold Landing was
gathered to watch the annual explosion of color and light,
while William stood so close to Amelia that he feared an explosion of another kind.

"Charlotte's probably in awe of you," Amelia speculated.
"She certainly doesn't have any trouble talking to me when I
visit her parents."

"Awe? I don't think so." William could not imagine anyone being in awe of him. Afraid, perhaps. But awe? Not likely.

They stood together on the riverbank, silently watching the
fireworks reflected in the water. It was odd. Although he had
minded silence when he was with Charlotte, it seemed different being here with Amelia. Comfortable. Peaceful. Right.

"Have you enjoyed your first Independence Day in Alaska?" he asked at last.

She nodded, although he could see a wistful expression in those beautiful blue eyes. "It was wonderful, but . . ."

"You're homesick?"

A light breeze soughed through the willows that grew near the water, setting their slender branches to dancing.

Amelia thought for a moment. "I guess so. Alaska is so incredibly beautiful that some days I can't believe it's real. I'm afraid I'll wake up and find it's a dream." Three firecrackers exploded simultaneously, lighting the sky with red, white and blue sparkles. Amelia sighed. "Oh, William, I love Alaska. Truly I do, but there are times when I'm reminded of home, and I wonder if I made the right decision, coming here."

As she pushed a stray lock of hair behind her ear, William wondered what she would do if he pulled the combs from her hair and let it tumble to her shoulders. Lord knew he had dreamed about doing just that.

"Does that sound strange?" she asked.

William shook his head, oddly touched by her words. In all the conversations they had had, it was the first time he had seen her vulnerable side. She had always seemed so strong, so convinced that the direction of her life was right; it was surprising to see her pain, her doubts.

"I think we all have doubts," he said slowly. "It's part of being human."

She shook her head, and the lock escaped again. "Not you, William. I can't imagine you ever questioning your decisions."

William gazed at her for a long moment. If only she knew! He was standing right next to her, wanting so badly to pull her into his arms, to discover whether her body was as soft as it appeared, whether her lips tasted as sweet as he had imagined. And he couldn't.

He shouldn't.

He did.

Chapter Nine

Belinda had told her it was like fireworks. *When a man kisses you—really kisses you—*her older sister had insisted, *you'll see shooting stars.* Amelia had laughed. She had been kissed more than once, and while the kisses hadn't been unpleasant, they certainly had not generated even a modest sparkle. As for fireworks, they were obviously a figment of Belinda's imagination. Or so she had thought.

Now she knew the truth. Belinda had not exaggerated. If anything, she had failed to explain just how wonderful, how powerful, a man's kisses could be. When William molded his lips to hers, the stars she saw were brighter than the ones Mother Nature hung in the sky. The roaring in her ears drowned the noise of the fireworks. And the warmth that went rushing through her from the top of her head, coursing through her veins until it reached her extremities, owed nothing to the sun.

When he wrapped his arms around her, she felt safe, protected and cherished. For the first time in her life, she felt like a woman—a real woman—and, oh, how glorious a sensation that was! Nothing mattered except the wonder of being in William's arms. The pain, the anguish of dreams that would never come true, disappeared, vanquished by the touch of his lips on hers. And somehow, the simple action of being held so close that she could hear William's heartbeat banished the blues. She had made the right decision. Coming to Alaska was her destiny. Being held in William's arms convinced Amelia of that.

It felt so good!

And then when she feared she might combust from the heat and the pleasure he was generating in her, he dropped his arms and took a step backward.

"I shouldn't have done that," William said, his voice

120

harsher than she had ever heard it. "I'm so sorry, Amelia." His gray eyes reflected pain and something else, something Amelia might have called confusion, had she not known that William was never confused. He took another step away from her.

Amelia stared at him. The fireworks continued. The river still flowed. The evening breeze had not diminished. Nothing had changed. Everything had changed. All in the space of a kiss.

Why had he stopped? Hadn't he enjoyed the kiss as much as she had? Of course he hadn't, or he would never have stopped. Men didn't just end a kiss with no reason, not if it was a pleasant experience. Lust was too strong an emotion to be turned off so quickly. The reason was obvious. She had done something wrong. She might be able to deliver a baby or suture a laceration, but she did not know anything about kissing. That was the problem. She had been so caught up in the magic of the moment, in the wondrous sensations William was sending through her, that she had not noticed he wasn't sharing the pleasure.

What a fool she was! For a moment she had deluded herself into believing she was like every other woman. She wasn't. She never had been. She never would be. The doctors in Philadelphia had made it clear that she lacked at least one critical element of a real woman. She had accepted their diagnosis that she would never be able to bear a child, and she had given up her hope of marriage, for her mother's words had rung true. A man wanted his wife to be whole. He expected her to give him children.

It was probably best that William hadn't enjoyed the kiss and did not want to repeat it. After all, they had no future together, for she wasn't his kind of woman. She wasn't anyone's kind of woman.

William was wise to back away from her. It was the right thing for both of them. Why, then, did it feel as though the sun had suddenly disappeared?

* * *

"Um, Doctor . . ." The way Carrie Gould twisted her hands in her skirt told Amelia she was nervous about something.

"Is there something else I can do?" Amelia asked as she completed her examination.

Carrie nodded again but did not meet Amelia's gaze. "Miz Brown is sick. Will you go there?"

Her hesitation surprised Amelia. Surely everyone in Shantytown knew she would treat anyone who needed her. "Of course I will. Where does she live?"

"End of the road, but . . ." Carrie's gaze remained on the earthen floor. "Doctor, her children are half-breeds. Her man was an Indian."

Carrie's face flushed with embarrassment, and Amelia was not certain whether it was generated by the thought of a white woman living with an Athapaskan or the fact that the half-breeds, as Carrie called them, lived so close to her own children.

Amelia knew of the ostracism that mixed marriages generated, and suspected that only the absence of other housing kept families like the Goulds living so near the Indians. Ella had told Amelia that the children of mixed marriages were shunned by both communities and that the prejudice against them was even stronger than that against the pure Athapaskans.

"If Mrs. Brown needs medical care," Amelia said firmly, "she'll get it."

She picked up her bag and strode down the street. Built of the same log construction as the Goulds' house, the Browns' was equally dilapidated. The front yard, if it could be called that, was nothing more than packed dirt, unrelieved by even a single flower.

Amelia knocked. "Mrs. Brown," she called as she opened the door. "I'm the doctor."

A coughing spasm greeted her. Amelia followed the sound to a pallet in the rear of the room, noting that two other pallets were arranged against a side wall. When her eyes had adjusted to the darkness of the cabin's interior, Amelia saw that her patient was a young woman, perhaps in her early twenties. At one time she might have been a pretty woman, but her blond hair was now matted and lifeless, her blue eyes dull with pain. Like Carrie Gould, she wore a faded cotton dress that had been patched repeatedly, and her feet were bare. Her one adornment was a brightly colored beaded bracelet encircling her left wrist.

"Ain't got no money to pay you," the woman said when she was able to speak again.

"Let's not worry about that right now," Amelia suggested. "Let's see what we can do to make you feel better."

But when Amelia had completed her examination, she realized there was little she or anyone could do to help Mrs. Brown. The woman had such an advanced case of tuberculosis that her life would be measured in days rather than decades. Amelia closed her eyes for a second and said a silent prayer that she would be able to give Mrs. Brown some measure of comfort.

If only they had had the clinic earlier! Mrs. Brown should have had medical care years before, when there might have been a chance to arrest the disease. Now there was no hope.

"It's bad, ain't it?" the young woman asked.

Amelia nodded, unwilling to lie to her patient. "I'm afraid so."

With a stoicism that surprised Amelia, Mrs. Brown simply bowed her head. "Figured as much. Coughs ain't supposed to be like this."

Amelia explained her diagnosis.

"What about my girls?" Mrs. Brown asked. Though her voice had betrayed no emotion when Amelia had given her prognosis, now it was laden with fear, a fear Amelia knew transcended whether they would contract the disease. For even if the girls escaped their mother's fate, their lives would not be easy. It would be difficult for them to gain acceptance with their father's people, since the Athapaskans believed that children belonged to their mother's tribe, yet it was unlikely that the whites in Shantytown would care for them. And at their ages—five and seven—they could not live alone.

As she left Shantytown, Amelia was frowning. Although her professors had claimed that years of experience made it easier to accept a patient's death, her grandfather had told her

123

that he had never been able to adopt such a philosophical attitude. He had viewed each one as a loss, a personal defeat. Amelia doubted she would ever become stoic enough to not feel the pain.

If only they had had the clinic. If only Mrs. Brown had come for treatment earlier. If only . . . Amelia shook her head. Since she could not alter the past, there was nothing to be gained by wishing it had been different. What she needed to do was ensure that the problems were not repeated. The clinic was the first step.

Two hours later as she crossed the bridge into Gold Landing, Amelia saw William walking toward her, a large basket slung from one arm. It was the first time she had seen him in the three days since the Fourth of July celebration, and for a moment Amelia was afraid he would turn aside when he saw her. But he continued in her direction, and if his smile was any indication, he was glad to see her. Maybe he had forgotten their kiss and what a failure she had been. Maybe he realized they were friends, and friendship did not demand that a woman know how to kiss.

"Amelia!" His smile widened to a grin as he greeted her. He doffed his hat, and she saw that his smile extended to his eyes. If he hadn't forgotten the kiss, he was at least willing to ignore it. "I hoped I could convince you to play hooky tonight."

Hooky! This wasn't a chance encounter; William had planned to meet her. Amelia's spirits began to soar. Why hadn't she noticed what a glorious sunny day it was, without a cloud to mar the sky?

"There's a place I'd like to show you," William continued, "and as a bribe"—he gestured toward the basket—"I brought supper for us."

The man must be a mind reader! How did he know that today of all days she would appreciate a break from her routine? She was tired, both physically and emotionally. An hour or so of diversion was exactly what she needed.

"That sounds wonderful."

William led the way back across the bridge, then turned left away from Shantytown and the Indian village. Amelia had never been in this direction. Unlike the forested area on the other side of Gold Landing, which teemed with plant and animal life, this side appeared barren.

She picked her way across the uneven terrain, surprised by how spongy the ground felt. "Where are we going?" she asked. Not that it mattered. Today it was enough that she had left Gold Landing and her problems behind, if only for an hour.

"There." William pointed at one of the streams that flowed from the ice fields into the river. "Look at this," he said as they approached it. From a distance, the riverbed appeared to be nothing more than a jumble of rocks with a narrow stream of water flowing through it. But as they drew closer, Amelia saw that the rocks, which from a distance had seemed lifeless, nursed tiny plants between them. Leaving her bag on the ground, she scrambled onto one of the large boulders.

"Oh, William, it's amazing!" She leaned forward and touched a yellow blossom that was smaller than her littlest fingernail. "Look at the way that plant clings to life." The plant, perhaps seeded by a bird, had taken root in a tablespoon of earth wedged between two rocks.

Amelia's smile was radiant. Bless William! He had found the perfect antidote to her afternoon with Mrs. Brown, showing her how life continued, even against seemingly impossible obstacles.

"It's beautiful," he agreed, "but the best is coming." They followed the stream for a few minutes more. Then William extended his arm. "Look," he said. For as far as she could see, they were surrounded by tundra. Amelia's expression must have revealed her confusion, for William grinned. "You'll see," he promised. Pulling a blanket from the basket, he spread it on the ground. "We need to be closer," he said.

He knelt on the edge of the blanket and motioned for Amelia to join him. "See this?" he said. With the tip of his finger, he pointed out a tiny white flower. Amelia gasped with pleasure. The bloom was perhaps a quarter of an inch in diameter, yet it was perfectly formed, its six petals cupped at the end, as if to catch every possible ray of sunshine. "And here." Only inches away, William showed her another miniature flower. This one was pale yellow.

"Oh, William, it's incredible. Alaska is so big, and these are so small!"

William grinned. "I come here every summer, and I'm always amazed." Amelia was amazed at the sight of William's big hand touching the petals so gently. "Someone told me the plants are hundreds of years old," he continued. "I don't know if it's true or not. All I know is they're mighty pretty."

It was Amelia's turn to be surprised. Somehow, she had not expected William to notice, much less enjoy, the beauty of the tundra's blooms.

Her hands moved through the short tundra plants, searching for new types of flowers. "Look, William," she cried when she found a small pink bloom. He shifted his weight, coming closer to her, and his hand brushed hers. It was the slightest of touches, and yet it ignited a fire that shone brighter than the most vivid flower, reminding her of the night he had kissed her.

It was foolish, of course. There would never be another kiss. She had seen to that with the way she had botched the first one. It had been so bad, he had even apologized. Still, when she was so close to William, when she could feel the warmth of his hand, the sweet smell of his breath so close to her, she could not help wishing things were different. It was only lust. She knew that, just as she knew how futile it was for her to wish that she could love a man like William, marry him and bear his children. Foolish, futile, and yet the fantasy refused to die.

"Were your parents born in Alaska, too?" Perhaps if she talked about something—anything—else, she would be able to forget how wonderful the kiss had felt and how the memory kept her awake at night.

The sun glinted on his hair, making it look more red than brown as he shook his head. "Polly said they came here for the ice business."

Amelia moved a few inches to the right. Maybe if she put

a little more distance between them, her pulse would return to normal.

"I heard people made fortunes doing that." Ice, Amelia knew, hadn't been as big an export business as fish or furs, but it had generated considerable wealth.

"Not my father." William laughed shortly. "The son of a bitch lost every piece of gold and every bit of family he ever had. He left my mother before I was born, and his sister hated him so much that Alex and I were grown men before we knew of each other's existence."

William's words confirmed the stories Amelia had heard. Her eyes misted with compassion, and for an instant the majesty of their surroundings seemed a cruel counterpoint to the suffering one young orphan must have endured. "I'm sorry."

But William dismissed her sympathy. "I survived. A good woman took me in and raised me." His eyes focused on the distant mountains, and Amelia watched a spasm of pain cross his face. It was gone so quickly she might have imagined it, for a moment later he turned back toward her. "Polly was the best mother anyone could want. Save your sympathy for someone who needs it."

His words were brave, his tone even, yet Amelia sensed there was more to the story than William was telling. Perhaps someday he would trust her enough to confide in her. Friends did that, didn't they?

Gloria was wrong. Oh, she was a smart lady, and she knew a lot about men. She wouldn't be such a successful madam if she didn't. But this time she was wrong. Plumb wrong.

William loved her. June knew that, even though he had never said the words. It was plain as could be. He needed her. Why else did he come to her when he was troubled? Others came to ease their physical needs, but William came for different reasons. June was sure of it. Hadn't he told her that he needed her? Everyone knew it was only one step from needing to loving, and one more from loving to marriage. William had already taken the first step.

Marrying William had been June's dream from the day she

had come to Gold Landing and seen him. The other girls talked about his money, but June saw beyond that. William was everything she wanted in a man: strong, handsome, kind. And she knew he loved her. It was just going to take a couple more months before he told her that.

June took her usual seat at the end of the porch. It was early evening, an hour or so before the regular customers began to visit them. June and several of the other girls would don their best clothes, then go onto the porch. Gloria said it was good advertising, reminding any of the men who passed by of the pleasures they could find inside.

A couple of men walked down the street, calling their greetings to the girls, promising to come back once they had eaten.

"Bet we won't see either of them," Sally muttered.

"Maybe not tonight," June agreed, "but they're regulars. They'll be here on Saturday." She leaned back in the rocker, pushing against the floor to set the chair in motion. William would come tonight. He wasn't one who waited for Saturday; besides, he was overdue for a visit. Things must be extra busy at the mine, because he hadn't visited June since before the Fourth. He would come tonight. For sure.

"Don't see that much." Louise pointed at a couple, approaching from the other side of the river. "Looks like they're lost." Women avoided this part of town, while the men found excuses to pass by.

As the man and woman came closer, June could hear the peal of the woman's laughter. Whoever she was, she sure was having a good time. Something about her looked familiar, but June's eyes focused on the man. He was big and tall and . . .

"Why, it's William Gunning and that lady doctor." Sally's voice registered her surprise. "I heard they couldn't talk to each other without fighting. What do you suppose they're doing together?"

June eyed the couple. It had to be a mistake. Probably William had met the doctor by accident and had been too much of a gentleman to let her walk home alone. That was it. He had been on his way to visit June, and he had gotten sidetracked by that lady doctor. He would be back.

But William did not come to Gloria's that night or the next or the next.

What a fascinating woman she was! William smoothed the wood with a plane, then took a step backward. Yes, the cradle was turning out nicely. Alex and Karen's baby would start its life in a pine cradle, not a laundry basket or an empty dresser drawer the way some children did.

William's hands moved carefully, shaping the soft wood. Normally, working with wood helped to soothe his thoughts. That was one of the reasons he had built a cupboard for his tools in the kitchen. He could sit in the room he considered the heart of the house and pull out a piece of lumber. When he was worried about the mine, he would begin carving, and soon he would have resolved the problem, almost without conscious thought.

Today was different. No matter what he did, he thought of Amelia. Try though he might, he could not forget the kiss they had shared by the river. Lord! Who would have dreamed that a man of his experience could learn something new from the lady doctor? But he had. Though he had kissed more women than he could count, there had never been a kiss like the one he and Amelia had shared. Just the thought of it set his blood to boiling.

It had been crazy, of course, kissing her out there where anyone could see them. Thank goodness he had stopped when he had, before someone had wandered by. That would have been a disaster. But somehow he had pulled away from those lips that were sweeter than Nellie Moore's blueberry pie.

William reached for a piece of sandpaper to smooth one corner. Amelia had looked surprised. Who could blame her? She had probably been shocked as all get-out that he had kissed her. But she was a real lady and had said nothing, either then or today.

William still wasn't sure how he had gotten through all that time on the tundra without kissing her again. It hadn't been easy, that was for sure. When his fingers had brushed hers, it had taken every ounce of control he possessed to keep from grabbing her hand, pressing kisses on that soft palm, then moving his lips up her arms.

He rubbed his hand over the corner of the cradle, checking for splinters, then buffed it with a soft cloth. Lord! He couldn't think straight when he was near that woman. But he had known that if he had touched her, he would not have been able to stop. One thing would have led to another, and that simply couldn't happen. A man had to show restraint. After all, a man didn't make love with a good woman until they were married.

Marriage. It was odd how often he had thought about that the past few weeks. A man needed a wife. Amelia would make a mighty fine wife. There was only one problem. When she married, and William knew it was only a matter of months until that happened, she would pick a man like Abe. Hell, she would probably pick Abe. She would want a man who talked about opera and ballet and books, the way that damned lawyer did. William sure couldn't oblige on any of those topics. He had never been to an opera or a ballet, and the last book he had read had been the one Polly owned. Growing up, there hadn't been time for nice things like reading books. He had been too busy surviving. Involuntarily, his hand touched the crescent scar.

William laid the cradle on the floor, testing the rockers. Fine. Just fine. He would bet that dandified attorney couldn't make a cradle. But when Amelia picked her husband, William knew she would choose book learning over manual skills.

It wasn't fair! *Life's not fair,* he could hear Polly saying, *so you gotta learn to handle that.* He would. He had set out to make Amelia his friend, and it looked like that plan was working. Now it was time for the next step. Perhaps he would be lucky. There were no guarantees, but maybe Abe Ferguson would be the one who learned that life wasn't fair. Oh, how sweet that victory would be.

William put his tools back in the cupboard as he considered what to do next. Amelia had liked the tundra. William knew that. And she had eaten every bite of the supper he had brought for her. If that and her dinners with Abe were any indication, she enjoyed having someone else cook. He wouldn't take her to the hotel, of course. Instead, he would plan something different. Maybe they would go to Pete's Roadhouse. Pete made a mean bear stew, and William would bet that Amelia hadn't been introduced to that particular delicacy. Yep, the roadhouse would be a good spot. He would take her there next week.

Amelia dragged the cabin's one chair next to the bed and held her patient's hand. It had been only a week since she had first met Mrs. Brown, but the woman's condition had deteriorated rapidly. The end was near.

"Oh, Doctor, it hurts so bad." Mrs. Brown's face was even whiter than it had been the first time Amelia had seen her, her blue eyes dull with pain. "I want it to end."

Amelia placed a comforting hand on her patient's arm. "I'll give you something for the pain," she said and reached for her bag.

The woman shook her head, spreading her matted hair on the dingy pillowcase. "Just stay with me. Please. I'm afraid to be alone."

Amelia looked around. The cabin seemed somehow emptier than it had on her previous visits. "Where are your daughters?" she asked, realizing that the girls' meager possessions were gone.

"To their father's tribe. No one here would take 'em." As a coughing spasm caught her, Amelia handed her a clean towel to wipe her face. "Their grandma said she'd raise 'em."

Amelia sensed that the older woman had been reluctant to accept her grandchildren. Though they were well mannered and attractive, their white blood would set them apart from the other children.

"They're fine girls," Amelia told Mrs. Brown.

The woman managed a faint smile. "They look like their daddy. He was the prettiest man I ever saw." Another coughing spasm shook her, leaving her weaker than ever. "I knew it was wrong," she told Amelia, "but I loved him so much."

131

She closed her eyes and sighed. "Three years. That's all we had."

The woman's breathing was labored, and Amelia knew that speaking must be painful. Still, she sensed that Mrs. Brown needed to talk. "What happened?"

"A hunting accident." Her blue eyes blazed with pain. "Oh, Doctor, it's so lonely without him. But I know he's waiting for me." She closed her eyes, and for a few moments the only sound in the cabin was her labored breathing. "If not for worrying about my girls, I'd be happy to be going. A woman ain't meant to live alone."

Amelia patted her hand, wishing there were something she could do or say to comfort Mrs. Brown. "Do you want me to give you something for the pain?" she asked.

Again the woman shook her head. "Just stay with me." She touched the beaded bracelet that Amelia had noticed on her first visit. "When I'm gone, take it." She coughed again, and Amelia knew the end wasn't far. "He gave it to me."

"I can't take that." Tears welled in Amelia's eyes at the thought of Mrs. Brown's generosity. "It should go to one of your daughters."

The woman shook her head. "You been good to me." She paused, drawing another breath, her lips pursed in pain. "Wanna pay for your care." She grasped Amelia's hand as she began to cough. "Take it. Maybe it'll bring you the happiness I had."

Tears began to roll down Amelia's cheeks.

"Don't cry, Doctor. Just tell me about that place you used to live. Phila . . . Phila somethin'."

Two hours later, Amelia left the cabin after making arrangements for Mrs. Brown's burial. The bracelet was in the bottom of her bag, wrapped in soft cotton. Although one day she might wear it, her pain was still too fresh to have the reminder of the woman's lost love in constant sight.

"Amelia, I was hoping I'd meet you."

Amelia looked up to see William approaching from the other direction, as he seemed to do so often these days. His gait was jaunty, his mouth set in a grin, while she could not muster a smile.

The sun had gone behind a cloud, leaving the sky as dreary as Amelia felt. Mrs. Brown's death had drained the last of her energy, leaving nothing but a fierce ache. It had happened before, and though Amelia's heart shrank from the knowledge, it would happen again.

Tomorrow would be different, but today she needed to mourn and to accept the fact that she had lost the most important battle she would ever fight. Only then would she be able to start again, fighting death and vowing that next time she would win.

"Amelia."

She nodded a greeting, still unable to speak. Her hand gripped her bag, and for a moment she was tempted to open it, to look at the brightly beaded bracelet. But if she did that, there would be no stopping the tears that even now threatened to spill forth.

"I wondered if you'd have dinner with me tonight." William's voice was vibrant, and on another day she would have found his enthusiasm contagious. Today it only added to her fatigue. "I thought we could go to Pete's Roadhouse."

As the clouds scudded by, Amelia heard the sound of distant thunder.

"I'm sorry. I can't." Even saying those simple words took so much energy.

William looked puzzled. "Is something wrong?" he asked.

Slowly, Amelia nodded. "I can't talk about it," she told him. "I just need to be alone." When he started to protest, she said simply, "Please."

With obvious reluctance, he turned and walked back into town, his gait no longer jaunty. Amelia remained on the outskirts, sitting on a boulder, staring into the distance, trying to regain her equilibrium. When at last she reentered Gold Landing, she was once more calm. Though she could not save Mrs. Brown, next time would be different.

She was almost home when a man greeted her. "You're

just the person I wanted to see. The new Dickens book arrived today.''

"I'm sorry, Abe, but I can't think about books today.''

The thunder was closer now, the air pregnant with rain. Though a few people remained on Main, most scurried for cover.

Abe took another step toward her. "What's wrong?'' he asked. His voice was low but fervent, those two simple words telling Amelia how much he cared. Suddenly the dam that had been holding back her emotions crumbled.

"Oh, Abe,'' she said as the tears began to roll down her cheeks. "One of my patients died this afternoon.'' Her voice broke as she pronounced the words, her anguish pouring forth. "It shouldn't have happened. I should have been able to save her.''

Abe reached for his handkerchief. "I'm so sorry,'' he said as he gently wiped the tears from her face. "I wish I could help you, but believe me, Amelia, I know that at a time like this there's no one who can help.'' He touched her cheek again. "Just know that I'm here whenever you need me.''

He had stopped at the office on his way back into town. Most days now he didn't go back in the evening, but he had been so restless after seeing Amelia that he had needed the distraction of worrying about the mine's production.

What was wrong with the woman? He had never seen her so quiet, so withdrawn. That wasn't like Amelia. When she was upset, she flared up like grease on a fire. She didn't get cold and quiet. Amelia was fire, not ice. But today the flames had vanished, leaving an empty shell.

Was it something he had done? William thought back, trying to remember whether he had said or done something that could have upset her. Whatever it was, he couldn't just leave things to fester. Maybe Ella knew what was wrong. He would go to their house and ask her. Maybe he would be lucky and Amelia would be there. By now, maybe she would be talking again. Maybe whatever it was had passed.

William strode down Main Street, pleased with his plan. If

he was lucky, the storm would hold off until he got to Ella and Amelia's house. Common courtesy would demand that they invite him in until the rain ended, and that would give him the time he needed with Amelia.

And then he saw them. There was no mistaking those profiles. Shameless fools! There they were in broad daylight right in front of the hotel where everybody could see them. Abe stood so close to Amelia that he could have kissed her without moving, and he was touching her face. Right there on Main Street. And she was letting him.

Damnation! She had lied to him. She had told him she wanted to be alone, when what she wanted was to be with that useless excuse for a lawyer. And to think he had worried about what might have been bedeviling her. The answer was plain as could be. She didn't want to be seen with William in public. That was why she hadn't wanted to go to the roadhouse. But she was willing to stand there in the middle of Main Street and let that cursed attorney paw her.

He should have expected it. Women like Amelia didn't spend time with men like him. Only a fool would have thought otherwise.

William turned and strode in the opposite direction.

"Where's June?" he demanded as he flung open the door to Gloria's house.

The petite blonde rose from the corner, a radiant smile on her face. "I'm here, William." She fairly flew across the room and laid a hand on his arm. "Oh, honey, it's so good to see you again!"

This was what a man needed, a woman who wasn't ashamed to be with him, a woman who told the truth.

"I need you, June," he said, putting his arm around her waist and leading her to the stairs.

When they reached her room, June turned to him. "I'll always be here for you, William. Always!"

An hour later, as he lay on June's bed, William closed his eyes. *I wonder where Amelia is spending her evening*, he thought.

Chapter Ten

She was a fool, Amelia told herself as she crossed the bridge to Shantytown. She shouldn't miss him. She had her practice to keep her busy, and dinners with Abe satisfied her need for polite conversation and masculine companionship. There was no point in craving something she could never have.

There was no reason to look for William each time she ended her rounds and headed back to Gold Landing. And yet she did. Each day her eyes would search the horizon, and each day they would drop in disappointment when there was no sign of his familiar figure.

She was a fool to want to trade her weekly dinners with Abe for one bowl of bear stew with William, to think that half an hour listening to William rant about the Alaska Syndicate's scheme to monopolize the railroad was preferable to Abe's learned discussion of Beethoven's sonatas.

Even a fool could learn, and she would.

As she walked down the narrow track that served as the primary thoroughfare in Shantytown, Amelia heard a woman call her name. "Would you look at my husband? He can't keep his food down." Amelia turned. This was the reason she had come to Alaska. Only a fool would forget that.

He was a fool. No doubt about it. He had let his anger overrule his common sense, and what had it gotten him? Seven days of pure misery. It had been a week since he had seen Amelia with Abe, a week of making sure his path didn't cross hers, a week of refusing to think about her when the truth was, he could think of nothing else.

He was a fool. Worse than that, he was a coward. Only a coward would give up so easily.

When the streams were played out, he could have moved on, declared Gold Landing's boom to be a bust. But he hadn't.

He had stayed right here, drilling for gold when everyone had told him there was no more. He had believed; he had persisted; he had won.

Why should this be any different, just because his heart and not his fortune was at stake? Was he going to let lily-livered Ferguson capture the prize of the decade?

Hell, no!

"What have you eaten that your wife didn't?" Amelia asked.

"Nothin'."

Unconvinced, Amelia turned to his wife. She shook her head. "There was a party last night. Kind of pot luck. Mr. Gunning sent some moose steaks, and everybody else brought something. I couldn't go, 'cuz the baby was fussy."

If Amelia's diagnosis of food poisoning was correct, there would be other victims. She went from house to house, checking on the residents. As she had expected, there was a small epidemic.

"Damned shame," one of the victims told her. "We don't have much cause for celebrating here with none of us working regular-like. Don't know what we'd do if it weren't for Mr. Gunning. He's got worries of his own, but he makes sure nobody up here starves. Never makes it seem like charity, neither."

So William Gunning, who claimed that he acted only for his own benefit, was taking care of the poor in Shantytown. Interesting.

By the time she descended the hill into Gold Landing, Amelia had spent twelve hours on her rounds. Her head ached and the muscles in her calves protested the time she had spent standing. By all rights, she should have been exhausted, yet fatigue had not caught her. She wouldn't let it. If she were tired, who would care for her patients?

Her eyes scanned the horizon as they did each day, looking for William. He wouldn't be there. She knew that, and yet she could not stop looking.

The sun was high, the sky blue and . . . He was there! She blinked, then looked again, afraid he would disappear. But he was still there. Her pace quickened as she moved toward him. Perhaps he had been working in the mine, and that was the reason she hadn't seen him. Perhaps they had just missed each other. Whatever the reason, he was here today, and for the moment that was all that mattered.

"You look tired," he said when he had greeted her. "Is Ben working you too hard?"

Amelia shook her head. "It's not Ben. There are just so many patients. But it'll be better when the clinic—"

Before she could finish her sentence, William grabbed Amelia's arm and pulled her to a stop. "Do you hear that?" he asked, his voice louder than normal. He drew a gun from his holster, pointing it in the direction of the noise.

"Don't move."

She couldn't have moved if she had had to. The sight of the weapon and William's obvious tension turned her legs to stone. As the low rustling in the brushes increased, Amelia heard an animal grunt.

"Bear," William announced, his eyes fixed on the swaying brush. "Don't move, or he might think we're threatening him."

A bear. Her mind knew they lived in the brush and came out to forage. Her heart didn't want to consider that she might be the bear's next meal.

"Keep talking, Amelia. Bears are shy. Normally they'll leave rather than confront man."

She managed a shaky laugh. "What do you want me to talk about, other than the fact that I have no desire to meet a bear and that your gun scares me?"

The brush stopped moving, as though the bear were listening to their conversation.

"Can you shoot?"

She shook her head.

"You'd better learn. You never can tell when you'll need to protect yourself."

Amelia had seen bears in the zoo. She knew that they looked like. What she didn't know was that their snorting would sound so fierce and that their smell was so pungent.

"I don't want a gun," she told William, trying not to think of the animal only a few feet away. "Abe doesn't carry one."

William's arm tightened. "Abe's a fool."

The rustling grew louder, then diminished. When the bushes stopped swaying, William reholstered his gun.

"He's gone," William confirmed. "It's safe to move now." But even though his gun was no longer drawn, he kept his arm around Amelia's waist as they walked down the path. "So, tell me about the clinic," he said.

The clinic. Of course. Surely she could form a coherent thought. After all, the adrenaline streaming through her veins was caused by the bear, not the fact that she was standing close enough to William to smell his woodsy scent and hear his heartbeat. She drew a deep breath.

"I'm planning to run some classes there—things like basic hygiene."

William raised a questioning eyebrow. "Something special make you think of that?"

They were out of the brush now, on open land with no place for a bear to hide. Amelia could feel her pulse begin to slow. Though she no longer needed the protection, when William dropped his arm from her waist, she felt oddly bereft.

"There was an outbreak of food poisoning in Shantytown last night," she managed to say.

"Food poisoning?" William stopped and faced Amelia, his gray eyes reflecting concern. "Don't tell me it was the moose steaks they ate."

Amelia smiled, a little amused by William's reaction. He would not volunteer the information that he had provided those steaks, but he was worried enough to ask if they had been tainted. And the man claimed he wasn't a hero!

"I doubt the steaks were the problem." She shifted her bag to her right hand, then extended her left, trying to ease the ache from her tight grip.

"Where did you get that?" he demanded, pointing to the bracelet on her left wrist.

A chill that owed nothing to the breeze penetrated her coat. "One of my patients gave it to me," she said, shivering as she thought of the day Mrs. Brown had died. The first fresh pain had diminished, and now she wore the beads as a talisman, a reminder that next time she would defeat death.

"Why do you waste your time on those animals?" William's words were as harsh as the bear's growl.

She wanted to ignore him, pretend she hadn't heard his question, but she could not. Amelia laid her bag on the ground and faced William. Since the day he had first shown his hatred for the Indians, Amelia had been careful not to raise the subject. Though some might call that cowardice, she preferred to think she was being prudent, waiting for the right time.

Her grandfather had told her that prejudice was usually the result of either ignorance or a painful experience. Since William was not an ignorant man, Amelia assumed something in his past had caused his hatred. One day he would tell her about it, or so she hoped, and so she was unwilling to pry.

"The Indians are not animals, William," she said as evenly as she could. "They're unfortunate people who live in the worst poverty I've ever seen, but they're not animals."

A ground squirrel scampered by, its mouth filled with berries. "That's an animal," she said.

William shook his head, and she saw that his eyes were as cold as a November day. "That depends on your definition. Did you know that the Athapaskans are cannibals?"

Amelia could feel the blood rise to her face. Where was the man who took time from his schedule to deliver moose steaks to the poor in Shantytown? That man, with his compassion, had disappeared. In his place was a stranger.

"Do you know that for a fact," she asked, "or is it only a scurrilous rumor?" She had heard the story herself when Ella had tried to dissuade her from treating anyone on the other side of the river. No one seemed to know any of the details, but the lurid tale refused to die. Keeping her voice as even as she could, Amelia asked William the same question she had posed to Ella. "Even if it's true, do you know the circumstances? Desperation will force men to do extraordinary things."

William picked up several small stones and began to hurl

them into the distance. "You call eating another human extraordinary?"

Perhaps the exertion would dissipate some of his anger. Amelia nodded. "In the true sense of the word, yes. It is out of the ordinary." She paused for a second as William flung the last pebble, then reached for more. "Starvation is a strong motivator. That's what led the Donner party to cannibalism," she said, referring to the pioneers who, when stranded on a mountain pass, had resorted to eating the weaker members of their group. "I'd like to point out that everyone in that party was white."

William dropped the stones, then grabbed Amelia's arm in a punishing grip. "I don't have your fancy education," he said. "I don't know anything about a Donner party, but I do know what those Indians are like. I've lived here for a long time. You haven't."

"Education has nothing to do with it," Amelia retorted. Though her arm ached, she would not give him the satisfaction of pulling away. "They're humans, just like you and me."

"No!" The word exploded from William's throat. "They are not like you and me. Those filthy animals commit atrocities a city person like you would never dream of." His free hand touched the crescent-shaped scar on his left cheek, and not for the first time Amelia wondered what had caused it. It had obviously been a deep laceration that had never been sutured.

"What happened, William? Why do you say that?"

A spasm of pain crossed his face, momentarily obliterating the fury. "You don't want to know."

"I do," she said softly.

"You wouldn't say that if you knew." He loosened his grip on her wrist.

"William, you're being unreasonable."

"So are you. It's like going out in the woods without a gun. You're risking your health—maybe even your life—on the dregs of society." William picked up her bag and handed it to her. "What will it take to convince you, Amelia?"

"A lot more than your ranting. I need facts, reasons."

He started walking, then stopped. "Trust me on this. I know

the Indians." His expression was bleak. "I just want to keep you safe. Stay away from them. Please."

Amelia shook her head. "I can't."

"How's the mother-to-be?" William put down the stain-soaked rag as his cousin entered the room. He had been working on the cradle for Alex and Karen's baby. Though it was supposed to be a surprise for Karen, Alex had seen it several times, and William suspected his reason for visiting frequently was to check on the progress.

Alex grinned. "Now that she's not getting sick every morning, she's a lot easier to live with. The doctor told her that the nausea would end after three months, but I don't think Karen believed her until it happened."

"And the doctor knows everything."

If Alex heard the sarcasm in William's voice, he ignored it. "She's a woman, isn't she? Karen figures about this time next year, she'll be having a baby of her own."

The last time William had heard, the speculation had centered on Amelia's wedding date. Now, it appeared, it had progressed to the next life event.

"And who's gonna be the lucky father?" he asked. "Or are we going to witness the second immaculate conception here in Gold Landing?"

As a young child William had learned not to share his innermost thoughts with anyone, and he wasn't planning to change now—not even to confide in Alex. Especially not to confide in Alex. No one in Gold Landing was going to speculate on his feelings for Amelia.

Alex chuckled. "No miracles. Abe can figure out how to do it the normal way."

"Abe?" No surprise there. Even Frank Stratton, who wasn't the brightest light in town, had repeated that piece of gossip. But so far no one had guessed how William felt.

"Who else? Everyone knows he's been courting her."

William studied the cradle for a moment, then rubbed one end, darkening the stain. "Courting, huh?"

"He buys her books and takes her to dinner at the Grand

almost every week. Yesterday he even ordered her some special candy from Boston, something he called saltwater taffy. If that's not courting, I don't know what is.''

''Seems like she could do better than that lily-livered lawyer.''

Alex reached out a hand as though to touch the cradle, then stopped when William frowned. ''You volunteering for the job?'' he asked.

''Hell, no! We'd kill each other before the ceremony was over.'' Besides, Amelia had made it pretty clear that she was unhappy with him over the Athapaskans. He would have to give her a while to simmer down before he saw her again.

''My point, exactly. Abe and the lady doctor are two of a kind.'' Alex swallowed a smile, then said casually, ''By the way, Karen wanted me to invite you to Sunday dinner.''

William groaned. ''Let me guess. She's got some eligible female she wants me to meet.''

''What can I say? Karen thinks everyone ought to be married.''

''You can tell Karen that I'll get married when I decide it's time, and I'll pick my own wife. I don't need her help. Or yours, either.'' William pointed to the door. ''Out. Now.''

Alex left.

He hadn't deserved it. William knew he had acted like a hungry bear, but it was blasted annoying. Every woman in Gold Landing and even some of the men thought they knew what was best for him. Damn it all! He didn't need someone picking his wife. He already knew who he wanted. He just hadn't figured out how to win her. And he sure as hell didn't need to hear every detail of Abe Ferguson's courting. Books, candy, fancy dinners. You would think a woman with Amelia's sense would see beyond that and realize that Abe wasn't a real man. But for some reason, she was blinded by all that window dressing.

William stormed out of his house and headed down Main Street. He would go to the mine. Good, physical labor always helped. But as he passed the general store, he paused.

''Hey, Herb,'' he said as he entered the store. ''I heard you got a shipment of books. Where'd you stash them?''

If Herb was surprised by William's request, he hid it well.

Ten minutes later William left, a copy of Jack London's *The Call of the Wild* under his arm.

''Let's get married at Christmas.''

Ella and Larry had left the musicale and were walking slowly down Main Street when he made the suggestion. It was becoming a familiar refrain. Ever since the Fourth of July celebration, each time she had seen him, Larry had pressed her to set the wedding date.

She wanted to marry him. She knew she did. Just not so soon.

''I thought next June would be nice,'' Ella said. ''We could get married when school ended.''

Larry stopped and stared at her, fingering his mustache. That was a sure sign that he wasn't happy. ''C'mon, Ella. I'm tired of waiting. Let's set the date sooner.''

''But I need time to get ready. You know that.'' Surely he could understand.

Larry shook his head. ''I've heard that before. What's the problem, Ella? You just never seem to get any readier.''

There was no problem. She had told him that. It was just . . .

''Oh, Larry. June is so beautiful. It's the perfect month for a wedding.'' Ella smiled at him, willing him to understand.

Larry was silent for a long moment, curling the end of his mustache around his finger. Then he nodded slowly. ''All right. But Ella, honey, you're so beautiful, it's powerful hard to wait.''

They had reached Ella's house and were standing on the front porch. Thank goodness Larry didn't ask to come inside. Ella didn't want another argument about why that wasn't proper. Then, so quickly that she had no chance to protest, Larry pulled her into his arms. Lowering his head, he crushed her lips with his. ''So sweet,'' he murmured as his hand moved to cup her breast.

''No, Larry! No!'' Ella spun out of his grasp. Flinging the door open, she ran inside, sobbing uncontrollably.

Amelia ran downstairs and switched on the light, finding Ella in the middle of the parlor with tears streaming down her face, her arms folded in front of her as if to protect herself from some danger.

"What's wrong?" Amelia looked around. Nothing seemed out of place, and Ella's cries sounded like fear rather than pain. Amelia hugged her friend. "You're safe," she said firmly. "Now tell me what's wrong."

But Ella refused to speak. Her body trembled, and Amelia's reassuring words did nothing to soothe her. Finally, she blurted out one word.

"Larry . . ."

No. Please, not that.

Amelia studied Ella. Though she was obviously distraught, her clothing was not disheveled, and she bore no outward signs of an attack. "Sit down," she said softly as she led her to the sofa. "You're safe now." She put her hand on Ella's, trying to comfort her. "What did Larry do?"

Ella shook her head, gripping Amelia's hand so tightly it hurt, while she continued to cry. When at last her sobs subsided, she turned a tearstained face to Amelia. "Larry . . . he . . . he kissed me."

For a moment Amelia was silent as she tried to mask her surprise. How could a simple kiss have caused hysteria? There had to be more to it than that. "Did he hurt you?" she asked.

Ella shook her head, then appeared to reconsider and nodded. "No. Yes. Oh, Amelia, I'm so scared." And she would say no more.

Chapter Eleven

Several of the men blinked as they emerged from the mine shaft into the bright summer sun. At this time of day, though the birds chirped their pleasure with the world, their songs were barely heard over the men's conversation. Shift change was a noisy time in Gold Landing.

William waited until the roar had subsided before he spoke. "Well, men, I assume you've all heard about the plans for the new clinic." The construction date had been established only after they had been sure that all the materials would be delivered.

Chet Wing chuckled. "I'll bet there's not a married man in town who could forget it. 'Pears that's all the women can talk about."

"It's not just the married ones," Jake Bolton chimed in. "Purty near every female in this town is talking about the lady doctor and her clinic."

One of the men scratched his head, then said, "I cain't figure that out myself. Sure, it's nice having the lady doc here. Hell, a purty lady's welcome anywhere. But why's there such a ruckus over a clinic?"

William was not going to admit that he had had similar thoughts himself. Amelia wanted a clinic, and that was all there was to it. There would be a clinic before the tundra turned red.

"Reckon the ladies care 'cause they need it more than we do," Chet speculated.

William rolled his shoulders, trying to relieve the tension he had felt for days. Mine production was at an all-time high, while expenses had remained flat. That translated into good profits. There was no reason why he should be sleeping poorly and waking up with a devil of a headache. No reason at all.

As a dark cloud scudded overhead, momentarily dimming

the sunlight, William spoke. "The clinic's for everyone—men as well as women. Of course, I agree with Chet. I figure none of us will ever need it." A murmur of assent told William his men were listening to him.

"Oh, I don't know," Jake countered. "It wasn't so bad having the lady doctor look at my throat the other day. She gave me the same medicine Dr. Ben always does, but she sure smelled a lot better than him."

As he pinched his nose, pantomiming the classic reaction to a foul odor, the other men laughed.

"A throat, sure. But do you want her looking at *all* of you?" Chet demanded. He stared at the portion of Jake's anatomy that had provoked his question.

William frowned. It was time to get this meeting on the right track. He hadn't assembled his men to listen to Jake and Chet's pathetic attempts at humor.

Jake responded with a broad grin. "Under the right circumstances, I surely would. In fact, I'd go so far as to say I might even let her *touch* me." He leered, leaving no doubt of what he considered the right circumstances.

Anger sharper than his whittling knife shot through William. "That's enough! She's a lady, and don't any of you ever forget it."

The eruption of ribald laughter died abruptly as the men absorbed his uncharacteristically sharp words.

"Sure, boss," Jake agreed, his face red with embarrassment. "No offense meant."

William accepted the apology. "You're probably wondering why I called this meeting. There was a reason, and it wasn't just so you'd have to listen to me jawboning. I'm here to tell you I'm closing the mine the day the clinic's built."

A round of groans and a few audible protests greeted his statement. "I need the money," more than one man muttered.

The thickening clouds brought with them the threat of precipitation. Rain was bad enough at any time, but it would be pure hell if it came while they were raising the clinic.

William held up a hand. "Hold your horses. I'm not finished. Just listen before you start moaning." The miners grew

147

silent. "You have your choice, men. You can stay home that day, but anyone who works on the clinic gets his normal pay."

The men were so quiet that William could hear the distant whine of Sam Baranov's sawmill.

"You're paying us to build the clinic?" Chet asked.

"That's what I just said. If you want to. The choice is yours."

As a round of cheers told William that his men had made their decision, the tension in his shoulders began to ease. At least now he didn't have to worry about how he was going to get Amelia's clinic built. As he had told his men, he did not expect to have any firsthand experience with the place, but if it would keep a smile on Amelia's pretty face, it would be worth the effort.

"Gonna be easy money," one man told the others.

He was wrong. "I wouldn't bet on that," William countered. "Building is hard work. Just as tough as mining, plus you get the sun and mosquitoes."

"Blasted birds."

As the first spatter of rain hit the ground, William grinned. It wasn't much of an exaggeration to say that the pesky insects were as large as small birds, and there were a lot more of them. He had seen swarms so dense they looked like a cloud, and had felt the bite of more than one greedy pest.

"I guess this means you're gonna be there." Chet phrased it as a statement rather than a question.

"Who do you think's in charge?" William demanded. It certainly had not been Amelia who had calculated the amount of lumber needed and who had arranged for Sam Baranov to cut it to size, nor Ben who had gotten Herb Ashton to sweet-talk the steamer captain into bringing a double shipment of nails.

Chet appeared to considered William's question. "I reckon it's Dr. Ben," he answered.

The idea was so ludicrous that William laughed. "Face it, men. Ben is a great doctor, but he doesn't know beans about building."

As he walked home, William grinned, ignoring the rain that

was now falling in earnest. Constructing that clinic was going to prove interesting. One thing was certain: at the end of the day, Amelia Sheldon would know how real men worked. She would have seen what muscles and brains and pure determination could do. That would give her something to think about besides her damned lawyer and his books.

That miserable excuse for a man probably got splinters just thinking about touching wood. As for doing something with it . . . William laughed out loud as he pictured Abe trying to build the clinic. Yes, Abe Ferguson ought to stick to his books.

Not that books were as boring as he had thought. William had to admit that that Jack London fellow knew how to tell a good yarn. He knew about real men and what they faced in Alaska. Maybe Amelia ought to read one of his books. Good idea. When he finished *The Call of the Wild,* he would offer it to her. Then he would have a reason for seeing her again, for of course they would have to discuss Amelia's reaction to the story. Books were even more useful than he had thought.

"I want you to know I don't use the term lightly," Gloria said as she poured Amelia a cup of tea, then refilled her own glass with something a bit stronger. "You really are a miracle worker."

Amelia raised an eyebrow. On a dreary day like this, she could use good news, but "miracle worker" was a definite exaggeration. "What makes you say that?"

Gloria sipped her drink slowly before she replied, and Amelia sensed that she was enjoying the delay, for Gloria, Amelia had learned, had a flair for drama. "I heard William Gunning is paying his men their normal wages if they help build the clinic."

"I wouldn't call that much of a miracle," Amelia said. "Ella told me William helped build the school, too."

Gloria shook her head, then drew the curtains closed. Though the sumptuous velvet did not obliterate the sound of rain on the glass, it did block the sight of gray sky. "That was different. William contributed a lot of the money for the school, and he was part of the work crew, but he didn't bring all his men with him.'' Gloria settled back in her chair. ''I wonder why he's doing this.''

''Probably his friendship with Dr. Ben.''

Gloria hooted. ''That's about as likely as the Tanana not freezing some winter. No, Amelia, if I were you, I'd look closer to home.''

It was a disconcerting thought. Setting her empty cup back on the table, Amelia said, ''I'd better check your girls now.'' The last thing she wanted was to indulge in speculation over William Gunning's motives, especially if they involved her. It was bad enough that she kept having those dreams about him—wonderful, terrible, disturbing dreams that always ended too soon, leaving her feeling unbearably empty.

''Rachel's with a customer,'' Gloria told her. ''The rest should be waiting for you in their rooms.''

Ever since Amelia had inadvertently interrupted one of the girls and her customer, Gloria had been careful to warn Amelia which rooms to avoid. Amelia hadn't been sure who was the most embarrassed when she opened the door. Celeste had laughed, but neither Amelia nor the man had found the situation amusing. It wasn't that she was a prude, Amelia told herself. It was simply that some things deserved to be kept private.

She knocked on the first door, then opened it.

''Go away.'' June Woods looked up from her mending.

Since it was still early in the day and few customers were expected, June had not curled her hair or applied her makeup, and she wore a cotton wrapper rather than her elaborate evening dress. Without the trappings of her profession, June looked younger than her twenty-six years, a fact underscored by her stubborn expression, which reminded Amelia of a rebellious teenager.

''If you're indisposed''—Amelia used the euphemism that the girls seemed to prefer—''I'll be back next week.''

''It's not that,'' June said, a pout emphasizing her petulant tone. ''I just don't want an exam.''

Amelia placed her bag on the floor. ''Why not, June?'' This

was the third day of rain, and Amelia wondered whether the inclement weather had caused June's mood.

The blonde shook her head. Keeping her eyes on the fabric in her lap, she said, "I don't want you to treat me."

Although Amelia had expected resistance to the regular exams when she and Gloria had instituted them, there had been surprisingly little. The girls had been almost grateful that someone worried about their health, and had consulted Amelia whenever they were ill. Amelia had been examining them all, including June, for several months now and had met no opposition.

"You know Gloria's rule. If you're not certified healthy, you can't work."

June shrugged. "If I have to, I'll go to Dr. Ben, but I'm not letting you touch me."

When she had finished her other examinations, Amelia returned to Gloria's office. "We have a small problem," she told the elegant madam.

Gloria listened, then said, "June's not usually moody. Let's give her a month. If she doesn't change her mind, I'll personally march her down the street to Dr. Ben." Gloria chucked. "It's probably just a passing megrim."

Amelia wasn't so sure. As she updated the patients' charts that afternoon, she told Ben of her experience at Gloria's. While she had not expected him to be overly concerned, his reaction managed to surprise her. Ben tossed his head back and laughed. "What's the matter, Dr. Sheldon?" He managed to infuse his words with mockery. "Are you losing your touch? I thought all the women idolized you."

Maybe the rain was affecting Ben's mood as well as June's. William said it bothered his men, even when they were deep in the mine shaft.

"Look, Dr. Taylor." If he wanted to be formal, two could play the same game. "I came here to tell you we might have a problem and to warn you what to expect. I did not expect to be jeered at."

"So—" Ben shrugged—"what do you want me to do?"

"I wondered if you had any idea why June might have

refused treatment," Amelia answered. "As you remind me so often, you've been in Gold Landing far longer than I have."

The swivel chair squeaked as Ben leaned back. "Just how am I supposed to know what one of Gloria's girls thinks? I'm not a mind reader."

"I thought you might have heard something," Amelia said.

Ben leaned farther back and stared at the ceiling for a moment. Then his laughter erupted again. "You mean you thought I might have heard something when I was frequenting Gloria's establishment for personal reasons?"

"Precisely."

"And now who's jeering at whom?" he demanded. "Although it's none of your business, I haven't been there in a while. I imagine June's problem is just normal female moodiness."

Amelia let the slur pass. "I'm not so sure." First Ella, now June. Amelia wondered if Gold Landing was experiencing a rash of emotional problems.

As he had expected, she was at the site before anyone else arrived, walking between the stakes, looking as though she were imagining the way the building would look at the end of the day.

"Are you sure this is where you want it?"

Amelia turned and smiled, her blue eyes warm with enthusiasm. Though she was dressed in her normal dark skirt and white shirtwaist, today William saw no sign of her medical bag. "Ben said this was a good spot," she told him, gesturing at the stakes.

Lord! She was beautiful, with those masses of dark hair that begged a man to run his fingers through them and those eyes that sparkled more than the Tanana on a sunny day. Which, thank God, it was. As for her scent! How could one woman smell so good?

William shook his head, as much to clear his thoughts as to disagree with her. "It's your clinic, Amelia, not Ben's. If you want to move those stakes, we can do it." Though he had to admit that Ben had chosen well. The small bluff was one

William had considered for his own home. Only its distance from the center of town had dissuaded him. When William had looked at the site, it had been wooded. In preparation for the clinic, many of the trees had been cut, leaving only a few to shade the back of the building.

"I like this spot." As Amelia started counting advantages on her fingers, William had a vision of another, more pleasurable use for those fingers. "It's away from the river, so it won't flood, and far enough out of town that I can keep patients quarantined here, yet it's not so far away that people won't come."

"It sounds as though you've got it all figured out." Maybe if he kept talking, he would be able to think about something other than how utterly desirable she was and how he wished they could spend the day alone together engaged in far more enjoyable activities than building a clinic.

"Look." Amelia walked between two stakes and motioned to William to follow her. "This small room will be the office," she said, pointing to an area to their right. "The one next to it will be the examination and treatment room. And this"—she gestured to the left—"is where we're going to have the two infirmary rooms. It'll be perfect, William. Just perfect."

William grinned, caught up in her infectious enthusiasm. "It doesn't take much to make you happy, does it?" Oh, how he wished that smile were for him and not for a building.

"Not much?" Amelia stopped and stared at him. "Don't you think that Gold Landing's first clinic is a major accomplishment?" Without waiting for his response, she said, "I do. I may have had the dream, William, but you're the one who's making it possible."

She smiled again, and this time William knew that the smile was for him. She was looking at him as though he were one of those heroes that Polly used to tell him about, a knight who slayed dragons and evil men. He was no hero, of course, but he wouldn't remind Amelia of that. Not today. It felt too good, basking in the warmth of her smile. Today he would build her the best clinic in all of Alaska, and then he would see about those dragons.

"The town is my responsibility," he said, his voice gruffer than normal.

No wonder Abe ordered books and special candy for her. That smile was enough to convince a man to do almost anything. As for her kiss . . .

"It was kind of you to organize the food brigade," Amelia told Bertha Langdon. Once the town had approved construction of the clinic, the minister's wife had volunteered to provide meals for the workers.

She had been the first on the site after Amelia and William, and Amelia had greeted her with mixed emotions. Of course she was anxious for the work to begin. After all, the clinic was the most important thing in her life. But those few moments with William had been special. They had shared a closeness, a camaraderie deeper and stronger than ever before. For the first time Amelia felt as though William truly understood how important being a doctor was to her.

That was what mattered. William's friendship was what she wanted, and yet there was no denying that her body wanted something different. When his eyes had met hers they were warm, igniting a fire that had not yet fully subsided. And though his eyes were intense, his lips had softened, curving so gently that for a moment she had thought he was going to kiss her. Then Bertha Langdon had arrived.

The minister's wife pulled a list from her pocket and began crossing off items. "I enjoy doing this," she said. "Besides, we'll all benefit from the clinic."

"And," Ella added as she joined them, her unfashionably long skirts swirling on the ground, "this is a good excuse for a party."

The morning was beautiful, perfect for a party. The rain had stopped two days earlier, giving the ground time to dry, and there was enough of a breeze that the mosquito plague would be less than normal. It was a great day to celebrate, but first they had a clinic to build.

Though Amelia had expected the volunteers to drift in, the majority of them came in a group, their overalls and sturdy boots confirming that they were ready to work, while the jaunty angles of a few caps said these men at least relished the break in their routine. Within minutes, the clinic was under way.

The scent of freshly sawed wood mingled with the honest odor of hard work, while occasional curses and outbursts of laughter could be heard over the steady sound of nails being hammered and beams being hoisted.

Amelia watched as the men dug holes for the foundation and started to frame the building. William did his share of the work—in fact, more than one man's share—yet at the same time he seemed to be aware of what everyone else was doing.

"Hey, Alex, bring those nails over here!" he called, scarcely breaking the rhythm of his hammering. Amelia hadn't expected Alex to be one of the workers. After all, how much heavy labor could he do with only one arm? But William had found a task—an important task—that Alex could accomplish.

Amelia looked around the site. Every male resident of Gold Landing was working, from Jethro Mooney, who was so old he claimed he had lost count of the number of winters he had spent in Alaska, to Frank Stratton, who had opposed the clinic and whose girth and general poor health probably made him more of a liability than an asset. Through it all, without being obvious, William appeared to be in the middle of everything.

"Ben," he called, "how about helping Abe hold that beam over there?"

Amelia smiled. Ben had been struggling to raise a beam single-handedly. She had seen the older man's face redden dangerously and had wanted to tell him to stop. But she couldn't, because that would have hurt Ben's pride. He would never have wanted to admit that there were tasks he wasn't physically capable of performing. William, it appeared, had seen the problem and had found a way to keep Ben from harming himself without making the man appear weak.

Ben would think he was helping Abe. The truth was, Abe needed help. Though he wore overalls and boots like the oth-

155

ers, it was clear Abe was unaccustomed to manual labor. Still, he had joined the crew of dirty, sweaty men who were turning Amelia's dream into reality.

By midday the rough framing was done, leaving the men more than ready for a break. Bertha Langdon's recruits had been working for this moment, raising a large tent and filling it with a seemingly inexhaustible supply of food.

"Thank you." Amelia greeted the workers as they entered the meal tent. Though they nodded and a few spoke to her, it was clear their attention was focused on the long tables laden with fried chicken, potato salad, baked beans and assorted beverages.

"What? No beer?" Trust Ben to be the one who asked that question. He mopped his brow, then settled his spectacles back on his nose.

Before Amelia could answer, Ella handed him a glass of lemonade. "Do you think we would risk Amelia's clinic by letting any of you drink? Not a chance! Besides, Ben, you don't need alcohol."

While others nodded their thanks for the cold drinks, Ben glared at the young schoolteacher. "What do you know about a man's needs?" he demanded.

"How about the fact that liquor isn't one you're born with?"

Ben looked at the lemonade as if it were a poisonous substance. "Is that so? Maybe I don't *need* a drink, but I sure as hell want one. And that's not the only thing I want." As he turned his glance back to Ella, a sly grin lit his face. "You know what else I want, Ella? I want to see you get rip-roaring drunk."

Amelia bit back a smile. Ben was in rare form today. Though the color rose to Ella's cheeks, she kept her voice calm as she said, "Prepare to be disappointed, Ben Taylor. That's one of your many cravings that will never be satisfied."

Ben harrumphed and left the food line, his glass of lemonade clutched in one hand.

"What's eating him?" William asked Amelia when he saw Ben's hasty exit. A streak of dirt and a spot of blood on his cheek suggested he had battled at least one mosquito. Amelia wanted to brush the dirt away. Instead, she reached for a clean glass and began to fill it. "Ben's suffering from absence of alcohol."

"He doesn't need it."

"Funny, that's what Ella told him, but Ben didn't seem to agree." Amelia handed William the glass she had just filled. "Your men have made good progress."

She had been surprised at how quickly the frame had risen and how well the men had worked together. There had been amazingly few disagreements and no mistakes that Amelia had seen. The credit, she knew, went to William. He had directed his men the way a skilled conductor did his musicians.

William nodded. "The men are glad to be outside. Working underground takes its toll after a while, and you have this craving to see daylight."

Cravings, it appeared, were a major topic of conversation today. Amelia wondered what William would say if he knew what she was craving. What would he do if he knew that she wanted nothing more than to be held in his arms and to feel his lips on hers, that she wanted to let the fire he had kindled this morning burn freely, igniting every one of her senses, destroying her fears and the last of her inhibitions, that she wanted her dreams, those wicked, disturbing dreams, to come true? He would be shocked. Ladies didn't admit to carnal cravings, and so she said, "Will you take an afternoon break?"

William reached for a piece of raisin pie, then shook his head. "We can't afford the time. We're going to be hard-pressed to finish today." He smiled at her again, then joined Ben at one of the tables outside the tent.

"He's a born leader, isn't he?"

Amelia turned to Ella, surprised that she had read her thoughts so easily. Next to William, every other man looked small, and it had nothing to do with physical size. William possessed what Amelia had heard described as presence. When he entered a room or joined a group, the others automatically deferred to him. She hadn't always admired that characteristic,

157

Amelia admitted, remembering Ella's party, but it served him well today.

"He certainly is."

"The men all follow him," Ella added.

"I was thinking that it's a bit like a symphony orchestra."

"With a good conductor."

"Exactly."

"Still, I have to admit that I was surprised," Ella continued. "I hadn't realized that Dr. Ben was so good at directing men."

"Ben?" Ella was talking about Dr. Ben!

"Naturally. Who did you think I meant? Abe?"

Amelia shook her head. "Of course not." Ella thought Ben was a leader! If her friend hadn't looked so serious, Amelia might have laughed. Instead, she helped clear the tables.

By nightfall, the clinic was completed. Amelia stared at the building, her heart so filled with happiness that she thought it would burst. Her clinic!

"You did a great job, men." Ben raised his voice to be heard over the congratulations that the women were bestowing on their husbands. "I couldn't have done it without you."

Ella beamed her approval while Amelia bit her tongue. Ben was acting as though he had been the leader, and for some reason William was not saying a word. Surely no one thought the clinic's success was the result of Ben's organizational abilities. William had done the work. He deserved the credit. She would see that he got it.

Amelia made her way to Ben's side. As she started to speak, the crowd fell silent. "To you, this may look like just an ordinary building," she said, "but I think it's the most beautiful one in all of Alaska, and I owe it to . . ."

Though dusk had begun to settle, she could see William in the back of the crowd, surrounded by a group of his men. When her eyes met his, he shook his head ever so slightly. For whatever reason, he wanted no public acknowledgment of his work.

"I owe it to each and every one of you." Amelia amended her words. "This was the finest teamwork I've ever seen, and

158

I want to thank all of you.'' She felt her eyes begin to fill with tears and, try though she might, she could not keep her voice from cracking. "What you did today has made me very, very proud to be a citizen of Gold Landing."

The men cheered. The women clapped. William smiled.

"Those were fancy words," he said. "I don't want to take anything away from them, but I'd like to show my thanks in a different way." He pointed toward the street. "That wagon that's coming down the road is carrying beer and whiskey. I'd be mighty obliged if you sent it back empty."

The crowd whooped.

"How could he do that?" Ella gripped Amelia's arm, her distress obvious. "Ben will drink too much."

Amelia merely smiled. William knew exactly what his men needed. He had given them both praise and a tangible reward.

While the men clustered around the wagon and the women headed home, Amelia remained in the clinic, too excited to leave. It was finished! Her dream had become a reality. She was picturing her young chicken pox patients in isolation, when she heard footsteps. They were too heavy to be Ella's, and Abe had left, obviously exhausted by the day's labor. Though it could be any one of the men, Amelia couldn't stop her pulse from racing with anticipation. She turned, happiness sweeping through her as she recognized the visitor. He was here!

"I thought you were with your men," she said, irrationally glad that he had left them, that they could end the day together where it had begun.

William shrugged. Though the light was quickly fading, she could see sawdust in his hair. "I had one drink with them—got them started. They won't miss me."

Amelia's happiness turned into bubbling laughter. "Oh, William, look." She grabbed his hand and dragged him from room to room, wanting to share her joy with him.

His hand tightened on hers, warm, calloused and so comforting. "One little building means that much to you?"

"Oh, yes." The words came tumbling out faster than the mountain streams when the snow began to melt. "This is so

159

much more than one building. It's what I worked for during all those years of school." As her eyes met his, the warmth that he had kindled earlier began to grow. "I owe it to you."

Amelia smiled, willing him to understand how important this was to her and how grateful she was. "You wouldn't let me say it in front of everyone, but now you can't stop me. Thank you, William. This means more than I can ever tell you."

He dropped her hand but did not move away. "If you mean it, how about a real thank-you?" And he pulled her into his arms, drawing her close to him. For a second they stood there, their arms entwined, their eyes saying what their lips dared not. Then William lowered his mouth to hers.

This was not the gentle, exploratory kiss he had given her after the Fourth of July celebration. While that one had been warm and comforting, this one was white-hot, a flame burning out of control. Wild and passionate, the kiss was the culmination of all the looks she and William had shared throughout the day. And, oh, how wonderful it felt!

The longings her dreams had raised were nothing—nothing at all—compared to those his embrace ignited. Amelia's pulse raced and she could feel heat radiate through every fiber of her being as William kissed her. She leaned into him, reveling in the feelings his touch aroused.

William was a mind reader. It was the only explanation. How else would he have known her secret cravings, the ones she had been afraid to voice? He must have read her thoughts, for how else would he have known that she wanted to be touched there, that she longed to be kissed in just that spot?

It was perfection, pure and simple. Not that there was anything simple about the way William made her feel. He aroused a maelstrom of emotions, filling her with longings at the same time that he satisfied her most elemental needs. For he was enjoying the kiss. She had incontrovertible evidence of that. She was not a failure!

This was the perfect ending to the perfect day. She was standing in the clinic of her dreams, being held by the man she loved. For a second, Amelia froze. She couldn't love him. And yet she did.

"Oh, William, I—"

Before Amelia could finish her sentence, the sound of men shouting and a woman's screams splintered the peace.

"Stop them!" the woman shrieked. Though distorted by fear, Amelia recognized the voice as Ella's. "Stop them! They'll kill each other."

"What the hell?" William released Amelia, and they raced out of the clinic, boots and shoes clattering on the freshly laid floor. Though the sun had set, the moon illuminated the yard surrounding the clinic. A small crowd had gathered to watch two men rolling in the dust, pounding each other with their fists, shouting imprecations between their groans of pain, while on the sidelines Ella screamed.

William and Amelia looked at each other for a split second, communicating without words. Responsibility to stop the fight warred with regret that their perfect moment had been shattered. William raised an eyebrow. Amelia nodded. He strode to the two men, grabbing one with each hand and separating them, while Amelia rushed to Ella.

"Are you hurt?" she asked. Ella's braids had tumbled from their coronet, and dirt stained one sleeve, but Amelia could see no sign of injury.

Ella continued to weep. Though her sobs were slowing, she was far from calm. A few yards away, William waited for Ella's reply, and Amelia had no doubt that if one of the men had hurt Ella, there would be swift retribution.

"No." Ella shook her head.

"Then why are you crying?" Amelia was concerned as both a friend and a physician. This was the second time she had found Ella crying almost hysterically for no apparent reason.

"Hitting . . . it was awful . . . so scared." Ella blurted the words between sobs. Whatever had happened, Ella had not been hurt. Amelia met William's eyes and nodded.

"Go home," he told the brawlers. "And if I hear you've caused any more ruckus, I'll fine you a day's pay."

The men slunk away, ignoring each other, and the small

161

crowd dispersed, leaving the evening silent, except for the sound of Ella's sobbing. Amelia put her arms around the schoolteacher. "It's all right now," she said softly, as though comforting a child. "They'll be all right. Just a few bruises." Though Ella's tears began to subside, she continued to sob.

Amelia looked at William, her eyes telling him how much she regretted the interruption, but all she said was, "Let's go home, Ella."

Chapter Twelve

"You'll have to lie." Lydia Sheldon's face was ashen, her expression more despairing than Amelia had ever seen it, worse even than the day Grandpa had died.

"Lie? What do you mean?"

When the doctors had summoned her into their consultation room and given their diagnosis, Amelia had had only one thought: to go home. Mother would know what to do. But Lydia had not reacted the way Amelia had expected. While Amelia collapsed on the brocaded chaise longue, her mother paced the floor, unable to offer the comfort Amelia sought.

"It's the only way." Lydia stared out the window, and Amelia sensed her reluctance to look at her, to see the imperfect woman who had come from her own body. "We'll tell no one. No one." Lydia repeated the words fiercely. "Not even your father or Belinda. Then, once you're married, you'll cry and pretend to be bewildered every month when your curse comes."

Amelia drew her knees up and wrapped her arms around them, trying to stop the trembling that had started when the doctors told her she would never be able to bear a child.

"I can't. No. I can't lie to the man I want to marry. It wouldn't be right."

Lydia swung around. "Do you think any man would marry you if he knew the truth?" she demanded, her blue eyes flashing with anger. "Men want children. That's the only reason they marry." Lydia pursed her perfectly shaped lips, giving Amelia the same disdainful look she had seen her bestow on a maid who had left a spot of tarnish on a gravy boat. "I don't know what I did to deserve a child like you. First you decide to be a doctor, and now it turns out you're not even a real woman. Thank God I have Belinda."

* * *

Amelia woke, her body trembling almost as violently as it had that day in Philadelphia. She had gone months without the dream, but tonight it had returned, more painful than ever. The reason was not hard to find, she realized as she pulled another blanket from the cedar chest and spread it on the bed. The day that she had learned she was barren, her pain had been caused by the loss of a dream, the dream of marriage to a man she had not yet met. But now that she had met the man she wanted to marry, the one man she could love for the rest of her life, the pain was far, far worse. Instead of the dull ache of emptiness, this was as sharp and deep as a razor's cut.

She could not lie to William. She *would not* lie to him. And that meant that they would never, ever have a future together. For William wanted children.

Amelia huddled under the blankets, shivering. The wise thing would be to avoid William, to make certain they were never alone again, that the kisses they had shared were not repeated. A wise woman would do just that, and Amelia was a wise woman.

She could not avoid him completely. In a town the size of Gold Landing, that simply was not possible. But she could keep their meetings as casual as her dinners with Abe. She and William could still be friends, just as she and Abe were. And somehow she would make sure they never crossed the boundaries of friendship. The thought did nothing to warm her heart or stop her trembling.

Amelia strapped the snowshoes onto her feet. Although they had felt awkward the first few times she had worn them, now that she had developed the proper rhythm, she found them surprisingly comfortable. And there was no denying the fact that they made walking through deep snow a lot easier.

The brief Alaskan summer had been followed by an even briefer autumn. Now, although it was only October, winter reigned, bringing with it a surprising calm. It was as though the frenzy that had characterized summer had burned itself out. Even Ella seemed to have regained her normal equilibrium. She had refused to discuss her outburst over the miners' fight, saying only that her nerves must have been on edge. But with school back in session, she was once more the calm woman Amelia had met her first day in Gold Landing.

Amelia's smile faltered as she climbed the last few yards to the Indian village. Ella might have regained her equilibrium, but she had not. It had been more difficult than she had dreamed to keep her distance from William, to treat him the same way she did Abe.

They were two such different men. Abe was her friend, and William was . . . her friend. Only her friend. Perhaps if she reminded herself of that every morning, one day she would believe it.

Amelia pushed the caribou hide aside and entered the hut. As she stripped off her mittens and laid her coat beside her bag, Amelia shivered. The wickiup, although covered with several layers of caribou hide, had no visible source of heat and felt as though it were only a few degrees warmer than outside.

Amelia examined her patient, a boy perhaps eight years old who lay on the traditional pallet of willow branches covered with furs and skins. Though Amelia was not an expert, it seemed to her that there were fewer furs than normal covering the child. Had his parents traded the others in Fairbanks? Ella had told Amelia that greedy fur traders encouraged the Athapaskans to wear cloth garments rather than their tribal furs and skins, since that increased the supply of furs to be traded. Never mind that the Indians needed the furs for warmth.

"I'd like you to bring him to the clinic," she told the boy's mother as she left the wickiup. Normally she would not have suggested an overnight stay for a simple fever, but the conditions in the wickiup were so appalling that Amelia feared the child's recovery would be delayed if he remained at home.

"Amelia!" His voice carried clearly down Main Street. As swiftly as an avalanche, Amelia's heart began to pound. It was foolish, of course, to react so to nothing more than the sound of her name. He was her friend. Just her friend. Yet if her life had depended on it, she could not have slowed her pulse.

"Amelia!" William finished buttoning his coat as he crossed the street, then thrust his bare hands into his pockets.

"Pete's making his special moose stew tonight, and I wondered if I could talk you into sampling it with me."

She smiled. "I'd like that." Oh, how she would like it!

Two hours later she and William were seated in Pete's Roadhouse, a large log cabin that had been serving travelers hearty meals for longer than Gold Landing had been in existence. Pete's moose dishes were famous, and Amelia had heard the women of Gold Landing sigh enviously over his biscuits. Today Pete could have been serving sawdust and river flour for all Amelia cared. She was with William. Her friend.

"It's hard for me to believe it's only October," she told William as he settled on the bench opposite her. She was glad she had changed into a fresh shirtwaist and had added a lace jabot, for William wore a spotless white shirt with one of the new rounded collars, and he had had his hair trimmed. "At home the leaves would be turning red and yellow; here we already have a foot of snow."

"At least the mosquitoes are gone." William gave Pete their orders, then leaned against the plank that served as the back of the bench. As conversations went, this one was light. How could a discussion of the weather compare to the analysis of literature that characterized her dinners with Abe? And yet Amelia felt a shiver of excitement that had nothing to do with the weather, and though the roadhouse lacked the comforts of the hotel's dining room, she would not have traded the unadorned wood bench and plain table for even the finest restaurant in Philadelphia or Boston.

When Amelia laughed, as much from pure enjoyment as William's quip about the pesky insects, he continued, "This is a harsh land."

"But a beautiful one."

"That, too. Of course, sometimes you forget the beauty when you're worried about survival." William's hand strayed to his watch fob, and Amelia wondered if he realized how often he did that.

As Pete placed bowls of the fragrant stew in front of them, Amelia sniffed appreciatively. "I've wondered about your watch fob,'' she admitted. ''Is it from the mine here?''

William shook his head as he dipped a piece of biscuit into the thick gravy. ''This was the first big nugget I found. It was probably foolish, because there sure have been times when I could have used the money it would bring, but I kept it. I suppose you'd call it a good-luck charm.''

''Then it's from Nome?''

It was the wrong question. A moment before, William had been smiling. Now his expression was empty as an abandoned mine shaft. ''Yes,'' he said simply.

''What brought you here?'' Perhaps the thought of Gold Landing would restore his smile.

William studied the bowl of stew. ''The gold was played out and there were stories of major strikes in the interior.'' It was a plausible tale, but the pain in his voice and his shuttered expression told Amelia there were other, more compelling reasons why he had left the coast. She wondered if those reasons were somehow tied to his hatred of the Indians.

Amelia shivered. Even though the roadhouse was well heated, every time the door opened, a blast of cold air swirled under her skirts. ''How do people survive the cold?''

''The miners get used to it. Cold is a way of life. Even in the summer, they're cutting through permafrost.''

Amelia shivered again, remembering her visit to the Indian village. ''I don't know how the Indians live,'' she said. ''The wickiup I was in this afternoon had no heat.'' If she and William were going to be friends, they could not ignore the fact that the small Athapaskan community was part of Amelia's caseload.

William took another spoonful of stew, chewing carefully before he spoke. ''The Athapaskans chose to live here,'' he said. He nodded a greeting to two men as they took seats at the other end of the long table.

''Weren't they here before the town?'' The Indians had certainly been in Alaska long before the white settlers came.

William shook his head. ''They used to be nomadic. It was only after we founded the town that they settled here.''

Nomads. That helped to explain why the Athapaskans had

167

so few possessions. If they were constantly moving, they would want to own only the essentials. Still, some of the wick-iups lacked even the basic necessities of life.

"They have so little," she said with a sigh. "I want to help them."

"I know you do." William reached across the table and placed a hand on hers. "Be careful," he said.

"What do you mean?"

"I wish you'd carry a gun," he said. "You could be in danger when you're out on your rounds."

Amelia knew he meant well, and there was no denying the fear she had felt the day she and William had heard a bear in the brush. Still, she did not believe she needed a weapon.

"I thought the bears were hibernating," she said.

"Bears are not the only danger." Although William looked as if he wanted to say more, he did not.

William changed the subject, telling Amelia of a new drill design he had heard about, and for the rest of the meal they discussed nothing more controversial than whether or not he should use dynamite to excavate the next shaft. It was a pleasant evening, listening to William talk about the mine, regaling him with the more humorous stories from medical school. Good food, good company, good conversation. It should have been enough, but though she felt replete from the stew and Pete's equally famous cranberry cobbler, Amelia was aware of an emptiness deep inside her, a need that, while it was physical, had nothing to do with sustenance. They were friends, nothing more, and she dared not forget that.

She was in the general store the next afternoon, bending down to see the pickled beets Herb Ashton had arranged on the lowest shelf, when two women came in.

"I heard the lady doctor had dinner with William Gunning last night," the first said, her boots clicking on the polished floor.

"I heard that, too. I have to tell you, Linda, I was mighty surprised. I didn't think those two had anything in common. Look at this, will you. Sprigged muslin."

"I wonder what Abe has to say about it." The woman named Linda appeared unimpressed with the yard goods. "He's sure been courting her."

The second woman's sniff was audible. "I don't imagine Abe's worried. A lady like Dr. Sheldon wouldn't be interested in William, even if he is richer than any two men have a right to be."

"She sure wouldn't be if she knew where he spent his nights."

"Now, Linda," the second woman admonished, "those are rumors, nothing more."

"That's not the way I heard it. I heard tell he visits Gloria's house regularly, and he always asks for June."

It was gossip, nothing more. In all likelihood, there was no more truth to it than to the story that Abe was courting her. Courting? Didn't the people of Gold Landing recognize simple friendship when they saw it? Besides, it didn't matter, even if it were true. Amelia didn't care whether William spent every night in a whorehouse and whether he had one girl or twenty. He was her friend. That was all.

William clenched his fist. Who would have thought it would be so hard? He had always prided himself on his self-control, but lately there hadn't been much to be proud of. After the way he had kissed Amelia in the clinic, drawing that delectable body close to his, tasting the sweetness of her lips, he had expected a bolt of lightning to strike him dead. That wasn't the way to treat a lady. When a man had needs, he visited Gloria. He didn't sully a good woman like Amelia.

It was plain as the hump on a moose's back that he had offended her. Oh, she hadn't said anything, but a lady like Amelia didn't need words to express her displeasure. Ever since that night she had been cool as springwater. She smiled when she talked to him, but make no mistake, she had hung a "do not touch" sign around her neck.

For a few weeks he had succeeded in keeping his distance. But William wanted to spend more time with her, and Lord knew no one stood outside in an Alaskan winter just to talk.

How much trouble could he get into at Pete's? The place was lit almost as bright as day, and there were no secluded booths. He would be all right at Pete's.

He had been so sure that he could resist touching her, but when she had started talking about those damned Indians, he couldn't help himself. The need to protect her, to warn her of the terrible risk she was taking, overruled his common sense. He had touched that soft hand of hers, and then he had been lost. All he had wanted to do was pull her into his arms and finish what he had started in the clinic.

Maybe then he would be able to sleep.

"We've got trouble, Amelia." Ella's lips trembled and her hands shook as she pulled out a chair. "There's something going on, but no one wants me to know what it is. They all stop talking when I walk into a room." She raised the mug to her lips, then placed it back on the table, untasted. "All I know is there's a town meeting tonight."

Amelia raised an eyebrow. "It's not time." Town meetings were held the third Wednesday of alternate months. Today was the second Tuesday of a nonmeeting month.

"It's a special one." Ella managed to sip the coffee. "This is the first time that's happened since I've been here. Oh, Amelia, something's wrong."

Amelia's uneasiness grew as she and Ella entered the church a few minutes before the meeting was scheduled to begin. Few citizens would meet her eye or return her greetings. She looked around the room. William was not present. Something was definitely wrong.

Amelia and Ella found a seat halfway down the aisle. Though people shifted to make a place for them, there were few smiles. Then the door opened again. The low murmur told Amelia that William had arrived. Instead of sitting in the last pew, he made his way forward and sat three rows in front of Amelia.

Promptly at seven o'clock, Glen McBride rapped his gavel. "Ladies and gentlemen, I call the meeting to order." He looked around the room, nodded at someone, then continued.

"According to our bylaws, this special meeting was called at the request of ten citizens. Frank, would you like to address the group?"

Frank Stratton, the man who had been vocal in his opposition to the clinic, strode to the front of the room. Without preamble, he began, "I told you all you were making a mistake—a big mistake—when you agreed to that damned clinic."

Amelia steeled herself not to react, but she could feel her heart begin to race. If Frank Stratton had initiated the meeting, it could bode no good for Amelia or the clinic. But what complaint could be serious enough that he had brought it to the whole town rather than to her and Ben?

"Now, Frank, watch your language," the mayor interjected. "This is a house of God."

"Right." Frank glared at Amelia, then continued. "The citizens of Gold Landing donated their time and money for that blamed clinic." He puffed out his chest and addressed the group. "I told you you were wrong."

Glen McBride raised a cautioning hand. "Get to the point, Frank."

"Right. That clinic was built for the people of Gold Landing. Now Dr. Sheldon is using it to treat those damned Indians."

The Indians. Amelia's heart sank as she guessed what was coming.

"Frank!" The mayor's admonition was drowned out by the cries of, "Yeah, no call to do that."

Thrusting back his shoulders, Frank Stratton said, "I make a motion that the clinic be used only for whites."

Amelia saw William clench his jaw. Surely he was not surprised by the motion? In all likelihood Frank had discussed it with him during one of their poker games.

"I second the motion," three men shouted at the same time.

"All in favor?" The mayor raised the question.

Before he could count the upraised hands, Amelia jumped to her feet. She could not let them destroy her dream without a fight. Though she knew prejudice was strong, surely the

171

people of Gold Landing, who had shown themselves to be so caring in other ways, would be swayed by compassion.

"I believe that parliamentary procedure says that motions can be discussed before a vote is taken. I would like to present my side."

"We know how you feel," someone jeered.

"Yeah, and you're wrong," another added.

"That may be your opinion," Amelia agreed as she walked to the front of the church, "but I would still like to remind you of a few facts. From the beginning, we said that the clinic would be for all the citizens of Gold Landing."

Frank glared at her. "You didn't make no mention of Indians." His face reddened dangerously, reminding Amelia that Ben had told her Frank suffered from a weak heart. Ben had given him digitalis on more than one occasion and had advised him to control his temper. Apparently Frank was ignoring his medical advice tonight.

"There was no reason to single out one group of people." Though she ached to shout at Frank, berating him for his prejudice, Amelia kept her voice level. "We agreed that the clinic would serve everyone, including the least fortunate."

"Not dirty Indians," one woman cried. "They might infect our children."

"They're not part of the town, anyway," another chimed in.

"Perhaps I was mistaken," Amelia said with glacial calm, "but I thought I was still in the United States. Didn't we found this country on some basic principles, one of which was 'all men are created equal'?"

The first woman shook her head. "That doesn't apply to Indians."

"She's right," another agreed. "The Nelson Act says so."

Amelia could feel the blood rushing to her face. She took a deep breath, then exhaled slowly before she spoke again. "Again, perhaps I was mistaken," she said, "but I thought the Civil War ended the idea that we had classes of people in this country."

"Don't be so hoity-toity, Amelia." Frank Stratton took a

step closer to her and started to put his hand on her arm. When she brushed him aside, he continued, "This is Alaska. We make our own rules here."

"If I've heard you correctly, those rules are based on ignorance and bigotry."

Though he had appeared unaffected by her physical rejection, Frank flushed at the insult. "If everything was so great in Philadelphia, why don't you go back there? It's clear you don't belong here."

Amelia's heart sank. She knew that when an argument degenerated to personal attacks, there was little chance of winning.

"Have you seen the conditions the Athapaskans live in?" she asked. "If you refuse them treatment, some of them will die needlessly."

Her words met silence. Amelia looked around the room. Surely someone would support her. Her eyes met William's. Though she saw pain reflected in his, it was clear he opposed her.

"May I have the floor?" Abe, who had been sitting near the back, rose and addressed his question to the mayor. When Glen nodded, Abe walked to the front to stand next to Amelia. Though he motioned to Frank, the other man refused to sit.

"There are a few facts I think we all need to consider." Abe paused, letting his gaze move slowly from pew to pew. "When she finished medical school," he continued, "Dr. Sheldon, like Dr. Ben, took an oath to help people. All people. She's doing that as best she can."

"We're not stopping her," the first woman answered. "We don't care if she treats the Indians. Just don't bring them into town. They don't belong here."

"Right." Frank spoke again. "They're not part of the town. They don't contribute anything."

Abe raised one eyebrow, as though questioning Frank's judgment. "How many of you have snowshoes?" he asked.

There was a low murmur. Though Amelia was not sure where Abe was leading, she doubted anyone in Gold Landing had less than one pair of snowshoes.

"Who makes those snowshoes?" Abe continued.

The murmur increased, as people admitted that the Athapaskans provided all of the town's snowshoes, bartering them for food and other goods from Herb Ashton's store. It was common knowledge that the payment they received was pitifully low for the quality of workmanship they provided.

Abe was not finished. "Who catches the salmon that we feed to our dogs? Or, for that matter, the salmon many of us eat?"

When the assembly had once again quieted, Abe asked, "Is there anyone here who can say the Indians have not contributed to the town?"

There was a general nodding of heads, and Amelia knew that even if the townspeople were not convinced, they were at least listening.

"Wait one minute." Frank Stratton was clearly displeased by the change in the tone of the meeting. "I want to know what Dr. Ben has to say about this."

Amelia knew better than to expect support from him. He had not set foot in the clinic since it had been built.

"I took the same oath as Dr. Sheldon." Ben remained seated as he spoke.

"You didn't answer my question, Ben." Frank was nothing if not persistent. "Would you treat Indians in the clinic?"

Ben chuckled. "That's a trick question, Frank. Everyone knows I treat patients in my office. I leave the clinic to Dr. Sheldon."

There was a moment of silence. While Ben had not supported her, he had not condemned her, either.

Frank was clearly not satisfied. He looked around the room, then said, "William, you helped build the clinic. What do you think?"

Like Ben, William remained seated. Amelia saw momentary indecision on his face. He knew how important the clinic was. Maybe he would support her.

"If you remember the discussion the night we voted to build the clinic, we all agreed Indians have no place in it." Though his voice was impassive, Amelia knew that his words had condemned her clinic. What she did not know was why William had taken this stand. He hated the Indians for some reason, but this seemed different. It was almost as though he was arguing a legal point the way Abe would.

"Perhaps you could explain to me exactly why not," she said.

"I'm afraid, Dr. Sheldon, that you agreed to exclude them."

"I did not!" How could he say that?

William leaned back in the pew, crossing his arms. To the casual observer, he appeared the picture of relaxation. Only Amelia saw the flash in his eyes and the momentary expression that, if she had not known better, she would have called pain.

"The Indians do not pay taxes," William said. "Everyone else in this town contributes to the mayor's salary and the general town budget. We used money from that budget to build the clinic."

All that was true, but Amelia did not understand why William thought it was relevant.

He fixed his gaze on Abe, who was still standing next to Amelia. "I may not have gone to a fancy law school like our attorney, but the way I figure it, if folks don't pay taxes, they're not citizens. You did claim the clinic was for all citizens, didn't you, Dr. Sheldon?"

Amelia nodded, remembering what she had said that night and again today, knowing she had been trapped by her own words.

"No one disputes your right to treat the Indians," William continued. "That's up to you. The only thing we're discussing is whether you treat them in the clinic."

If his words were supposed to placate her, they failed.

"If there's no more discussion, let's vote on the motion." Glen McBride took control of the meeting again. When Amelia, Abe and Frank had taken their seats, he continued. "All in favor of the motion, raise your right hand."

Amelia looked around. Though there appeared to be a forest of hands in the air, not everyone was in agreement.

"One hundred twenty-two," the mayor announced. "All

opposed.'' This time she didn't look around. She knew Abe was voting for her. The rest were a gamble, and Amelia was not a gambling woman.

The mayor counted once, shook his head, then counted again. "One hundred twenty-four."

Amelia let out a sigh of relief. Somehow something she or Abe had said had touched a few hearts or consciences.

"Well, folks, the motion is defeated. Meeting adjourned."

Ella gripped Amelia's hand. "You won!" Her face was wreathed in a smile.

Amelia shook her head. "I don't think there were any winners tonight."

As she made her way out of the church, Amelia saw William standing in the middle of a small group of people. She approached him, and the others backed away.

"Did you come to gloat?" His eyes were filled with so much pain that Amelia wanted nothing more than to put her arms around him and comfort him. "For the second time you and that lawyer friend of yours talked the town into doing things your way."

She knew William was a complex man with firm opinions of what was and was not right, but she still did not understand what had formed those opinions or why he was suffering tonight.

"No, William, I'm not gloating, and I'm not celebrating. What I am is hurt. I can't believe you'd be so . . ." She stopped, momentarily at a loss for words.

"I believe the words you used before were 'ignorant' and 'bigoted.' Was that what you meant?"

She shook her head. Though she had once thought of William in those terms, she knew she had been wrong. "I just don't understand how you can be so cruel. You know that without the clinic, people will die who could otherwise have been saved. Yet you still opposed giving them treatment."

"You think I'm cruel?" William's finger traced the scar on his cheek. "Amelia, you don't know the first thing about cruelty. I could tell you stories that would put you on the next boat back to Philadelphia."

The church was empty. No one would overhear. Perhaps now William would confide in her. Perhaps he would trust her with his secrets. "Then tell me. Please, William, help me understand. I know there has to be a reason why you feel this way. Tell me what it is."

His eyes were bleak, his expression haunted. "I can't."

Without another word, Amelia walked away.

William stared at her back for a moment, then turned and strode in the opposite direction, ignoring his friends' calls. The last thing he needed now was to talk to anyone. He had hated to hurt her. The way Amelia carried on about that clinic, one would think it was her child. She took the slightest criticism personally.

William crossed the street to avoid Frank Stratton. If there was one person he did not want to see tonight, it was Frank. If he had known what Frank was going to do, he might have been able to stop him, but once the mayor got involved, it had been too late.

Frank wasn't wrong. The Indians should not be allowed into the clinic. The risk was too high.

William climbed the stairs and let himself in the front door. It was ironic. Amelia claimed that innocent people might die. He did not disagree. She was right; the irony was, she didn't understand that she might be one of those innocent people. Tossing his coat and hat onto the rack, William strode toward the kitchen. He needed a drink, a good, long drink, to help him forget.

Maybe Frank was right, and she didn't belong here. Things appeared to be different in Philadelphia. They had fancy houses, fancy ideas and fancy people. Not like Alaska. Everything was real here, not pretend. And some of that reality was mighty ugly.

He grabbed a bottle and a glass. Maybe he should have told her. She might have understood if she knew what had happened, what still could happen. William shook his head, picturing Amelia's face as she listened to his story. He couldn't do that. Not to her. Not to him. Some things were too horrible to be put into words. A man had to protect his woman.

177

But Amelia wasn't his woman. William slammed the glass on the table.

They were wrong. Sally and Louise said that William was interested in that lady doctor, but it wasn't true. June knew that. Oh, he might talk to her. Gentlemen did that, and William was certainly a gentleman. He might walk with her occasionally, just to keep her safe, of course. That was another thing that gentlemen did. But he didn't love Amelia.

He couldn't, because he loved June. He had told her in so many ways. William was different from the other men. Even though he was the strongest, the bravest, the most handsome man in Gold Landing and probably in all of Alaska, he never took advantage of a girl. He always asked what she liked. He never hurt her. And he always said nice things, like how her hair reminded him of sunshine. He wouldn't say that if he didn't love her.

Being William, he had not actually said those three overused words. Most men used the words because they thought it was what a girl wanted to hear. June knew better. She knew just how meaningless they were. Love was about other things. Like the way he made sure she didn't get pregnant. Most of the men expected the girl to take care of that, but William had told her from the beginning that he did not want any bastards, and he wasn't taking any chances. Of course, if she got pregnant, the baby would not be a bastard if he married her.

When he married her.

Chapter Thirteen

It was surprising how quickly the anger died, while the hurt remained like a sore tooth, a dull ache that the slightest wrong move could turn into agony. For a week after the town meeting, she had seen fewer patients than usual at the clinic. Mothers who would normally have brought their children to the clinic asked Amelia to make a house call, while the miners sought Ben's aid, refusing to enter the clinic, even outside Ben's office hours. Gradually her practice returned to its pre-meeting levels, yet she still sensed nervous undercurrents whenever she suggested that a child should stay overnight.

Though it hurt to realize that at some level the citizens of Gold Landing did not trust her, with the approach of Christmas that pain was almost forgotten.

"This will be my first Christmas away from home," Amelia told Ella as the two women sat in the parlor, hemming angel costumes. "I hadn't realized I'd miss it so much."

"Alaska's different," Ella agreed. "I've gotten used to most things, but the long darkness still bothers me." Ella shuddered. "I don't know how you can go on your rounds. Aren't you frightened?"

Amelia shook her head. "No. I feel safe." Even without the gun William thought she needed, she did. It was foolish, of course, to remember how comforting it used to be when he would join her on her rounds during the summer, telling her she needed protection from the wild animals: the bears and wolves and snakes. As though she were such a *cheechako* that she thought there were snakes in Alaska! It was his companionship she missed now, not the physical protection, but that was foolish, too. How many times did she have to tell herself she wanted William as a friend, nothing more?

Amelia shook her head again, trying to dismiss the thoughts of Gold Landing's most disturbing citizen. It was bad enough that she dreamed of him, waking in the middle of the night, her arms flung wide as though reaching for him. She could not control her dreams, but she most definitely ought to be able to stop these nonsensical thoughts.

"How does this hem look?" she asked. Perhaps if she concentrated on the sewing, she would be able to keep those errant thoughts in line.

Ella inspected the small garment, then smiled. "The children are so excited about the pageant." Each year the school-children presented a Nativity pageant two days before Christmas, and each year there was great rivalry over who would play Mary and Joseph. The younger children had the less demanding role of angels, content to stand in a row and smile at the baby in the manger.

"You mean to say you don't think the parents are excited?" Amelia's patients had been more anxious than normal when their children had developed fevers. She had reassured them, but her comfort had been bittersweet, filled as it was with the knowledge that she would always be on the outside, that she would never know firsthand the joy of seeing her child don an angel costume.

"Do you suppose this is one of the parents?" Ella laughed as someone pounded on her front door.

"Pauline's in labor." Though the bearded, hooded figure in the bulky parka could have belonged to half the men in town, Amelia recognized Joe Feehy's voice. "She needs you, Doc."

Amelia grabbed her bag and dressed for the trip to the Feehys' cabin. She had made numerous house calls there, for Pauline Feehy was a high-risk mother, a woman who had already had three miscarriages. Amelia had urged her to come to the clinic, telling her she could have constant care there, but Pauline had refused. Even though her cabin was far outside town, nestled in the middle of the forest, she was determined to have her child at home. Clinics, she had told Amelia firmly, were like hospitals. They were places where people went to die.

"How frequent are the pains?" Amelia asked Joe as she took her place on the dogsled. Though normally she traveled to the cabin on foot, she was grateful for the ride today. If

180

Pauline's labor was as long and difficult as Amelia feared, she would need to conserve her strength.

More than twenty-four hours passed, and the sun was setting for the second time, when Pauline and Joe's baby was born. Though Amelia's fears of a prolonged labor had been founded, young Joe was healthy. Pauline, exhausted but radiant with happiness, held him in her arms. "He's a miracle, Doctor, my very own miracle."

Amelia had to agree.

"I'll take you back into town," the proud father offered when Amelia had cleaned her instruments and was ready to return home.

She shook her head. Joe needed to stay with his wife and son, and though she was tired, she could walk. Even in deep snow, it would take less than half an hour.

Afterward Amelia had no idea how it had happened. Perhaps it was fatigue. Perhaps the fading light. Perhaps the simple fact that she was thinking about how wonderful it had felt to hold young Joe in her arms, pretending for a moment that he was her child, not simply her patient. All Amelia knew was that she had been walking for far longer than the half hour it normally took to get home, and she was still in the forest. The light snow that had been falling when she had left the Feehys' cabin had intensified, obliterating any signs of a trail, and night had fallen.

There was no doubt about it. She was lost.

Amelia stopped and looked around, searching for a familiar sight. In the darkness, the trees all looked alike. *Don't panic,* she told herself. *You'll find the trail.* How? Despite her fierce admonitions, panic welled up inside her. She had to get home.

She stopped, disoriented. Had she seen this stand of trees before? Was she walking in circles? *Keep moving.* Amelia knew she could not stand still without risking frostbite, yet each step she took drained more of her ebbing strength. If only she had accepted Joe's offer of a ride! She was tired, so tired. All she wanted to do was sink to the ground and sleep. Just a minute or two; that was all the rest she needed. Then she would continue.

Amelia brushed the snow from her face. She could not stop. She didn't dare, for if she did, she might never rise. Amelia had heard the tales of people who succumbed to sleep and then froze to death. And so she kept walking, putting one foot in front of the other, although she feared that no matter how much she forced herself to move, the end was inevitable.

The snow intensified, driven now by the north wind, whose power she had learned to fear. Amelia could see only a few inches in front of her, and snow caked her eyebrows and lashes, making it even more difficult for her to keep her eyes open.

Three more steps, and then she would rest. Her fingers were losing all feeling, and she knew it was only a matter of minutes before she was forced to drop her bag. Three more steps. She could manage that.

She lifted her head, searching for the trail. Then she blinked, trying to clear her blurred vision and muddled head. At first she thought it was an illusion, the product of her wishes and prayers. But when her hand touched the logs, she knew the cabin was real.

Amelia pushed the door open. Though it was dark and only a few degrees warmer than outside, at least the walls provided protection from the wind. She stripped off her mittens and lit one of the matches that she carried in her bag. Thank God! There was a small supply of wood next to the stove. If she was frugal, it might last the night.

With hands that shook from the cold, she built a small fire. It felt good, so blessedly good. Her fingers and toes tingled unpleasantly; her head was light from fatigue and hunger, but at least she was alive. Minutes later, Amelia fell asleep.

"If you want my advice," William told Ben as he collected his winnings, "you'll find a new game. You seem to have lost your touch at poker." After Alex and Frank left, William remained to talk to his friend.

"Who asked for your advice?" Ben took a long swallow

of his drink, then leaned back. "Maybe I lost the game on purpose, so you'd feel good."

The wind howled, rattling the windowpane but failing to drown out the annoying sound of that blamed cuckoo clock that Ben refused to mute.

William pocketed the money. "And maybe that's not a snowstorm we're having tonight."

"Ben!" A woman's voice carried from his office into the doctor's modest living quarters. "Are you home?"

Ben muttered a few obscenities. "Just the person I don't need."

"What's wrong with Ella?"

"You'll see." He took a firm grip on the whiskey bottle, as if he thought Ella had ventured out in the blizzard to wrest it from his grasp.

Ella marched into the room, and a man did not need a medical degree to see that she was upset. "You must do something, Ben," she announced. "Amelia's out in the storm."

Amelia! William could feel his blood begin to rush. "How do you know?"

"Simple." Ella glared at Ben. "She hasn't come home from delivering the Feehys' baby." Snow dripped from her parka as she shook her fist.

"Calm down, Ella." This time Ben spoke. "She told me it was likely to be a long labor. She's probably still there, waiting for the baby."

Ella shook her head. "She's not. Joe came into town an hour or so ago to tell everyone that he's a father. He stopped by my house to thank Amelia again and couldn't understand why she wasn't there." Ella's voice broke. "Joe said Amelia left them a couple hours before that. She's lost. I tell you, she's lost."

William heard the panic in Ella's voice, and his stomach tightened. She might be overreacting. But if she wasn't . . .

"She probably went back after Joe left." Ben sounded so unconcerned that William wanted to throttle him. An Alaskan snowstorm was serious, and Ben knew it.

183

"Maybe she wanted to check the baby again," Ben suggested.

"She could have gotten lost." William agreed with Ella's assessment. "It's easy enough for anyone to lose their way in that forest, especially a *cheechako*." He made a quick decision, then looked at Ella. "Go home and pack some of her warmest clothes. Ben, give me whatever medicine Amelia might need."

"What are you going to do?" Ben demanded.

"Find your assistant. What else?"

"C'mon, Nugget," he called to his lead dog. "You can do it!" William gripped the back of the sled, urging the dogs forward. They were a powerful team, the best in Gold Landing. No one could get to Amelia faster. He knew that. But he also knew that it might be too late. She could be hurt, lying somewhere on the forest floor. She could be worse than hurt. William pushed that thought aside. She was fine. Ben was right; she'd gone back to check on Pauline Feehy.

But she hadn't. A weak Pauline opened the door and confirmed what her husband had told the men at the saloon. "Is she all right?" Pauline asked.

William nodded, as much to convince himself as Pauline.

It seemed that he had been searching for hours when he smelled it, the unmistakable odor of smoke. With the wind-driven snow, he had seen no plumes, but not even the snow had been able to destroy the smell.

"That's it, Nugget. She's there!" The cabin had been abandoned last spring. If someone was there tonight, it had to be Amelia. It just had to.

William halted the team in front of the small cabin, then flung the door open. By the light of the embers, he could see a form lying near the stove.

Amelia! He would know that slim body anywhere. She was asleep. Or was she . . . ? He refused to complete the thought.

William crossed the room in three strides, then knelt next to her. "Amelia!" His heart pounded so fiercely that he could not hear her breathing, if she was indeed breathing. She had to be. He would not consider the alternative. William bent over her, and as he did, a lump of snow slid from his parka onto her face.

"What?" Her eyes flew open, and she looked around, clearly disoriented. "William?"

He nodded, careful this time to push his parka hood back. "Are you all right?"

Amelia struggled to a sitting position. "I was so lost and cold and afraid," she confessed, her voice husky with remembered fear. "Oh, William, I didn't want to die."

Putting his arms around her, William drew her close. He could feel the cold radiating from her body and knew that he needed to stoke the fire. In a minute. First he was going to hold her until he had convinced himself that she was real, not a figment his imagination had conjured to allay his fears. He would breathe in the flowery scent of her hair and listen to the beating of her heart for another minute. Then he would warm the room.

"You're safe now," he said as her breathing grew more regular and the color returned to her cheeks. She had been terrified, justifiably so. As he had told her that night at Pete's, Alaska was a harsh land, unforgiving of mistakes.

For a moment they sat silently. Then William said, "I'm going to feed the fire. Then I'll feed us." Reluctantly he released Amelia and stood. "We'll go back in the morning."

Even in the dim light he could see Amelia's eyes widen in surprise. "Why not tonight?"

Of course she was worried about the propriety of spending the night alone with him. Amelia was a lady, and ladies did not risk their reputations. But tonight there was no alternative. William had lived in Alaska too long to mistake the fury of the wind and snow.

"The snow's turned into a full-fledged blizzard," he told her. "I hardly made it here. Trying to get back would be suicidal."

Though she nodded, her blue eyes sober as she realized the severity of the situation, he could see that she was nervous.

She was probably remembering the way he had kissed her that night in the clinic. He knew *he* was.

The prudent course was to wait out the storm in the cabin, then take advantage of daylight to return to town. That was what a prudent man would do, and no one had ever accused William of being anything other than prudent. They would stay in the cabin. The question was, how would he get through the night, having Amelia so close and not being able to touch her? Prudence be damned!

William threw a log on the fire and strode to the door.

By the time William had returned from feeding and caring for the dogs, Amelia had made a pot of coffee and unwrapped the ham and biscuits that Ella had packed for them. She had found a lantern among the supplies, delighting in the way it banished some of the shadows.

Perhaps the light would help dispel her uneasiness, an uneasiness that had nothing to do with the storm buffeting the cabin and everything to do with the man who was sharing that cabin with her. How was she going to spend the night so close to him and not betray her feelings? How on earth would she manage to keep a distance between them? Though her mind knew he was simply a friend, her body had other ideas.

The small cabin was sparsely furnished, with only two chairs, a table and a single bunk. Amelia tried not to think about the bunk. Instead she set the table, placing the chairs so neither of them faced the bed.

"I heard the Feehy baby was a boy," William said as he took another biscuit from the plate she had set in front of him.

Amelia nodded, although next to tonight's sleeping arrangements the last thing she wanted to discuss was babies. But William had no such compunctions. "I guess Joe was like most men, wanting a son."

"Is that what you'd like?" Only a fool would ask a question when she did not want to hear the answer, but Amelia seemed to be doing a lot of foolish things today, starting with getting lost in a blizzard.

William slapped a piece of ham on the biscuit. "I can see myself teaching him to hunt and fish," he told her.

186

The wind buffeted the small cabin, driving snow through the chinks between the logs.

"And mine gold?"

"Is there something wrong with that?" When his words came out harshly, Amelia sensed that she had somehow insulted him. Did he think she regarded mining as less rewarding—less worthwhile—than being a doctor? He could not be more wrong.

"Of course not. I only asked the question because I assumed you would be like many fathers and want your son to follow in your footsteps."

When the wind subsided for a moment, Amelia heard William's dogs howling, perhaps in response to a distant wolf.

He remained silent, his eyes searching hers as if for proof of her honesty. "What I'd want if I had a son," he said at last, "is for him to be happy."

"Are you?" The question came out unbidden.

William closed his eyes as an expression of pain flitted across his face. She watched him clench his jaw, then open his eyes again. "I could be," he said simply.

What would it take to make him happy? Though she longed to know, Amelia dared not ask the question and risk more heartache, for she knew she could not make one of his most important dreams come true.

When he had eaten the last of the biscuits, William brushed the crumbs from his hands, then rose. "We'd better get to sleep now. You take the bunk. I'll keep the fire going." He tossed three blankets onto the floor.

If anyone had asked her, she would have said it was impossible that she would be able to sleep so close to William, remembering how wonderful it had felt being held in his arms, yet unable to ask for that comfort. She would have been wrong. Her fatigue was so great that she was asleep within minutes of wrapping herself in a blanket.

The sound was soft, unfamiliar but not unpleasant, more suitable for a lullaby than a morning's wake-up call. For a moment Amelia was not certain where she was. Then she remembered. The cabin. William. A rush of hot blood stained her face at the thought of spending the night so close to him. He was obviously awake, but since he said nothing, he must not realize she was no longer sleeping.

Amelia opened her eyes. William was seated on his blanket, a piece of wood held in his left hand while his right wielded a knife. She lay quietly for a moment, content to watch him as he whittled. Gone was the strain she saw so often on his face. Instead, although he regarded the wood intently, he appeared to be at peace with himself, a man who knew what he wanted and was fortunate enough to be doing it.

Amelia felt a momentary pang, wondering if she would ever feel that same level of satisfaction. Though her practice brought her great joy, there was no denying the emptiness that haunted all too many of her nights.

Unwilling to succumb to self-pity, Amelia sat up. "Good morning," she said, straightening her garments before she unwrapped the blanket.

William turned toward her, and she had the feeling he was studying her as carefully as she would a patient. "It's morning," he agreed with a wry smile. "You may change your mind about the 'good' part when you look outside. The storm's worse than ever."

As if to underscore his words, a blast of wind rattled the door. Though the cold did not reach the bunk, Amelia shivered.

"We have to get back," she told William. She buttoned her shoes, then shook out her skirts when she stood. "I have patients, and there's Ella's pageant. I promised I'd help her."

"Spoken like a *cheechako*." William rose to stoke the fire while Amelia measured coffee into the pot. Bless Ella for grinding coffee in advance!

"The pageant will be postponed," William continued. "No one in their right mind is going out in this snow. It's too easy to get lost."

"I guess I am a *cheechako*," she admitted. She looked out the small window. William's dogs lay curled on the snow, their tails covering their noses. "When I left the Feehys', all

I could think was how beautiful the snow was. I didn't even consider the danger." One of the dogs stirred, looked up at the cabin, then closed his eyes again.

"You were lucky, Amelia, damn lucky that you found this cabin in time."

Amelia turned, startled by the emotion she heard in William's voice. "Believe me, I know that." She would never again underestimate winter's power. "I also know how lucky I am to have friends like you and Ella. You didn't have to come out in the storm to rescue me."

"Yes, I did."

Amelia's eyes widened in surprise at both William's words and the ferocity in his voice. She stared at him for a long moment, trying to understand what he was saying. Though the words were simple, she sensed that the emotion behind them was far more complex.

"I mean it, Amelia. I couldn't have lived with myself if I hadn't tried to find you." As if he had said too much, William returned to his seat on the floor and resumed his whittling, while she set the table for breakfast.

"What are you making?" Though it was not the question she longed to ask, Amelia realized that William wanted to change the subject, and if she were wise, she would not explore his feelings. They were friends. Why couldn't she remember that?

"It's going to be a whistle." William held it to his lips, grinning when the sound he produced was anything but melodic. "Theo will like it, though I suspect his mother will banish him to the barn when he uses it."

Amelia laughed. "What do you bet Theo thinks that's a good thing?"

"You do understand little boys, don't you?" William held the whistle at arm's length, as if trying to decide how to improve the sound.

"Boys, girls, I think all children enjoy playing without adult supervision."

As the coffee brewed, Amelia walked to the window and looked outside again. The swirling snow was so thick she

189

could see only two rows of trees, and the dogs' fur was caked white. "When I was a child, I always wanted snow for Christmas," she told William. "Belinda and I used to say we would trade our presents for enough snow to make a snowman."

"Looks like you're getting your wish this year, and you don't even have to barter anything. This will be the Christmas of your dreams."

Amelia doubted that. Not wanting to talk about her own dreams, she turned away from the window and sat in a chair next to William. "What was Christmas like when you were a child?" He would probably refuse to answer, as he did so often when she asked about his past. But maybe today would be different.

A fierce gust dislodged a piece of moss chinking, sending it to the floor with a soft plop.

William was silent for a long moment, and Amelia was sure he would shake his head. Instead, he said, "My Christmas wasn't much like yours, I'm sure. Nothing you'd want to hear about."

It was the opening she had sought. "But I do. I wouldn't have asked otherwise."

William's eyes dropped, and he studied the half-finished whistle as if it held the answers to Amelia's question. "Unlike you," he said slowly, "we had lots of snow but no presents. No stockings. No tree." He cut a shallow groove in the whistle. "I don't think anyone in my house ever believed in Santa Claus, although we'd heard of him. He was just another story. The truth was, we had no money, and that meant no gifts." For a moment his eyes had a distant look, and Amelia realized he was remembering those Christmases past. She hardly dared to breathe, lest the wrong move stop the flow of William's words. This was what she had wanted for so long. She could let nothing jeopardize it.

William laid the whistle on the blanket. "We may not have had presents, but there was always a cake." He looked at Amelia, his eyes glistening. "To this day, I don't know how Polly did it. She must have hoarded sugar all year to make that cake, but she made sure we had one."

At the sight of William's bittersweet smile, Amelia's heart reached out to the man who had never known a child's wonder over gaily wrapped packages. No wonder he was taking such pains with Theo's whistle. Amelia would bet that it would be wrapped and tied, maybe even stuffed in a stocking, on Christmas morning.

"We would gather around the table and sing carols, and all the while, we'd be looking at that cake and thinking about how good it was going to taste."

Tears sparkled in Amelia's eyes as sorrow mingled with another emotion. "It sounds beautiful."

When William's eyes met hers, they were once more devoid of emotion. "You don't need to patronize me. I was there. I know what it was like, and it wasn't beautiful."

He didn't understand.

"I wasn't patronizing you, William. I was envying you." William's expression registered disbelief. "Oh, you're right in thinking my family had more money than yours. We had material things, but we never had a tradition like you did. I don't remember us ever singing carols, and I doubt we enjoyed any of my mother's banquets as much as you did your cakes." As the aroma of fresh coffee filled the cabin, Amelia looked at William. "I think you had the real Christmas."

She poured them each a cup of coffee, then impulsively, instead of handing one to William, she placed them both on the floor. Kneeling next to him, she put her arms around him and hugged him. She meant to comfort him, to banish—at least for the moment—the memory of Christmases without presents, but as William's arms reached out to enfold her, she could not have said who was comforting whom. All she knew was that she was warm and happy.

Perhaps the snow would never end.

She was afraid the snow would never end. Ella had spent hours staring out the window, wondering where Amelia was, whether William had found her, and when she would be home again. Without her, the house seemed empty and, worse than that, lonely.

191

When she heard the knock, Ella jumped to her feet, her heart thudding. Amelia would not knock, but if she were injured and William was bringing her home, he might. Ella flung the door open, expecting to see William and Amelia. Instead Larry stood on her front porch, his parka so coated with snow that it looked white rather than its normal dark brown.

"Have you heard anything about Amelia?" Ella shivered as the snow swirled on the porch, then drifted into the house.

"It's too cold to be outdoors," Larry announced as he entered the house. "I don't know anything about Amelia," he admitted. "I just wanted to be sure you were all right." He started to unbutton his coat.

Ella stared at him. What was he doing? "I'm fine," she said. Suddenly the room, which had felt empty only a few minutes before, seemed crowded.

"I don't like you being here alone," Larry continued, as though Ella had not spoken. He tossed his coat onto the rack.

"Larry, you've got to leave." Ella's gaze moved nervously between Larry and the front door. "It's not proper for you to be here."

"Who's gonna know? There's nobody out in this storm."

"But, Larry . . ."

"I'm not leaving without a kiss." Before Ella had a chance to protest, he pulled her into his arms and lowered his mouth to hers. His lips ravaged hers, while his arms held her so closely that she could scarcely breathe.

"Larry!" Ella gasped when he pulled away long enough to take a breath. Though the room was brightly lit, she could feel darkness begin to encroach. "You can't—"

"—wait." He finished the sentence. "You're damn right about that." With one arm, he pulled her close to him, while the other grasped her breast, squeezing it until she cried out in pain. *It was dark, so dark, and she couldn't stop him.*

"Stop!"

But there was no stopping Larry. *He was so big, and she was so little.* He grasped her shirtwaist in his fist, tugging until it ripped and gave his hand access to her flesh. *He tossed her night shift onto the floor.* As his fingers kneaded her soft skin, his lips continued their assault on her mouth. *"Don't make a sound, or I'll hurt you more!"* Then his hand moved lower, grasping her skirt and hiking it around her waist. *He thrust his fingers deep inside her.*

For an instant Ella stopped breathing. *No! Not again!* She closed her eyes for a second as the waves of almost unbearable pain swept over her. *No!* she cried, but no sound came from her mouth. She forced her eyes open. This was Larry. Not *him.* He wouldn't. But he did.

Terror lent strength to her arms, and she shoved at him, trying to break his grasp. He was too strong, just like *he* had been. She couldn't stop him. She had to stop him! In desperation, she reached for his face, clawing at his eyes. Her nails ripped, and she felt blood on her fingertips. *Blood. There was so much blood.*

As blood streamed down Larry's face, he pulled back for an instant. It was all the time Ella needed. She spun out of his grasp and grabbed the heavy pottery vase that Amelia used as an umbrella stand. Raising it over her head, she brought it down on Larry's skull.

"Get out of here!" she shouted when he stared at her, momentarily dazed. "Don't you ever come back."

When Larry slammed the door behind him, Ella dragged the sofa in front of it, then crumpled to the floor.

The house was strangely quiet when Amelia entered it the next morning. At last the storm had subsided, and she and William were able to return to Gold Landing. Amelia had expected to hear carols on the Victrola while Ella put the finishing touches on angel costumes or baked cookies for the pageant. Instead, she had found the house dark and apparently empty.

Where was Ella? Her coat was on the rack. Surely she hadn't gone outdoors without a coat. The house did not feel empty, but she could hear no sound. Ella's door was closed. That was odd.

"Ella?" Perhaps she was asleep, although it seemed unlikely. This close to Christmas, Ella would have no time for a nap. When there was no response, Amelia opened the door to her friend's bedroom. She stopped on the threshold. Sunlight flooded the room, leaving no doubt that something was terribly amiss. The room that was normally painfully neat was now in shambles, with clothing spread on the floor and the bureau shoved halfway to the door. In the midst of the chaos, the young schoolteacher lay curled on her bed in a fetal position, her eyes staring blankly at Amelia.

"Ella?" Amelia moved to the side of the bed and touched her shoulder. "What happened?" Still there was no sound. Then Ella started to sob, a low cry that reminded Amelia of an animal's keening. Amelia drew her to a sitting position and wrapped her arms around her friend, trying to comfort her. It was then that she saw Ella's torn clothing.

"Who did this?" she demanded, her heart thudding at the evidence.

Ella shook her head. Though she refused to speak, Amelia noted with relief that her eyes had lost their glassy stare. Now they were brimming with anguish.

"You've got to tell me what happened." Amelia was not sure whether Ella had been raped, but it was clear she had been assaulted.

"I can't. It's too awful." At least she was speaking.

Amelia kept her arm around Ella's shoulders to comfort her as she spoke firmly. "Whatever happened will be like a festering sore. You need to lance it and let the poison drain out. It won't heal otherwise." She stroked Ella's head gently. "Let it out, Ella. Tell me who hurt you."

Ella looked at her for a long moment, and the pain in her eyes made Amelia want to cry. No one deserved to suffer like that, especially not sweet, gentle Ella.

"Tell me," she said.

Ella shuddered. "Larry." She sobbed and buried her face in Amelia's shoulder. "He tried to . . . you know. He tried to hurt me."

"Did he rape you?" Though Ella was reluctant to say the word, as both her friend and her doctor, Amelia had to know what had happened.

"No." *Thank God!* "But I was so scared. It was like before."

"What happened before?" When Ella refused to answer, Amelia helped her bathe, then made her a cup of tea. "Tell me," she said. "What happened before that scared you so much?"

Ella stared at the tea. "I didn't even remember it," she told Amelia, "until he tore my clothes."

Under Amelia's gentle questioning, Ella told how a neighbor, a man she had believed a friend, had beaten and raped her when she was a young child. Though Ella's story angered and saddened Amelia, it also answered many questions. No wonder Ella had reacted so violently to Larry's kiss and the miners' fistfight. No wonder she had been so reluctant to marry. The horror of her childhood rape had been locked deep inside her, but violence of any kind and the threat of physical intimacy had broken the seal, letting memories escape to torment her again.

"You can't tell anyone," Ella insisted.

It was a normal reaction, the injured person fearing rejection and renewed pain if her secret were known. But Ella had to know that she was not to blame. And Larry needed to be stopped.

"It's not your fault, Ella. You were the victim. There's no reason to be ashamed."

Ella shook her head. "You can't tell anyone. No one," she repeated. "I'd die if anyone knew."

Slowly, Amelia nodded. Though she wanted to see Larry brought to justice, her friend's health was more important. Ella's emotional wound was still an open sore that only time would heal. Unfortunately, Amelia feared it would be a very slow healing process.

Chapter Fourteen

There were few things Ben enjoyed less than the annual Christmas pageant. He wasn't sure which was worse: all those children or the doting mothers. If there had been a way to avoid the pageant, with its reminders of what might have been, he would have taken it. But Ben knew there were some things a man just had to do, especially if he wanted to remain on good terms with the adults of Gold Landing. Since they were his livelihood, he had no choice.

When he arrived at the church two minutes before the pageant was scheduled to begin, he found children and parents milling around in small groups and a noise level decibels above normal. Ben checked his watch. It must be running fast, because he knew the routine. This chaos should have ended half an hour ago. By now everyone should be seated, the church filled with an expectant hush.

Ben spotted William standing in one corner and made his way to him. The simple process of moving from one side of the church to the other reminded Ben of salmon swimming upstream. It was a journey filled with hazards, confirming that something was amiss. Ella would never allow such obvious disorganization.

"What's going on?"

William shrugged. "Apparently Ella's not here. From what I can gather, Amelia is trying to run the show."

"Amelia." Ben's chuckle threatened to turn into a full-fledged guffaw. "Looks like I'm in for more entertainment than I'd expected. The woman's a damn fine physician, but I can't picture her shepherding two dozen youngsters."

William raised one brow. "That's where we differ, my friend. I can see her with the children, but I'm still not convinced she's a real doctor. There are just some things women can't do."

Ben tried to mask his surprise. Though he knew William had felt that way originally, he had thought that he had changed his mind once he had gotten to know Amelia. Apparently he had not.

Eventually the players took their places and the pageant began. If there were more mistakes than normal, no one seemed to mind. Indeed, when the postperformance party started, the mood was jovial, and people were telling each other that this had been the best pageant ever. Ben, who heard the same words every year, sniffed, but he followed William toward the center of the room, where Amelia was talking to several parents.

"Nice job, Amelia."

Though William grinned when he spoke, two spots of color rose to Amelia's cheeks. "You can save the sarcasm, William," she retorted. "I know just how bad it was."

"And what makes you think I was being sarcastic?"

Ben looked from Amelia to William and back again. Apparently the stories he had heard about sparks flying every time they met were true. It was odd. William was slow to anger, and though Amelia could be as fierce as a mother bear protecting her cubs, Ben had never seen her fury directed at a person unless she felt one of her precious causes was being threatened.

Perhaps it wasn't fury he saw, but another basic emotion. Ben swallowed a smile. Wouldn't that be an interesting turn of events?

"If that wasn't sarcasm," Amelia said, "I'll be forced to think you've imbibed a little too heavily and have lost your senses." She continued to stare at William, seemingly unaware of Ben's existence. "The pageant was dreadful. I don't know how Ella keeps those children under control."

"Where is she?" Although the magnetism between William and Amelia was intriguing, Ben had other, more important concerns. Like Ella. He could not imagine why she had missed the performance. The pageant was one of the highlights of her life, or so he had thought. It would take an emergency of gargantuan proportions to keep Ella away.

Amelia turned, as if surprised to see him. "She's home."

Home! That wasn't much of an answer. "Is she sick?"

Amelia appeared to hesitate before she said, "She's indisposed." The tone of her voice told Ben there was more to the story than she was admitting. Must be some sort of female ailment. Odd, though. He hadn't thought Ella suffered from such problems.

Ben glanced around the room and saw Larry Wilson standing so close to Charlotte Langdon that he would have been hard-pressed to slide a hypodermic between them.

"That man of Ella's sure isn't indisposed." Ben's lip curled. "Look at him pawing Langdon's daughter just because Ella's not here. Someone ought to rearrange his face."

"The engagement is over." Though Amelia spoke quietly, Ben saw her look at his hands. Realizing he had balled them into fists, he forced himself to relax.

So Ella had broken her engagement. Now, why would she have done a thing like that? Though Larry Wilson was as useless a piece of protoplasm as Ben had ever encountered, Ella seemed oblivious to that particular fact. So why had she suddenly ended the town's longest engagement?

Three days later, Ben was more puzzled than ever. Ella had been conspicuous by her absence from Christmas Eve and Christmas Day church services, leaving the good matrons of Gold Landing to speculate on why a fellow pillar of the community had missed such important events. For his part, Ben wasn't buying that "indisposed" story Amelia was telling. Something serious was wrong with Ella, and it did not take a genius to figure out what it was.

She had not broken the engagement. That overly pretty boy with his underdeveloped brain had jilted her, leaving Ella too hurt and humiliated to face her friends. That had to be the reason she had not left her house. Amelia would not confirm it, of course, but Ben recognized the symptoms. He also knew that the time for action was now. The wound could not be allowed to fester.

Ben let himself in the front door. As he had expected, the

door to Ella's room was closed. She probably had the curtains drawn, too, but the house was as neat as ever, proof that nothing, not even personal trauma, interfered with Ella's domestic routine.

"Okay, Ella. The choice is yours," he announced. "You can come out, or I'm coming in."

There was a moment's silence, and Ben wondered if she might be sleeping.

"What do you want?" There was neither anger nor curiosity in her voice. It sounded flat, devoid of emotion.

"I want to talk to you."

Another long silence told Ben she was having trouble formulating a reply. How well he knew that state!

"I don't want to talk to you." Her response was predictable. In all likelihood, Amelia had let her get away with the silence and self-pity. But Amelia did not have the firsthand experience to know how wrong that treatment could be. Strong measures were needed. Ben knocked on Ella's door.

"Well, now, that's too bad, isn't it, because we're sure as snow going to talk. I told you before, we can do it one of two ways. You come out, or I come in. You've got one minute to decide."

Ben heard the sound of a drawer closing. A few minutes later, Ella entered the kitchen. He forced himself not to react. She looked terrible. Her hair, normally confined in neat braids, hung limply beside her unnaturally pale cheeks. The worst were her eyes. Ben would have called them dull and lifeless, had they not been so full of pain. As a physician, he worried that her emotional devastation would lead to physical problems. As a man, his heart ached for her.

She stood in the center of the room, facing him, her arms folded in front of her as though for protection. "All right, Ben. Say what you want, and then leave me alone."

He was not going to let her get away so easily. "The least you could do is offer me a drink."

A spark of animation lit her face, making Ben glad he had chosen that ploy. "That's the last thing you need, Ben Taylor."

"I meant coffee."

"Sure you did." She remained motionless.

In response, Ben rummaged through her cabinets until he found the pot. When he started searching for coffee beans, Ella protested. "Just talk," she said. "You don't need coffee." As if to encourage him, she pulled out a chair and sat. "Now, what do you want?"

Ben took a seat opposite her at the small table. "I heard about you and Larry."

Ella reacted as if he had hit her. What little color there was drained from her cheeks as she gripped the table's edge. "She promised she wouldn't tell!"

The woman was overreacting, but it was not the first time Ben had seen a woman close to hysterics. "I didn't give her much choice. I asked Amelia point-blank what was wrong, and she told me your engagement was over."

As a hint of color chased the pallor from Ella's face, she relaxed her fingers. "That's true," she admitted.

Ben took a deep breath. He had known this conversation would not be easy, but the reality was worse than he had expected. "I came here today because I know how you're feeling."

Ella's head jerked up, and she stared at him, her eyes now blazing with pain and something else, perhaps anger. "You couldn't possibly know how I'm feeling," she cried. "No man could."

She was wrong. Absolutely, completely wrong. He knew that, but he also knew it was a symptom of just how deeply she had been hurt that she believed her pain to be unique.

"Pain is pain, Ella, and loss is loss. It doesn't matter whether you're male or female. You still hurt."

She shook her head wildly, her hair beating against her cheeks. "You don't understand."

"I think I do." Ben lowered his voice, trying to calm her. He had hoped to avoid this. Though no man liked baring his soul, it was clear Ella would not accept his advice unless he displayed his credentials.

Ben pushed his spectacles back and looked directly at Ella.

"Did you know I was married once, before I came to Alaska?" It took a moment for the words to register. When Ella shook her head, he continued. "Julia—that was my wife's name—was a pretty little thing. But that's not what's important." He paused for a moment, trying to brace himself for the next part of his story. "I loved Julia very much, probably the way you loved Larry."

Though she stiffened, Ella remained silent. "We dreamed of having children, but month after month went by, and Julia didn't conceive. Then after we'd been married for five years she became pregnant." It might have been his imagination, but Ben thought some of the pain had left Ella's eyes. "I was sure we were the happiest people on earth. But it ended. Julia died in childbirth, taking the baby with her."

Ben lowered his face to his hands, as the memories that even now had the power to reduce him to tears swept through him. Then, ashamed of his momentary weakness, he raised his eyes to Ella's. "So you see, Ella, I do know how you feel. I know what it's like to lose a loved one."

She stared at him, tears in her eyes. "I'm so sorry, Ben."

This was not turning out the way he had planned it. He had come here to comfort her, to help her overcome her loss, but somehow his plan had gotten off track. Ella was trying to comfort him. Ben rose and walked to the other side of the table. Kneeling next to her, he put his arms around her waist. "Oh, Ella," he said, his voice brimming with emotion.

In a movement so swift he had no way to anticipate it, she jumped to her feet, thrusting him away from her, knocking the chair over in her haste to free herself from his embrace. What had gotten into the woman?

"You're just like every other man, Ben Taylor." She looked around wildly, then picked up the coffeepot and held it in front of her as if it were a shield. If she hadn't been so angry, Ben would have laughed. "You've only got one thought on your mind," she said through clenched teeth. "Now, get out of here." Ella pointed at the door. "Get out!"

Ben stared at her for a second. This was his payment for trying to be kind to the ice maiden. He had bared his soul to

201

her, dredging up memories that he had spent years trying to drown, and what had he gotten in return? Rejection.

"I beg your pardon, Miss Roberts." The sarcasm was deliberate. "For a moment, I thought you were a real human being with normal emotions. Please forgive me for such an inexcusable mistake." She flinched at his words as she would have from a whip. "It's obvious you don't have warm blood in your veins. Hell, you probably don't have blood at all. You're just a dried-up old prude."

Her cheeks flamed, and her eyes sparkled with anger. The lethargy that had worried him half an hour ago had disappeared, destroyed by the force of her wrath. "Do you honestly think I care what you call me?" This was an Ella he had seen once before, the day the mine had collapsed on Alex Fielding.

"Why should I care about you? You're nothing but a broken-down old man who drinks to forget what a failure he is." She plunked the coffeepot onto the stove, apparently no longer needing its protection. "Maybe you can fool others, but I see you for what you really are. And let me tell you, Ben Taylor, I don't like what I see."

"This has got to stop, Ben," Amelia said when she found him in the same position he had been in every morning for the past two weeks, prone on the examining table in his office, clutching his head and moaning. "I thought you hired me as your assistant. Now it turns out that I'm taking care of the whole practice."

Ben forced one eye open a slit. "You should be happy. This is better than a dime novel. Amelia the heroine strikes again, going where that dastardly Ben Taylor can't."

The room reeked of liquor and Ben's unwashed body. Though it was January and the mercury had not been over freezing in months, Amelia flung the window open.

"Stop making a joke of it, Ben. This isn't funny. You haven't done a minute's work since Christmas."

"Are you complaining, Dr. Sheldon?" Ben shivered, and Amelia closed the windows. Even the brief airing had helped. If any patients came, they would not be assaulted by noxious odors. "I thought that's what you wanted," Ben continued, "your own practice."

"I do want my own practice," Amelia admitted, "but not this way. You're too good a doctor to waste yourself like this. Whatever it is that's bothering you, you know liquor's not the cure."

"But it sure helps the symptoms."

"What's wrong, Ben? Why are you doing this to yourself?"

Ben closed his eyes and rolled onto his side, facing the wall. "Get the hell out of here, Amelia," he muttered. "Go home to that priggish schoolteacher you live with or try to practice medicine on people who want to get well. Just get out of here."

Amelia did.

According to the calendar it was spring. But the calendar, it appeared, had failed to notify Mother Nature, and Gold Landing was still in winter's icy grip. The only sign that the seasons were changing was that the days were growing longer. Which, Amelia had to admit, was a major blessing. Though she still did her rounds on snowshoes and carried extra provisions, just in case she was caught in a remote cabin during another blizzard, at least now she could complete most of her rounds during daylight.

"It's going to be any day now," Martha Johnson informed her when Amelia had finished examining the baby. Young Rachel Amelia had gone from vigorous crawling to trying to pull herself upright, leaving her mother convinced that she would be walking soon. Each time Amelia visited, Martha speculated on how much longer it would be.

"Probably another week or two," Amelia said. The baby was doing well, but her legs still were not strong enough for walking.

"Not that long. There's too much noise."

Noise? Amelia saw no correlation between the fact that Rachel was pounding the floor with a wooden spoon and her imminent walking. She looked at Martha. "Are we talking about the same thing?"

Martha shrugged as she gently pried the spoon from her daughter's hand. "I thought so. The ice breakup, right?"

Amelia laughed. For the past month, the Tanana's annual breakup had been the major topic of conversation in Gold Landing, the source of more betting than Amelia had seen, even at the Saratoga racetrack. She should have realized that was what Martha meant.

"Wait till you see it. It's a sight—and a sound—you'll never forget," Martha promised. "Someone told me the chunks of ice cover an acre."

It was more than Amelia could imagine. But then, a year ago, she had never seen a river freeze solid and remain that way for months. During the winter, dogsleds used the ice as a road; with its breakup, boats would soon be able to ply the river again, and that meant the return of fresh produce and goods from the south.

"At least the river won't wash our bridge away," Martha continued.

"Why would it?" Surely bridges were designed to withstand normal annual events.

"Beats me," Martha confessed, "but I hear tell that the one in Fairbanks gets destroyed each year. It gives them two things to bet on: the time of the breakup and how long it'll take to rebuild the bridge."

"It's going to be soon," Ella announced the next morning as she and Amelia ate breakfast together, and this time Amelia had no doubt of the subject. As the months had passed, Ella's trauma seemed to fade. She was quieter than before, and there were times when her eyes reflected pain, but she appeared to have regained most of her zest for living.

"The children and I heard the creaking yesterday," Ella said.

"Have you canceled school?" Amelia asked.

Ella nodded, then shrugged. "I'm not going to fight the inevitable. No one would come, anyway, so you and I might as well go enjoy the sight."

By the time the two women reached the riverbank, it seemed

half the town was there. Men held their watches ready to mark the exact minute of the breakup, while the more adventure-some edged out onto the ice to see it happen. Women held their children by the hand, lest their curiosity cause them to follow the intrepid.

Amelia nodded as Abe tipped his hat to her, while her eyes continued to scan the crowd, looking for William. He was at the center, surrounded by a group of his miners.

"Any second now," one man cried.

"Listen!" another voice rang out. The noise was changing, becoming more a grinding than a creaking. Amelia stared, fascinated.

A man broke out of the crowd and began to cross the ice.

Ben! Amelia's heart thudded as he wove his way unsteadily toward the middle of the river. What was he thinking? Even she knew he had gone too far.

"Get back!" She heard William shout the warning.

Ben turned and waved. "I'm not missing this." His voice, slurred from the whiskey that was the staple of his diet, was almost drowned by the noise of the ice. "Not for anything." Ben staggered a couple more steps and stared down at the frozen river.

"Don't be an idiot! Come back!" William moved to the edge of the ice as he shouted to his friend.

The creaking was louder than before, a sound unlike any Amelia had ever heard. "Soon!" she heard someone say. And then it happened. An explosion that reminded her of a gunshot, only a hundred times more powerful, was followed by a tremendous crunching. It was ice; her rational mind knew that. Only her imagination thought the sound was of thousands of bones crunching together. Huge pieces of ice started to move, crashing into each other, piling together, as if hurled by an unseen giant. And in the middle of what had been a frozen riverbed, water started to flow.

"Look at that!" Ben's words could barely be heard over the noise of the ice that plunged downstream. He stood on the edge, peering into the dark water. A sober man might have been able to step backward in time. Ben had no chance. As

205

the ice shifted beneath him, he slid forward, his right leg falling into the nearly freezing water. A second later, one of the huge ice floes crashed into him, throwing Ben's body back onto the ice, leaving his leg pinned between two enormous frozen chunks. The crowd, which had been shouting, fell silent at the sound of Ben's cry of agony.

It happened so quickly that only later was Amelia able to piece the events together. Somehow, when the ice moved, Ben slid into the water. A second later, William lay stretched out on the ground, reaching his arm toward Ben. Heedless of the ominous creaking, Amelia began to run toward the two men.

"Take my hand," William shouted. "I can hold you."

And he did. As Ben gripped William's wrist, the miner started to haul his friend out of the water. *Thank God!* Amelia continued to run toward them, knowing that Ben would need immediate medical care. Even seconds could make a difference when a man had been in water that cold. But before she could reach them, Ben slid back into the frigid water, dragging William with him.

Amelia stared, horrified. She heard the crowd's gasp, then a few shouts as several of the miners edged onto the ice, trying to reach the men.

Ben began to sink.

"Let me go," she heard him say. "Save yourself."

William ignored him. Though Amelia knew his own limbs must be near freezing, he wrapped his arms around Ben's legs, thrusting him upward and out of the water onto the sheet of ice. Half a dozen other men grabbed Ben and pulled him away from danger.

"Wrap him in your coats and get him to the clinic," Amelia ordered. She would follow in a minute, once she knew that William was safe.

One of the miners lay on the ice, extending his hand as William had done a minute earlier. But as William reached out, the ice behind him shifted. Two sheets collided, and as one buckled from the force, a huge chunk broke off.

"No! Oh, God, no!" Amelia screamed, but it was too late. William, his reflexes slowed by the frigid water, was unable to react. Amelia watched, horrified, as the ice knocked him on the back of his head. Without a sound, he sank into the black water.

Amelia's knees threatened to buckle, and there was a collective gasp of horror from the onlookers. A second later, William's head bobbed to the surface. He drifted for a few yards, then grasped one of the outstretched hands and clambered onto the ice.

"It'll take more than a little ice to kill a bastard like me," he said, his teeth chattering but his spirit obviously unharmed.

He was alive! Thank God! As the adrenaline began to course through her veins, Amelia ran to William.

"Bring him to the clinic," she said to the men who were wrapping coats around him. "I need to look at his head."

"There's nothing wrong with my head, Amelia. Thought you knew it was harder than granite." Though he shivered, he managed a smile. "Go take care of Ben."

William was right. She had another patient waiting for her.

"Drinks on us," one of the men cried as he and two others helped William to his feet. "Meet us at the saloon."

She found Ben lying on one of the treatment tables in the clinic, a whiskey bottle by his side.

"Can you hear me?" she asked.

A deep snore was Ben's only response. Just as well. The next hour was not going to be a pleasant one. She cleaned his hands, then wrapped them in thick bandages. Thank goodness the abrasions weren't too deep. With proper care, they would heal with only minor scarring, and Ben would be able to continue his practice. Though the injury to his leg was more serious, Amelia knew Ben's hands needed immediate care. He could work with only one leg, but permanent damage to either hand would mean the end of his career.

Amelia cut Ben's pants away and studied the wound. His flesh was gashed, badly lacerated by the ice. That damage was minor, compared to the ravages the ice had wreaked on his leg. The femur was broken, the two pieces obviously misaligned. Amelia shuddered.

207

"Need some help?"

His voice startled her so much that she almost dropped her scalpel.

"What are you doing here? I thought you went to the saloon." Though William had changed into dry clothes, his hair was still wet. She looked at him carefully, checking his color and the size of his pupils. By some miracle, the blow he had sustained appeared to have done no serious damage, although she suspected his head ached fiercely.

"Go to the saloon and leave my friend to your tender mercies? Not likely. I want him to keep his leg."

Amelia took a deep breath. She needed all her energy to deal with Ben's injury; there was none to spare for arguing with William. Though they were friends and agreed on many other things, it was obvious the man was never going to believe that she was a doctor—a real doctor. The sooner she accepted that, the better.

"In that case," she said mildly, "I suggest you start praying. The bone's so badly broken that prayer may be the only thing that saves it."

She looked at the wound again, deciding how best to treat it. William took a step closer. She could feel his warmth, and her own traitorous body reacted with a warmth of its own.

"If you're not going to pray, you might as well help me." This time her voice was tart with strain and anger. How dare she forget—even for a second—that she was a doctor and that a man's future depended on her?

"Hold Ben's leg." She reached for her scalpel.

"What are you doing?"

Without stopping to look at him, Amelia made a deep incision. "There are bone fragments in there," she told William. "If I don't get them out, even prayer won't save his leg. Gangrene is a painful way to die."

It was painstaking work, reaching for the tiny shards of bone, plucking them from the tissue, a job that was made infinitely more difficult by the knowledge that William was watching, expecting her to make a mistake. But she would not make a mistake, for, whether he believed it or not, she was a competent surgeon.

Only when she was convinced that she'd found the last fragment did she turn back to William. "This is going to hurt," she said, "so hold him still." As William kept Ben's upper body immobilized, Amelia gripped the two sections of the femur and jerked them into alignment. Ben groaned, then fell back into merciful unconsciousness. The worst was over. A few minutes later, Amelia finished suturing the incision. Her hands were bloody, her back ached and she could feel wisps of hair matted on her neck where they had escaped from the back combs. Still, she let out a deep breath as she placed a splint under Ben's leg. He would not lose it.

"We're going to have to put his leg in traction," she told William, who had stood silently throughout the operation.

When she had ordered the equipment, Ben had scoffed, telling her it was an unnecessary expense. Amelia could imagine his reaction when he regained consciousness and discovered he was the first to use what he had called a useless contraption.

"Ben's gonna hate this," William said as Amelia adjusted the pulleys, suspending Ben's leg from the ceiling. William was stating the obvious. Amelia could imagine the abuse Ben would heap on her when he woke.

"He'd hate being a cripple even more," she said mildly, and started cleaning her instruments. The inevitable aftermath of surgery had begun, and she could feel her hands start to tremble. It was always this way—a sense of relief mingled with the fear that she had made some irreversible error. Today her reaction was magnified by the horror of the accident, the sight of Ben's leg being crushed and that terrible, heart-stopping moment when William had been hit.

William's footsteps rang out as he left Ben's side. "That was mighty fine work, Amelia." She could hear the smile in his voice.

No! Not now!

Amelia spun around, her eyes narrowed in anger. If there was one thing she did not need, it was William Gunning's sarcasm, not now when her nerves were so badly frayed that she questioned her own skill.

"Let me tell you something, mister. It *was* fine work, and I don't need your caustic comments. Just get out of here."

There was no hope for the woman. She was a damn fine doctor; the way she had fixed Ben's leg was proof of that. Oh, William admitted, he had had his doubts at first. Hell, he had had his doubts even today. But now that he had seen her in action, there was no denying it. She was a skilled physician.

If he hadn't seen her operate, William would not have realized how much skill, effort and, yes, courage, was needed to turn that mangled piece of flesh and bone back into a leg. But William *had* seen it, and what he saw filled him with admiration. He had tried to tell her that. But she hadn't cared. Amelia did not want to listen to him; she did not care about his opinion. All that mattered was Abe and what he thought. To hell with both of them, he thought, striding out of the clinic toward Gloria's.

"Oh, William, I was so worried about you." June put her hand on his arm and gazed up at him. William smiled. At least this woman would not reject him. "I heard you fell into the river," she continued. "You must have been so cold."

It *had* been cold, and for the first hour, he had felt chilled to the bone. Now the cold was gone, replaced by an unpleasant warmth.

"I'm not cold now," he told June. "Kind of hot, in fact."

June laughed and tossed her blond hair. "I know just how to treat that heat. Come with me, big fellow. I'm what the doctor ordered."

With a grin William followed her up the stairs. "You might be, at that."

When they reached June's room, William stood in the doorway, gripping the frame. It was ridiculous. He had climbed those stairs more times than he could count, and he had never felt tired.

"That bed looks mighty inviting," he said.

June laughed again. "It's supposed to."

With a lurch, William collapsed on the mattress, overwhelmed with fatigue.

"C'mon, William," June coaxed. "Let's get those clothes off you."

"So tired," he muttered. "Need half an hour's sleep. Then good as new."

But he wasn't. Though William fell asleep immediately, it was a restless slumber. He thrashed from one side of the bed to the other, then sat up and stared directly at June. "Amelia!" he called.

June put her hand on his forehead. His head was terribly hot. "Lie back," she said, pushing him down. "You need to rest."

He would be better in a few hours. But he wasn't.

As the night passed, William's fever rose. He would sleep for a few minutes, then waken long enough to call for Amelia.

"I'm here," June said. "June will help you."

"Amelia. I want Amelia."

June's eyes darkened with hatred. *Damn her! Damn that woman to hell!*

Chapter Fifteen

The man had pneumonia. There was no doubt of that. Amelia
had seen the symptoms too often to be mistaken. As if his
dangerously high fever and pulse rate weren't enough, he was
complaining of severe pain on both sides of his chest, and he
had started the telltale coughing. Double pneumonia. Though
her heart ached at the thought that the man she loved above
all others was so ill, she willed her hands to remain steady as
she pulled the quinine out of her bag and began to measure
it. This was no time for emotion. A man's life depended on
her skills.

Her patient stirred. "How did I get here?" William demanded, punctuating his words with a racking cough.

Amelia turned, her eyes assessing his condition. William
had kicked the quilts to the floor and lay covered with only a
sheet, despite the cool air.

"Gloria didn't think you would agree to go to the clinic, so
she had a couple of the men bring you home. Then she called
me."

Amelia did not want to remember how the summons had
frightened her. Her initial fear that he had suffered a delayed
reaction to the blow he had sustained had proven unfounded,
but pneumonia was equally serious. She stirred quinine into a
glass of water.

"What on God's earth was that—rat poison?"

For the first time since she had entered William's house and
seen how ill he was, Amelia smiled. William's bad humor was
a good sign. "Believe it or not, the quinine will help reduce
the fever."

William leaned back on the pillows she had propped against
the sturdy wooden headboard. Though his bedroom was the
largest Amelia had seen in Gold Landing, the furnishings were
plain, clearly chosen for function rather than beauty. A chest

of drawers was pushed next to one plain white wall, a wardrobe by another. The only color in the room came from the brightly patterned quilt that lay in a tangle on the floor.

"I'd rather die," he announced as he handed Amelia the empty glass.

Amelia stared at him for a long moment. Of course he didn't mean it. "That's not going to happen if I can help it."

He was a strong man, one who had survived a harsh childhood and, from all accounts, an even more difficult adolescence. If anyone had a chance of surviving this, it was William. Still, the ice bath he had taken in the Tanana did not help. Men died from simple exposure; combine it with pneumonia, and the odds were not good.

William lay back on his pillow, visibly exhausted by the effort to speak. "Why do you care?" he asked.

It would be unprofessional to admit that he was more than a patient to her, that, though he had never asked for it, she had given him her heart months ago. And so Amelia shrugged. "You never can tell when I'll need you to help me in surgery again," she said as lightly as she could. "I'm not going to let you go, William. Good assistants are too hard to find."

As she had hoped, he managed a grin, then fell asleep. Amelia remained at his bedside, sitting in the rocker that she had dragged in from the parlor.

His breathing was shallow, but at least he was still alive. The man was ornery; he was stubborn. God willing, those traits would keep him from succumbing to the disease Amelia and her fellow medical students had nicknamed "the Grim Reaper's apprentice."

"Will he be okay?" Alex entered the room so quietly that Amelia had not heard him.

"It's too soon to tell, but I hope so." Somehow her voice sounded normal. Thank goodness Alex would never guess that William was not an ordinary patient, that she cared about him in ways that could never be described as professional. It was, Amelia knew, a dangerous situation. When a doctor was emotionally involved, she was supposed to hand the case over to another physician. The problem was, with Ben incapacitated, there was no one else. And that frightened Amelia almost as much as William's pneumonia. What if she made a mistake?

She could tell Alex none of that. Instead, she said, "He's a strong man. That helps. And he's got reasons to live—like Hannah." Though Amelia knew William loved children, she had been surprised at the joy Alex and Karen's daughter gave him. If she had not known better, she would have believed William to be the girl's father, the way he doted on the baby.

Alex stared at the floor, his expression grim. Then a smile cracked his face. "William's too cussed ornery to die," he announced.

Amelia returned the smile. "Did you go to med school? That was my diagnosis." She reached for a piece of paper that she had left on the dresser. "Would you mind taking this to Ella?"

Half an hour later Ella arrived with the medicine Amelia had requested and a scowl on her face.

"You can't ask me to do this," she announced when Amelia told her what she needed. Her brown eyes flashed, and Amelia knew the color in her cheeks was caused by something other than the exertion of walking from the clinic.

"It was bad enough just getting the right bottles," Ella continued, gripping the back of a kitchen chair. "I thought I was in mortal danger. That man was so angry, if he could have killed me, he would have."

Amelia suppressed a smile. If the situation had not been so serious, she would have been amused by the anger in Ella's voice and the way she had dramatized the scene at the clinic. *Mortal danger!* Only William faced that. Still, Amelia could not help feeling that something good had come from today's accidents if Ella was finally displaying emotion. "I need you, Ella. There's no one else who can do this," she said firmly.

"But I don't know how," Ella protested, her lips pursed in disapproval.

"Think of Ben as one of your students. A slow learner. The subject you're going to teach him will be staying in bed and getting well." Not that Ben had any alternatives. With his leg in traction and both hands wrapped in thick bandages, he was helpless.

"Amelia . . ." The anguish on Ella's face almost made Amelia relent.

"I'm desperate, Ella. I can't be in two places at the same time. William's condition is critical, but I can't take care of him properly if I'm worried about Ben. That's why I need you to help me with him." Amelia looked at her watch. She had already been away from William longer than she wanted. "Please, Ella. You saw Ben. He can't do anything for himself." And, oh, how Ben would hate that.

"You're not giving me much choice, are you?" Ella listened while Amelia described what needed to be done. Then, with a surprising bounce in her step, she headed for the clinic.

Amelia's smile vanished when she reentered William's room. Even without her thermometer she could see that the quinine had failed to reduce his fever, and his breathing was so shallow she wondered if he was getting any oxygen to his lungs. She mixed another dose of quinine.

"Drink it all," she said as she put her arm around his shoulders to keep his head upright while she held the glass to his lips.

Though he grimaced at the bitter taste, William said nothing.

It was not a good sign.

"Get out of here! You're the last creature on earth I want near me."

Ella stared at her patient, her hands on her hips in her best disapproving schoolmarm stance. "For once we're in agreement on something. You're the last person on earth I want to be near."

"So leave." As Ben jerked his head toward the door, Ella felt a twinge of sympathy for him. It couldn't be easy, being trussed like a Thanksgiving turkey. And to have someone else see him that way—Ella knew she would die of sheer mortification if she were in Ben's predicament.

"Leaving is a tempting thought," she agreed, "but I can't.

215

I promised Amelia I'd make sure you're okay.''

"Well, Miss Schoolmarm, you sure failed that test. Any fool could see that I'm not okay. Look at this contraption she's put me in. It's worse than the rack.''

Though Ella had heard Amelia wax eloquent over the traction pulleys when she planned the clinic, today was the first time Ella had seen one in operation. Ben's description was accurate, not that she had any intention of giving that cantankerous old man the satisfaction of knowing she agreed with him.

"I don't imagine Amelia had medieval torture in mind when she put you here,'' Ella said mildly. "As I understand it, the alternative was amputation.'' Ella tried to ignore the vivid picture her imagination conjured. Amelia would not want her to alarm Ben. "Would you like me to have her try that? Maybe she could work on your tongue, too.''

Ben's growl reminded Ella of a moose warning other males to stay out of its territory. "When did you develop that sour attitude?'' he demanded.

Amelia was right. He was like her younger students, striking out at the closest person when things didn't go his way. "If I have a sour attitude, it started when Amelia told me I had to take care of you. Now, are you going to drink your medicine, or do I have to force it down your throat?''

"You wouldn't.''

"I would.''

Ben looked younger, less formidable, without his spectacles. Not that she would tell him.

"Just give me some whiskey,'' he demanded. "That's what I need, not Amelia's damned medicine.''

Whiskey. Of course he would ask for whiskey. "Not one drop.''

He glared at her. "You're enjoying this!''

Ella took a step closer to the bed and stared down at him. "Maybe I am,'' she admitted. How odd. If anyone had told her she would enjoy being with a man, sparring over nonsensical things like his childish refusal to take medicine, she would have said they were demented. And yet, there was no

216

denying the fact that it felt good to be the one who gave Ben Taylor orders.

If Ella was happy, Amelia was not. The days passed, and William's condition worsened. His lucid periods grew shorter as the pain intensified. Though he rarely slept, Amelia wasn't certain he knew where he was, for he would sit up, his eyes open but focused on some distant point, and cry out, "Polly! No, Polly, no!" The words were always the same, his voice so hoarse with pain that Amelia felt as though something were being ripped out of him. Perhaps it was, for each time he would clap his hand to his scarred cheek as if trying to stanch bleeding.

Amelia knew that Polly had been his stepmother, the woman who had raised him, but she had no idea what caused his nightmares. All she knew was that she had never before heard a man in such agony.

"Let me die!" he shouted. "Dear God, let me die!" He gripped his chest in a vain effort to stop the pain.

He couldn't die. She would not let him. Her mind balked at the realization that the decision wasn't hers, that no matter what she did, she might still lose him.

Amelia laid her hand on William's forehead, gently pushing him back onto the nest of pillows she had arranged so that he could lie half-reclined. With his lungs as congested as they were, that position was his only hope for sleep.

"Don't you dare die, William Gunning," she told him, her voice low but fierce. "I won't have it. Do you hear me? I'm not going to lose you." *I love you,* she added silently.

Though he gave no sign of hearing her, for a few moments his limbs stopped thrashing, and he seemed calmer.

Amelia remained by his side, feeding him liquids when he was awake enough to swallow, pressing cold compresses onto his head to reduce the fever. There were times when she thought he recognized her, when his grimaces could almost be construed as smiles, but those times were fleeting. Most of the time he was incoherent.

He was strong. She repeated the words so often they became

217

a mantra. But as the days passed, his strength ebbed, and Amelia knew that the Grim Reaper would have little difficulty in harvesting William. Even the strongest of men could not forever resist a disease as virulent as pneumonia.

She splashed cold water onto her face in a vain attempt to rinse away her fatigue. She had long since given up trying to keep her hair neat. Locks had escaped from her combs to droop onto her neck, while her once spotless shirtwaist bore quinine stains. Though she opened the window daily, even the breeze could not banish the rank smell of disease.

William was ill. Dangerously so.

"I won't let you take him," she cried, and redoubled her efforts, increasing the dosage of quinine and administering carbonate of ammonia to protect his heart. But the horrible, racking cough that sapped his strength continued, and the fever that dried his skin and left his eyes glassy continued unabated.

"No more!" William sat up and stared at the opposite wall. "No more!"

Amelia placed her hand on his forehead. It was hotter than before, and there was nothing more she could do. William's fate was out of her hands.

"Please, God, spare him." She joined her prayers to William's, holding his hand in hers.

Afterward Amelia could not have said how long she sat there, William's big hand clasped between both of hers, staring at the face that had haunted her dreams for so many months. All she knew was that suddenly the room seemed to have grown colder and the hand she held was no longer burning with fever. Fearing the worst, Amelia turned William's hand upward and pressed her fingers to his pulse. Tears filled her eyes and began to leak onto her cheeks. It was over.

"Oh, Amelia." When Ella entered the room, she saw Amelia slowly rocking, not trying to disguise her tears. William lay on the bed, his eyes closed, his face peaceful. Ella knelt in front of Amelia and grasped her hands. "I'm so sorry."

Amelia blinked her tears away. "It's not what you think. The worst is over. Oh, Ella, William's fever broke. He's going to be okay.'' Though her voice was shaky, Amelia smiled. ''Chalk the tears up to fatigue.''

''And no wonder.'' As if she were one of her schoolchildren, Ella led Amelia out of the sickroom. ''You haven't had any sleep in days. Let me help you.'' She led Amelia into the kitchen. ''Sit down,'' she said. ''I'm going to help.''

Amelia didn't know whether it was fatigue or sheer relief that made her legs so wobbly. She did know that it felt good to sit at the table and watch the sun stream onto the floor, all the while knowing that in a matter of days William would sit in the same chair and see the same sunshine.

Amelia accepted the cup of cocoa that Ella offered her. ''You are helping,'' she told the other woman. ''Taking care of Ben is an enormous responsibility.''

Ella's braids bounced as she shook her head. ''That's why I came here this afternoon, to tell you I just can't do it anymore. Today that obnoxious man tried to spit food at me.''

Amelia couldn't help it. She laughed. Ella pursed her lips. ''I'm not laughing at you,'' Amelia was quick to reassure her. ''But didn't I tell you that he would be like one of your worst schoolchildren?''

''He's worse. I tell you, Amelia, he's less mature than the youngest child I teach. And his manners . . .'' She shuddered.

''Please, Ella. It'll only be a few more days. Now that William's fever has broken, he'll start to mend and I'll be able to leave him.'' When Ella nodded reluctantly, Amelia said, ''There's just one more thing I need you to do.''

How on earth was she going to do it? Amelia had been so calm when she had told her. A bed bath. She had made it sound like the easiest thing in the world. *Easy, my grandmother's hairpiece.* Amelia had been to medical school. She had been trained to do things like that. Ella had not, but it was Ella who was going to have to look at that man and touch him . . . all of him. She couldn't. She simply could not.

''If it isn't Little Miss Sunshine.'' Ben greeted her as if he hadn't tried to spray chicken soup at her the day before. ''Or is it Madame Vinegar who's come to play Florence Nightingale today?''

Ben peered at her through the spectacles she had given him two days ago. Though they should have improved his disposition, they obviously had not. He was still as cantankerous as ever, determined to annoy her. Unfortunately for Ben, he had picked the wrong day to employ that caustic tone with her.

Amelia was right. She could do this. She would do it. One way or another, Ben Taylor would learn not to underestimate her.

''If I were you, I'd be careful or I just might use vinegar when I bathe you.''

Ella wished she could capture the look of horror that crossed Ben's face.

''Bathe?'' He pronounced the word as though it were a curse.

Ella nodded. ''That's exactly what I said. Personal hygiene. Cleanliness. Surely you were introduced to those concepts in medical school.'' She turned and started to heat the water. Though there would be a certain satisfaction in using cold water on him, she had no desire to put her hands in it.

''I don't need a bath.''

''Oh, Dr. Taylor, not only do you need one, but you're going to get one.'' If she admitted that she was dreading the whole experience as much as he was, she would be lost. The only hope was to feign sangfroid. How appropriate! On at least one occasion Ben had accused her of being cold-blooded. Now she could show him just how cool she could be.

''Don't do it.''

She ignored him. With the water heated and the towels ready, she stared at Ben, deciding where to begin. The feet. At least they could spit nothing at her. She tugged on the pulley and lowered Ben's injured leg. Uncovering his feet, she cleaned each one carefully, making sure to dry between his toes. To her amazement, he said nothing until she had put clean socks on him.

''Are you finished?'' he demanded.

Rather than reply, Ella pulled the sheet so that his legs and half of his thighs were exposed. Ben hissed. "Stop right now."

"And risk gangrene? I can't do that."

"It's my leg. If I want gangrene—"

"You have no choice." Ella moved her washcloth up his right leg, cleansing carefully around the wound, then repeating the process on his uninjured left leg. She ought to continue working up his body, but that would mean looking at and touching . . . Refusing to complete the thought, Ella moved to the head of the bed. Surely it was her imagination that Ben sighed in relief. Whatever the reason, he remained silent.

"Close your eyes," she cautioned, "or you'll get soap in them." His face bristled with whiskers, catching on the soft cloth, but she continued, then pulled the sheet down a few inches so she could wash his neck and shoulders. Lowering the sheet to his waist, she turned her attention to his chest.

Odd. Whenever she had pictured a man's body, it was ugly and threatening, an instrument designed to inflict pain. But there was nothing ugly about Ben's arms and chest. They were actually nice to look at, and there was nothing even remotely threatening about them. She drew the cloth downward until she reached his navel. All that was left was . . . Surely she didn't have to wash that.

Apparently Ben agreed. "Satisfied?" he demanded. "I feel as clean as a newborn."

"I'm not finished." Ben's complaint stiffened her resolve.

"Yes, you are."

"Amelia said I had to wash *all* of you." Ella repeated the words as if they were part of a lesson she was drilling into her students.

Quickly, before she could lose her nerve, she pulled the sheet aside, replacing it with her cloth. There! He was decent. She swirled the cloth, then picked it up again. And as she did, she sneaked a look. Ella felt the color rise to her cheeks. *That* was what she had feared all these years? Why, there was nothing terrifying about that piece of flesh.

Could it be that Amelia was right and that men weren't inherently brutes?

*   *   *

"I feel like someone's been pounding on my chest with a pick." It was the first time in days that William could remember sitting upright in the bed. When he had wakened, Amelia had been sitting in the rocking chair that somehow had gotten from the parlor to his bedroom, her foot moving slowly but rhythmically as she turned the pages of a book. At the sound of his voice, she laid the book on the floor and walked to his bedside.

Lord, she was pretty! That dark hair of hers sat on top of her head like a halo, but to William's way of thinking, she would look more angelic with it tumbling down her back. As his thoughts continued to their logical conclusion, William figured he was recovered. A sick man wouldn't feel that way.

"A pick or an ax might have been less painful," Amelia told him as she stuck a thermometer under his tongue. "You had a bad case of pneumonia."

Memory came flooding back, reminding William of all that had happened the day of the ice breakup.

"How's Ben?" he muttered around the thermometer as he remembered the contraption Amelia had attached to his friend's leg.

Amelia smiled, and William noticed the circles that lined her eyes. Though he was the one who had had pneumonia, Amelia looked as if she had been ill. She was still the most beautiful woman he had ever seen, and she smelled nice, too, but something was definitely wrong.

"Ben's mad as a hornet, or so Ella says." *Ella?* What did Ella have to do with Ben? "Ella's been taking care of Ben while I was here."

For a moment the intriguing question of Ben and Ella was forgotten as fragments of memories danced in the back of William's head. A woman's hands, soft and soothing. A woman's voice, first soft and entreating, then fiercely demanding. A woman's tears. Had Amelia been that woman, or had it been part of his dream, memories of Polly, mingled with the present? William didn't know, and he would not ask. What he did know was that no woman since Polly had cared for him enough to stay with him when he was sick, and Amelia had done just that.

"I can't imagine Ben and Ella together," he said, swallowing the lump that had somehow formed in his throat. "Ben's probably turning the air blue with curses."

The air in his own room was fresh and smelled of sunshine and mud, the normal scents of an Alaskan spring.

Amelia's lips curved in what could only be called a sly smile. "That's what I heard. But Ella got her revenge, in the form of a bed bath."

Ben Taylor submitting to a bed bath! The idea was ludicrous. William laughed, an act his chest protested. Though it hurt like the fires of hell, his mirth was quelled by more than the pain in his lungs. He had been sick for a week, and here he was wearing nothing more than a nightshirt. William looked at the quilt that covered his lower body. It was thick and concealing. But . . . it had been a week, and he could remember very little of those days. What if Amelia had bathed him? Suddenly the picture of Ben and Ella wasn't so amusing.

As if she could read his thoughts, Amelia said sweetly, "You don't think I'd let you go for a week without proper hygiene, do you?"

She had! William could feel the blood rise to his face. It shouldn't matter. More than one woman had seen him naked and enjoyed both seeing and touching his body. This was different, though. She had no right to stare at him when he was unconscious.

"Relax, William. I'm a doctor."

He could not meet her gaze. "You're also a woman," he muttered. As if he could think of anything else. "The skirt was a giveaway." Somehow he managed to keep his voice light and joking, as though the thought of her touching him hadn't stirred him in ways he would prefer she not notice. She was a woman, all right.

William woke the next morning to the smell of frying bacon. Lured by the aroma, he made his way on shaky legs to the kitchen.

"Where's Amelia?" he demanded, surprised to see his cousin Alex wielding a frying pan. In all the time Alex had lived with William, he had never once cooked. Perhaps marriage was changing him.

"If she's smart, she's getting some sleep. Everyone's talking about it, wondering how she survived, because she didn't leave here once until yesterday." Alex pushed the strips of bacon to one side of the pan and broke an egg into it. "Abe got the women to bring food every day, so she didn't have to cook. Good thing, considering she would hardly budge from your bedside."

Abe. How he hated that name! That was probably where she was today, meeting Abe and talking about one of his fancy books.

He was wrong. Half an hour later when he had collapsed on his bed, shocked by the magnitude of his fatigue, Amelia poked her head into his bedroom.

"I brought you a visitor," she said. "Theo's here."

The young boy grinned, then walked to the bedside. "I'm glad you're better," he said. Pulling an object from behind his back, he handed it to William. "This is for you." It was a carved walking stick, similar to the one he had made for Amelia the previous summer.

William turned it over in his hands, fingering the crude carving. "It's fine work, son."

Amelia's gaze flew to William, surprised that he had called the boy "son."

"Ma said you'd be weak after the new . . . new—." He turned to Amelia. "What was it you called it?"

"Pneumonia." She pronounced the word slowly, then let him repeat it after her.

"I figured you might need this," Theo explained. "To get to the mine, you know."

William smiled. "That was good thinking, Theo. I sure can use it." William reached out a hand and tousled the boy's hair. "Thanks, son."

There it was again, that word.

When Theo had left, Amelia returned to William's room.

"I hope you didn't mind my letting him visit you. He came every day that you were sick, but he refused to leave the walking stick without seeing you."

William smiled. "I like the boy. It's tough on him, not having a father."

"So you're the surrogate."

William stared at the wall, a clear sign that he was uncomfortable with the conversation. "A boy needs a man's influence," he told Amelia.

It was nothing she had not surmised. She knew that William had felt the lack of a father deeply. Though he had talked occasionally about Polly, the unspoken words were that Polly had done as well as any woman could, but a man would have been better. No wonder he felt such a strong need to have a child of his own. And, oh, how that knowledge hurt!

"I hear William's back at the mine."

The second woman nodded as she leaned forward in one of the comfortable chairs Gloria had ordered for the girls' common room. "They say he woulda died if it hadn't been for Dr. Sheldon."

"If you ask me, Sally, it was a lucky thing for the doctor." The first woman frowned at the rent in her dress. "I hear folks are upset that she's been treating Indians in the clinic. 'Course I reckon now that she saved William's life, they'll cool down a mite."

Sally nodded again. "She's a pretty good doc, even if she does have some peculiar ideas. Imagine, Louise—Indians in the clinic."

They meant no harm. June was sure of that. Neither Sally nor Louise had any way of knowing how painful those words were. They were merely repeating the tales being circulated by virtually every citizen of Gold Landing. Dr. Sheldon, the miracle worker. Her name was on everyone's lips. Everyone's except June's, that was.

"I haven't seen William here lately," Louise said. She turned to June. "Do you know why?"

It was a question June asked herself each night when an-

Amanda Harte

other day passed without William coming to call. There was
an answer, but it was so unthinkable that she would not admit
it, even to herself.

"He's probably so busy after being out of the mine that he
doesn't have time for anything else." That was what she
wanted to believe, because the alternative was unbearable.

"Seems odd. I reckon he used to have plenty of time to pay
a call or two."

But that was before that wicked woman got her claws into
him. It was all Amelia's fault.

Chapter Sixteen

There were some things a man did not want to think about. Unfortunately, some could not be avoided forever. His bout with pneumonia, the little he remembered of it, had made him realize that he could not afford to wait. It was time to talk to Abe.

"Lookin' for the lawyer?" Herb Ashton stood in front of his store, either enjoying the sunshine or hoping to lure customers indoors. Since William's knocking on Abe's office door made the question rhetorical, Herb continued, "Just missed him. Closed up shop about a quarter hour ago. Took off."

"Did he say where he was going?" It was ironic. He had waited all these years to write his will. Another hour or even a day would not matter, but now that he had decided it was time to put his affairs in order, to make sure that baby Hannah never wanted for anything, William begrudged a moment's delay. Why the hell had Abe picked today of all days to close early?

Herb pulled a packet of tobacco and a piece of paper from his pocket. "Headed up the hill. Figure he went to meet the doctor." Keeping his eyes on the cigarette he was rolling, Herb continued, "Reckon he'll be popping the question pretty soon."

So let him! If Amelia was foolish enough to marry that dandified lawyer, she deserved everything she got. All that William cared about was tracking down Abe and getting the man to write his will. That was the only reason he found himself climbing the hill. It had nothing—absolutely nothing— to do with the fact that Abe had gone to meet Amelia.

By now she should be coming back from the Feehys' cabin. William knew that she liked to make it her last stop so that she would have a long, uninterrupted walk home. "Clear-my-head time," she called it. And, if she had no one waiting for her at the clinic, she would frequently detour to follow the streambed. It was not the most direct route, but Amelia had told him it was the most scenic.

Abe would probably take the direct path. William walked swiftly, determined to catch up with him. It was not that he was trying to prevent Abe from spending more time with Amelia. Only a jealous man would do something like that, and William was not jealous. No, sirree. The simple fact was, he needed to talk to Abe.

But there was no sight of either Amelia or the lawyer. Though Amelia might have been delayed at the Feehys' or with one of her earlier patients, that did not explain why Abe had disappeared. He rarely left town, and to William's knowledge, he never climbed the hill. If he was looking for Amelia, surely he would stay on the open tundra as long as he could. He would not walk through the brush or venture into the forest any sooner than necessary, because that would make finding Amelia more difficult.

They had to be somewhere. William quickened his pace, looking in all directions, searching for a glimpse of the white shirtwaist Amelia always wore for her rounds. He had almost decided that she must still be in the cabin when he heard voices. They were too far away for him to distinguish words, but he could tell that they belonged to a man and a woman. The fools were in the brush.

Moving with the silent tread that he had been taught as a child, William made his way through the thicket. In the middle of the underbrush was a large clearing, probably a spot where moose had once made their beds. What he saw made William's blood run cold.

"Dear God, no! Amelia! No!"

She was the most fortunate of women. Not only was she lucky enough to be living her dream of helping people, but she had wonderfully generous patients. It wasn't that they were wealthy. Some, in fact, lived in deplorable conditions. But what little they had, they shared with her. She pulled the golden object from her pocket. Lord only knew how the Fee-hys had kept an orange so long. So what if the skin was shriveled and the meat was likely to be dry? At this time of the year, the fruit was worth more than gold. Amelia suspected the orange had been part of a Christmas celebration and that Pauline had hoarded it, saving it for a late-winter treat. Though she had tried to refuse it, telling Pauline that Joe had paid her fee when the baby was born, the woman had been adamant.

"I want you to have it, Doctor," she had insisted. "It's to thank you for all that you've done for me."

Her patients appreciated her. The people of Gold Landing were healthier than they had ever been, and a few of the Indian mothers had mustered enough courage to bring their children to the clinic, despite the obvious disapproval they met from some of the townspeople.

She ought to be filled with happiness. So why did she feel empty? And why, oh why, did she keep dreaming of William? She had done everything she could to prevent the dreams, everything from deliberately thinking about Abe before she went to sleep to refusing to walk along the streambed where she and William had spent so many pleasurable hours. Nothing had worked. There was, it appeared, no way to inoculate herself against William.

She was almost out of the forest when she saw him. "Abe!" Amelia's eyes widened at the sight of the lawyer walking up the hill toward her. "What are you doing here? I thought you had office hours today." Though William used to meet her outside town, Abe had never joined her on her rounds.

She searched his face, wondering what emergency had brought him to her. But, far from appearing distressed, Abe looked relaxed. His smile was as warm as ever, although it seemed somehow tinged with self-consciousness. "I closed the office," he admitted.

There must be something in the air that was making people behave strangely. How else could she explain her doldrums and the fact that Abe, the man who *never* closed his office, the man who had informed her that keeping to a schedule was essential, had evidently played hooky?

"Am I permitted to ask why?"

"Not only are you permitted, but I'll even answer. It's simple. Today's a beautiful May day, and I wanted to spend it with you."

There was definitely something in the air, but Amelia was not complaining. Perhaps Abe's company would help her recover her equilibrium.

"Your timing is perfect. I just finished my rounds, and there's no one in the clinic, so I don't need to rush back." She and Abe walked slowly, talking about the last book they had shared, until they reached the edge of the forest.

"Would you like to see one of my favorite spots?" Amelia asked. No one, not even William, knew that she had found a private refuge outside of town.

Abe nodded. They headed across the tundra toward a cluster of bushes a few hundred yards away. A narrow track, obviously used by animals, led through the thicket. "We're almost there."

Amelia used her bag to part the bushes where they had started to overgrow the path. "Look." In the center of the thicket was a small meadow ringed by bushes. A patch of flowers brightened one area, while on the other side a narrow stream cut through the grass, then disappeared into the brush.

"It's beautiful," Abe said.

"And so peaceful." Amelia sank to the ground. "I know it's fanciful," she told Abe, "but when I'm sitting here, I feel like I'm in a castle." She laughed. "I can picture my mother's and sister's expressions if they saw me here. They would be horrified. Belinda would scoff at the idea that these bushes are castle walls, while my mother would shudder at the thought of grass stains on my skirt."

The sun glinted off Abe's spectacles. "And you love it, anyway."

Amelia nodded as she pulled the orange from her pocket. "If I remember the stories correctly, since you're visiting my castle, I should offer you a feast. I'm afraid this is all I have."

When she started to peel the fruit, Abe held out his hand. "Let me. If I'm the knight in this tale, I need to perform some heroic task.'' Carefully, as if he were unwrapping a priceless treasure, Abe stripped the skin from the orange. He tossed the peels over his shoulder, then separated one of the segments. ''My lady,'' he said, touching Amelia's lips with the succulent fruit. When she had eaten her piece, she reached for the orange. Pulling off another segment, she fed it to Abe.

There was a rustling in the bushes, as if the wind had suddenly gusted, but Amelia hardly noticed it. She watched Abe's smile deepen and his eyes grow dark with emotion as he laid the orange on the ground and moved closer to her.

''Amelia, love,'' he said, ''do you know why I came here today?''

Before she could answer, he put his arms around her, drawing her close to him, lowering his lips to hers.

The world exploded with two fierce roars.

''William!'' Amelia's eyes flew open at the sound of his shout. She saw him standing at the edge of the clearing, his face contorted with rage. Why was he here? How had he found her? And what had made the other cry? The thoughts swirled through Amelia's mind faster than dry leaves before a storm.

''Lie down! Play dead!''

In the instant before she complied, Amelia saw the reason for William's command. A bear cub lay on the grass only a few feet behind her and Abe, busily shoving orange peels into his mouth, while his frantic mother burst through the bushes to protect him.

A second later, the bear was gone.

Her ears still ringing with the sound of the gunshot, Amelia rose on shaky legs. The cub scampered away, leaving only a solitary peel as a reminder of how close she had been to danger. Though Abe tried to support her, Amelia brushed his arm aside. The expression on William's face told her he was as filled with fury as the mother bear had been and as close to exploding with violence. Knowing the animosity between the two men, she would not antagonize William by letting Abe help her.

''Why did they come?'' she asked. ''I've never seen bears here.''

William pointed to the one remaining scrap of orange peel. "The smell must have attracted the cub. City folks like you"—he included Abe in his condemnation—"probably don't know much about bears, but they love to eat, have a keen sense of smell and are extremely curious. I don't need to tell you what happens when you separate a mother from her cub."

Amelia shuddered.

"You could have killed that animal." Abe's voice was low but angry.

"Damn right I could have. And I would have if she hadn't left." William holstered his revolver. "I suppose you would have preferred to be the one who died?"

Abe bristled. "Of course not, but there had to be another way."

" 'Fraid not, Mr. Lawyer. This was one time when negotiations wouldn't work."

Amelia was treating the last of her patients when William appeared at the clinic the next day. She looked up, startled. Like most of the men in Gold Landing, William had not set foot inside the clinic since the day he had helped build it.

She bandaged the little girl's leg, then shook her head when the mother offered payment. "You've already paid," she said. "Follow-up visits were included." The mother nodded gratefully, a shy smile lighting her brown face as she gathered the girl into her arms.

"Still treating the Indians, I see."

Amelia looked at William. Though he was leaning against the door frame, his posture apparently relaxed, his eyes seemed to bore into hers. "Did you come here to criticize my medical care?" she asked.

He shook his head. "We've got something more important to talk about." William reached into the sack he had brought with him. "This is for you," he said, handing her a revolver.

Amelia stared at it. The gun was similar to William's but smaller, obviously designed for a woman's hand. For months he had tried to convince her to buy one. Today he had taken the next step, and today Amelia would not refuse. Her mind had replayed the scene in the clearing countless times, and with each repetition, she had trembled, realizing that William had been right. She needed to be able to protect herself.

"I've never used one," she said. "Never even held one."

"That's about to change." He placed the gun in her hand. "If you're through here, it's time for your first lesson in firearms."

"Thank you." Amelia smiled at William. "You know how hard it is for me to admit this, but you were right. Alaska isn't Philadelphia."

As William smiled, his eyes lightened until they reminded Amelia of mercury. "C'mon. Let's turn you into Annie Oakley."

The noise was almost deafening; the recoil hurt her arm; her eyes stung from squinting at the target; but what Amelia remembered most about the afternoon was the feel of William's arms around her, his hands positioning hers on the gun, showing her how to hold it, how to squeeze the trigger. It felt so good, so right to be cradled next to him, their hands moving together as if they were one, even their breathing synchronized as William taught her to inhale deeply, then expel the air slowly as she fired.

In her dreams they touched, but not even her dreams could compare to the reality of being held by William. If only they had a future. If only her dreams could come true. If only.

That night her dreams were not of William. Those dreams were warm and rose-colored, promising greater happiness than she had ever known. The one that wakened her was dark and ominous, filling her with dread. She woke, trembling, her mouth dry from an unknown fear. Amelia could remember nothing of substance. All she knew was that something was wrong.

She sat up and listened. Perhaps it had not been a dream at all. Perhaps she had heard a noise outside the house, and that was what had wakened her. Pulling on a wrapper, Amelia went to the front door.

Smoke! Huge, billowing clouds of smoke rose in the distance. Her heart faltered, then began to race, and the dread she had felt in her dream intensified as she realized what was burning. The clinic was on fire!

Amelia shouted for Ella, then ran down the street to the church and tugged on the bell rope. Within minutes, a fire brigade was in place, but they were too late. By the time the first buckets of water were thrown, Amelia's clinic was little more than charred rubble.

"What could have caught fire?" Ella, shivering in the cold, turned to Ben, who had somehow materialized at her side when the last of the flames had been doused.

He shrugged. "Almost anything. Amelia kept an oil lamp there. Maybe it tipped over." Even though Gold Landing had electricity, she had insisted on the lamp, telling Ben it was for backup in case the power failed, as it was wont to do during rainstorms. "Could have been some of the medicine, too," Ben added. "I don't know."

The crowd began to disperse. A few of her patients tried to comfort Amelia, but most echoed the common sentiment that if anything had to burn, it was lucky it was an empty building. Fires, they pointed out, were as much a part of life in Alaska as snow and mosquitoes.

An empty building. That was all it was to most of them. It was not a dream now reduced to rubble. Though the sky was light, the smoke clouds gone, the smell of fire lingered, as Amelia knew it would. She walked around the shell of what had been her clinic, trying to salvage some of the contents.

"Over here, Amelia." William stood near what had been a corner of the building. His hair was mussed, his face and hands covered with soot, his clothes grimy. Amelia knew she must look the same, but surely her expression was not as grim. Though he had been one of the first on the scene and had worked tirelessly in the futile attempt to save Amelia's dream, this was the first time they had spoken.

"Did you leave that here?" William asked, pointing to the

charred remains of a five-gallon oilcan. Even with the label missing, the shape was unmistakable.

"No," she said, puzzled by the can. What was it doing here? "I don't use much, so I buy oil in one-gallon containers."

William's lips thinned, and he drew her aside where his next words would not be overheard. "I can't prove it, but I'd say that's what caused the fire. The oil was spilled and lighted."

Amelia looked from William to what was left of the clinic, then back again, and the horrible dread that had wakened her grew more intense. She had thought nothing could have been worse than seeing the clinic burn. Now she knew she was wrong. "Someone did this deliberately." Her voice was flat, as though she did not want to admit the truth of her words, but she knew this was no nightmare; it was reality.

"Looks like it."

She gripped William's arm, her eyes filled with anguish. "How could they? How could anyone destroy the clinic?" Though it was truly unthinkable, someone had done this. Someone she knew. Assailed by another thought, she asked, "What if patients had been there? They would have died. Oh, William, why would anyone do this?"

It was a question that haunted her days and nights, making her inattentive during the day, waking her only minutes after she had fallen into a disturbed sleep. If the fire was not an accident, and she knew William was right in his assessment, then there was only one reason for the arson, and that saddened her as much as the loss of the clinic. The people who had opposed her treating Indians had chosen violent means to stop her. She would never be able to prove it, but in her heart, Amelia knew she was right.

The question now was, how could she continue to live and work in Gold Landing, surrounded by hatred?

William worried about her. A week had passed since the night they had stood together in the ruined clinic, talking about prejudice. He had seen her only briefly since then, but every time he had, she looked worse. The spring had disappeared from her step, and she walked like an old woman now, her shoulders stooped as though she bore the weight of the world. William understood grieving. He had done his share when Polly had died, but that had been different. Polly had been a person; this was a building.

"It can be rebuilt," he told Amelia as he joined her at the end of her rounds. In the past she would have greeted him with a smile. Today Amelia barely acknowledged him.

She faced him, her cheeks pale, her expression so despairing that it wrenched his heart to look at her. "No," she said simply.

"But it can, Amelia. My men and I'll do it. We'll have a new clinic before the snow flies." It would be difficult, but he would do it. He would do anything to chase the pain from Amelia's face.

She shook her head slowly. "I know you mean well, and I appreciate that." The words came out sounding as colorless as her face. "I don't want another clinic."

The rumor mill had told him that, but he had not believed it. "Why not? The town needs a clinic. You convinced us of that last year, so what's changed that you don't want me to rebuild it?"

She was silent for a moment, as though considering his question. "I guess I'm the one who's changed. Didn't you tell me that I was too idealistic and needed to face reality?" Her laugh held no mirth. "I've faced reality, and I don't much like what I've seen."

That was something William could understand. Lord knew, there were days when he wished there were a way to avoid the harsh truth that the world was a less than perfect place, but he had learned to live with the imperfection, not run from it.

"It was only one person—maybe two—who were responsible for the fire. Are you going to judge the whole town based on them?"

Her head snapped up, and this time when she spoke, he saw life in her eyes. They blazed as hot as the fire that had destroyed her clinic, and William feared that the aftermath would be the same: total ruin. He could not let that happen. There had to be a way to help Amelia.

"I don't know that it was only one or two people," she said, her voice telling William that this was the source of her pain. "Don't forget that the nonwhite motion was defeated by only two votes. That means that almost half this town hates the Indians. Maybe one or two people spilled the oil and lighted it, but how do I know that a hundred didn't plan the fire?"

"Wait a minute." William held up a cautionary hand. "Just because someone voted against the motion doesn't mean they would burn the clinic. It doesn't even mean they hate Indians. I voted against it, and I sure as hell didn't burn that building."

"But you hate Indians, don't you?"

He couldn't deny it.

Chapter Seventeen

Gradually the pain subsided. Though it was there, reappearing at unpredictable intervals, it was no longer a constant part of her life. She could go whole hours without thinking of the clinic. Someone—perhaps William—had removed the charred remains. Now the only reminder that there once had been a building on that lot was the scorched earth. Eventually Mother Nature would heal the scar; in the meantime, bare ground was easier to accept than charred timbers.

Amelia knew the healing process would have been longer had it not been for Abe. He alone of her friends never talked about the clinic, never asked how she was feeling. He simply acted as though nothing unusual had happened. They met for their weekly dinners, just as they always had. They discussed books and the libretto from the opera Abe received each week. Somehow he seemed to sense when she most needed companionship, and he was there. Though some of the citizens of Gold Landing might regard him with scorn, Amelia knew Abe for what he was: a true friend.

Amelia finished bandaging Vera Kane's burned hand and accepted the widow's offer of a glass of iced tea. She had just settled back in her chair when the older woman leaned across the kitchen table and asked, "So, when is the wedding?"

For a moment Amelia looked at her blankly. "Whose wedding?" She could not recall any recent engagements.

Vera chuckled as she patted Amelia's hand. "Why, yours, of course. I heard you were going to marry Abe Ferguson."

Amelia gripped her glass as she stared at the window. Abe? People thought she was going to marry Abe? She started to bristle, then forced herself to relax. Everyone knew Vera Kane's primary topic of conversation was marriage. If she could not convince Ben to marry her—and it appeared she had been unsuccessful with that plan—she would turn her

238

hand to matchmaking. Besides, gossip was one of the favorite pastimes of the townspeople, and there had been little cause for speculation once people decided they'd never know who had started the clinic fire.

"Abe and I are friends," Amelia said simply, hoping that would satisfy Vera.

It did not. "The way I heard it, you're a lot closer than that."

This time Amelia did bristle. "I'm afraid your sources are wrong. Abe and I are just friends."

In all the time she had spent with Abe, he had never shown her anything other than common courtesy and friendship. Except, of course, for that day on the tundra when he had kissed her. But since he had never alluded to that, she knew that it had affected him as little as it had her. Although they shared many interests and enjoyed each other's company, they were not in love.

That evening as they sat at the kitchen table, Ella cut a piece of pot roast and laid it on her plate. "The rumor mill hasn't been this active since you came to town," she said.

Amelia laid down her fork, her appetite disappearing. After her discussion with Vera Kane that afternoon, she had a good idea what Ella was going to say, and it was not a topic she wanted to discuss.

"People are actually betting on your wedding date." Ella confirmed Amelia's fears. Though she suspected Ella had been one of the last to be included, the fact that she knew about the rumors told Amelia speculation was rife. It was not a pleasant thought, for it meant that her dinners with Abe would become awkward affairs as everyone watched them and tried to guess when their nonexistent nuptials would occur.

"They can bet on anything they want." The words came out more sharply than Amelia had intended. She tempered her next statement with a smile. "The simple fact is, I'm not getting married."

It was Ella's turn to smile. "That's what you say now." She buttered a biscuit, then continued, "It hasn't escaped the eagle eyes of Gold Landing's matrons that you and Abe have been together more often than usual these past few weeks. Besides, Abe would be a good husband.''

Amelia pushed the green beans from one side of her plate to the other, as if that would restore her appetite. "I agree," she said at last. "Abe will be a wonderful husband. Just not for me."

Ella looked up, surprised. "Why not? You two have so much in common."

The window was open. Outside a bird trilled, and Amelia heard children playing. It was an ordinary day in Gold Landing. It was only she who found this conversation so unusual and so unsettling.

"Abe and I have a lot in common," she admitted. "I enjoy his company very much, but that does not mean I'm going to marry him."

Ella paused, obviously considering Amelia's declaration. She laid her fork and knife down, and Amelia suspected she was not the only one who had lost her appetite.

"I think you're making a mistake, Amelia," Ella said. Her lips thinned, and the look she gave Amelia was so disapproving that Amelia understood why Ella had few discipline problems in her schoolroom. "You'll never find a better husband than Abe."

But Amelia was not a schoolgirl to be chastened. "Haven't you heard what I said?" She knew her voice was harsher than she had intended when Ella flinched, yet she continued. They needed to resolve this today. "I'm not going to marry *anyone*. Besides, Abe hasn't asked me."

"He will."

He did.

It was their usual night for dinner and, as they often did during the summer, they walked along the river after they had finished eating. In the past, Amelia had enjoyed the stroll. Tonight, though, mindful of the gossip that was so rampant, she felt awkward. Curse the rumor mill! She wasn't going to let it or anything else destroy her friendship with Abe.

And yet she had to admit that the gossip had already affected her. Perhaps it was only her imagination, but their dinner conversation had seemed a little constrained, and she had been aware of curious looks from the other diners. In all likelihood, people had been giving her and Abe the same speculative glances for weeks; the only difference was that tonight she was aware of them.

As for Abe, he seemed preoccupied. Though they talked about the opera, his attention wandered, and she had had to remind him twice that this week's libretto was *Barber of Seville,* not *Madame Butterfly.* Something was definitely wrong. But now, thank goodness, they were out of the hotel. Surely they would be more at ease now.

They walked slowly, talking about inconsequential things. When they reached the bend in the river, without warning Abe dropped to his knees in front of her. "Amelia, I love you. Will you make me the happiest man on earth by becoming my wife?"

Abe wanted to marry her? Though the rumor mill had foretold it, she had not believed it was true. Abe was her friend, her very dear friend. But her lover? No. Surely he knew that. Aware of the picture they made and the rumors that Abe's kneeling would generate, she tugged on his hand, urging him to his feet. "I love you, too," she said softly, "but . . ."

Abe interrupted, grasping both of her hands. "Then you'll marry me."

Amelia looked past Abe at the swiftly flowing river. Though normally the sight of the current soothed her, reminding her of the constancy of nature, today she derived no pleasure from it. She had believed her friendship with Abe to be like the river, changing forms with the seasons but remaining basically immutable. Abe's proposal changed all that, and she feared that their friendship would not withstand her refusal. For refuse she must. Though she would do almost anything to avoid hurting him, she could not marry Abe. Somehow she had to find the words to convince him he was mistaken, that they were friends, good friends, best of friends, but nothing more.

"Oh, Abe, I wish there were an easy way to say this." She tried to free her hands, but Abe would not let go. "I care about you. Truly I do, and I wouldn't hurt you for anything on earth, but I can't marry you.''

Abe blinked so rapidly that Amelia wondered if he was fighting tears. Surely not. Surely she hadn't caused him that much pain. ''You said you loved me.''

The cracking of Abe's voice sent a stab of pain through Amelia. This was far worse than she had dreamed possible, having to hurt a man she cared for as much as she did for Abe.

''I do love you,'' she said as gently as she could, ''but as a friend, not a husband.''

His face brightened. ''Friendship can grow into love, Amelia. That's what happened to me. I didn't plan to fall in love with you. It just happened.'' Abe pressed her hands to his lips and kissed them. ''Marry me, and I'll make you love me.''

Amelia shook her head. Tonight was turning into a nightmare. No matter what she said, Abe was going to be hurt. But she could not marry him.

''Abe, a marriage like that wouldn't be fair to you. You deserve a wife who can give you her whole heart, and I can't do that. Eventually we wouldn't be friends anymore.''

Amelia swallowed deeply, trying to keep her composure even though she saw the now unmistakable tears in Abe's eyes. ''It's better this way,'' she said softly. ''Someday you'll meet a woman who loves you the way you should be loved.''

Abe released her hands, but though his shoulders slumped, he kept his eyes fixed on her. ''I don't want another woman,'' he said, his voice filled with emotion. ''I only want you, and I'll take whatever piece of you you can give me.''

Tears filled Amelia's eyes. ''I wish I could love you that way, but I can't. Oh, Abe, I'm so sorry.''

''I heard you lost the bet.'' Jake Bolton swung his pick at the hard earth.

A few yards away, Chet Wing shoveled rock into a cart. ''The way I hear it, we all lost.''

It was a mistake working near Chet and Jake. Although they were good miners, they talked too much, and today William had no desire to listen to his men chattering like a bunch of birds. He growled, but neither man paid him any attention.

"You sure it's true?" Jake asked.

Chet's grunt sounded like an affirmation. "You seen him lately? I never saw the man so ornery. Thought he was gonna take a swing at me this morning, and all I did was say 'hello.' "

Jake chuckled. "I heard they didn't have dinner together yesterday. Bet that's why he was so riled."

As he recognized the subject of his men's speculation, William's scowl turned into a grin. Even though it was raining, it looked like today might be a good day after all.

"So, what's going on?" he asked.

Without breaking the rhythm of his strokes, Jake said, "It's what's *not* goin' on that we're talking about."

This was getting better by the second. "Okay. So, what's not going on?" William stared at the rock as though the only thing that mattered was whether his drill brought out ore. If either Jake or Chet realized how interested he was in their tale, he would never live it down.

"I heard old Abe popped the big question." It was Chet who answered, but Jake who finished the explanation.

"Reckon Dr. Sheldon gave him the wrong answer."

William bent his head, lest the men see his widening grin. No one—least of all the biggest busybodies in the mine—needed to know that Amelia had given Abe precisely the right answer, or that William's heart was pounding faster than it had the day he pulled Ben out of the river.

Instead he said, "That's a real shame."

Jake appeared to miss the sarcasm in William's words. "You can say that again. I was counting on the money from the pool."

"So how come the lady doctor turned him down?" Chet asked. "Anyone know that?"

For the first time, Jake put down his pick. "Hey, fellas, what do you say?" He called to the men who were working a few yards away. "Wanna start a pool to see who guesses the answer?"

The enthusiasm with which William wielded the drill had nothing to do with the prospect of a new pool. So Amelia had refused the honorable Abe Ferguson's offer of marriage. There could be a dozen reasons, as his men were speculating. But maybe, just maybe, there was only one. And maybe it was the right one.

The only way he would know was to ask her. That was the tricky part. He couldn't just walk up to her and say, "So, tell me, Dr. Sheldon, why did you make that miserable excuse of a lawyer even more miserable than normal?" No, he couldn't do that. Amelia was a woman, and a man could not forget that women preferred a gentler approach.

William grinned. He knew what he would do.

That evening he paid a visit to his cousin's house. As he entered the kitchen, he sniffed. "Something sure smells good, Karen."

She smiled and offered him a piece of peach pie. "Mighty good." William made a show of cleaning the last flake of crust from his plate. "Almost as good as those chocolate cakes of yours."

As Alex entered the kitchen, his daughter cradled in his good arm, he raised an eyebrow, then handed the baby to William. "What's the occasion?"

William ignored him, talking instead to Hannah, who fixed her blue eyes on his face as though she understood his words.

Karen laughed. "Your cousin seems to have a hankering for home-baked chocolate cake. At least I think I just heard a not-so-subtle request for one."

William plastered an innocent expression on his face. "I thought your wife might take pity on a helpless bachelor," he said.

Alex groaned. "Go ahead, honey. If you don't, we're likely to have the man here every night, and then I'll never get a chance to hold Hannah. Lord knows what the tyke sees in an ornery critter like him."

"Charm, Alex, charm. It works on the ladies every time."

But it was a man whom William approached next. "I'm

getting mighty tired of my own cooking," he confessed to Herb Ashton as he paid for his purchases. "A man can only eat so many canned beans." He pointed to the ten cans that were lined up on the counter. "Lately I've been having a hankering for potato salad, but that doesn't come in tins. Do you suppose your wife would show me how she makes hers?" William asked the question as if the thought had just occurred to him.

Herb leaned on the counter. "Maybe on her deathbed. Sorry, William, but she guards that recipe closer than the gold in Fort Knox." When William's face reflected disappointment, Herb thought for a moment longer. "I might be able to convince her to make some for you."

"Every week?"

"Don't press your luck. Even I don't get it that often."

Thursday morning, William collected the chocolate cake, potato salad, fried chicken and biscuits he had persuaded Gold Landing's matrons to provide. By midafternoon, he was ready. Swinging the picnic basket from one hand, he climbed the hill outside of town. If all went well, he would have his answer today. Before the sun set, he would know why Amelia had declined what Gold Landing considered a great honor: the opportunity to become Mrs. Abe Ferguson.

"Hello, Amelia." As he had planned, she had finished her rounds and was heading home. One of the many things he liked about Amelia was that she was predictable. When she was on her rounds, she walked quickly, as if an extra minute reaching a patient would make the difference between life and death. But once she had visited the last one, her pace slowed to a stroll and she would look around her, as if suddenly aware that she was walking through some of the most beautiful land God had created.

"Thank goodness I found you." William laid the basket on the ground and faced Amelia. She was wearing her usual dark skirt and white shirtwaist, and today she had a little straw hat perched on top of her head. Her eyes were as blue as ever, and her cheeks as rosy as could be. As for those lips . . . William pushed that thought firmly aside. "I was hoping you would take pity on me."

Just as he had planned, Amelia laughed. "Pity is the last thing you need, William."

He shook his head. "Save your judgment until you've heard my tale of woe." He pointed to the basket. "The women of Gold Landing must have decided that I'm malnourished. Food just keeps appearing at my house. Good stuff, judging by the smell, but it'll spoil before I can eat it all, and you know I can't insult the ladies by throwing it out." He gave Amelia his most persuasive grin. "I thought maybe you could help me eat some of it."

She looked from William to the basket and back again. "I suppose it's pure coincidence that you happened to have the food with you."

It looked like his strategy was a sound one. She was doing exactly what he had hoped she would. Now, if only his luck continued.

"As a matter of fact, that was deliberate. I figured it would be harder for you to say no this way."

Amelia laughed. "You were right. I won't say no."

William picked up the basket, and they walked for a few minutes until they reached the spot along the stream where he had first shown her the tundra flowers. When he spread a blanket, Amelia knelt on the edge, peering at the tundra. Lord, she was beautiful! Tendrils of that dark hair had escaped from her pompadour to lie softly on her neck. It took every ounce of self-control William possessed not to brush the errant locks aside and kiss her neck.

"I remember the first time you did that," William said softly.

She turned and smiled at him, her expression so sweet that his heart threatened to break through his chest. "It was almost a year ago," she said.

"A lot has changed since then. You're no longer a *chee-chako*; now you're a sourdough."

Amelia was silent, her smile fading until she looked not quite sad, but nostalgic. Hell, he hadn't meant to make her sad. Bringing her here was supposed to remind her of happy times. If he lived to be a hundred, he would never understand women and the way their minds worked.

This probably wasn't the right time to ask her. Maybe he ought to wait. Then again, maybe there would never be a right time. The only thing that was certain was that he had to know.

"I heard a rumor," William said, "and I wondered if it was true."

Amelia sat upright, her expression unreadable. The breeze stirred her few loose strands of hair, once again tempting William to touch her. He clenched his fists.

"What rumor?" Amelia asked.

"That Abe asked you to marry him, and you said no."

Her eyes looked sad, and for a moment William thought the gossipmongers were wrong. Then she said, "It's true."

Elation filled his veins. It was true! She was not going to marry Abe! And yet her voice had sounded sad, as though she regretted the decision.

She had answered one of his questions; now came the second, even more important one. Softly William asked, "Why won't you marry him?"

He had thought she might be reluctant to tell him. He had even considered that she might refuse to answer at all. What he had not anticipated was what she did. Amelia jumped to her feet, clearly agitated. "Don't tell me the same thing everyone else in Gold Landing does! I couldn't bear it," she cried. Twin spots of color rose to her cheeks as she clenched her fists. "I'm tired of hearing that Abe is the perfect husband for me."

The hope that had been growing deep inside him began to flower. Slowly, carefully, he said, "That's the last thing I'd tell you, Amelia. I don't believe Abe's the right man for you."

She looked at him for a moment, as if trying to assess the meaning behind his words. He met her gaze and hoped his eyes did not reflect the excitement he could feel building within him. "Then we're in agreement," she said at last.

He waited until she had relaxed her hands before he continued. "Is that why you refused Abe, because he wasn't per-

247

fect?'' She probably thought he was prying, and that he was like the other busybodies, seeking to satisfy idle curiosity. She had no way of knowing how important her answers were to him.

"Perfection has nothing to do with it. Abe's a wonderful man.''

Wonderful, but she would not marry him?

"Then why . . . ?''

William saw the confusion on her face, and he sensed that she was battling some inner demon, trying to make a decision. *Please, Amelia, tell me,* he exhorted her silently. But she said nothing, just kept looking at him with those blue eyes that were now clouded.

A bird flew out of the bushes, its wings beating even faster than William's heart as he waited for her reply. With a small sigh, Amelia tipped her head to watch the bird's flight. Only when it had disappeared from view did she turn back to him. Her eyes were once more clear, her expression resolute, and suddenly he did not want to hear her answer. How would he bear it if she destroyed his dream?

"If you must know,'' she said finally, "the reason I won't marry Abe is that it wouldn't be fair to him. I can't marry him when I love you.''

William stared, unable to believe his ears. "What did you say?'' he asked. His words sounded embarrassingly like a croak. Could it be true? William had never believed in miracles, but it looked as if he might have to reconsider.

As he reached forward to take Amelia's hands in his, she stepped back. "Don't you dare laugh at me, William. I didn't want it to happen.'' She took another step away from him. "You're the last man on earth I thought I'd fall in love with. But I did.''

It was true! Joy rushed through him, leaving him more light-headed than his first drink of whiskey had. Amelia loved him! Dreams *could* come true.

With one long stride William reached her and drew her into his arms. He touched her hair gently, then cupped her chin, turning her face toward his. "I'm not laughing at you, Amelia.

I only asked you to repeat your words because I couldn't believe they were true.'' His finger traced the contours of her face, then lingered on her lips, and all the while his heart thudded, sounding as loud as a miner's pick. ''I didn't think you could love me. I'm not educated like Abe. I don't know anything about ballets or operas.''

''As if that mattered!'' Amelia's eyes sparkled as they met his gaze. ''You're ornery and opinionated and far too sure of yourself. So am I.'' When she laughed, William was certain there was no sweeter sound on earth. ''We're probably too much alike, but I don't care. The fact is, I love you in spite of—or maybe because of—what you consider your shortcomings.''

''Oh, Amelia.'' William could wait no more. He wrapped his arms around her, pressing her against the length of his body, then lowered his lips to hers. When they were both breathless, he ended the kiss. ''Say you'll marry me.''

Amelia shook her head and tears filled her eyes. ''My love, I can't.''

Chapter Eighteen

"What do you mean?" As she watched, the blood drained from William's face, and confusion clouded those gray eyes that she loved so much. "You've just told me you love me." William shook his head as if to clear it. "Why won't you marry me?"

Amelia closed her eyes, wishing she were somewhere—anywhere—else. She had known it would not be easy, telling a man why she couldn't marry, but she had never dreamed it would be so difficult. The reality was worse than anything she had imagined, and it was all because of William. When she had thought about marriage in the past, it had been to a nameless, faceless man. Now that the man had a name and a face, the thought of giving up a life with him was more painful than her worst nightmares.

"I can't marry anyone," she said simply.

Another bird flew by, its cry so plaintive that Amelia wondered whether it had lost its mate. It was nonsense, of course. Only she was fixated on mating.

William stared at her, clearly perplexed by her statement. Finally he asked, "You're not already married, are you?"

The thought was so preposterous that Amelia might have laughed if the situation had been less grave. "Of course I'm not married," she replied.

"Then why won't you marry me?"

That was the question, the one that kept her awake at night and caused her so much heartache. If only there were an easy answer.

"Because I love you too much."

William grabbed Amelia's forearms, and for a second she thought he was going to shake her. "You're not making sense, woman. Now, what's going on? What kind of a game is this? Either you love me or you don't. And don't give me any of that nonsense about loving too much. That's not possible."

Amelia blinked back her tears. Maybe she should follow her mother's advice and say nothing to William, pretend that she did not know. But Amelia knew her conscience would not permit that. She could not lie, especially not to William.

"This is no game, William," she said slowly. "You deserve a whole woman."

His eyes moved slowly from the crown of her head to her toes. "You sure look like a whole woman to me."

If only!

"As a physician, I have to tell you that appearances can be deceptive. On the outside, I look fine. It's what is inside that's the problem."

The little remaining color left William's face, and his eyes widened in shock. He pulled her into his arms with a motion that seemed almost a reflex action. "Don't tell me you have some incurable disease," he said fiercely as he tipped her face toward his. His fingers were rough and callused, and Amelia was certain she had never felt anything as wonderful as their touch on her face. "I couldn't bear to lose you," William said fiercely.

Amelia laid a comforting hand on his cheek. "I'm not going to die anytime soon," she told him, although her heart ached so much she almost believed death would be a relief. When he muttered, "Thank God," she swallowed deeply, then forced herself to utter the words that had caused her incalculable pain since she had first heard them. "I can't have children."

Surely there should have been thunder, lightning and torrents of rain to match the tumult in her heart. But the day remained sunny and cool with only a light breeze.

Though William said nothing, she watched his eyes darken as the import of her words registered. "William, I know how much you want children and what a good father you would be. I've seen you with Hannah and Theo." And, oh, how that wrenched her heart. "That's why I can't marry you. I won't let you settle for less than you deserve."

William continued to stare at her, and she sensed he was

trying to marshal his emotions. A muscle in his cheek twitched, distorting the scar. "I've always wanted children," he said at last. "That's true. I would be lying if I said children didn't matter or that I wanted a marriage without them."

"I know that. That's why—"

He laid a finger across her lips. "Let me finish. You said you wanted to be fair to me and make sure I had what I deserved. Do you really mean that?"

"Of course I do. I love you, William, and I want you to be happy."

"Do you?" He raised one brow. "Would you ask me to marry someone I didn't love just to have a child? Is that what I deserve—a loveless marriage?"

"You know I don't mean that, but children are an important part of marriage."

For the first time since she had refused his proposal, William smiled. "You won't get an argument from me on that. I definitely want children to be part of our marriage. But Amelia, there are other ways if you can't bear a child."

He released her, then sank to the blanket. "Come here, sweetheart," he said, pulling her onto his lap and cradling her in his arms. "There are children already born who need parents. We could adopt one. Look at me." When she did, she saw that his eyes reflected the sorrow she had seen in them so many times. "Where would I be if Polly hadn't taken me in? She didn't give birth to me, but Polly sure as summer sun was my mother."

Amelia shook her head. William's argument was persuasive; she had played it in her mind a thousand times. The problem was, she did not believe it was the answer. Not for William. Though some men might be content with adoption, William was not one of them. Amelia knew how deeply he felt the lack of a father and how much he wanted to give a son everything that had been missing from his own life.

"You think you would be happy with an adopted child, and maybe you would be for a while. But eventually you would resent me because I was the reason you didn't have your own child." Amelia's voice broke as she confessed her worst fear.

"William, I could not bear to watch your love die."

He pulled her closer and pressed his lips to her neck. "How can you think that would happen? It wouldn't. Amelia, I love you. You, not your womb. I do not want to marry anyone else, even if she could give me a hundred children." His voice was fierce, his eyes dark with emotion. "How many times do I have to tell you? I want to marry you, even if you'll never bear me a child."

He sounded so sure of himself. But that was William, supremely self-confident and convinced that he knew best. It would be wonderful if it were true. For a moment Amelia let herself hope. Then reality intruded.

"You say that now."

"And I'll be saying it for the next thirty years. Marry me, Amelia."

Oh, how she wanted to! The spark of hope that refused to be extinguished flared again. William had not reacted the way she had expected. She had thought that when he learned she was barren, he would agree they could not marry. But he hadn't. Maybe her mother was wrong. Maybe she was wrong. Maybe . . .

"It's a big decision, William. You need to think it through carefully."

William made a show of staring into the distance for five seconds. "I've considered it. I still want to marry you."

She could not help it. Amelia smiled. The man was incorrigible, impossible and utterly lovable. "I want you to be very sure this is what you want from your life."

"I'm sure."

This time Amelia placed her fingers on William's lips. "Listen to me, William. I won't let you make a hasty decision that you might regret for the rest of your life. You need time to think about it and be sure you'll be happy."

"I'm sure."

Amelia smiled. "I hope you're right. If you still feel the same in a year, I'll marry you."

"I will. I've already told you I won't change my mind, so why are we waiting?"

"Because I'm just as stubborn as you, and I said we had to wait."

"Six months."

"A year."

"Nine months."

"A year."

"You won't give up, will you?" William grinned. "Well, neither will I."

Amelia met his smile with one of her own. "Then we'll marry next June."

"Oh, Amelia, I swear there's no one who could love you more than I do."

William pressed his lips to hers, sealing their engagement as lovers have throughout the ages. This was no gentle kiss but rather a fierce declaration of their decision. His lips plundered hers, his tongue invading the sweet recesses of her mouth, sending waves of warmth coursing through her veins. Amelia stretched one arm around his waist, drawing him closer to her, while she traced the contours of his face with her other hand.

This was William, her beloved, the man who had haunted her dreams for so many months. Though she had not believed it possible, somehow, despite everything, it looked as though those dreams might come true. Who said that miracles didn't happen?

With a groan, William wrenched his lips from hers. "I will not change my mind," he said, his voice hoarse with passion. "Ours will be a wedding no one in Gold Landing will ever forget."

"There's never been a party like this," Ella told Ben as she looked around in wonder. William had spared no expense for his engagement party. He had ordered a huge tent and colored lanterns from Fairbanks, a band from Anchorage. The flowers, great masses of red, pink and white roses, had come all the way from Portland, Oregon. And the food had been shipped in from so many different ports that even Herb Ashton had lost count. All Herb could report was that William had been adamant. No one in Gold Landing was to work in any way, form or fashion on the day of the party. That, rather than disdain for the goods and services available in Gold Landing, had been the reason he had ordered everything from outside. Today was a day of celebration, pure and simple.

And celebrate they did. The party had started at high noon with a feast of gargantuan proportions, followed by an afternoon of games for all ages, designed, or so Herb had alleged, to counteract the effects of the midday meal so that the guests could enjoy dinner. Now that dinner was concluded and the children were drifting to sleep on quilts in one corner of the tent, the dancing had begun.

"I've never seen William looking so happy." Ben frowned. "Poor fool. He doesn't know what he's getting into, or he sure as hell wouldn't be celebrating."

Ella bristled. You would think Ben could shed his cynicism—or at least hide it—for one day and let Amelia and William enjoy their party. "Not everyone shares your opinion that marriage is a mistake." If her voice sounded tart, it was no more than Ben deserved.

He peered over his glasses, staring at her as if she were a specimen under his microscope. Oh, no! Would he notice that she had finally listened to Amelia and shortened her skirts? It felt so odd, not having them touch the ground. But surely Ben had not noticed. Amelia had assured her that men did not pay attention to that sort of thing.

Apparently she was right, for when he had completed his study, Ben said only, "I don't see·you rushing into wedded bliss."

As the band began to play a Strauss waltz, Ella's foot started to tap, keeping time with the music as she had taught her pupils to do.

"There's a difference between us," she told Ben. "I'm not opposed to marriage; I simply haven't found the right man."

He gave her another appraising look. "And what kind of man would that be? Surely not one like Larry Wilson."

Ella blushed. Trust Ben to embarrass her by talking about Larry. At least the man was no longer in Gold Landing. He had left town suddenly a week after they had broken their engagement, telling no one where he was going or why he was leaving. Since Larry had few close friends, no one worried overly much about his destination, but his clandestine departure had provoked half a dozen contradictory explanations of why he had left. Ella hadn't cared why; she was simply relieved that he was gone. And now Ben was reminding her of him.

She smiled a greeting at Bertha Langdon as she and the reverend waltzed by, then turned her attention back to Ben. At least her cheeks had cooled.

"The man I marry will be kind, patient, a good provider, and he'll love children." Ella ticked off the items on her fingers.

"Children, huh? That leaves me out of the running."

The nerve of the man! As if she had ever considered him in that light. "You were never *in* the running, Ben, so you can't be out of it now." As Ben raised his eyebrows in that condescending way he seemed to have perfected, Ella continued. "Maybe I should have added a fifth criterion: I want a man who doesn't rely on whiskey to solve his problems."

The barb hit home, for his lips thinned with barely concealed anger. "And if I were going to remarry, I would want a woman with warm blood in her veins, not ice water like yours."

She had only meant to needle him, but he obviously sought to wound. He succeeded. "What makes you think my blood isn't warm?" Ella asked.

Ben shrugged. "You don't do things that normal folks do."

That hurt. Oh, how it hurt to have him say that she was not like other women. "What sort of things don't I do?"

"You don't dance. Look around, Ella. Everyone else in town is out there, kicking up their heels to the best music Gold Landing has ever heard, and you're standing here like a wallflower."

The band switched from the smooth sound of a waltz to a turkey trot's faster pace. Ella watched Amelia dancing with William, her sapphire skirts swirling, and she felt a stab of envy. It must be wonderful to move so gracefully.

"There's a reason I don't dance," she told Ben.

"Yeah, I know. You don't approve. Your puritanical background has you convinced that anything that's as much fun as dancing must be a sin. Right?"

"Wrong." She wasn't sure why she bothered explaining to him, but somehow it seemed important that Ben understand. "It's not that I disapprove," she said. "The reason I don't dance is a lot simpler than that. I don't know how."

"Everyone knows how."

Ella shook her head. "I don't." It was not necessary to tell Ben she had never learned to dance because the mere thought of a boy touching her used to make her physically ill.

"Do you want to learn?" Ben peered over the top of his spectacles. It was odd, but she thought he looked a little wistful. That was not an adjective she had ever associated with Ben Taylor.

Though it was a lie, Ella shook her head, while her foot continued to keep time with the music.

Ben gave her another appraising look, his gaze lingering on her foot. "Tell you what. I'll make you a bargain. We'll go outside the tent where no one can see us, and I'll teach you to dance, but only if you agree to come back here and dance with me."

As the turkey trot ended, Ella felt a momentary panic. "In front of everyone?" How was she going to learn to dance well enough that she would not embarrass herself and Ben?

"In front of everyone." Though the lanterns provided subdued lighting, Ella could still see the twinkle in Ben's eyes.

"Are you sure it won't hurt your leg?" She wasn't simply searching for an excuse. He had limped ever so slightly since the cast had been removed, and Ella did not know whether he should dance.

"My leg will be fine. It's your courage that seems to be lacking." Ben smiled, his brown eyes as mischievous as one of her pupils'. "What's it gonna be, Ella? Do we have a deal?"

Ella tipped her head, considering. "All right," she agreed,

"but I have a bargain of my own. Instead of one, I'll dance two dances with you if you agree not to take another drink tonight."

"Starting now?"

It was worth it, just to see the horrified expression on Ben's face. She nodded.

"You drive a hard bargain, lady."

Ella smiled smugly. "Take it or leave it."

"I'll take it."

He was right. Dancing was fun. Oh, there were awkward moments when she forgot which direction her feet were supposed to be moving and others when, even though she knew where they were supposed to go, her feet somehow landed on top of Ben's shoes. But the moments in between were glorious. She felt as though she were a bird drifting through the air when Ben swung her around. And when he pulled her close to him as the music slowed, she was filled with such a sense of belonging that her face flushed, and she could feel her pulse grow erratic.

It had to be magic. Nothing else could explain the way she felt.

"It must be magic." As she twirled in William's arms, Amelia gazed around her. It was a tent. A big one, to be sure, but only a tent. The lanterns were ordinary paper ones, designed to cast a pretty glow, and the roses, although magnificent, were only flowers. The ingredients were all common. The effect was anything but. From the moment she had set foot inside the tent, she had felt as though she were a princess in a fairy tale and this was her happy ending. She was dancing with Prince Charming on a night that would never end.

"Magic? What do you mean?"

"This has been a perfect day. No one's gotten sick, not even a scraped knee."

William chuckled. "I don't think anyone would dare. They all know this is your day."

"Our day," she corrected. "But whether it was your threats

or magic, it's wonderful. I never realized I could be so happy.''

"You?" William pretended to scoff at her. "I'm the luckiest man alive."

Amelia curtsied, while William executed a deep bow, then drew her into his arms for the next dance. Though Ella had suggested Amelia order a new dress for the party, she had decided to wear the blue silk that she had first worn at Ella's party. It seemed somehow appropriate that she celebrate her engagement to William in the same gown she had worn when she met him. They had come so far!

"Everyone looks happy," Amelia said as they waltzed. "Oh!" Her eyes widened at the sight of the couple who had just entered the tent and started dancing. "Look, William." Somehow she managed to keep her feet moving in time to the music though her mind whirled in her surprise at what she saw. "Ella's dancing with Ben."

William raised a brow. "I didn't think she approved of dancing."

Ella's face flushed with exertion, but even from the other side of the tent, there was no mistaking her smile. It was one of pure happiness. There had to be a touch of magic in the air to make Ella look so happy.

"She told me she had never learned how to dance," Amelia said. "I offered to teach her, but she didn't seem interested."

William watched the couple execute the dance steps. "Looks like she's interested now."

"And look at Ben. He's staring at her as if he just discovered she was a woman."

William chuckled. "Maybe he—" Whatever William saw startled him enough that he lost his train of thought. "I didn't expect to see *him*."

Turning in time to the music, Amelia saw the reason for William's surprise. Abe, his face ashen, his eyes ringed with deep circles, stood in the entrance to the tent. Since the day she had refused his proposal, Amelia had seen him only from a distance, and no one had discussed him in her hearing. Poor

Abe! Tonight he looked like a man suffering from a terminal illness.

"Oh, William!"

He pulled her closer than the dance demanded and whispered fiercely, "Now, don't get all weepy. You picked the right man."

Her eyes sparkling with unshed tears, Amelia managed a smile. "I most certainly did."

It was one of the most difficult things he had ever done, coming to Amelia's engagement party. Damn it all! It should have been *their* party. For the life of him, Abe could not understand why she had agreed to marry William. It made no sense at all. She had turned *him* down, and then less than a week later she was engaged to that arrogant mine owner. Why?

Surely Amelia was not so impressed with the man's wealth that she could overlook the fact that he was crude, uneducated and patently incapable of carrying on a civilized conversation. Amelia wasn't shallow, and if money had mattered to her, she would not have come to Alaska. But if money wasn't the reason, what was? The whole thing was inexplicable, and that made it even more difficult to accept.

"Give me another drink." Abe held out his glass to the stranger who was tending bar. The only good thing he could say about the party was that the liquor was first-rate.

"It's a party, Abe. Can't you at least manage a smile?" Herb Ashton stood beside him.

Smiling was one thing Abe could not do. He had considered leaving Gold Landing, at least temporarily, but the thought of being branded a coward had been as distasteful as the prospect of seeing Amelia with William. Besides, if he stayed, there was always the possibility she would come to her senses. If the stories were true, they were not getting married for a year. That gave him twelve months to help her change her mind.

"Don't ruin Amelia's day. If you can't smile, go home." Though Herb kept his voice low, his words were more command than suggestion.

Abe emptied his glass, then turned away without a word.

He blinked once, then twice. Was that Ella Roberts dancing? And with Dr. Ben? The world really had turned upside down. Abe made his way across the dance floor and tapped Ben's shoulder. As he swung Ella into his arms, she made a moue of distaste.

"You've been drinking."

"How astute of you to notice." As Ella flinched from his sarcasm, Abe continued, "Surely in your vast experience of life, you must have smelled liquor before." Dimly, in the back of his mind, he knew he would regret his cruelty tomorrow, but tonight his pain was so great, all he wanted to do was inflict it on someone else. It was not fair that everyone else was happy when he was miserable.

"Go home, Abe." Ella's smile looked forced. "If you love Amelia, you won't spoil her day."

Love! How dare that old-maid schoolteacher talk to him about love? "What do you know of love?" he demanded. "You're nothing but a dried-up spinster."

Ella's smile faltered, and tears filled her eyes, ready to spill onto her cheeks. Good. Someone else was hurting.

Ella blinked and started to pull away, but Abe would not release her. One woman had rejected him; he was not about to let another compound his misery.

"Get out of here!" Seemingly from nowhere, Ben materialized at his side. Gripping Abe's shoulder, he propelled him outside the tent. The air was surprisingly cool. "Go home and sober up," Ben ordered, "but whatever you do, don't show your face here again."

As if he would come back! As he walked away, Abe heard Ben try to comfort Ella. "He didn't mean it," the doctor said. "It was just the liquor talking. Now, come back inside and dance with me."

He was not going home. No, sirree. There was nothing for him in that empty house except unhappy memories, and he sure as hell didn't need those. His feet moved, almost without conscious direction, turning onto Second Street, his pace quickening as he approached the house with the red and gold trim.

"Why, Abe, I'm surprised to see you here." Though Gloria's smile was welcoming, Abe could see the question in her eyes. So what if he had never been there before? There was a first time for everything.

"This visit is quite overdue," he said, trying to keep from slurring his words. He looked around the room, noting the velvet upholstery and the deep carpet. Gloria's house was more tastefully decorated than he had expected. A man, even an educated man such as himself, would feel comfortable here. "This is a mighty elegant establishment you've got," he said.

She smiled, and again Abe had the thought that she was assessing him, trying to determine why he had come tonight of all nights.

"We're not too busy this evening," she said. "Is there any special girl you would like to keep you company?"

Abe looked around. Though he had heard that Gloria employed a dozen girls, only three were in the parlor: a blonde, a brunette and one with fiery red curls. The brunette and the redhead flashed him sultry smiles. Although the blonde managed a smile, Abe could see the sadness in her eyes. Here was a woman who looked as miserable as he felt.

"That pretty blonde would suit my fancy," he told Gloria.

The blonde shook her head.

"I'm afraid she's not seeing gentlemen tonight," Gloria said. "But if it's blondes you fancy, I can call Susie."

Abe shook his head. "Perhaps I should have made my intentions clear. I'm interested in conversation tonight, nothing more."

Surely that was not pity he saw on Gloria's face. People admired Abe Ferguson. They envied him. They did not pity him.

As Gloria nodded, Abe took a seat next to the blonde. Close up she was prettier than he had thought, even though a man did not need a college degree to realize her smile was a fake. "What's your name?" he asked. Though she said she was not working, her dress was obviously designed to inflame a man's passions. Not that Abe cared. There was only one woman for him, and she wasn't a whore.

She kept her eyes on the floor. "June," she said with a faltering smile.

June. The name sounded familiar. Abe ordered drinks for both of them. Where had he heard that name? That's right. One of the miners had mentioned that when William frequented Gloria's house, it was June he visited. Abe looked at her again. So this was William's girl.

"I guess you don't feel much like celebrating tonight, do you?"

She shook her head and sat quietly while Abe gulped down his drink and ordered another.

The front door opened and three men entered the parlor. From the ease with which they moved around the fancy furniture and made their way to the bar, Abe guessed they were frequent visitors.

"A round for me and my friends!" The leader put his elbows on the bar and grinned. He was a short, stocky man whom Abe recognized as Jethro Mooney, one of the miners. When he and his companions held drinks in their hands, Jethro turned and raised his glass. "A toast to William, the best mine owner in all of Alaska, and his lovely bride-to-be!"

Abe glowered as the three men cheered and downed their drinks. He remained seated, his drink placed firmly on the table in front of him and June, while the other couples rose and joined the toast.

One of the men nudged Jethro and pointed at Abe.

"Say, man, what's the matter with you? How come you didn't toast with us?" Jethro glared at Abe.

For a moment Abe considered not answering. He owed no explanations, especially not to these uneducated boors. Then he said in his most condescending tone, "I don't care to celebrate the forthcoming nuptials."

"No, Abe." June put a hand on his arm. "Don't do this." Abe ignored her.

Jethro hooted and turned to his friends. "Did you hear those fancy words? Nup . . . nup . . . What was that word? 'Sore loser' is what I heard."

"That, sir, is your opinion." And if Jethro Mooney thought he cared one whit, he was sadly mistaken.

"Never could figure out what the lady doctor saw in you," Jethro sneered. "Now, William's a real man."

The cretin thought he had delivered an insult; that much was clear, even through the alcohol-induced fog that surrounded Abe.

"Feel free to impugn my manhood," he said with a magnanimous gesture. "I assure you, you would not be the first."

"Abe, please." He brushed June's hand aside.

Jethro's companions muttered something incomprehensible. The miner silenced them with a frown, then said, "Maybe I'll be the last." Grabbing his own full glass, he approached Abe. "Here." He shoved the glass at him. "Now drink a toast to William and Amelia."

Abe rose, towering over the miner. "Perhaps you are hard of hearing," he said. "Or is it only that you are slow to comprehend? I said no."

"And I said yes."

Afterward, no one was certain who swung first. All they knew was that one minute the two men were standing; the next they were on the floor, punching each other and shouting obscenities.

"Stop it!" June shrieked. An instant later the bartender had grabbed each man by the neck, separating them. Attracted by the commotion, Gloria entered the room. "Get out of here," she said in a voice that brooked no dissent.

Jethro and his companions swaggered toward the door as if a fistfight were a daily occurrence. Abe followed, limping slightly.

"Wait." June put her hand on Abe's arm. "I've got something that will help your face."

Abe could feel the blood oozing from a cut. "Thanks."

He followed June as she climbed the stairs and opened the door to a small room, furnished with a bed, a plain chest of drawers and a chair.

"Sit down," she said and motioned him toward the chair. While she cleaned his cuts and applied a soothing salve, she spoke. "You shouldn't have riled Jethro like that. He's one of the mean guys here—likes to use his fists."

"My face is testimony to that particular fact."

June smiled. "Your fancy words didn't help, either, but it sure was funny watching Jethro try to figure out what you were saying." She sat on the bed, facing Abe. "You should have drunk that toast, you know."

He looked at her, his eyes reflecting a pain that had nothing to do with the bruises he had sustained. "Would you have done it?"

She was silent for a moment, thinking. "No, I wouldn't. I guess we're in the same boat tonight." Two lonely people, suffering the loss of a dream. Slowly, deliberately, her hands reached for the first button on her dress. "Come here, Abe," she said and patted the bed. "Let's help each other forget."

He was a surprisingly gentle lover, caressing her skin, whispering fancy words in her ear, telling her she was beautiful. And for a few minutes, it worked. For a few minutes, she felt beautiful. For a few minutes, she was able to forget why she and Abe had drunk more than they should have. But when he reached his release, the fantasy shattered.

"Amelia, my love!"

Damn the woman! She thought she was so special, bewitching all the men in Gold Landing. June had tried every way she knew to get her to leave, but even burning down that clinic that she loved so much had not worked. She would find another way, and the next time, it would work.

Chapter Nineteen

"Oh, William, I don't want to go home." Amelia looked around the tent, now empty of everything except memories. The crew had dismantled the tables, and the extra food had been taken to the church hall, where it would be packaged and distributed to the unemployed miners on the other side of the river.

"I don't want the day to end," she said softly, laying her hand on William's arm and gazing at his beloved face. "This has been the most wonderful day of my life, and I want it to go on forever."

William smiled, his gray eyes sparkling with happiness. His hair was slightly mussed, and this time—away from prying eyes—Amelia indulged one of her fantasies, extending her hand to smooth it.

"If you think this is wonderful, wait until we're married. Then we won't have to say 'good night.' " As if to give her a taste of pleasures to come, he drew her into his arms and pressed his lips to hers. Amelia closed her eyes, indulging in the pure delight of being kissed by William. Sparks, brighter than the fireworks that had celebrated their engagement, appeared behind her eyelids, while the flames of desire raced through her veins. The lingering fragrance of roses mingled with William's own woodsy scent, surrounding Amelia as completely as his arms did. He was hers, now and forever!

William drew her closer, letting a soft groan escape when she opened her mouth to his sweet invasion. "Oh, Amelia, I want you so much," he said, his voice ragged with emotion. "How am I going to wait a year?"

Though their watches said almost midnight, the sky was still bright. Amelia stepped back a pace so that she could see William's expression. How would he react to her proposal? "Who said we had to wait?" Her voice was low and sultry.

William's eyes widened in surprise, and it was clear he had not expected that response. "You did."

"Yes, I did." She nodded. "I said we had to wait a year to *marry*." Amelia emphasized the last word, then watched as confusion clouded William's eyes. His arms tightened, drawing her back against him.

"I don't understand."

She smiled sweetly. "Yes, you do."

William shook his head. "Don't you want to save—" He broke off, obviously embarrassed by the direction the conversation was taking.

How odd! The man, though so worldly in many ways, had a conservative streak. How endearing!

"I thought that was important," he continued.

"Saving my virginity?" There, the word was out in the open. "Yes, it is important," Amelia agreed. "I was raised to believe that it was the finest gift a woman could give the man she loved. William," Amelia said softly, "you're the man I love. The gift is for you."

The smile that lit his face was almost blinding in its brilliance. "Then why are we waiting to marry?"

That was the question, the one he had asked her so many times.

"Marriage is different," she said. "It's forever and for children, and you already know I can give you only half of that." Tonight the pain seemed less intense, diminished at least momentarily by the sheer joy of their engagement. "Before we marry, I need to be sure you'll be happy with me the way I am. But I love you, William—only you. If I don't marry you, I won't marry at all." She put her hand on his arm again, willing him to understand what she was saying. "You're the only man I'll ever love."

His eyes blazed with love and the desire neither of them wanted to deny. "And you're the only woman I'll ever love."

Oh, how she hoped that would be enough! "Then why are we waiting?"

William groaned. "Don't make this any harder than it already is. I want you so much that it's taking every ounce of self-control I possess to keep from tossing you onto the ground.'' As if to underscore his words, William traced the lines of her cheek, then drew his fingers over her lips. "Your first time has to be perfect. You deserve a soft bed and candlelight—not dirt and colored lanterns. Besides, I can't expose you to gossip. I won't have your gift besmirched by wagging tongues.'' William pulled her close, and for a moment the only sound she heard was the pounding of his heart and his ragged breathing. "Give me a few days, Amelia. I'll find a way."

It was four days later, and, though Amelia hated to admit it, she was growing impatient. She had hardly seen William since their engagement party, and when she had seen him, he had seemed preoccupied. Fortunately, her practice demanded much of her attention during the day. It was the nights that were difficult, for she would toss for hours before falling asleep, and when she did sleep, it was fitfully, her rest disturbed by dreams of William.

Today was her day to visit the Indian village. She had saved Mrs. Gray Eyes until last, knowing she might require more time than her other patients. The young Indian woman's pregnancy had been a difficult one from the beginning.

"The pains are real bad, Doctor,'' the woman said as Amelia examined her.

Amelia frowned. "You're having contractions. This baby's impatient."

"But it's too early."

That was the problem. According to Mrs. Gray Eyes' calculations, she was only in her fifth month of pregnancy. If the baby was delivered now, its chances of living were almost nonexistent.

"We need to slow him down.'' Mrs. Gray Eyes always insisted that the child would be a boy. To humor her patient, Amelia referred to the fetus as a male.

"How can we do that? When a baby wants to be born, it's born."

"Maybe.'' For the hundredth time since it had burned, Amelia wished she had the clinic. The treatment she was going to prescribe would be much easier to monitor if she had overnight facilities for her patients. "We're going to make it difficult for this baby to find his way out. I want you to stay in bed all the time. No work, not even cooking." Keeping Mrs. Gray Eyes in bed would not be easy. She took pride in keeping her wickiup spotless, and Amelia had heard that she frequently prepared meals for other families.

Mrs. Gray Eyes nodded and put a protective hand on her rounded stomach. "I want this baby so much." When Amelia had first met her patient, she had told her that her husband had been killed by a bear. "This baby is all that I have left of him," she had said, tears welling in her eyes.

"We'll do our best," Amelia said, touching the woman's hand in a comforting gesture. She only hoped her best would be enough.

When she left the Indian village, William was waiting on the path. Amelia's heart soared with anticipation. William never came this close to the village. The fact that he was here must mean he was as anxious as she. Tonight! She smiled.

William returned the smile. Though a fleeting frown crossed his face as he looked at the circle of wickiups, he said nothing. Instead, he swept his hat off in a courtly gesture. "I wondered if I could invite you to join me for dinner this evening," he said.

Dinner. Though it was most definitely not ladylike of her, she had hoped he would suggest they share something much more intimate than a meal. Still, dinner was better than nothing. Amelia nodded. "I don't see a basket. Does that mean we're going to Pete's?"

They crossed the bridge leading back into Gold Landing, greeting several of William's miners, whose freshly washed hair and embarrassed expressions left no doubt that their destination was Gloria's establishment rather than the mine shaft.

"Not Pete's," William said. "I thought we would go someplace more private."

Amelia shivered, more with anticipation than from the cool air. Indeed, her body temperature rose several degrees as she realized he had something other than dinner in mind. "I think I'm going to like this."

He grinned. "I sure hope so!" He tipped his hat to Bertha Langdon, and Amelia felt her cheeks flush. Could the minister's wife guess what she and William were planning?

To Amelia's surprise, rather than stopping in town, William led her beyond it into the forest. He refused to answer her questions about where they were going, merely shaking his head and counseling patience as he talked to her about the weather, his mine, her patients—everything except the evening to come.

The forest was dark, cool and deliciously pine-scented, but Amelia cared little for her surroundings. How much longer would they walk?

As the path bent sharply to the right, a small log cabin came into view. When William stopped, Amelia realized it was the one where they had been snowbound. William had said he wanted to shield her from prying eyes. Though this remote cabin would certainly accomplish that, she wondered if there had been another reason he had chosen this particular spot. Perhaps William cherished the memory of the time they had spent here as much as she did.

"I told the owner that I wanted to buy a hunting lodge, but the truth is, I figured we could use a place where no one could find us," he explained.

"Like my patients."

"And my miners. Besides, this cabin brings back good memories."

She was right! Though William would deny that he had a romantic bone in his body, he was as sentimental about the spot where they had been snowbound as she was.

"It's perfect."

A pinecone plopped to the ground, while a squirrel shrieked as it jumped to an adjacent branch.

William laughed. "How can you say it's perfect? You haven't even seen the inside."

He opened the door, then before Amelia could enter, he swept her into his arms and carried her across the threshold.

"Oh, William!" As he set her on her feet, Amelia stared at the room, unable to believe the transformation. Fresh white curtains hung at the window, while a thick rug covered half the floor. The old table was set with plates and cups, and a new rocking chair stood next to the stove. He had even brought a begonia, centering it carefully on the chest of drawers. Though by rights the cabin should have been musty with disuse, the clean scent of pine needles told Amelia he had swept it with fragrant boughs. It *was* perfect.

Self-conscious, she eyed the bed. *Ah, the bed.* Instead of the moth-eaten wool blanket that had once covered it, it was neatly made with a snowy white chenille bedspread, and she could see the outline of two plump pillows. William had thought of everything.

"It's so beautiful." She put her arms around him and kissed him. "I can't believe you did all this in four days. It's like a fairy tale."

He smiled, his pleasure evident. "I told you I wanted your first time to be perfect." Then, as if he had said too much, he dropped his gaze to the floor. "Um . . . er . . . Would you like dinner now?"

Amelia shook her head. Though she had been ravenous when she left the Indian village, her hunger had disappeared, replaced by another elemental need. As the blood reached her cheeks, she lowered her eyelids.

William laid a finger under her chin and tipped it so that her eyes met his. "Nervous?" he asked.

She nodded. "I'm afraid I won't please you."

His hoot of laughter echoed off the log walls. "Not please me?" He laughed again. "Trust me, Amelia. You have no cause to worry. Just looking at you pleases me so much that I can't sleep at night."

She stared at him, momentarily surprised. "You, too? I thought I was the only one who had those dreams."

William chuckled. "Sweetheart, I'll match my dreams against yours any day—or night."

The warmth of his voice sent shivers of anticipation through her body. This was William, the man she loved, standing only inches from her. There was no reason that her mouth should have dried up or her palms grown moist. How could she be afraid of a man who loved her so much that he had transformed a simple log cabin into a romantic bower for her pleasure? There was no reason to be nervous. And yet . . .

"I don't know what to do," she confessed, forcing herself to look directly at him. "I mean, I understand the basics. After all, I'm a doctor. But I've never . . ."

There was no laughter in his gray eyes, only a smile of pure delight at her renewed admission of innocence. William drew her into his arms. "Don't worry, darling. I'll teach you."

Amelia nodded, her heart pounding with longing. William was the only teacher she wanted.

"The first lesson," he told her, "is that you're wearing too many clothes."

She moved out of the circle of his arms, feeling oddly bereft as she left their comforting warmth, and reached for the first button on the back of her shirtwaist.

"No, sweetheart. Let me." William turned her so that her back faced him. For a moment he stood silently, his arms wrapped around her waist as though he knew she needed reassurance. Then he pressed a kiss on the nape of her neck, and his fingers slipped the first button out of its loop. "Umm . . . sweet." He spread the high collar, caressing the tiny stretch of exposed skin with his fingers, then moving his lips over it, circling the patch of flesh with the tip of his tongue.

Had she thought she was cold? With each button that he released, William raised her temperature, and when he unhooked the shirtwaist, sending her skirt sliding to the floor, a new wave of heat flooded through her. The summer sun paled next to the warmth William's touch engendered.

"My turn," she said, facing him. Though her fingers shook with nervousness, somehow she managed to loosen the first button on his shirt. Following his example, she parted his collar and leaned forward. His skin was tempting, so tempting, and so she kissed it, laving it gently with her tongue.

William shuddered.

Instantly, Amelia dropped her hands and felt a flush rise to her cheeks. "Did I do something wrong?"

William chuckled. Taking her hands in both of his, he drew them back to his chest. "No, darling, you did something very, very right." Before she could anticipate his move, he pulled her close to him and pressed his lips to hers. His fingers raked through her hair, sending the last of her combs tumbling to the floor as they ignited sparks of pleasure that coursed swiftly from her crown through her veins, warming every molecule of her body. When at last he wrenched his lips from hers, they were both breathless.

"Way too many clothes," he said, eyeing their disheveled clothing. This time William's fingers moved swiftly, divesting Amelia of the last of her garments, then shucking his own.

When she stood in front of him, clad only in a smile, William was silent for a long moment. His eyes moved from the top of her head to the tips of her toes, then met her gaze again. "Oh, Amelia, you're even more beautiful than I imagined!"

Her smile matched his. "It's you, William. You make me feel beautiful."

Laying his hands on her shoulders, he gazed into her eyes. "If you feel beautiful," he said softly, "you're ready for the next lesson. I want you to feel loved."

He flung back the chenille spread, then swept Amelia into his arms and placed her on the bed. A second later he lay beside her. Though she could feel the warmth of his body, he left a space between them, and Amelia knew he was waiting for her to take the next step. His ragged breathing and the pulse that beat at the base of his throat told Amelia how much the restraint cost William. And still he waited, giving her the chance to change her mind.

"I love you, Amelia. Let me show you how much."

She placed her hand in his, entwining their fingers. "Yes, my love. Teach me!"

It was magic, pure magic, as his lips and fingers caressed her, as she reveled in the sensation of his hardened muscles pressing against the softness of her curves, as the sound of his breathing made her pulse race. But nothing, not even her most vivid dreams, had prepared her for the reality of William's lessons in love. For when their bodies joined, Amelia felt beautiful, she felt loved, and more. She felt complete.

The vague emptiness, the sense that somehow she was lacking an essential element, disappeared. Here, in the tiny cabin that had been her refuge against the storm, Amelia found what had been missing from her life. She found William's love.

The brief Alaskan summer turned to fall, the tundra blazing with autumn's fiery colors before the first snows covered the mountaintops and dusted the ground. She had seen it before and had reveled in the beauty of the changing seasons, but last year it had not seemed so magnificent. Last year she had not been with William.

She had not realized she could be so happy. Oh, she had thought she had experienced happiness before, but the past paled compared to the present. What she and William shared was so wonderful it almost defied description. They met in the cabin as often as they could, in trysts that combined passionate interludes with quiet meals and companionable hours spent talking, trading stories of their days apart. Amelia grew to know the miners' individual foibles, while William learned of her patients.

It was a golden autumn, a time of almost unblemished happiness. Though Amelia's heart ached when she saw Abe and knew that she was responsible for his grim expression, she also knew her decision was right. Someday Abe would find the woman he deserved, just as someday her mother would understand why she had been unable to lie to William.

The one blot on the virtually perfect slate of Amelia's life was Mrs. Gray Eyes. Though the woman's contractions had eased, hers was still a high-risk pregnancy, and Amelia feared that the child would be dangerously premature. Gold Landing had no facilities to care for a tiny neonate, and even if the child were born alive, it might not survive those perilous first few hours.

Amelia had begun a consultation with Lou Mitchell, a Fairbanks doctor whom Ben had declared the best in Alaska. Dr.

Mitchell, concurring with Amelia's diagnosis, recommended sending Mrs. Gray Eyes to Fairbanks a month before term so that the child could be born there and have access to the city's more complete medical facilities.

"There's a doctor in Fairbanks who specializes in difficult pregnancies," Amelia told Mrs. Gray Eyes that afternoon. "I want him to deliver your baby."

As blood drained from the woman's face, she shook her head. "Me? Go to Fairbanks?" Amelia nodded. "I don't want to go. I'm afraid."

Amelia held her patient's hand. "I know how important this baby is to you. Dr. Mitchell is your best chance at having a healthy son."

Tears welled in the pregnant woman's eyes. "I want this baby. I do. But I'm so scared." She gripped Amelia's hand. "Why can't you go with me? I wouldn't be scared then."

Why not? It would be for only a few days. Amelia had no other critical cases, and Ben could handle her routine patients. "All right," she agreed.

"You're doing what?" William laid down his fork and stared at Amelia. She had waited until after they had made love to tell him her decision, and she had made one of his favorite meals, hoping that would soften his response.

"You heard me the first time, William. I'm going to Fairbanks with one of my patients."

"An Indian." He spat the words as if they poisoned his mouth.

Although Amelia was not surprised by his reaction, his virulent hatred saddened her. William was so generous, so understanding about most things, but where the Indians were concerned, he would not listen to reason. "She's a woman who needs me," Amelia said softly.

"I need you, too."

Unable to eat, Amelia took a swallow of coffee, trying to ease the lump in her throat. How she hated confrontations with William! "Not in the same way. Mrs. Gray Eyes' life and her baby's are at stake."

William pushed back his chair and stood. "Women have been having babies without help for centuries," he announced.

"And they've died doing it. That's what would happen to Mrs. Gray Eyes, or to her baby." Amelia shuddered. Life—any life, but especially a baby's—was precious. Why couldn't William see that? Why did he let his prejudice cloud his reason? "That's not going to happen, not if I can help it."

William reached for Amelia, drawing her out of the chair and holding her close to him. He stroked her hair gently. "I don't want you to go," he said. "Traveling this late in the season is dangerous. You shouldn't risk your life for an Indian."

"Let's not argue, darling. I love you very much, but I can't ignore my conscience, and it tells me I need to go to Fairbanks with Mrs. Gray Eyes."

Though the cabin was warm, Amelia shivered when William released her. "You're saying that an Indian means more to you than I do." His eyes were cold, his expression unyielding. When she reached out to touch his cheek, he stepped away.

"No, I'm not saying that. I'm a doctor, William. I need to do what's best for my patients."

"So you would leave me and everything we've shared here for some ignorant savage."

Amelia shook her head. It was obvious there would be no reasoning with William tonight. "I'm sorry you feel that way, but I have to go."

He stared at her for a long moment, then grabbed his coat. "Don't expect me to be here when you get back."

"I heard the lady doctor went to Fairbanks," Louise said as she brushed the mud from her skirts. She, Sally and June were seated in the big common room where Gloria's girls ate their meals, mended their clothes and gathered during the long months when they could not be outdoors.

"Sure did. I saw her get onto the boat with some Indian woman. Looked like the woman was ready to drop her brat." Sally was quick to provide the details that Louise craved.

June bent her head over her sewing. Though the arrival of a boat was always a big event and one that most of the girls attended, June had not cared enough to go outside. Ever since William had gotten engaged to that woman, she hadn't felt like doing much. Oh, she made sure she entertained her gentlemen callers properly. There was no choice about that. After all, she could not lose her home. But life hadn't been much fun.

"Say, what do you think, Louise?" Sally poured a glass of milk and took a long swallow. "Reckon William will come a-visitin' now that the doctor's gone?"

June's heart began to pound. Maybe he would. Maybe now that the witch was gone, her spell would weaken and William would realize how much he missed June.

"Don't know. He's been a different man since they got engaged."

"A real gentleman." Sally managed to infuse the word with scorn.

"Or a fool."

"Same thing!"

As Louise and Sally laughed, June's thoughts began to spin. She was beginning to think God had not heard her, but maybe those hours she had spent on her knees had been worth it. Maybe her prayers had been answered after all. She did a mental calculation. The timing was right. In fact, it was perfect. She had thought and thought ever since the horrible day she had learned William was engaged to someone else, and she had realized there was only one way to bring him to his senses. This was her chance.

"Gloria, I've got to go out for an hour or so," she told the madam. She had put on her prettiest hat and a dress she knew William liked.

Gloria raised a perfectly groomed eyebrow. "Does this have anything to do with the fact that William Gunning is sitting in the saloon drinking himself blind?"

June feigned innocence. "I didn't know that," she said, while her heart rejoiced. She had not been sure where to find William, but Gloria's words meant she wouldn't have to waste any precious time. It was a sign. June knew that. She was meant to be with William today.

"Be careful, June."

She nodded. "I always am."

When she reached the saloon, William was there, just as Gloria had said, his elbows propped on the bar, a half-filled glass in front of him.

"Mind if I join you?" June took the stool next to him, leaning forward so he would have a good view of her breasts. William had always admired them, especially in this dress. Tonight, though she moved so that his head was practically in her cleavage, he said nothing.

Draining his glass, William turned to June. "She left me. Can you believe that, June? She left me here and went away with a stinking Indian."

Amelia! June was sick to death of the woman. Maybe the boat would sink or she would discover she liked Fairbanks better than Gold Landing. It didn't matter how it happened; all that mattered was that that snooty doctor never return to Gold Landing and William. Then June's dreams could come true.

She put her hand on William's arm and moved closer, snuggling next to him the way he had always liked. "Aw, honey," she said in her softest voice, "you deserve better than that. You deserve a woman who really loves you. A woman who loves you would never leave."

William's eyes narrowed as he considered her words. "You're damn right, June. That's what I deserve."

She put her arm around him and nuzzled his neck. "Come home with me, darlin'. I'd never hurt you."

He shook his head. "Can't do that." Though his words were slightly slurred, his eyes focused clearly. "Wouldn't be right."

June motioned to the bartender to fill William's glass. "Drink up, honey," she said. When he had finished half of the potent liquid, she said, "You know what isn't right?" Without waiting for his answer, she continued, "It wasn't right that she left you."

This time William seemed to have trouble meeting her gaze. " 'S true. Say, June, when'd you get so wise?"

She smiled, then pressed a kiss on his lips. "When I started lovin' you."

William grinned, a silly, lopsided grin that should have looked foolish but set June's pulse racing. "Bet you say that to all the men."

She shook her head and traced the outline of his lips. "Only to you, darlin'. You're special." When he continued to grin, she said, "To show you how special, I won't even charge you for tonight."

William shook his head. "Don't have to do that."

"I want to."

"Then what are we waiting for?"

William stumbled as he climbed down from the stool. When his first step was little more than a lurch, June put her arm around his waist and led him toward the door. He might be drunk, but he was hers. At least for tonight.

The dawn had not yet broken when he woke. June, who had slept little, preferring instead to spend the hours watching his beloved face, smiled at him.

"Where am . . . ?" As his eyes focused, William shuddered. "What the hell happened?" Brushing aside her arm, he leaped out of bed, his face turning bright red as he looked down and recognized his nakedness.

The pounding of June's heart echoed in her ears. This was not the way it was supposed to be. Many was the night William had spent in her bed, and he had always been proud of his body. He would walk around the room as easily nude as when fully clothed. Not today.

"Oh, my God, what have I done? What am I going to tell her?"

The pain in his voice told June more clearly than any words that it was over. Her dream had ended, for William would never return to her. The memory of last night was all she would ever have.

"Nothin'," she said. "Don't tell her nothin'."

"What if she hears?"

This was William, worrying about that woman, not his own reputation. For a moment, June considered her choices. She could flaunt William's indiscretion, but what good would that do? It wouldn't bring him back. It would only cause him pain. Amelia could rot in hell for all she cared, but William was different. No matter what happened, June did not want to see him hurt.

"I'll deny it," she offered.

The hope that lit William's face hurt almost as much as the knowledge that he was leaving. If only he had cared for her the way he did for that woman! She would have been the best wife any man could ever want. A far better wife than Amelia Sheldon could even dream of being.

"Thanks, June." William finished dressing, then tossed a gold coin onto the bureau. "You're a good girl."

When he left, June picked up the coin and hurled it against the wall. "You stupid, stupid man," she cried. "It's not your money I want. It's you!"

Chapter Twenty

Amelia was exhausted by the time she arrived home. Mrs. Gray Eyes' son had been born the day after they had reached Fairbanks. As Amelia had feared, it had been a difficult birth, and the neonate had hovered between life and death. Thank God for Dr. Mitchell! He and Amelia had spent three sleepless nights giving the baby the constant care he demanded, but now the child was out of danger, and Amelia could return to Gold Landing. Though Mrs. Gray Eyes would stay with her baby, Amelia wanted nothing more than to be home—with William.

If he was there. The memory of their argument haunted her, and with each mile that the boat traveled, she wondered whether William would carry through with his threat. Though she doubted he would actually leave Gold Landing, he might refuse to see her.

As the boat rounded the final bend, Amelia saw him on the bank, and her heart began to race. He was waiting for her! She waved. He waved. She smiled. He smiled. And when the captain lowered the gangplank, she raced down it into William's open arms.

"Welcome home, sweetheart. I missed you so much." William whispered the words in her ear, then—heedless of the audience that had come to meet the boat—he kissed her.

Though the chill of autumn filled the air, William's kiss warmed Amelia, chasing away the doubts that had weighed so heavily on her heart. Their love could overcome the undeniable obstacle of their strong wills. She knew it.

"Oh, William, I missed you, too." Amelia linked her arm in his as they walked back into town. She needed to see Ben, to learn what had happened to her other patients while she had been gone. And then she was going to bed. But first, she and William had to talk. She wanted him to understand the obligation she felt to her patients at the same time that she reaffirmed how much she loved him.

"Thanks to Dr. Mitchell, both Mrs. Gray Eyes and her son are alive."

Though she half expected a disparaging remark, William said only, "I'm glad you're back. When you've seen Ben—"

"I'm exhausted. I need some sleep."

William chuckled, his lips curving into the mischievous grin that she found so endearing. "Me, too. Of course, I did have something else in mind first."

"Maybe I'm not as tired as I thought." She would show as well as tell him the depths of her love.

William was waiting when she arrived at the cabin. He had lit the stove, and although the room was still chilly, the worst of the cold had been chased away. As he opened his arms, Amelia slipped out of her coat and ran into them. Laying her head against his chest, she smiled. She was home, where she belonged, in William's arms.

At first she thought it was her imagination. Surely William didn't hold her tighter than before. Surely his kisses could not have changed. There was no reason his embrace should seem filled with a wildness that she—if she had not known better—might have called desperation. And yet William *was* different. When they made love, he clung to her as if afraid she would leave, and he told her repeatedly how happy he was that she was home. Though Amelia wondered if this was his way of apologizing for their argument, she did not ask. It was enough that he listened when she told him how important the trip to Fairbanks had been for her and that he smiled when she declared her love.

September drifted into October, the days growing shorter, the temperature barely rising above freezing, even on the sunniest of days. Alaska's winter had begun. Though she missed the long summer days, Amelia found the snow-covered landscape beautiful and more than a little awe-inspiring. This was the

Alaska of her dreams, a land of vast expanses and magnificent splendor.

Unfortunately, the snow was a mixed blessing. Now that she had to do her rounds on snowshoes, it took longer, and that meant she had less time to share with William in their cabin. Still, despite that and the fact that Abe was visibly unhappy, so much so that he kept his office open only three days a week, Amelia was happy.

"Oh, Ella, sometimes I can't believe it's true," she told her friend one evening. "It seems like every dream I've ever had—except one—is coming true."

"It's wrong of me. I know that. But I can't stop myself from envying you." Ella laid down the skirt she was hemming and looked at Amelia. "Larry wasn't the right man for me, but sometimes I can't help wondering whether that right man exists."

Though Ella's words were despondent, Amelia viewed them as a positive sign. The healing process was beginning, and Ella's fears of intimacy were receding if she was worrying about finding a husband. Truly, life was good.

"The right man does exist," she told Ella, "and you'll—"

Before she could complete her sentence, someone knocked on the front door. A tall, gaunt Athapaskan stood in the doorway. "Adam sick, Doctor. You come?" Although Amelia recognized the woman, she was surprised to see her. Spring Flower never asked for help. She would nod solemnly when Amelia passed her wickiup, but even when she herself was visibly ill, she insisted she needed no medical care. Her son's condition must be serious if she had come to summon Amelia.

An hour later, when she had finished examining the boy, a youngster who Spring Flower told her had seen seven summers, she turned to his mother. "I can't be sure," she admitted. "The fever and weakness could be several things. Until I'm sure, we need to isolate him." Again Amelia wished she had the clinic. Isolation and, if it was needed, quarantine would have been so much easier there.

"No place." Spring Flower shook her head.

Amelia spoke slowly so that the other woman would understand her. "You can help Mrs. Gray Eyes with her baby. I'll stay here with Adam."

Though the woman protested, not wanting to leave her son, Amelia was adamant. If the child's illness was what she feared, the fewer people who were exposed, the better.

By morning Amelia's fears were confirmed. Adam had diphtheria. There was no mistaking the gray false membrane that even now impeded the boy's breathing. Her spirits sank. Without a miracle, she would have an epidemic on her hands.

Amelia scribbled a note and asked one of the children to take it to Ben. She already knew that their small supply of antitoxin serum would be inadequate, and she could only hope Ben could locate more in time to save the village.

Afterward, Amelia had few distinct memories of the week that she spent in Spring Flower's wickiup. When she thought about it, all she could remember was that she was constantly cold, while Adam and the four other children who had contracted diphtheria burned with fever. The initial dose of serum had little effect, and Amelia was forced to give them a second, even though it meant using the last of her supply.

Please, Ben, she prayed. *Send me more.* Instead Ben sent the message that there was no diphtheria antitoxin to be found anywhere in Alaska. He had ordered more from the States, but with the river's freezing, no one could predict when it would be delivered.

Amelia redoubled her prayers, this time begging that the disease would not spread. Those prayers were answered. When she was certain that no one else had been infected, she picked her way across the river, so weary that the effort of carrying her bag made her arm ache.

"Thank God you're back!" William knocked on her front door five minutes after she arrived. As if from a distance, Amelia noticed that his face looked haggard, and his eyes glistened with unshed tears.

Her own eyes had trouble focusing. Fatigue. That must be the reason William's face seemed to sway and why her head ached so horribly. Amelia nodded slowly. The room was terribly warm, and all she wanted to do was sleep.

"The children will be fine," she told William, vaguely surprised at how much effort it took to speak.

William kissed her forehead. "Darling, you're the one I was worried about. I don't give a damn about the Indians."

She sank onto the sofa, too weary even to remonstrate against his declaration. "It's sweet of you to be worried, but I'm all right. I'm just tired."

She was wrong. By the time Ella returned from school, Amelia knew that she had more than a simple case of fatigue.

"Don't come in," she said when Ella opened the door. "Just get Ben."

Within ten minutes, Ben arrived, accompanied by William.

"I thought you were supposed to be curing illness, not contracting it." Ben's sober mien contrasted with the deliberately light tone of his words. "How did you manage to get so sick?"

It was a rhetorical question. With a thermometer stuck in her mouth, Amelia could not have answered, even if she had had the energy to form the words.

William, however, had no compunction about replying. "She got sick by treating those no-good Indians, that's how."

Amelia's eyes flew open, and she stared at William. "No!" She shook her head, then sank back in weariness. After Ella left, she had climbed the stairs to her room, resting after each step, and with what felt like a herculean effort, she had hoisted herself into bed.

Ben laid his hand on her forehead as though to calm her. Then he turned to William. "You had better leave. I can't have you upsetting my patient."

William remained motionless.

"Out!" Ben pointed toward the door. "You're making her worse. You can wait for me downstairs, if you insist."

"Take care of her," William said as he left the room, "or you'll answer to me."

Ben didn't spare William a glance. Instead, he simply muttered, "That's my job, and I'm good at it."

Her eyes glassy with pain and fever, Amelia focused them on Ben. "I sure hope so. I've never felt this bad."

It was hours later when Ben came downstairs, his face haggard, his forehead creased with worry.

"Tell me she's going to be all right." William rose from the sofa. Ben might look awful, but he felt worse. At least Ben had been doing something. William had been left on his own, with nothing but his thoughts for company, and tonight those thoughts were poor companions.

Ben shuffled his way into the kitchen, then sank onto one of the wooden chairs. "I've never lied to you, William, and I don't aim to start now." He stared at the table, seemingly unwilling to look at William. "It's a bad case. I can't guarantee anything. If I had the serum, I wouldn't worry, but without it . . ." He let his words trail off.

William clenched his fists, not sure which was stronger, his fear or his anger. Amelia, the woman he loved more than any other person on earth, was in danger, and he was powerless to help her. "She risked her life for an Indian. How the hell could she do that?"

This time Ben met his gaze. "Amelia's a good doctor and a caring woman. Isn't that why you love her?"

Of course that was why he loved her—part of the reason, anyway—but it did not excuse what she had done. Ben missed the point. "She shouldn't have been treating an Indian."

The doctor poured himself a glass of the grape juice that Ella kept for special occasions, then took a long swallow. "William, I'm going to put this as plainly as I know how. I've got a very sick woman up there. Just keeping her alive is going to take every bit of skill and energy I possess. That means I don't have time to deal with your problems. My professional advice is, go to your mine. Work off some of your anger there." He took another swallow, then laid the empty glass on the table. "You might try praying, too. That never hurts."

But William did neither. A crime had been committed, a deadly serious one. While there was no way it could be undone, he would make damn sure that the guilty parties knew just what they had done.

Fighting back his revulsion, he crossed the river and entered the Indian village for the first time. Though he had known the Athapaskans lived in poverty, the reality was worse than William had imagined. The out-of-work miners' huts seemed palatial when compared to the hide-covered wickiups. But William had no time for pity.

"Where's Spring Flower?" he demanded of the first person he saw.

He stormed into her wickiup, then stopped, assailed by the odors. How could anyone live like this? A tall woman, who looked as if it had been months since she had eaten a regular meal, stood before him, surrounded by her meager possessions. He had been wrong in thinking that the Indians lived like animals. Even his sled dogs had better homes than this.

"You Spring Flower?"

She nodded, and William's eyes continued to search the wickiup. He found his quarry crouched on the other side of the hovel. "Then that must be your brat. He's the reason the doctor's sick."

Spring Flower recoiled from the anger in William's voice, and it took a second before she understood what he had said.

"Dr. Amelia sick?"

"Damn right, she is. She came here and risked her life for no-account scum like you and that whelp of yours, and what happened? Your brat is alive, and my woman's going to die— all because of useless animals like you."

William's anger exploded at the thought of Amelia lying still and lifeless. He lunged for Spring Flower and, lifting her until her feet were inches above the earthen floor, began to shake her. "You killed her. Now you're going to pay!" Her head jerked and she whimpered, but William, blinded by rage, ignored her cries.

"Leave my ma alone!" The boy launched himself at William, grabbing the man's legs and pounding on them. "She didn't hurt you." He flailed his fists in the air, then resumed his attack on William's legs. "Leave her alone!"

Though the boy's blows were not painful, they forced William to look down. As he narrowed his eyes at his small assailant, the fury that had blinded him to everything but his own fear began to subside. William saw a frightened child, tears of anger and terror streaming down his face, and for the briefest of moments, he was not certain whose face he saw: Adam's or his own.

No! Polly, no!

With a horrified groan, he released Spring Flower. *My God,* he cried to himself as he fled from the wickiup, *I'm as bad as they are.*

Fueled by anger, remorse and a fear so deep it seemed to have settled in his bones, William raced to the cabin. There he would find sanctuary. There he could put the horror of Spring Flower's wickiup out of his mind. But instead, all he found were memories of Amelia.

The happiest moments of his life had been spent in this room. Though they had shared so many joyous hours here, today he could recapture none of them. The only memories he could conjure were of the times he had disappointed Amelia, when he had said or done something that had not met her image of him as a dragon-slaying knight. The truth was, he did not deserve peace. His armor was tarnished, and so was his soul.

How could he have done it? How could he have treated Spring Flower the way he had? He had hurt her—deliberately hurt her—and frightened a child. Why? They had committed no crime, done him no harm. Being ill and calling for Amelia was not a sin. But hurting Spring Flower and Adam was.

William sank to the floor and rested his head in his hands. Amelia was right. The past had blinded him to the simple truth: Spring Flower and Adam were not animals or lesser creatures simply because they were Indians. They were human beings, a woman and her child. They made mistakes, like every other human. They felt pain and joy like every other human. They were no different from William and Amelia, no different from him and Polly.

Polly. The pain threatened to engulf him.

William closed his eyes in a vain attempt to block out the past. But his moments of violence in the wickiup had resurrected memories he had spent half a lifetime trying to bury. For years, he had kept them at bay, fighting them when they tried to surface in his nightmares. But today those memories had returned, more vivid and painful than ever. Would it ever end?

William forced his eyes open. His rational mind told him he was an adult, sitting in the cabin. But as William watched, the cabin was transformed, and he was back in Nome, a child once more, trying to protect Polly.

His stomach churned. Though he closed his eyes, trying to stop the waves of pain from overtaking him, memory was like the tide, inexorable. Why wouldn't that day die? William clenched his teeth.

It had been a school day and he was coming home, whistling as he thought of ways to avoid the afternoon chores, but his whistling had died abruptly when he heard Polly's cries of pain. With the brash confidence of youth, William burst into the cabin, ready to help her. Nothing in his experience could have prepared him for the horror within.

Three Indians, lured by tales of the white man's wealth, had broken into the cabin, demanding that Polly give them her stash. Though there was no money, the men would not believe her denials. The white woman, they were sure, needed only a little persuasion to give them her coins. By the time William arrived, they had hacked off two of Polly's fingers and had sliced the soles of her feet to ribbons.

Though William tried to defend her, a small boy was no match for three grown men emboldened by liquor. One of them had carved William's cheek with the same knife he had used on Polly; then another tossed him aside like a sack of flour, hurling him to the ground with such force that he had lost consciousness. When he woke, Polly was dead, and so was a part of William. His face healed; his heart did not.

In William's young mind, Indians were forever associated with the horror of Polly's death, and nothing could convince him otherwise. Any Indian, every Indian, shared the blame for killing the only mother he had ever known.

Amelia had tried to tell him he was wrong, but he had not wanted to listen. Just as he had refused to grow a beard lest it hide the scar that reminded him of all he had lost that day, he had refused to view Indians as anything other than savage murderers. Memories of that day blinded him to the truth, tainting all of his interactions with the Athapaskans, and for years he had been certain he was right. Until today. Today's act of senseless violence had stripped the scales from his eyes. At last he understood what Amelia had tried to tell him.

Amelia. It all came back to her. Somehow she loved him even though his armor was tarnished, and in loving him, she had given him a new reason to live. William rose and began to pace the floor. He needed Amelia, needed her desperately. But if Ben was right, he might lose her before the night was over.

William had not felt this helpless even when Polly died. At least he had tried to help his foster mother. He might have failed, but he had made an attempt to save her. Today he could do nothing. There were no intruders for him to fight, and he had no weapons to defeat germs. William Gunning, the man whose word was law in Gold Landing, was powerless to determine whether the woman he loved lived or died.

He groaned in agony. There had to be something. He had told Ben he would go anywhere to get the serum, but Ben had shaken his head. There wasn't time. Amelia needed a miracle, and she needed it tonight.

You might try praying. Ben's words echoed in his mind.

Prayer. William stopped pacing and stared out the window, as if the forest held an answer. All he saw was a clump of snow sliding down a tree bough.

Could prayer help Amelia? William watched the snow clump tumble to the ground and break apart. Polly had set a lot of store in prayer. She had insisted that William pray every night before he went to sleep, and because it had made her happy, he had done it. But the day Polly died was the day

William stopped praying. He figured that if there really was a God, He would not have let Polly die.

God doesn't stop evil. He just helps us bear it. William could hear Polly as clearly as if she stood next to him. Had she told him that when he was a child? William couldn't remember. All he knew was that that was her voice he heard, and the words made sense.

Slowly, he sank to his knees next to the bed, and for a moment he was back in Nome, a child once more, with Polly smiling as she listened to his prayers.

"Polly said we couldn't bargain with You." He spoke aloud, as he had done then. "Trouble is, I don't feel right asking for something and not giving anything in return. So let me tell You what I want. That's Amelia's life. I'm asking that You let her live, and if You do, I'll try my best to make up for all those years of hatred. I'll do my best to help all Your creatures."

There was no answer, but he had not expected one. God had never answered his prayers before. Why would He start now? And yet, as he rose and extinguished the fire, William realized that the anger that had been a part of him since Polly's death was gone. In its place, he felt a deep sense of peace.

The decision about Amelia was made. Though he could not say how he knew it, William was sure that Amelia's illness had reached its crisis. Perhaps his feeling of peace was because she was living; perhaps it was the knowledge that she had passed to a better world. All William knew was that he had to see her one more time.

When he reached her house, he found Ben sitting in the kitchen, an empty glass in front of him. Though his heart plummeted, wrenched by the fact that Ben was no longer at Amelia's bedside trying to save her, William tried to tell himself there might be a good reason. The doctor turned to look at William, and his eyes, ringed with deep circles, mirrored his exhaustion but gave no clue to Amelia's condition.

"How is she?"

When Ben rose and clapped his hand on William's shoulder,

William was not sure whether it was to steady himself or to comfort William.

"I don't know how to tell you this," the older man said. "That gray membrane just about filled her throat, and she was barely breathing. I knew the end was near." Ben's brown eyes were sober, and William saw water spots on Ben's spectacles, as though he had wept. "She stopped breathing. I didn't want to believe it, but she was gone." Ben shuddered, and William knew he was reliving Amelia's death. Though he heard Ben's words, his heart refused to accept them. The pain would come. He knew that. But for the moment the blessed calm protected him.

Ben wiped his eyes. "I don't know how long I sat there. Finally I got up to pull the sheet over her, and she started to breathe again. Only this time, it was normal. I tell you, William, I've never seen anything like it."

The calm shattered. Amelia was alive! He was swept by a surge of joy so powerful he felt he had been hit by an avalanche. Amelia was alive! Ben had gotten the miracle he needed.

Could it be?

"The crisis. When did it happen?" William asked. Ben would never know just how important his answer was.

The doctor pulled out his watch and studied it for a moment. " 'Bout an hour ago, I guess."

William closed his eyes. *I told you so, boy.* Polly's voice echoed in his mind. An hour ago, he had been on his knees, praying for Amelia's life, and his prayers had been answered.

Thank you, God.

Chapter Twenty-one

Though never uncertain, Amelia's recovery was slower than she had expected. The disease, coupled with the hectic schedule she had maintained all fall, had weakened her so much that it was two weeks before she could walk downstairs. Each day she remained out of bed a little longer, but Ben insisted that she not resume her practice for another month.

"What about my patients?" Amelia demanded.

"Believe it or not, Amelia, I can care for them." Ben chided her gently, his brown eyes sparkling behind his glasses. "Somehow I managed the whole practice before I had the good sense to hire you."

Amelia rested her head on the pile of pillows that also served as her backrest. Her room, with the cabbage-rose wallpaper and crisp muslin curtains that she had once found soothing, seemed to shrink daily. "I know that, Ben, but I also know you don't like maternity cases, and Susan Whittaker's due soon."

His reaction was stronger than she had expected. Ben flinched as if she had thrown a sharp object at him. "I thought you said Susan wasn't due for another month."

"That's her official date, but if she's carrying twins, you know they're liable to come early."

Ben muttered something under his breath. The only words Amelia could understand were, "If they know what's good for them, they'll wait for you."

The sound of boots on the stairs signaled the arrival of a visitor.

"William!" Amelia did not try to conceal her joy as he entered the room.

Ben looked from Amelia to William, then picked up his bag. "I can tell when I'm not needed." His statement went unchallenged.

"Oh, William, I'm so glad to see you."

He pulled a chair next to the bed and studied her for a long moment, his gray eyes serious, though his lips curved in a smile. "How are you feeling today?"

Amelia laughed. "Bored." She leaned forward and touched William's hand. "I'm suffering from what we in the medical community call a severe case of cabin fever," she admitted. "I can't wait to leave this house."

"To resume your practice?"

Amelia nodded, then added, "And to visit a certain cabin in the woods. Of course, I wouldn't want to go there alone."

William's chuckle reverberated against the wall. "You're turning into a wanton woman."

"Are you complaining?"

"Not one bit. I'm looking forward to meeting that wanton woman again and maybe teaching her a few new things."

As Amelia raised one eyebrow, William nodded. "You didn't think we had exhausted our classes, did you? Now, whose turn is it to read?"

Since she had been well enough to sit up in bed, William had brought a stack of books, and they had taken turns reading them aloud. They had finished every Jack London book William could find, and had moved on to Edgar Allan Poe. By tacit agreement, the one author they did not choose was Charles Dickens. Everyone in Gold Landing knew that Abe and Amelia had shared his books, and neither she nor William wanted any reminders of how unhappy their engagement had made Abe.

He had visited Amelia once since her illness, bringing her a new book and a box of candy. But when Amelia had asked him about his practice and the week's opera libretto, Abe had shaken his head. "They're not important," he told her. He had wiped his spectacles, then fixed his blue eyes on her. "Are you happy?" And when Amelia nodded, Abe had been silent for a long moment before he said, "That's good," sounding as though he meant the opposite.

"My turn," Amelia told William, and reached for the book.

He settled back in his chair, pulling out a block of wood and his carving tools.

"What are you making?" Amelia never tired of watching William whittle.

"It's going to be a rabbit," William said. When he held it up for approval, Amelia saw little more than a rounded block, though she knew that by tomorrow the animal would be recognizable. "I'll put wheels on the bottom and tie a rope to the front so a child can pull it."

"Is it for Hannah?" William had made so many toys over the past few weeks that Amelia wondered how any one child could use them.

He shook his head. "Someone else."

As frustrating as it was being bedridden, Amelia did not know how she would have survived without seeing William. Though the gossips' tongues might wag over the dubious propriety of their being alone together, she didn't care. William was the best medicine she could have, and every doctor knew the importance of daily doses of medicine.

It was even more difficult than he had expected. William loaded the goods he had gathered onto the sled and harnessed the dogs. He spoke to each of the animals, checked the load twice, then shook his head at himself. As embarrassing as it was to admit it, he was procrastinating. There was no reason to check and double-check the ropes, and the dogs had made longer, more strenuous trips than this many times. The only reason he was delaying was fear of the reception he would receive. Knowing he would deserve every humiliating snub didn't make the prospect any easier to bear.

"Mush!" The command was meant for his feet as well as his dogs. The dogs were eager. His feet were not. But the snow was packed, the trail well marked, and in only a few minutes he approached his destination.

Fresh snow had done little to camouflage the poverty. William could see that many of the caribou hides were thin, undoubtedly providing only a poor barrier against the cold and wind. As he entered the Indian village, the few residents who were outside scattered, fleeing as if he were the devil himself. William could not blame them. It was no more than he had expected, less than he deserved after the way he had treated Spring Flower.

He guided the dogs to her wickiup. "Spring Flower." Last time he had barged in, too angry to adhere to accepted social behavior. This time he stood at the entrance to the wickiup. He would not enter until he had received permission.

There was no answer. William repeated his call, then heard the soft murmur of voices inside the teepee. A moment later Adam poked his head past the bear skin that covered the door. "Go away," he said, his eyes fixed on a point beyond William. "I won't let you hurt my ma." Though his words were fierce, the boy's voice trembled, as if he remembered William's violence.

William regarded the child with respect. He was doing exactly what William would have done under similar circumstances, protecting his mother. "I don't want to hurt her. Or you, either." William kept his voice low and even.

Adam emerged from the wickiup and spat at William's feet. "You lie."

He was only a child. His rejection should not hurt. But it did. William gestured to the sled that stood a few feet behind him. "I brought food for the village, and blankets." There were toys, too, carved animals and games that William hoped the children would enjoy, but he would not tell Adam of them. They were to be a surprise.

As Adam shook his head, William sighed, remembering how obstinate a young boy could be. Though the supplies were meant for everyone, it was essential that Spring Flower receive them, that she be the one who distributed them to her neighbors. It wasn't just Athapaskan etiquette. Common decency decreed that since Spring Flower had been the one he had harmed, she had to pardon him before he could approach the others. And before he could see Spring Flower, he had to convince her son of his goodwill.

"Bad man. Go away."

Adam slipped back into the dwelling. William would wait

a few minutes longer. Then if Spring Flower continued to refuse to see him, he would go home. But he would be back tomorrow and the next day and the day after until she agreed to see him.

The dogs whimpered, eager to run. The short trip to the Indian village had excited them, readying them for a long run. "Later, boys," William said.

The layers of caribou hide did little to mask the soft murmur of voices within the wickiup. A moment later, Spring Flower pulled the bear skin aside and motioned to William to enter. She was as gaunt and the dwelling as pathetic as he remembered.

"Doctor dead?" Spring Flower asked, her face white with fear, reminding William that he had accused her of killing Amelia. Did she and her son think he had come to exact more retribution?

William shook his head. "No. Dr. Amelia will be fine. The other doctor helped her."

The haunted look began to fade from Spring Flower's face. Though it had been over a week since Amelia's illness had reached its crisis, no one had thought to notify the Indian community. *Stupid!* William chastised himself. *You should have realized they would be worried. They love Amelia, too.*

"Good." Spring Flower spoke rapidly to her son. Though the boy shook his head, obviously disagreeing with something she said, he moved to the back of the wickiup.

Now. William took a deep breath, then began to speak. "Spring Flower, I came to tell you I am sorry about what I did. It was wrong to hurt you."

She nodded, acknowledging the truth of William's words, then looked at her son. "Scared boy."

Adam stood at the far edge of the wickiup, a tree branch in his hand. Though it was not much of a weapon, William was saddened by the knowledge that the boy believed it necessary. *What did you expect?* he asked himself.

"I know, and I'm sorry for that, too." Sorrier than he would ever be able to tell her. "I brought some things for you . . . and for him."

297

"Go away," Adam said from the other side of the dwelling.
Spring Flower spoke to him again. This time her words
were slower, her voice persuasive, but to no avail. The boy
shook his head a second time, and Spring Flower turned back
to William. "No."

William watched the play of emotions on the young
woman's face. He sensed that she wanted to accept his gifts
for her son, and yet she was reluctant. Pride, William realized.
She was unwilling to accept charity.

"I will be shamed if I take them back with me," he said,
speaking slowly so that she would understand him. "This is
white man's potlatch. A celebration that I want you to share."

"Celebration?" Spring Flower appeared to know the word,
but it was evident she questioned the reason for William's
rejoicing. He should not have been surprised. In all likelihood
the only cause for celebration he could give the Indian village
would be his permanent departure from Gold Landing.

"Dr. Amelia's going to be my wife." Even though he had
said the words a hundred times, they brought a flush of happiness he made no attempt to disguise.

Spring Flower's thin face broke into a smile. "Doctor marry
you?"

Though William kept his gaze fixed on the woman, he heard
a gasp of disbelief from the other side of the wickiup. "Yes,"
he said solemnly.

At Spring Flower's urging, Adam came to her side, the
branch still firmly clenched in his fist. There was a moment's
silence as the two Indians looked at each other. At last Spring
Flower nodded. "Yes," she said to William. "Take potlatch."

As William unloaded the sled, he mused. It was humbling
that for the first time since he had founded Gold Landing, he
had not been accepted for himself. It was only his position as
Amelia's fiancé that gave him entrée to the Indian village.

"Were you expecting William?" Ella asked when someone
knocked on the front door.

Amelia shook her head and started to rise. At Ella's frown,
she sank back into her chair. *Foolish woman, trying to do too*

much! Still Ella couldn't help smiling. That was Amelia, always trying to help.

"Mr. Whittaker." Ella opened the door wider when she recognized the man. "What's wrong?"

"My wife's having pains. The baby's coming."

This time Amelia did rise. "Why don't you go back home?" she suggested. "Dr. Ben will be there in a few minutes."

As the man shut the door behind him, Amelia said, "I told Ben this would happen." She frowned. "He's going to have to deliver the babies, and I'm afraid you're the one who has to tell him that. I doubt he's going to be happy."

Ella could not disagree. After Ben had told her how his wife died in childbirth, she knew he would not want to attend any delivery, especially a high-risk one like Susan Whittaker's. Ella reached for her coat. "I'll make sure Ben goes." In her best imitation of Amelia's voice, she said, "Don't wait up for me." As she had hoped, Amelia laughed.

Ben did not.

He was sitting behind the desk in his office, a thick book in front of him when she entered the room.

"What's wrong, Ella? Is Amelia sick again?"

Ella saw that his hair was neatly combed and his eyes clear, as if he had not begun to drink. Thank goodness! Now if only she could keep him sober. "Amelia's fine," she said to reassure him. "Get your bag, Ben. Susan Whittaker needs you."

Ben muttered something under his breath and opened the bottom drawer.

Not tonight. She could not let him jeopardize those babies' lives. Before he could reach inside, Ella moved to the other side of the desk and closed the drawer. As she had suspected, it contained two bottles of whiskey that Ben used for his own nonmedicinal purposes.

"You're not taking that, Ben."

"You don't understand." There was no mistaking the pain in his eyes, but he was wrong. She did understand. Ella knew about pain and how to conquer it. After all, he had taught her that lesson.

"I know that you're a fine doctor," she countered. "You don't need liquor as a crutch."

Ben opened the drawer again. Grabbing one of the bottles, he laid it in his medical bag. Ella pulled it out and placed it beyond his reach. "No," she said simply.

With a chuckle, Ben closed the bag. "You win, Ella. I'm not going to fight with you anymore. Besides, Bart will have a good supply."

She shook her head, then led the way outside. They had crossed the first hurdle. The night was cold and moonless, a time when no one stirred unless necessary. When Ella did not turn down First Street toward her house, Ben asked her where she was going.

"Why, to the Whittakers', of course." They lived on Third between Main and River.

Ben stopped abruptly. His eyes widened, and he blinked twice. "Why on earth would you go there?" he demanded.

To keep you from drinking.

"Because I enjoy the pleasure of your company," she replied sweetly. "Why else?"

As she had hoped, that made Ben laugh. "Better be careful. I could take my scalpel to that tongue of yours." He started walking again, his stride so long Ella had to take two steps to every one of his. If he thought that would discourage her, he was mistaken.

It was her turn to laugh. "Why is it that your threats remind me of one of the passages I make my students memorize: '. . . full of sound and fury, signifying nothing'?"

"Is that what you think? I wouldn't be so sure, Ella. You might just find out you're wrong."

All laughter ceased when they entered the Whittakers' house and heard Susan's cries from the back bedroom. There was no sign of Bart and the two boys.

"We're here, Mrs. Whittaker," Ella called, shedding her coat.

The laboring mother's only response was another groan. Though Ben said nothing, Ella could see him recoil from the sound of Susan's pain. "I'll go in with you," she said, and took a step toward the bedroom. "Maybe having a woman nearby will help her." If the jumble of toys and unwashed clothes on the floor was any indication, Ben might need help clearing a path to his patient.

He appeared shocked by her suggestion. "It wouldn't be proper. You're an unmarried woman."

Ella opened the bedroom door. A quick look told her that although Susan Whittaker did not appear to equate cleanliness with godliness, the floor was bare save for a braided rag rug. "Have you forgotten that this unmarried woman took care of you when you were an invalid? Somehow I survived that lapse of propriety. I imagine I'll survive tonight, too."

"This is different," Ben warned her. "I don't want to hear any complaints."

"You won't."

They spoke to Susan Whittaker for a few seconds, confirming that Bart and the boys would not return until summoned. Then Ella stood at Susan's side, holding her hand while Ben draped a sheet over her and examined her. Though the woman flinched at a contraction, she did not cry out again.

"Is Dr. Amelia right?" Susan asked. "Am I having twins?" Though strands escaped from her blond braids, and caked blood on her lower lip told Ella she had bitten it, she was still a pretty woman.

Ben nodded. "You sure are. I can feel both of them, and they're anxious to come out."

As another contraction swept through her, Susan groaned and gripped Ella's hand. "I'm scared. The pain wasn't like this with the others."

"That's natural." Ben's voice was soothing. "You've never had twins before. Now, when that next pain comes, push."

Susan did, again and again, but the babies showed no sign of being born. After two hours, Ben told the young woman to rest. "No pushing for a few minutes," he said and walked toward the kitchen.

Ella gave Susan a drink of water, then followed Ben. As she had expected, he was rummaging through one of the cupboards. When he found a bottle filled with amber liquid, he reached for it.

"You're not going to drink it."

Ben turned. "How did you know what I was looking for?" His guileless expression did not fool Ella.

"I didn't have to be Sherlock Holmes to solve that mystery. I thought you agreed you weren't going to drink tonight."

Ben lifted one brow. "That's where you went wrong. You told me not to drink. I never agreed." But he put the bottle back in the cupboard and closed the door.

Another hurdle overcome. Ella grabbed a cloth and wiped jam off one of the chairs before she sat. Ben took another. "I'm worried," he told her. "The labor isn't going the way it should. By now they ought to be born, but those babies just aren't moving into the birth canal."

"What's wrong?"

Ben's eyes were wild and haunted when they met hers. "I wish to God I knew what was wrong. The only thing I'm sure of is, she's going to die. I'm going to lose Susan and her babies." He rested his face in both hands, and his shoulders slumped.

Ella had never heard such pain in a man's voice. Poor Ben! She knew Susan Whittaker's condition was tangled with memories of his wife, but somehow he had to get beyond that.

"You will not lose them," she said firmly. "You're going to save all three of them." Ella reached across the table and laid her hand on Ben's arm. He seemed surprised at her touch, almost as surprised as she was that she had done it. It was the first time she could remember touching a man voluntarily.

Perhaps it was her imagination, but his haunted expression seemed to have lessened. "You're a good doctor, Ben," she said.

"But Julia—"

"Susan isn't Julia." Ella spoke calmly but firmly, as she would have to one of her students. "You can do it."

Though he looked dubious, Ella saw a glint of hope in Ben's eyes. When they returned to the bedroom, there was no change in Susan's condition. Ben examined her again, then moved to the head of the bed. He took one of Susan's hands between both of his.

"Susan, I'm going to have to perform a cesarean section," he told her. "Do you know what that is?"

Her eyes widened, and Ella saw tears fill them. "You're going to cut me open?"

Ben nodded. "It's the only way to save your babies."

The young woman whimpered at another contraction, then turned beseeching eyes on Ella. "Stay with me, please."

"Of course." There was nothing that would have gotten her to leave Susan's side now. "I'm going to help Dr. Ben."

She watched as Ben placed a few drops of chloroform on a pad, then laid it over Susan's nose. When the woman was unconscious, he pulled a scalpel from his bag and began to sterilize it.

"I need a drink," he said and turned toward the door.

"No, you don't." Ella put a restraining hand on his arm. "Stop stalling, Ben. I want to see those babies."

The procedure was faster than she would have thought. Ben disinfected Susan's abdomen, then picked up the scalpel. Though Ella saw him hesitate for a second, once he made the first incision, he moved quickly, his skill apparent. In what seemed like only seconds, he had brought the first baby out and handed it to her to clean.

Ella gathered the tiny girl in her arms, heedless of the blood that covered the baby's skin. She was a miracle, this little scrap of humanity who had caused her mother so much pain.

Ella shivered. She had never realized how much joy there could be in watching a life begin. No wonder Amelia had become a doctor. And Ben! Who could ever doubt that he was one of the world's finest surgeons? No matter how old she lived to be, Ella knew tonight was a night she would never forget.

When he finished suturing Susan, Ben turned to Ella. She stood on the other side of the room, a baby in each arm, looking down at the two squalling babies as if they were her own personal miracle. For an instant, Ben was speechless. Ella's expression could only be described as beatific, and she resembled a Madonna with her head bent over the two infants.

"Ella."

She looked up at him, her face radiant with happiness. She was beautiful, Ben realized, truly beautiful. Why had it taken him this long to notice that?

"We did it!" he said.

"No, Ben," she said, smiling jubilantly. Her eyes were fixed on him in an expression he had never seen before. It was almost as though she were seeing him for the first time. "You did it," she said. "I knew you could."

Her voice was warmer than the summer sun, and like the sun it started to thaw fears that had lived within him for years. Ella was right. He had done it. He had defeated the Grim Reaper by saving Susan and the babies. Somehow with the help of the woman who even now looked at him as if he could slay demons, he had delivered not one but two babies.

Ben grinned. "This calls for a celebration."

Ella pressed a kiss on each of the babies' heads, then laid them in their crib. "I saw some grape juice in the pantry. I'm sure Susan wouldn't mind if we had some."

Leave it to Ella to suggest grape juice. Ben doubted there was another woman in Gold Landing who thought that was the proper beverage for a celebration. "Grape juice isn't what I want."

"It's what you need." She followed him into the kitchen and poured two glasses of the purple liquid. When she handed a glass to him, her eyes were luminous. "Don't spoil the day, Ben. You were wonderful. Why do you want to ruin your success with drink?"

Ben took the juice. Whiskey might taste good, but it was not worth seeing the light in Ella's eyes dim. He would let her think he was the hero she imagined him to be, a man who was strong enough to resist temptation. At least for tonight. After all, he could wait until he got home to have the real stuff.

But when he was back in his office and reached for the

bottle, his hand hesitated. Instead of the oblivion that the whiskey would bring, he saw Ella's face and heard her words, *You were wonderful.*

Ben put the bottle back and closed the drawer.

Chapter Twenty-two

The days were short, with the sun hovering near the horizon for only a few hours. Though Amelia missed the summer sun, Alaskan winters had a beauty of their own. She loved the way the snow settled on the branches of the evergreens and the contrast of the blue sky against the white ground, but most of all she loved the northern lights.

The first time she had seen the colored bands of light, she had stopped, afraid that her imagination was playing tricks on her. Surely nothing could be that vivid. Abe had told her that once she had seen the northern lights, she would never forget them, but she had not expected anything so vibrant.

She had thought that the lights would be like a rainbow, a breathtaking arch of muted colors. She had been right about the beauty. It did indeed steal her breath, but there was nothing muted about Alaska's winter spectacle. Ribbons in every shade of blue and green were followed by reds and yellows. They sparkled and glowed like a rainbow, but unlike a rainbow, they were not content to rest in the sky. Instead, they danced. Others might say they shifted or pulsed, but Amelia knew the Indians were right when they said that the lights danced in celebration of the beauty of the great land.

When she pushed open the door to the cabin, Amelia's smile was as bright as the northern lights. The weeks since her recovery had been the happiest she had ever known as her love for William grew, expanding into new dimensions. How could she have ever believed that what she felt for him was nothing more than lust? Oh, there was no denying the physical attraction that drew her to him like bears to a salmon run. But what she and William shared was more than that, much more. They were not just lovers; they were friends, and that knowledge filled Amelia with a deep contentment.

"Hello, love," William said as he brushed the snow off his

coat and hung it on a peg. "I missed you." He punctuated his words with a kiss.

Amelia tipped her head back to look up at him, and her smile was mischievous. "It's been two days."

"Forty-six and a half hours. That's about forty-six hours longer than I should have been away from you," he announced as he drew her closer. Though his skin was still cold from being outdoors, there was nothing chilly about his kiss. When they broke apart, both of them were breathless. "Now, won't you reconsider? A Christmas wedding would be nice."

Amelia shook her head. The idea was tempting, so tempting. But she had to be sure William would not regret his decision, and it was simply too soon to be certain. "A year is twelve months long."

"Things are different in Alaska."

"Not that different. Even Alaskans can't change the calendar."

"I can try, can't I?" When Amelia continued to shake her head, William said, "I won't change my mind, Amelia. I love you, and I want you as my wife—for now and forever."

"I hope so." Oh, how she did!

William kissed her again, then began to unbutton her shirtwaist. His eyes, which had been warm with desire, narrowed as he touched her necklace, and Amelia felt herself stiffen. She should have taken it off before he arrived, but she had forgotten, and now she would have to pay the price. William's caustic comments would dull the luster of their happiness.

"Where did you get this?" he asked.

She would not even try to lie. There was only one source for jewelry like this. "It was a gift from Spring Flower." Amelia waited for his response. When he said nothing, she continued, fingering the pendant, "She told me it's a caribou tooth. I'm afraid I wouldn't know a caribou's tooth from a bear's, and I really don't care to get close enough to either one to learn the difference. Can you imagine looking into their mouths?" Amelia knew she was babbling, trying to postpone William's anger.

To her surprise, he chuckled. "Whoever polished it did a

nice job. Now, let's see what else you have hidden under there.''

Later, as they shared a cup of coffee before returning to Gold Landing, William said, "I saw Ben today. Can't put my finger on it, but he looks different.''

Amelia raised her mug to lips still swollen from William's kisses. "He is different.'' Though the external changes had been subtle, she had noticed Ben's new attitude immediately. "He hasn't had a drink in a month.''

"That's got to be some kind of record. Any idea why he's not drinking?''

"I'm not sure.'' Amelia had known better than to ask Ben directly, but when her subtle questions had elicited no real information, she had begun to speculate. "Since it started right after the Whittaker twins were born, I imagine there's a connection. I just don't know what it is.'' She set the mug on the table and looked at William. Ben was not the only one who had changed. Ever since her illness, she had noticed a difference in William. Though he denied anything had changed, he had seemed more relaxed, as if he were at peace with himself.

"It's strange about Ben," she continued, "because I know he hates maternity cases.'' Though Ella had been there that night, she said little about what had happened other than informing Amelia that Ben was a first-rate doctor and that watching him operate had been nothing short of miraculous.

William shook his head. "Polly used to say that this time of the year was the season of miracles. I never put much stock in that—never did see any Christmas miracles, if the truth were told—but if Ben Taylor has stopped drinking, then maybe Polly was right.''

A season of miracles. What a lovely thought.

The last of the students had left, and Ella was packing papers into her satchel when she heard the door open. She looked up. "Ben!'' Ella felt her face flush. Could the man tell that she had been thinking about him? It was odd. In all the time she and Larry had been engaged, he had not occupied her thoughts

as often as Ben had in the past month. Ever since that magical
night when they had worked together to deliver the Whittaker
twins, Ella could not stop thinking about Ben. At the oddest
times she would find herself remembering how gently he had
held the babies and the smile of pure joy he had worn when
they had toasted their health with grape juice. And now he
was here, in her school.

"Is something wrong?" she asked. Ben rarely came to the
school, and today he looked different, oddly nervous as he
hung his coat on one of the hooks. "Has something happened
to Amelia?"

"Amelia?" For a second Ben acted as though he had never
heard the name. "She's fine," he said at last. He removed his
spectacles, polished them, then stared at the plants lining the
windowsill as if he had never seen a red geranium before.

Something was definitely amiss. He was not drunk, but he
certainly wasn't the Ben Taylor she knew. "What's wrong?"
she repeated.

"Nothing . . . well . . . er . . ." Abruptly, Ben knelt on the
floor in front of her and clasped her right hand between both
of his. "I love you, Ella. Will you marry me?"

The silence of the schoolroom was broken only by the
sounds of the fire and their breathing. Then Ella's heart began
to pound. Her ears had betrayed her. It was not possible. But
he was there, kneeling at her feet. Ben Taylor loved her? He
wanted to marry her? How wonderful! How glorious! How
awful! For an instant hope as brilliant as the northern lights
filled her heart. Then it disappeared as quickly and completely
as the lights did.

How could she even contemplate marriage? Ben might think
he loved her, but when she learned that she was damaged
goods, that love would soon evaporate.

"I'm sorry, Ben. I can't." Ella kept her eyes on the floor,
not wanting to let him see the misery reflected in them. If she
looked at him, the tears that prickled the inside of her eyelids
would surely fall.

He rose and tipped her chin up, forcing her to look at him.
"I don't understand. I thought you cared for me."

"I do." Tears began to trickle down her cheeks.

"Then—"

"I can't marry you, Ben. Please don't ask me to explain.

Amelia sat in the small room that Gloria used as an office sipping a cup of coffee. It had become a ritual. After Amelia finished her monthly examination of the girls, she would spend half an hour with Gloria. Sometimes they would discuss Gloria's girls, but more often their conversation ranged from the weather to the latest fashions. Today, however, Amelia needed to tell Gloria what she had learned.

"Your girls are all fine, except . . ."

Gloria set her glass on the table so quickly that the liquid sloshed onto the highly polished top. "I was right then."

Amelia nodded. "June's pregnant. She won't confirm the date, but I'd say she's two months along. Other than the predictable morning sickness, she seems healthy."

As though she needed fortification, Gloria took a slug of her whiskey. "Will you perform the abortion?"

Gloria had hung a new picture on the wall, a delicate watercolor of a Parisian street. Amelia stared at it for a moment then shook her head. "I can't." It wasn't just her Hippocratic oath to do no harm that stopped her. She could not destroy life. Babies were far too precious.

"Besides, June doesn't want an abortion. She says she's going to keep this baby." Amelia had been surprised by June's reaction when she confirmed the pregnancy. Instead of the dismay she had expected, June had seemed pleased, almost smug in her satisfaction.

It seemed to take Gloria a minute to absorb the news. Then she asked, "Did she tell you who the father is?"

Again Amelia shook her head. "I didn't ask." It was cowardly, and Amelia knew it, but she had not wanted to spend any unnecessary time with June. Though Amelia couldn't approve of June's profession, it was giving her the one thing in life Amelia wanted and would never have.

"Then she probably doesn't know who he is." Surely it was only Amelia's imagination that Gloria sounded relieved.

When she had finished her rounds, Amelia returned to Ben's office. "One of Gloria's girls is pregnant," she told him as she filed the charts for that day's patients.

Though he asked the woman's name, Amelia sensed that, as usual, he had no interest in pregnant women.

"June Woods."

Ben's head shot up, and he stared at Amelia for a moment. He opened his mouth as if to speak, then merely cleared his throat and continued to stare, a puzzled expression on his face. He swallowed once more before he said, "I want to talk to you about Ella."

Either the man was crazy or he did not want to discuss the pregnant prostitute. "What does Ella have to do with June Woods?"

"Nothing, but I need to talk to you about her."

Amelia laid the last charts on the desk, then moved to the other side to face Ben. "What about Ella?"

As Ben made a show of polishing his spectacles, Amelia smiled. It was his favorite delaying tactic. How well she knew him.

"I asked her to marry me."

Ben marry Ella? Amelia revised her opinion. She did not know him at all.

Her mind whirled, considering the possibility. Ben and Ella. Ella must be the reason Ben had not been drinking, and Ben was the cause of Ella's recent absentmindedness. Though she had denied that anything was wrong, Amelia had caught Ella daydreaming with a secret smile on her face. Ben and Ella. They would be so good for each other.

"Wonderful!" Amelia repeated the word, savoring the thought.

"It's not so wonderful. She refused me." A flush of embarrassment colored Ben's face, and Amelia realized how painful the admission must be.

"Did Ella say why?" Amelia leaned her arms on the scarred desk. Though she wanted to put them around Ben to comfort him, she was certain he would hate that.

Ben shook his head. "She wouldn't tell me. All she did was

311

cry and say she couldn't marry me. Hell, Amelia, I hate i'
when a woman cries, and I sure as blazes don't like being the
cause of it.''

Amelia was silent for a long moment, considering. There
was only one reason she could imagine for Ella's refusal.

"You weren't the cause of her tears," she said. She shifted
uneasily, her discomfort caused by more than the hard wooden
chair.

Ben seized her words gratefully. "Then I was right. I figured if anyone in Gold Landing knew the reason Ella won't
marry me, it would be you. Tell me, Amelia."

He looked so earnest, so eager, so . . . loving. There was
nothing Amelia wanted more than to see two of her dearest
friends happy together, and yet . . . "Oh, Ben, I can't." Prom-
ises were sacred. Amelia remembered Ella's anguish the day
she had confided her secret, how adamant she had been that
Amelia could tell no one of her rape. Now Amelia faced a
dilemma. If she told Ben, she would be breaking a trust. If
she did not, she might be condemning Ben and Ella to a life
apart, a life of unrequited love.

"I promised. . . ."

"For God's sake, Amelia, if you know the reason, tell me."
Ben's voice was harsh, mirroring his anguish. "I love Ella,
and I want to make her happy. Hell, I'm even conceited
enough to think I *can* make her happy."

He would. She knew it. Amelia reached across the desk,
and this time she touched Ben's hand. "Is Ella the reason you
stopped drinking?" So many pieces were starting to fit together.

The cuckoo clock ticked, filling the short silence. Ben nodded. "She believed in me. I couldn't face delivering Susan
Whittaker's twins, but Ella told me I didn't need liquor. She
wouldn't let me touch the bottle, just kept telling me it was a
crutch I didn't need." Ben shook his head in wonder. "You
know what, Amelia? Ella looked at me like I was some sort
of hero. God knows I'm not, but she made me see myself
differently. Every time I wanted a drink, I thought about how
disappointed Ella would be, and somehow whiskey didn't look

so good anymore.'' Ben's spectacles slid down his nose. He pushed them back impatiently, saying, ''I love Ella, and I don't want to lose her over some misunderstanding.''

Amelia made her decision. ''It wasn't a misunderstanding.'' Slowly, she told Ben what had happened to Ella. As she spoke, Ben's face turned white, then red with rage.

''The bastard!'' He pounded the desk with his fist. ''I'll kill the bastard!''

Amelia reached for Ben's hand, forcing him to unclench it. ''Ella's frightened. She's afraid of intimacy—which is understandable—but even more than that, she probably thinks you won't want her because she's not a virgin.''

''That's ridiculous! Of course I want her. Being raped wasn't her fault. I love her; it's that simple.''

''Then tell her.''

Amelia made it sound simple. *Just tell Ella you love her and that nothing that happened to her could change that. Tell her you understand her pain, and you want to help her get over it. Tell her you love her.* It sounded simple, but Ben knew that with Ella, very little was simple, and the direct approach was unlikely to be successful. He would have to try a different tactic.

He met her coming out of the general store. To the casual passerby, it would appear a chance meeting. No one needed to know that he had been standing inside his front room, watching through a crack in the curtains, waiting for her to leave so he could just happen to be on Main Street at the same time.

''I've come to apologize,'' he said as he matched his step to hers.

''Apologize? Why would you do that?'' Her breath turned frosty in the winter air, but Ben was willing to bet the red that colored her cheeks was caused by something other than cold. Ella looked downright uncomfortable.

''A gentleman always apologizes when he insults a lady.''

Ella stopped so abruptly that one of her packages tumbled to the ground. She reached for it, but Ben was faster. With a small bow, he handed it back to her. "Let's go inside the hotel," he said, "before Amelia has to treat both of us for frostbite." He had picked the hotel because it was one of the few places in town where he could talk to Ella without offending her sense of propriety.

When they were seated opposite each other on the matched set of horsehair settees in the hotel's small parlor, Ben continued, "Ella, I'm sorry."

She leaned forward, fixing her gaze on his face. Her eyes were troubled, and the way she clasped and unclasped her hands told Ben just how uncomfortable she was with him. Damn that nameless man! Death was too good for him. He deserved a lifetime of slow, infinitely painful torture.

"What are you talking about?" Ella asked. "What makes you think you need to apologize for something?"

From the corner of his eye, Ben saw two women approach, then turn away as the desk clerk ushered them into the larger parlor. Good man. He had earned his generous tip. Ben managed a small smile. "You're being too gracious, Ella. I can't even blame my disgraceful behavior on drink. All I can tell you is, I should never have insulted a fine young lady like you."

Ella's eyes widened, and she started to protest.

"Let me continue," he implored, holding up his hand to silence her. "I don't know what I was thinking. The effrontery of it! Imagine asking you to marry a broken-down old man like me."

When she opened her mouth to speak, he shook his head. "I know my flaws. I'm weak; I used to drink to excess; I'm not young or handsome; I was married before." He took a breath, then continued, "Truly, Ella, I did not mean to insult you. It's just that I love you so much." He shook his head as if in dismay. "I should not be burdening you with my problems. I know I'm unworthy of you, and I promise I will not insult you that way again. Please, just tell me you forgive me."

As Ben watched, Ella's eyes filled with tears. Damn it! He

hated it when a woman cried. She was not supposed to do that.

"You're wrong, Ben. You're not unworthy. You weren't the reason I said no. I was!"

Though his heart began to pound with elation that she had started to confide in him, he shook his head again. "Don't try to spare my feelings, Ella. I know I'm not good enough for you." And that was no exaggeration. Though he had planned his speech to break down her barriers, he knew how little he deserved this wonderful young woman.

"It's not that." Ella leaned forward and laid her hand on his, apparently heedless of the fact that someone might see her gesture. It took all the strength Ben could muster to keep his hand motionless. Hers was so soft, it practically begged a man to grasp it in his, then drag it to his lips.

"Ben, the problem is me, not you. I'm not worthy of you." Her voice cracked, and Ben feared she would shed those tears that hovered on the edge of her lids.

He gave in to temptation and took her hand between both of his. Fixing his gaze on hers, he said, "That's nonsense. The problem is, you're much too good to be my wife. Believe me, Ella, I know that. There's nothing you or anyone else could say that would stop me from loving you and wanting you to be my wife."

As the front door opened, the desk clerk rushed to greet the newcomers and steer them in the other direction. Apparently oblivious to everything else, Ella remained silent for a long moment. When she spoke, it was so softly he could barely hear her words. "I'm not a virgin."

Ben knew how much courage it took for her to utter that sentence. Though he wanted to gather her in his arms and banish the memory of her pain and humiliation, he settled for squeezing her hand and saying, "Neither am I."

Ella gasped softly. When she raised her eyes to meet his again, he saw wonder shining from hers. "You're not shocked?"

Without betraying Amelia, he could never tell Ella that he knew the whole sordid story, and so he countered her question

315

with one of his own. "Do you want me to be shocked?" When she shook her head, he continued, "I told you that I loved you, Ella, and I do. I love you, the whole woman, just as you are. Everything that has happened to you has made you the woman I love."

Ella's hand, which had been lying passively between his, gripped his. "You don't want to know what happened?"

Ben shook his head. "If you want to tell me, I'll listen, but I don't need to know. I know I love you, and that's enough for me." He carried her hand to his lips and pressed a kiss on the palm. "Will you marry me?"

Though her smile was tremulous and tears still pooled in her eyes, Ella's voice was clear. "Yes, Ben, I will."

It was a beautiful wedding. Once Ella had agreed to marry him, Ben had insisted that they not wait. And, to Amelia's surprise, Ella had consented to a Christmas Eve wedding. "Ben says I'm going to be his Christmas present," she had told Amelia, blushing.

Though William had tried his best to convince Amelia they should make it a double wedding, she had refused. It was endearing, the way the man told her at least once a week that he wanted to marry her, but Amelia still was not sure his ardor wouldn't cool when he accepted the reality of her infertility.

"Oh, Amelia, I'm so happy!" Ella's face glowed. She and Amelia had retired to the small room that served as the minister's office, where Amelia was helping Ella into her traveling clothes.

"You deserve to be happy," Amelia told her friend. "And I know you will be. Ben's the perfect husband for you."

Ella blushed and stared at the floor. "I'm a little scared about tonight," she confessed.

Amelia was not surprised. Most young women had bridal jitters as they faced their marriage beds. In Ella's case, the fears were based not on ignorance but on the knowledge of just how painful intimacy with the wrong man could be.

"Talk to Ben," Amelia advised. "He's probably as scared as you."

Ella's head jerked up. "Ben's not scared of anything."

"Except losing you. I've never seen a man so in love. He looks at you as if you're a china figurine that he's afraid will break."

Ella's smile told Amelia she had said the right thing.

"Hurry up." William knocked on the door. "I've got an impatient bridegroom out here."

"We're almost ready." Amelia straightened Ella's hat and kissed her cheek. "Merry Christmas, Mrs. Taylor."

For an instant Ella looked confused. Then she smiled. "That's me, isn't it?"

"Sure is!"

Once Ben and Ella had left Gold Landing, the crowd of well wishers made their way back to the church for the traditional Christmas Eve service. Amelia felt her heart fill with joy as Reverend Langdon told the story of the Christ child's birth, reminding the congregation that this was a season of peace, happiness and, above all, rebirth. How true that was. Ella had been able to cast aside her fears, and Ben had conquered his weakness. Neither had done it alone, but together they had been able to overcome their pasts and forge a new relationship, one filled with love and hope.

When the service was over, William and Amelia returned to her house.

"Merry Christmas, Amelia." He reached into his coat pocket and handed her a square package.

As she unwrapped it, Amelia gasped. "It's beautiful!" She had no doubt that she was holding William's handiwork. The wooden box was carefully crafted, sanded smooth and polished to a high sheen. By itself it was a beautiful piece, but what made it special was the carving on the top. A wreath of flowers surrounded an intricate *A,* and as she looked more closely, Amelia saw that the blossoms were those of tundra plants.

"Oh, William, it's magnificent!"

"Open it," he urged her. As she did, she saw that he had lined the box with velvet. "I wanted you to have a place to

317

put the jewelry your patients gave you. The velvet will keep the beads from getting broken.''

For a moment Amelia was speechless. Though the gift was priceless, his words were even more precious. ''You mean you don't mind that I wear their gifts?''

William shook his head. ''My ring is going to be on your finger. Everything else is your choice.''

''But . . . I thought . . . you said—'' Amelia found it difficult to form a coherent thought.

He took her hands in his and looked into her eyes. ''I was wrong, Amelia, and you were right. Indians are God's creatures, too.''

As he lowered his lips to hers, Amelia's last rational thought was that William's Polly had been right: this truly was the season of miracles.

Chapter Twenty-three

No one would ever call an Alaskan winter short, and yet this, her second winter in Gold Landing, seemed to pass in half the time of the previous one. Perhaps it was all the changes in her life; perhaps it was the fact that her practice had almost doubled in the past year. Amelia was not sure. All she knew was that time seemed to have accelerated.

By the first week in June, Amelia's life had reached a frenzied pace. If she had not known the condition was not contagious, she would have declared that Gold Landing was having an epidemic of pregnancies. Martha Johnson and Karen Fielding were expecting their second children, while Susan Whittaker, whose twins were less than a year old, had surprised everyone with the announcement that she and Bart were planning another addition to their family.

To Amelia's delight, her sister had agreed to come to Alaska a few weeks early to help with the wedding preparations, for William had been determined that his and Amelia's wedding would outshine their engagement party. "There won't be a person in Gold Landing who doesn't know how happy I am to be marrying you," he declared.

Amelia had laughed. "At the rate we're going, there won't be anyone in Alaska who hasn't heard about our wedding."

"All the better."

Today she had reached the cabin before he did and had laid out the simple supper she had brought. They had agreed that when they married, Amelia would move into his house, using the residential portion of Ben's house for a clinic. But, though their official residence would be the big house on Main Street, neither William nor Amelia wanted to give up the cabin. They knew their rendezvous there would be less frequent, but neither doubted the need for a place where they could be together without interruptions.

319

"Why, Dr. Sheldon, you look happy," William said as he entered the cabin. "Is that possible?"

Amelia grinned. "Tell me, Mr. Gunning. Why wouldn't I be happy? It's only three weeks until our wedding, and you haven't changed your mind."

He pulled her into his arms and kissed her soundly. "It gives me great pleasure to say, 'I told you so.' From the very beginning, I told you there was no need to wait. But you, stubborn woman that you are, wouldn't listen."

"You know the reason why."

"And I also know that we've wasted a year when we could have been together."

"Soon."

"Not soon enough." With a wry glance at the plates on the table, he asked, "Do we have to eat?"

"You need your energy."

"Oh, I think I have enough for what I had in mind."

Amelia laughed. "Have I told you how much I love you?" she asked. "Or how happy I am?" Amelia laid her palm on his cheek. "Oh, William, everything is so perfect that sometimes I'm afraid it can't continue."

"Nonsense." William looked at the table again, then shook his head. "Love doesn't end, and you can't deplete it," he told her as he led her toward the bed. "Now, let me show you just what I mean."

For months, Amelia had planned the welcome she would give Belinda when her boat arrived in Gold Landing. She would gather flowers and make a garland for her head like the princesses in the stories she and her sister had read as children. Then, once her trunks had been delivered, she would take Belinda out onto the tundra and show her the beauty she had discovered. That night, because her sister would be tired from the long journey, they would have a simple dinner with William, and then the visits would start.

It was all perfectly planned. Unfortunately, June's baby had other ideas.

"Oh, Ella! I hate to do this to you."

Ella shook her head. "It's no problem. The schoolchildren will be excited when I tell them we're taking an hour off from lessons to meet the boat, and your sister can spend the day with us. I know it's not what you planned, but she'll understand. Babies can't be scheduled the way boats can."

By the time Amelia reached Gloria's house, June's labor was advanced.

"Oh, Doctor." She groaned as the pain subsided. "I'm going to die. I know it."

Amelia shook her head. "You are not going to die," she announced. "You're just having a baby—a big one." She had known from previous exams that the child was large. Though she had been concerned about whether June would need a cesarean section, today everything was progressing normally.

Gloria had had a small room in the attic prepared for June's labor. Though the room was warmer than Amelia would have liked, she could not fault Gloria's logic in keeping June far enough from the other girls' rooms that her cries would not be overheard. Amelia suspected that the sounds of a woman in labor would dampen most customers' ardor, and Gloria—the consummate businesswoman—would not allow that.

"I knew the baby would be big," June said as she caught her breath between contractions. "His father was."

Amelia continued her exam, not voicing her puzzlement. Throughout the pregnancy June had insisted she had no idea who the child's father was. Now it appeared that she knew his identity. "Let's get this baby into position," she said, matching her actions to her words. "I want you to push."

As Amelia watched, she saw the baby's head crowning. "He's coming. Push, June, push." Birds twittered on a branch outside the small window.

June took a deep breath, groaned, then screamed. "William! Oh, William! Help me!"

For an instant, Amelia's hands faltered. *William?* Why was June calling him? *Silly,* she chided herself. *There is more than one William in the world, even if there is only one in Gold Landing.* June meant someone else.

"It's a boy," Amelia said as she cut the cord and cleaned

321

the baby. "A healthy boy." As if on cue, the infant began to howl. The birds, disturbed by the unfamiliar sound, flapped their wings loudly and flew away.

Amelia looked at the new mother. Though her hair was matted and her face covered with perspiration, June's smile was one of supreme satisfaction.

"I knew it would be a boy." As June gloated and extended her arms toward Amelia for the baby, Amelia felt a sharp stab of envy. June, whom the good women of Gold Landing reviled, had a son, while she, who had once been called the town's heroine, would never know the joy of motherhood. Gloria had been right when she'd told Amelia that life was not always fair.

When Amelia handed the baby to June, the young mother studied his face carefully, tracing his features with one finger. "He looks like me." June sounded disappointed. For her part, Amelia could see no resemblance to anyone.

"Then he's a fortunate boy," Amelia said. Now that the delivery was complete, she wanted to leave, to escape the reminder of her own failure. "You're a pretty woman, June, and he's lucky to have your features."

June touched one of the baby's ears, tracing its outline. "I wanted him to look like his father. You know, Doctor, his daddy is the most handsome man in all of Alaska, and when he sees this beautiful baby, he's going to marry me."

It was not William. Though Amelia knew he had had a relationship with June at one time, it had ended before they were engaged. William had told her that. And this baby had most definitely been conceived during their engagement. If the father's name was William, he was another man, someone who had been passing through Gold Landing. In all likelihood, June had called for William only because of their past. It had nothing to do with the child she now held in her arms. Nothing at all.

"Have you picked out a name?" Amelia asked. Despite her rationalizations, she was almost afraid of the answer.

June smiled. "Yes. I'm going to name him after his father.

Joshua." Amelia relaxed. She had been imagining things. William was not the boy's father.

"Joshua William," June added.

"It feels good to be here." There was no disguising the mixture of excitement and fatigue in Belinda's voice.

Amelia studied her sister carefully. By the time she had arrived home, it was early evening, and Belinda had already been in Gold Landing for half a day. They had hugged and kissed and chatted about inconsequential things for a few minutes. Then Amelia had led Belinda into the small sitting room so they could have a long talk. No matter how tired she was from her day's work or how the questions about June's baby's parentage bothered her, and no matter how tired Belinda was from her journey, she wanted to feast her eyes on her sister and hear her voice again.

"You should have warned me about the welcoming committee," Belinda said. "It seemed like half the town was there."

"At least half," Amelia confirmed. "I'd tell you that meeting the boat is a Gold Landing tradition, but it's not confined to us. The arrival of a boat is a big event anywhere in Alaska."

"Like the first motor cars in Philadelphia?"

Amelia smiled, remembering how she and Belinda, along with all of their neighbors, had lined the street, curious to see Henry Ford's new invention.

"I met hundreds of people." Belinda shrugged, her smile telling Amelia she knew she was exaggerating. "All right. Dozens of them. Mostly women, though. There were a few men, but they stood on the side and didn't come for introductions."

Amelia nodded. That, too, was typical of Gold Landing. The men would have been ill at ease being introduced to a single woman.

"I saw your intended, though," Belinda continued. "He's even more handsome than I'd expected from your letters."

Amelia was surprised. William rarely met the boat. Perhaps he had gone today to greet his future sister-in-law. "William

323

was supposed to join us for dinner tonight.'' Amelia explained the plans June's baby had disrupted. ''Now we'll have to wait until tomorrow for you to meet him.''

Belinda chuckled. ''I can wait. The question is, can you? And why on earth did you insist on such a long engagement? I'd have snapped him up in a minute.''

Amelia grinned. ''Don't get any ideas. There are plenty of other men in Alaska.''

''But probably none so distinguished-looking. If I didn't know better, I would have thought he was a lawyer, not a miner. He looked so scholarly.''

A thought assailed Amelia. It was not like William to have remained on the sidelines. Surely he would have introduced himself to Belinda. ''What did he look like?''

''You want me to describe the man you're going to marry?'' Belinda didn't bother to hide her incredulity.

''Humor me, please.''

''He was tall and . . .''

By the time Belinda finished, Amelia was laughing. ''You were partially right, sister of mine. The man you saw *is* a lawyer, but he's not my fiancé. That's Abe Ferguson, Gold Landing's only attorney and my very good friend. I'll introduce you to him.''

And she did.

''Your baby seems healthy,'' Amelia told June when she had completed her examination. ''Is he eating well?''

Joshua slept in one of the bureau drawers. That and the wooden bed were the only pieces of furniture in the small room that Amelia suspected had been designed for storage, for its plain whitewashed walls and unpainted floor were far different from the rest of Gloria's house.

June smiled and nodded. ''He sure is. Josh is one hungry baby. I figure he's in a hurry to grow up big and strong like his father.''

There it was again, the reference to Joshua's father. Though it seemed as if June raised the subject frequently, as if to needle her, Amelia said nothing, merely continued to examine June.

"You're healing well," she told June, "but I don't want you to go back to work for six weeks. Gloria already knows that, and she's agreed to keep paying you."

June sat up, leaning against the headboard. Although without her makeup she looked young, no one would make the mistake of calling her innocent or defenseless. June's blue eyes were filled with knowledge and determination. "I may not go back to work at all," she said. "I've got my son to think about now. It wouldn't be fitting for him to grow up in a place like this, would it?" She gestured toward the white walls, which were, in Amelia's estimation, preferable to the flocked paper in June's other room.

June's words surprised Amelia. She had heard of whores who raised their children while practicing their trade, and had assumed that June would continue to work.

"Where would you go?" she asked.

"I don't rightly know. I reckon I can get some advice, though." When Amelia turned in her direction, June smirked.

"Gloria may be able to help you," Amelia suggested.

"Maybe." June sounded dubious. "I figure I need a man's advice. Maybe I'll ask William. He'll know."

Amelia clenched her fists. William. It always came back to him. Though she did not believe he had fathered June's baby, there was little doubt June was goading her, introducing his name every time they met. What Amelia did not know was why.

When Amelia arrived home that afternoon, she found Belinda pacing the floor of the small parlor, obviously distraught.

"What's wrong?" she asked. Though Amelia loved her sister dearly, she was not sure she had enough energy to deal with another problem today. The puzzle of June and William remained in the back of her consciousness, nagging her when she least expected it.

Belinda's eyes were red-rimmed, as though she had been weeping, and she seemed reluctant to meet Amelia's gaze. "I

325

heard some horrible gossip this morning. I know it's all lies, but it still hurt to hear it.''

It could not be the same story. And yet . . . As her legs threatened to buckle, Amelia collapsed in one of the wing chairs, motioning Belinda to the other.

"Gold Landing is like most towns," Amelia told her sister in a voice that was amazingly calm, considering how her emotions roiled. "We have an active rumor mill, but don't be too quick to discount it. I've found that the tales are frequently true."

Belinda shuddered and dashed a tear from her cheek. "Not this time. It can't be."

"What did you hear?" The last thing Amelia wanted was to hear the gossip, particularly if it confirmed what she had begun to fear. But she had learned long ago that bad news did not go away simply by ignoring it.

Her sister dropped her gaze to the floor, as if unwilling to face Amelia while she spoke. "I heard one of Gloria's girls— Jane, Jean . . ."

"June?" The sick feeling in the pit of Amelia's stomach began to grow.

"That's right. Her name was June. I heard she had a son and . . ." When Belinda looked at Amelia, her eyes filled with tears.

"What about June's son?" Amelia prompted her sister.

"It's too awful!"

"Tell me."

"They say William's the father."

When she realized she was pacing the cabin floor, Amelia willed her feet to be still. Worrying accomplished nothing. She had done what she had to, and in a few minutes, she would know the truth.

"This is an unexpected pleasure," William said as he entered the cabin and tossed his hat onto a hook. "I thought we had agreed we were going to wait until after the wedding to come back here. Not that I'm complaining." He grinned and reached for Amelia.

This was the same William she had seen yesterday, the man she loved, the man she was going to marry. Surely if the stories were true, he would look different. Guilty. Ashamed. Different.

"We need to talk."

William nodded, his face once again solemn. "I figured we would have this talk once more, just so you would be sure." Without waiting for confirmation, he said, "I still want to marry you, Amelia. I have not changed my mind."

The scent of pine trees filled the room, reminding Amelia of the first time William had brought her here, when he had cleaned the cabin with pine boughs to create the perfect bower for their love. Dear William!

"It's not that." Amelia took a deep breath, trying to slow her pulse. If only it were that simple! "There's an awful rumor going around Gold Landing," she said. "I don't want to believe it, but I need to know the truth." He would deny it, and then everything would return to normal. Those horrible, insidious doubts would be vanquished forever.

"What is it, love?"

"People are saying you fathered June's baby."

It was only her imagination that all sound ceased, that her words fell into a vacuum. But as Amelia watched, William's smile faded. "When I heard she was pregnant, I couldn't believe it. Whores are supposed to know how to prevent pregnancy, so how did she get caught that time?"

He had not denied it. Amelia clutched the back of a chair to keep her legs from collapsing.

"Are you saying the baby's yours?"

It could not be true! This was all a nightmare. Any minute now she would awaken, and it would be nothing more than a bad dream.

William was silent for what seemed like an eternity. "It's possible," he said at last.

Amelia could feel the blood rush from her head, and the buzzing reminded her of a swarm of bees. *No!* her mind shrieked. *It's not true!* William couldn't have left her bed to go to June's. He had told her he loved her and that he would never want another woman—not even one who could give him a child—and, fool that she was, she had believed him.

"When did it happen?" Even to her ears, her voice sounded dull and lifeless. This was insane, asking for the details, and yet she could not help herself. She heard the soughing of the pine trees, the chirping of a bird and the soft rustle of a ground squirrel. Everything was the same; nothing was the same.

"When you went to Fairbanks with your patient." William's gaze met hers, and his eyes were filled with pain. "Hell, Amelia, I was hurt, thinking that you cared more for an Indian than you did for me."

He was hurt! "So you decided to get even by hurting me?" How could he have gone to June? Amelia remembered the argument they had had that day and William's threat that he would not be waiting when she returned. She had been tortured with fear that he was serious, but never—not even in her darkest moments—had she thought he would seek solace with a prostitute.

"It wasn't like that." When William reached for Amelia, she backed away. "I got drunk that night and don't remember much of what happened except that I woke up in June's bed."

"And Joshua William is the result." She stared at William. He looked like the man she loved, the one who said he loved her, but he certainly had not acted like a man in love. How could he? With one act, he had destroyed the foundation of their marriage and her happiness. And this was the man who only minutes earlier had declared his love for her!

"Don't look at me like that."

"Like what?"

"Like I'm some sort of monster."

"What would you call it?" she asked. "The man who said he loved me—only me—went to a whore the minute I was gone."

"I told you it wasn't like that. I was drunk, for God's sake."

Amelia closed her eyes, not wanting to see the room where she and William had spent such joyous hours. It was all a sham. Her worst fear had become reality. "Maybe the baby wasn't an accident.'' She opened her eyes and looked directly at him.

William recoiled as if she had struck him. ''What do you mean? Do you think June planned it?''

Seemingly without volition, Amelia's eyes turned toward the bed. She shuddered. ''No, I think you did.'' When William started to speak, Amelia held up a cautioning hand. ''June could give you something that I couldn't—a child of your own flesh and blood. That's why you slept with her, isn't it?''

William reached out as if to touch her, but she shook her head. ''Of course not,'' he said. ''I love you, Amelia.''

''You have a strange way of showing it.'' Amelia clenched her fists to keep from hurling something at him. ''You said all the right words, and, God help me, I believed you. But the truth is clear. You wanted a son of your own so badly you would let a whore be his mother.''

William's face whitened, and she saw lines of strain near his mouth. ''It was a mistake!'' William took a step toward her as he shouted the words. ''Haven't you ever made one?''

Amelia would not give him the satisfaction of stepping back, no matter how menacing his scowl was. She stood her ground and spoke softly. ''Of course I've made mistakes. But not one that hurt someone else that way. I don't know how you could have lied to me.''

A muscle in his cheek twitched, highlighting the scar that stood in sharp contrast against his tan. ''Of course you don't.'' William flung back some of his anger. ''You're the perfect woman. You don't make mistakes, so you have no compassion for any kind of weakness.''

She had not thought a heart could actually break, but if hers wasn't broken, it was badly wounded. Nothing else could hurt so much.

''I know one mistake I won't make.'' She spoke slowly and deliberately, forcing herself to enunciate each word. ''I won't marry you.''

Chapter Twenty-four

"You look awful." Ella did not mince her words. That was one of the changes Amelia had noticed since Ella and Ben's wedding; marriage seemed to have helped her friend gain a new sense of self-confidence. Ella Roberts would have couched her thoughts more carefully, lest she irritate Amelia. Ella Taylor was less timid.

"I feel awful," Amelia admitted. The two women were in Ella's kitchen, Amelia sitting at the table sipping coffee while Ella peeled vegetables. "The pain is almost physical—as if a part of me were amputated."

Ella's hands stilled as she turned to look at Amelia. "It doesn't have to be that way. Ben says William is just as miserable as you are. Can't you find it in your heart to forgive him?"

If only it were that simple. "It's not a matter of forgiveness, Ella. Oh, I know everyone thinks I'm angry because he went to June's bed. That hurt. I'd be lying if I claimed it didn't." Amelia placed the mug on the table, turning it so that the handle was parallel to the table edge, as if the act of arranging a piece of crockery would somehow put her life back in order.

She looked up at Ella. "The fault was mine for believing William could love me the way I am."

Ella's eyes widened, her confusion evident. "What do you mean? Why wouldn't William love you?"

"I'm not a whole woman." After everything that had happened, the words should not have been so painful, but they were. Simply uttering them sent a new stab of loss through her. "I can't have children."

Ella dropped her knife. "Are you sure?" Her face turned red, then white, and she lowered her gaze, apparently no longer willing to meet Amelia's.

"There's no doubt. One of Philadelphia's finest physicians

confirmed it. That's the reason I insisted on a long engagement. William said it didn't matter to him, but I wanted him
to be sure.'' Amelia closed her eyes for a second, remembering
William's protestations. "Obviously, it did matter.''

Giving up all pretense of paring carrots, Ella took a seat
opposite Amelia. "It doesn't make sense. Even if William
wanted a child, I can't believe he would want June to be the
mother.''

"As Abe would tell us, the evidence says otherwise.''

Ella put her hand on Amelia's. "Maybe it was a mistake.''

"It was a mistake, all right, but the mistake was mine. I
thought he loved me enough to overlook my barrenness.''
Amelia's eyes filled with tears. "For a while, I thought I had
everything. Now I know it was a lie. I didn't have anything
at all.'' She laid her head on the table and began to sob.

By the time Amelia left Ella's house, her tears had subsided,
though her eyes were still reddened. The sun, which had been
playing peekaboo with the clouds earlier that day, was now in
hiding, and rain seemed imminent, gray weather that suited
Amelia's mood far better than the brilliant summer sun of the
past few days.

"Amelia!'' Ben was whistling as he turned the corner. He
stopped when he saw her, and his expression grew serious. "I
see Ella told you.''

She looked at him blankly as a few fat raindrops hit the
street. "Told me what?''

"Ella's pregnant.'' Ben sounded as somber as the weather.

For the first time that day, Amelia smiled. "That's wonderful!'' If there was anyone who should have children, it was
Ella, and Ben would be a good father.

"It's not wonderful.'' Ben glowered as he looked at Amelia.
"In fact, it's the worst thing that could happen. I figured that's
why you looked so sad.''

Amelia shook her head, puzzled by Ben's words. "I'm sad
because I made a mess of my life, but this is the best news
I've heard in weeks.'' She ducked under the church portal to

avoid the rain. "Ben, you'll be wonderful parents. Why would you think Ella's pregnancy is bad?"

He dried his spectacles on his shirtfront. "I can't bear to lose her."

Amelia sighed. Several of her patients' husbands had voiced the same fear. Babies were blessed events, but they did force changes in a couple's everyday life.

"Of course the baby will take time," she said, "but Ella will still have plenty to spend with you. You won't be losing her; you'll be gaining a child." It was the advice she gave her patients, advice Ben himself had probably offered on numerous occasions.

Ben shook his head. "Hell, Amelia, if time was all I was worried about, I'd be grinning like a jackal."

"Then what is it? What are you afraid of?"

The rain came down in torrents, splashing on the street, even reaching Ben and Amelia under the portal. Ben looked at his trouser legs in disgust.

"I'm afraid that Ella will die the way Julia did."

"Julia?" That was a name Amelia had never heard.

"My first wife." Ben's eyes were bleak as he remembered. "After she and the baby died, I didn't want any reminders. That's why I came to Gold Landing."

So many pieces started to fit together. Amelia knew Ben had lost a wife, but he had not confided the details. "And that's why you wanted me to handle all the births." No wonder Ben had turned to drink when he had had to deliver a baby; he had sought courage or perhaps oblivion.

"That's right."

Amelia's smile was designed to reassure him. "Ben, there's nothing to worry about. Ella and the baby will be fine."

"I wish I could believe that."

"You can."

How long was she going to punish them? William used the plural pronoun, because there was no doubt Amelia shared his pain. He had seen her walking down Main Street, returning from her rounds, and she looked as miserable as he felt. Knowing that she was suffering was no consolation and did nothing to fill the gaping hole where he used to have a heart. She refused to talk to him; she sent his letters and gifts back unopened; she even had her sister inform him that if he needed a doctor, he would have to contact Ben.

A doctor was not what he needed. A wife was, but thanks to one stupid mistake, it appeared he was not going to have one. Amelia was stubborn and proud, and what he was about to do would only fuel her anger. Still, a man had responsibilities.

He turned down a front walk that had not felt his footsteps in close to a year.

"Is June in?" To William's surprise, Gloria opened the door herself.

Her welcoming smile faded, and for a moment William feared she would close the door in his face. Instead, she gave him a long, appraising look, then said, "June won't be entertaining callers for another few weeks."

Even William knew that. Hadn't he heard Alex grouse about the six weeks of celibacy after Hannah's birth? "It wasn't entertainment I was looking for. I need to talk to June."

Gloria's expression was grim. "I'll bet you do." She propped her chin on one hand, considering. "That's a real cute baby June's got," she said at last.

The baby. Of course Gloria knew that was the only reason he was here.

"Let me be straight with you. I don't know if he's mine or not. Hell, I don't know how she could tell who fathered the child."

Gloria raised a carefully sculpted brow. "You'd be surprised. Women have a sense about these things. And there are ways . . ." She let her words drift off, then asked briskly, "So, what are you going to do if he is yours?"

"I don't know." If Gloria thought he was going to offer to marry June, she was wrong. He would not subject June and himself to a loveless marriage just for the child's sake, and yet . . . "All I do know is how hard it is for a boy to grow up without a father."

333

Apparently satisfied, Gloria ushered him into a small room that he had never seen before and summoned June and her baby.

She was dressed in a simple wrapper that did nothing to flatter her body; her face was devoid of makeup, and her hair hung in lank strands. This morning June was no man's fantasy, and yet her smile as she looked at the baby in her arms transformed her face, making her more beautiful than William had ever seen her.

"You came to see Josh." It was a statement, not a question.

William nodded and took a step closer to the boy who might be his son. He stared at him, searching for a resemblance. The child had pale blond fuzz that would someday be hair, and blue eyes. Look though he might, William could see nothing of himself in the baby's features. "He looks like you, June."

As she moved closer to William, a ray of sunshine lit her face, and William realized how young she was. He had always considered June mature; today she seemed like little more than a child herself, despite the baby in her arms.

"That's what everyone says." June did not bother to hide her disappointment. "Do you want to hold him?"

Did he? William was not sure, but he reached for the boy, transferring him into the crook of his arm. With one finger, he traced a line down the child's cheek, watching him smile instinctively. Josh opened his eyes and stared at William. Though it was foolish to think that the infant recognized him, William felt an unfamiliar warmth begin to spread throughout his body as he looked down at him. He had held Hannah and other babies, but he had never felt this way. Was this a parent's instinctive recognition of his child? Or was it nothing more than the knowledge that Josh and he shared a common bond, the lack of a father? William wished he knew the answer.

"I never thought I'd say this, but you're stupid." Belinda stood in the doorway to Amelia's bedroom, watching as her sister unpinned her hair and began to brush it.

Amelia met her sister's gaze. "Just what did I do to provoke hat criticism?'' It was not like Belinda to be so blunt, and unlike Ella, Amelia could not attribute her sister's frankness to a recent marriage.

"Look at you, Amelia. You're throwing yourself into your work as if that'll make you happy. If that's not stupid, I don't know what is."

Amelia bristled. Of course she was working hard, but it was not for the reason Belinda thought. "I came to Alaska to be a doctor," she told her sister, drawing the brush through her hair with more force than usual. "That's what I'm doing."

Belinda's expression said she was not convinced. "You can try that story on someone else, but I'm not buying it. I saw how you worked last month, and it wasn't like this. You've gone crazy. And don't try to convince me that everyone in Gold Landing has suddenly developed a disease that you have to cure."

Amelia fixed a cold stare on her sister. "You know nothing about my patients. Nothing."

In the past Belinda would have backed off when Amelia used that tone of voice. Not today. "Perhaps not, but I know you, and I know you're using your patients as a shield because you're afraid to face the mess you've made of your life."

Her words struck a painful chord, and Amelia lashed out in retaliation. She flung her hairbrush onto the dressing table. "I can handle my life quite well, Belinda. I don't want your advice."

"That's clear, but I'm going to give it anyway. Older siblings have some prerogatives, you know."

Amelia stared at her sister, then asked in a weary voice, "When are you going home?" She was not sure how much more of Belinda's company she could face, particularly now that her sister was asking questions Amelia had no desire to answer.

Belinda smiled sweetly. "I came for your wedding. I certainly can't think of leaving until after that."

"If that's what you're waiting for, you'll be here forever."

"That suits me fine."

Before Amelia could respond, Belinda turned and flounced out of the room.

If there had been another way to get to the bridge, Amelia would have taken it, but Second Street was the only road at this end of town. And so she was forced to walk past Gloria's house each time she visited her patients on the other side of the river. And each time she did, she thought of the small boy who slept in a bureau drawer on the third floor, the boy who looked like his mother but bore his father's name.

Today she was not the only pedestrian on Second Street. As she walked toward the bridge, careful to remain on the opposite side of the street from Gloria's, she saw a man emerge from the whorehouse. There was no mistaking that tall figure, and—though she fought it with every ounce of self-control she possessed—her heart leaped at the sight of William.

He strode down the walk, then stopped when he saw her.

"Hello, Amelia."

She brushed a mosquito away. Though she was sorely tempted to ignore William, to pretend he was a momentary annoyance like the mosquito, part of her could not help asking, "Were you visiting your son?" The answer was obvious, and her question did little more than needle him and cause her own stomach to knot. Yet still she asked it.

"I was with June's boy," he replied. The front curtains parted, and two women peered out, obviously intrigued by the drama unfolding on their doorstep.

"We're talking about the same child, aren't we?"

William gave her a long look, then took her arm and led her a few steps down the boardwalk, where they would not be overheard.

"I love you, Amelia," he said, "and it's killing me one inch at a time that I hurt you the way I did." His gray eyes were solemn as they met hers, and Amelia knew the pain that radiated from them mirrored her own anguish. "I would do almost anything not to have hurt you, but I can't wish that Josh was dead."

The circles that ringed William's eyes and the lines of fatigue creasing his forehead told Amelia that William slept as poorly as she did. He paused for a moment, and Amelia sensed he was searching for strength to continue. He looked at the sky as a cumulus cloud drifted by, momentarily blocking the sun. "You once told me that everyone was put on earth for a reason. I believe that, too. Little Josh has his reason. I don't know what it is yet, but I do know that he deserves love and happiness like the rest of us."

He was right, of course. She could not hate Josh. She didn't hate Josh, and yet it was so hard to view him as just a boy. Each time she came to Gloria's house and examined him, she saw not a patient, but a symbol of her own inadequacy. Each time, she faced the painful realization that June, though she lacked Amelia's education and social standing, had the one thing Amelia wanted most: a child.

Jealousy, Amelia was discovering, was a nasty illness, and she had developed a serious case.

Amelia was returning from her rounds the next afternoon when she heard a woman shouting.

"Quick, Doctor! It's Frank. He's having another attack."

Amelia turned, recognizing the woman as Muriel Stratton. Though Amelia had never treated Frank professionally, she was aware of his bad heart, and adrenaline began to course through her veins as she ran the last few feet to the Stratton house. Speed was vital.

She found Frank Stratton clutching his chest. "It's bad, Doc." His face was ashen, his eyes wild with fear. "Help me."

Amelia grabbed his wrist, placing her fingers on a vein. She counted, then forced a serene expression onto her face. As she had feared, Frank's pulse was dangerously irregular.

"Do you have pain in your arm?"

Frank nodded as he grimaced. "Arm . . . chest . . . can't breathe." He pronounced the words with obvious difficulty.

"Help him!" Mrs. Stratton leaned over Amelia's shoulder.

"Would you boil some water?" Amelia did not need boiled

water; what she needed was a reason for Frank's mother to leave the room. Her hovering would not help her son.

Amelia opened her bag, pulling out her mortar and pestle. Thank goodness she carried a supply of medicines whenever she left the office. She knew Ben treated Frank with digitalis.

"Try to relax," she said as she measured the powerful drug into the mortar. "I'm going to give you something for the pain."

"Hurry, Doc. I'm gonna die. Never been this bad."

Amelia checked his pulse. Though it was erratic, it had not worsened.

"You'll be all right. Dr. Ben has given you this medicine before." She measured the last grains, then began to grind. When she had made the tincture and administered it, she took Frank's pulse again. His color was returning, and his pulse slowed. The digitalis was working. His condition had stabilized.

Amelia cleaned the mortar and pestle, then turned back to her patient. *Oh, God, no!* Frank's face bore a bluish cast, and his breathing was now so shallow she could barely see his chest rise.

Amelia grabbed his wrist, searching for a pulse. Where was it? There had to be a pulse. When she finally located the beat, it was dangerously slow.

No! It couldn't be. But as she held his wrist, Frank Stratton's pulse slowed again, then stopped. Though Amelia tried every lifesaving procedure she had been taught, they had no effect. Frank Stratton was dead.

"What is it, Doctor? What's wrong?" Muriel burst into the room at the sound of Amelia's cry. After one look at the doctor's somber expression, she ran to her son's bedside and touched his face, then recoiled when she realized he was gone.

"Frank, oh, Frank. What am I going to do without you?" The woman began to keen, a loud wailing that rang in Amelia's ears.

"I'm sorry," she said. "His heart just gave up."

But Muriel Stratton wanted no comfort. "Get out of here!" she shouted. "You killed him. You killed my Frank." She kept one hand on her son's body as if she thought Amelia would try to wreak further harm. "Get out before I kill you the way you killed my son."

As Amelia gathered her instruments, she heard Muriel mutter, "Dr. Ben could have saved him."

When she returned home, Amelia found the house empty. Belinda had left a note that she had gone to supper with Abe, and there were no patients waiting. Slowly, wearily, Amelia pulled Frank Stratton's chart from the files and made the final notation. As she had been taught, she inscribed the dosage she had given him, then opened her bag and pulled out the vial of digitalis, counting the remaining tablets to confirm what she had written.

She counted once, then a second time. There was no mistake. She was short two tablets.

As Amelia stared at the medicine, she heard a roaring in her ears, and the room began to darken. Instinctively, she lowered her head, tying to prevent herself from fainting.

She could not deny the evidence or the implication. She had given Frank an overdose of one of the most potent drugs known.

Muriel Stratton was right. She *had* killed him.

Chapter Twenty-five

"Where's Ben?" Amelia demanded as she burst into Ella's house. She had to talk to him, to tell him what had happened.

Ella came into the hallway, wiping her hands on her apron. "It's poker night, so he's at William's." She looked at Amelia. "What's wrong?"

Amelia shook her head. "I've got to see Ben," was all she would say.

She opened the back door of William's house, knowing the men usually played in the kitchen. It was the first time she had been in the house since William had recovered from pneumonia. When she had left that day, she had been ebullient, thrilled that she had been able to nurse William through his crisis. That seemed like a hundred years ago. Then she had believed herself to be a competent physician. Today she knew different.

"Amelia, what's wrong?" William jumped from his chair. Ben, Alex and Sam Baranov nodded a greeting but remained seated.

"Ben," she said, her voice sounding as lifeless as she felt, "I've got to talk to you. Now."

"Party's over." William nodded at the two other men. He gestured toward Ben. "You can use the parlor."

Amelia walked on legs that would barely support her weight, then sank into one of the chairs. "Oh, Ben," she said, "Frank Stratton's dead. I killed him."

Ben pulled the pipe from his mouth, gripping it so tightly Amelia could see his fingers whiten. "What happened?" he asked.

The words tumbled out as Amelia explained what she had done, concluding, "Muriel said I killed him, and she was right."

Ben made a show of tamping the tobacco into his pipe and

lighting it. Then he shook his head. "That dose shouldn't have been lethal. I might have given him that much myself, especially since he told you the pain was worse than normal."

Amelia was certain Ben was trying to help her, but he was wrong. "I knew better," she said. "We were taught to start with a small dose, then give the patient more if needed."

Ben exhaled smoke rings. His pipe, he had told Amelia, helped him to think clearly. "That's a good policy," he agreed. "But Amelia, this was your first time dealing with a bad heart. When there's an attack like that, everything happens so fast that it's frightening."

He was right. She had been frightened, but that did not exonerate her. She should have followed procedure. Amelia could feel her whole body begin to tremble. *Shock,* her mind told her. *Delayed shock.*

"Don't try to rationalize it, Ben," she said, forcing the words through clenched teeth. "I made a mistake, and a man's dead as a result. I can't ever undo that."

There was a moment of silence as Ben continued to smoke. Then he said softly, "All of what you've told me is true. The question is, what are you going to do now?"

Amelia took a deep breath, trying to still her racing heart, before she answered. "There's no choice. I'm going to leave Alaska and stop practicing medicine."

"I never thought you were a coward."

The voice came from the doorway. "William!" Amelia turned to stare at him. "How much did you hear?"

"Enough to realize that you've suddenly become a coward."

For once she could not read his expression. Though he appeared sad, she was not certain what had caused his sorrow, whether it was the knowledge that his friend was dead or something else.

"I'm not a coward," she said. "I'm a realist, and I know I can't trust my own judgment. Just ask Muriel Stratton."

In three quick strides William crossed the room and pulled Amelia to her feet. "Look at me," he said, tipping her chin upward. "How many babies have you delivered?" When she

341

remained silent, he continued. "How many lives have you saved—including mine?" She could not answer, could not form the words to tell him that none of that mattered. "Are you going to forget all that? You made one mistake, Amelia. One. That's all."

He did not understand.

She forced herself to speak. "I'm a doctor, William. A doctor can't afford to make mistakes."

Slowly, William shook his head. "Amelia, you're human. That means you make mistakes. We all do. Only God is perfect."

His words echoed in her head as the days passed. Though Ben and Belinda insisted that she return to her practice, she refused to leave the house. How could her patients trust her when she did not trust herself? But finally, when Ben told her that patients were suffering because he couldn't treat them all, she resumed her rounds.

Belinda told her it was her imagination, that people were not actually staring at her and calling her a murderer, but the feeling lingered, and she was hesitant each time she made a diagnosis, worrying that she would be wrong.

Worst of all was the knowledge of how she had hurt William. What a fool she was! She had rejected William because he had made a mistake, and when he had asked if she had ever made one, she had been adamant, telling him she had never hurt anyone with her mistakes.

How arrogant she had been, so convinced of her own superiority that she had refused to see the truth. The newest grave in the cemetery bore testimony to just how wrong she had been. How ironic. She had berated William, but his mistake had created a life, while hers had ended one. Knowing that, how could she face him or anyone else again?

But face them she did. And if she was less confident of her diagnoses, more tentative in her treatment, she tried to hide it. Her patients paid her to heal them, and part of that healing was instilling in them the belief that they would soon recover.

"Oh, Doctor, I'm glad you came today," Martha Johnson said when Amelia entered her cabin.

"Problems?" Martha's pregnancy had progressed smoothly, and she had passed the first three months with nothing more than occasional morning sickness.

Martha shook her head. "Not me. It's Rachel. She's been coughing. I'm real worried."

She had reason to worry, Amelia soon discovered. The little girl's painful cough and the blue tinge that even now colored her face told Amelia she had developed pneumonia. It was a virulent disease, particularly for the young or elderly. Though her heart was heavy, Amelia tried to mask her fear that the first baby she had delivered in Gold Landing would die.

"I want Dr. Ben to treat her," she told Martha as she explained her diagnosis. What if she was wrong and it wasn't pneumonia but something else? Amelia would not risk Rachel's life.

Martha Johnson put her hands on her hips. "What for?" she demanded. "Rachel knows and trusts you. She would be afraid of Dr. Ben."

But Amelia was adamant, and finally Martha sent Emil into town to call Ben.

"This had better be important," Ben groused when he arrived at the Johnsons' cabin. "Ella made moose stew for dinner, and you know I like that." Though his tone was exasperated, he could not hide the twinkle in his eyes when he spoke of his wife.

"How can you make light of the situation?" Amelia demanded. "A child's life is at stake. I think she has pneumonia."

"You've handled pneumonia before." Ben made no move toward the child's bed.

"But what if I'm wrong?"

"You aren't."

He was not listening. "Ben, I need to be sure."

This time when he peered over the top of his spectacles, the twinkle had disappeared. "All right," he agreed with obvious reluctance. As she watched, Ben performed a perfunctory examination. "You're right, Amelia. Rachel has pneumonia. Now I'm going home to my wife and my moose stew."

"But Ben—"

"What do you mean, 'but Ben'? It's simple. The girl does not need more than one doctor. She needs the best that Gold Landing can offer, and that's you."

"But Ben . . ." How could he forget what had happened to her last seriously ill patient?

"Would you stop that 'but Ben' routine? Be sensible, Amelia. You know more than I do about pneumonia. That means you are the right person to stay with Rachel."

She did, caring for the young girl at the same time that she reassured Rachel's anxious parents and tried to quell her own doubts. Three days passed before Rachel reached her crisis, three days in which Amelia slept for no more than minutes at a stretch. But at last the girl's fever broke, and she began to breathe normally.

Amelia grinned, her elation bubbling to the surface. "Rachel's going to be fine," she told Martha and Emil.

Emil grinned. Martha began to weep. "You're the best doctor Gold Landing has ever had," she said as she brushed the tears from her cheeks.

Amelia's smile was bittersweet. "I only wish that were true."

Though Emil offered to drive her home, Amelia walked, needing the time alone. She had saved a patient, and it felt so good, so very, very good. She tipped her face up and let the sun caress it. How long had it been since she had been able to enjoy the simple pleasure of being alive on a beautiful day? Though nothing could erase the pain of knowing she had caused Frank Stratton's death, saving Rachel helped to even the scales. It reminded her of why she had become a doctor. She could make a difference.

The apathy that had been her constant companion dissolved, and for the first time in weeks, Amelia felt a bubble of excitement. Life could be wonderful, if only she could share it with William.

Oh, how she missed him!

Without William, nothing else mattered. The satisfaction she felt over defeating death paled without William at her side to share it. Even the agony she had endured after Frank's death would have been easier to bear if she had been with William. But she had turned him away. Every time he made an overture, she rejected him. She had hurt him in so many ways that the damage might be irreparable.

Still, she had to try.

Though her heart pounded and her hands trembled, she forced her feet to keep moving. She had to see William, and even though there was a chance he would refuse to talk to her, she had to try to explain just how wrong she had been. Then the choice would be his.

He was sitting behind his desk, staring at a sheaf of papers, when she entered the mine office. Amelia looked at him, cataloging his beloved features, committing them to memory. If he turned her away, she would leave Gold Landing, perhaps Alaska. Living here without William would be impossible.

"Amelia!" William rose to greet her. He looked puzzled, and his hand touched the scar on his cheek. "Is something wrong?"

He walked in front of the desk, extending his hand toward her. "Come, sit." Before he could touch her, Amelia shook her head and dropped to her knees.

"What the—"

"Oh, William, please forgive me," she said. Though her eyes were brimming with unshed tears, she refused to let them fall. Amelia knew William would do almost anything to prevent tears, and she would not take advantage of his weakness.

He looked stunned. "Forgive you for what?" He reached down, trying to pull her to her feet.

She shook her head again. Her heart thudded, and she could taste the fear, a fear so great she thought it might overwhelm her. When he heard everything, would he reject her? "For so many things, but mostly the cruel words I said about you and June. I know the night you spent with her was a mistake. I should have known that from the beginning, because you

345

wouldn't have hurt me deliberately. But I didn't believe you. Instead, I lashed out in my pain.''

When William started to speak, Amelia shook her head, silently pleading for him to let her continue. ''It was my own weakness and fear that made me blame you. I know that now. You're the best thing that's ever happened to me.'' She closed her eyes, hoping to keep the tears from falling. ''I was so afraid I'd lose you when you saw me the way I saw myself—as half a woman.''

He stared at her for a moment, as if absorbing her words. ''Is that what you think I would do?''

''Let me finish, please.'' She met his gaze, and the love she saw blazing in his eyes was so strong that despite her resolve, tears began to course down her cheeks. ''I know I can never undo the words I've said. All I can do is hope that you'll forgive me.''

William drew her to her feet. Catching her hands in his, he said, ''Sweetheart, I'm the one who should ask for your forgiveness. I hurt you horribly.'' His gray eyes were serious as he said, ''We've both hurt each other, but I'd like to think our love is strong enough to survive it. For I love you, Amelia, and I always will. Nothing you can say or do will change that.'' He drew one of her hands to his lips and pressed a kiss on it. ''I know you loved me once. Do you still love me?''

''Oh, yes, William. I do!''

A smile lit William's face and chased the shadows from his eyes. ''Then marry me.''

He loved her. Somehow, despite everything, he loved her. Amelia threw her arms around him. ''Oh, William, I love you.''

''Confound it, woman. Answer my question. Will you marry me?''

Amelia laughed. ''Yes, yes, a thousand times, yes!'' she said, and punctuated her words with kisses.

''It's about time!''

Chapter Twenty-six

The first frost had already turned the tundra flaming red, and the willows had begun to shed their leaves. Though some might view the advent of autumn with regret, sorrow had no place in Amelia's heart. The happiness that filled it left no room for even a seed of discontent to take root, for today was her wedding day.

"You're going to be the most beautiful bride Gold Landing has ever seen," Belinda told her as she arranged her hair in sausage curls, a style that was years out of fashion but the only one Amelia would consider.

Amelia answered with a radiant smile. For the first time in her life, she felt beautiful. William's love had banished the last of her insecurities, leaving only contentment in their wake. Though the tundra flowers might be dying, Amelia was blossoming.

"It's the dress," she said. She wore her grandmother's wedding gown, a magnificent concoction of ivory satin and lace with the fitted bodice and hoop skirt of a previous era. At Amelia's request, Belinda had brought the dress and their grandparents' wedding portrait with her and had just spent hours coaxing her sister's hair into the style shown in the daguerreotype.

"You always said you wanted to wear Grandma's dress." Belinda took a step backward to admire her handiwork.

"And you were going to wear Mother's."

Belinda laughed. "Abe won't wait long enough for it to be shipped here." She touched Amelia's hand. "Are you sure you don't mind?" She and Abe had announced their engagement three days earlier, sending Gold Landing's rumor mill into overdrive.

If it would not have dislodged some of the curls that Belinda had so painstakingly arranged, Amelia would have shaken her head. As it was, she flashed her sister a reassuring smile.

"From the beginning, I thought of Abe as a brother, and now you're going to make it official. How could I be anything but happy? I just hope—"

Amelia's words were interrupted by a woman's cry.

"Dr. Sheldon! Dr. Sheldon!"

"What's wrong, Sally?" Amelia recognized the visitor as one of Gloria's prostitutes. Beneath the heavy makeup, her face was white.

"Gloria thinks one of the girls drank poison. She's mighty sick."

Instinctively Amelia reached for her bag. Though Belinda had chided her for keeping her medical bag at her bedside rather than in the office, Amelia had been summoned in the middle of the night too many times to have it more than an arm's length away.

With a restraining hand on Amelia's arm, Belinda faced Sally. "Call Dr. Ben. It's my sister's wedding day."

As if that mattered. A woman's life was at stake. "Tell William what happened and that I'll be there as soon as I can."

"But Amelia—"

"Who's sick?" Amelia hiked up her hoop skirt as she climbed into the buggy. While Gold Landing's residents made their way to the church for what everyone knew would be the most elaborate wedding of the year, the bride was racing in the opposite direction.

"It's June." Sally maneuvered the buggy around a small group of pedestrians.

June. Of all the girls, Amelia would have thought her the least likely to harm herself. She alone had a child, and from what Amelia had seen, she was devoted to the boy.

"Let's hope you're not too late," Gloria said as they climbed the stairs to June's third-floor room. Though she was as impeccably groomed as ever, lines of worry creased the madam's face and added years to her appearance. "Josh is downstairs. I didn't think he should be with his mother if . . ."

Amelia nodded and opened the door. Her first sight of her

patient confirmed the gravity of her condition. June's face was gray, and even from the door, Amelia could see that her breathing was shallow. She grasped the woman's wrist and took her pulse while she monitored her other vital signs.

"What did you drink?"

June shook her head weakly, her blond hair fanning out over the pillow. "Doesn't matter. I'm gonna die."

Amelia's hoop skirt swayed, the satin rustling softly as she mixed a solution of ipecac. "I need your help," she told Gloria. "We have to get the poison out of her system."

"No." June's voice was weaker than before.

Amelia nodded at Gloria. "Ready?" Together they propped June into a sitting position; then Gloria held June's arms while Amelia forced the liquid down her throat. When the medicine had done its work and June had vomited the remaining contents of her stomach, Amelia wiped her patient's face.

"Why are you torturing me?" Though still weak, Amelia noted that June's voice seemed stronger, and her color was improving. "Don't you understand? I want to die."

Gloria gasped, frown lines appearing between her eyes. In response to Gloria's unspoken question, Amelia shook her head. June would not die.

"Why?"

"I have nothing. Nothing." June repeated the word, struggling to a sitting position as she fixed her eyes on Amelia. "I hate you, Amelia Sheldon. You've taken the only thing I ever wanted. You stole William." Her voice was venomous, and her eyes narrowed as they focused on Amelia's dress, now spotted with blood and vomit.

Amelia's legs threatened to buckle. It was normal for her to feel drained after she had fought a particularly difficult battle, but this was different. This was the first time her patient had been angry because she saved a life, the first time Amelia had faced recrimination rather than joy over a successful treatment.

"I never thought he would marry you," June said, her face contorted with pain. "If you had left when you were supposed to, he would have married me."

Gloria stroked June's forehead, brushing a tendril of hair from her face. "William never promised to marry you," she said, and Amelia sensed that she was trying to help June face reality.

"He would have. I know it. Only she was here." June glared at Amelia. "I tried to make you leave. That's why I burned the clinic."

There was a moment's silence as June's words registered. Stunned, Amelia sank onto the plain wooden chair that Gloria had dragged in for her, her heart thudding as she recognized the depth of June's hatred. It was frightening to realize she had had no inkling of June's feelings, and yet June's confession sent hope rising like the proverbial phoenix from the flames.

Like most of Gold Landing, Amelia had thought that one of the men, or perhaps a group of them, had started the fire to prevent her from treating the Indians. Now she knew the truth. It was jealousy, not prejudice, that had caused her to lose her clinic. The fire had been directed at her, not her native patients. Though nothing would restore the clinic, June's confession lightened Amelia's spirits.

Gloria's reaction was far different. She pulled her hand away, as if flames were shooting from June's forehead. "What kind of monster are you?" she demanded. "How could you do something like that?"

Amelia shook her head. "It doesn't matter now. What's important is keeping her alive. Let's get her walking."

Though obviously reluctant to touch June, Gloria helped Amelia force her patient to her feet.

"I told you, I don't want to live."

Amelia pushed June, prodding her to walk. "And I said I am not going to let you die." Amelia felt almost giddy with the knowledge that she could rebuild the clinic and not worry about another case of arson.

June stiffened her legs, trying to defeat Amelia. "You won't win. You may keep me alive today, but I'll try again tomorrow. And tomorrow I'll succeed."

Amelia shook her head. "Think about Josh. He needs you."

As June took another step, Amelia watched emotions play across her face, sorrow, pain and then hope.

"Promise me you'll take him." June's blue eyes filled with tears. "Take Josh and raise him as yours."

"You're not going to die," Amelia said firmly. "Josh won't need a guardian."

The stubborn expression Amelia had seen so often settled on June's face. She pointed at Amelia. "You want me to live. Well, I want something, too. I want to leave Gold Landing."

It was the perfect solution. June could start a new life, and Amelia would not be faced with the reminder of William's mistake.

"I can arrange that," Gloria said, and if her voice betrayed eagerness, Amelia couldn't blame her.

"I want my son to have a better life than I ever did. That's why I need her to raise him." June jerked her head in Amelia's direction.

What she was asking was impossible. June could not realize how painful Amelia found her visits to Gloria's house and how she sought ways to avoid little Josh. How could she possibly live with him, see him every day, and every day face that living, growing reminder of her own inadequacy? How could she even consider raising him as her child?

Adoption was one thing. She and William had planned to adopt a child, a stranger's child. This was far different.

She couldn't!

"You're an unnatural woman, June." Gloria's voice resonated with anger, and her heels clicked on the floor as she tried to force June to walk more quickly. "How can you give up your own child?"

"Stay out of this, Gloria. It's between the doctor and me. She takes Josh and I leave, or I finish what I started."

Amelia stared at June's face, searching for a sign as she searched her own heart. She did not think June would follow through with her threat to kill herself. As the poison loosened its grip on her, June was regaining her normal composure. If Amelia had to guess, she would say the woman was anxious to leave Gold Landing. With the money William would give her, she could invent a past that did not include prostitution.

Josh was another story. Amelia's palms dampened at the thought of the baby.

"Let's go into the hall," she said, suddenly unable to bear the small room any longer. As she strode down the corridor, setting a pace that even Gloria had trouble matching, Amelia tried desperately to quench her anger and her envy.

How could she raise Josh, knowing how much his mother hated her? And yet, how could she deny William his son? If Amelia refused June, she would probably take the boy with her. Knowing William, there would be no mention of the child or the emptiness in his heart wrought by Josh's absence.

William was a strong man, a man who had dealt with loss before. He would deal with this. There would be no words of recrimination, no indulgence in the game of "if only." William would accept June's departure and the loss of his son stoically. He and Amelia would adopt another child—perhaps two or three—and build a family together. They would be happy, for William would never know that he had had the chance to raise his son.

But Amelia would.

Her feet moved slowly and deliberately, forcing June to keep walking, while her mind continued to whirl. If she loved William—really loved him—how could she deprive him of the joy of seeing his son grow? How could she take away something that she knew was vitally important to him? How could she destroy his chance to guide Josh's childhood as he wished his father had guided his own?

She could not.

"Keep walking," she ordered when June's feet faltered. "A few more minutes," she told Gloria, whose face showed signs of strain.

The sound of her own kid slippers on the floor was oddly comforting, helping her marshal her thoughts.

It would be difficult. She knew that. There would be days when she resented Josh's presence in their lives and when the pain seemed overwhelming. There would be days when she hated herself for having a constant reminder of her own inadequacy. There might even be days when she hated William for the mistake that brought Josh into their family. But balancing that would be the knowledge that she had been able to turn one of William's dreams into reality and give him a son. Love, the all-encompassing, overwhelming love she felt for William, would help her endure the pain.

"Yes," she said, "I'll take Josh."

June smiled smugly, as if there had been no doubt of Amelia's answer.

"Are you sure?" Gloria asked. Her eyes searched Amelia's face, seeking confirmation that Amelia recognized the gravity of her decision.

Amelia nodded. The calm that even now was displacing her anger told Amelia she had made the right decision. "If William agrees."

"Amelia!" She heard his voice at the same time that heavy footsteps sounded on the stairs. "What happened?"

As William rounded the corner, June stiffened, then let out a soft moan at the sight of his wedding suit.

Amelia flashed William a smile. He filled the small corridor with his presence, and the faint woodsy scent that always clung to him helped dispel the rancid smell of sickness.

"I heard that June . . ." Though he spoke of the young prostitute, his eyes never left Amelia's face.

"June's going to be all right," Amelia told William, "but there are some things we need to talk about."

When June was once more seated on her bed and Gloria had left, Amelia turned to William, suddenly conscious that she was wearing her wedding gown. It was wrinkled and stained, and a few of the pearls that her grandmother had so painstakingly sewn to the skirt lay on the floor. This was not the wedding day she had dreamed of.

She laid her hand on William's arm, needing the reassurance of his warmth and strength. "June wants to leave Gold Landing and start a new life somewhere else," Amelia told him.

The sorrow flitted across his face so quickly that she might have missed it if she had not been watching closely, for he quickly replaced it with a calm, almost stoical expression.

"It's better for the boy," William said quietly.

"He's not going." June spoke for the first time since William had arrived.

"What does she mean?" William demanded. His eyes darkened, and Amelia caught a glimpse of hope in them.

"June has asked us to take him."

"Us?" It was one word, but it was so filled with wonder that Amelia felt tears prick her eyelids. She had made the right decision.

She nodded. "I told June we would raise him as our own, if you agreed."

William looked at June for a moment, as if assuring himself that she was serious. Then he turned and placed his hands on Amelia's shoulders. "You would do that for me?" His voice cracked with emotion.

June sobbed, covering her face with her hands. Despite everything June had done, Amelia wished there were a way to spare her the pain, but what mattered now was William.

She laid her hand on his cheek. "Yes, William. I love you, and I'll love your son as if he were mine."

"Oh, Amelia!" Heedless of the woman who sat on the bed, William drew her into his arms, and Amelia was unsure whose heart beat faster or whose tears moistened her cheek.

"He's not William's son." June's voice, harsh with tears, shattered the silence.

As if one, Amelia and William turned toward her. "What did you say?" It was William who asked the question.

"He's my son."

"Of course he's yours." Amelia understood what June was saying. She wanted them to recognize her as the boy's mother.

"Just mine," June insisted. Her face, though tearstained, was set in the stubborn lines Amelia had seen so often. "Not William's."

Maybe she had not understood June's statement. Amelia and William exchanged puzzled glances. "But I thought . . ."

June stretched her hand toward William. With an apologetic glance at Amelia, he took it.

354

"I wanted you to think you were the father," June explained. "I pretended he was yours, because more than anything on earth, I wanted that to be true." Tears welled in her eyes. "Josh is not your son."

"How can you be so sure?" William asked.

Dropping his hand, June leaned back on the pillows, as if her announcement had drained her remaining strength.

"How much do you remember of that night?" she asked, keeping her eyes fixed on William, making no attempt to hide the love she felt for him. Under other circumstances, Amelia would have been embarrassed by June's candid lust for the man who would soon be her husband, but that seemed of little importance now. What mattered was Josh's paternity.

"Not much." William spoke slowly. "I remember coming here with you and waking up in your bed. Nothing in between."

"That's because there *was* nothing in between." June's smile was bittersweet. "I tried to seduce you, but you were too drunk to do anything. Still, I figured if I got pregnant, I could pretend he was yours and you would marry me for the baby's sake."

Before William could speak, Amelia put a restraining hand on his arm. She knew William would not have married June; there was no point in hurting the woman by having William say the words aloud.

"Who is Josh's father?" she asked.

June shook her head. "I don't know. All I know is it's not William. Now, do you still want to take him?"

Amelia turned to William. Though she knew she should be happy that he had not betrayed his love for her, Amelia felt a deep sadness that now William would never have a child of his own. Still, Josh was a boy who needed their love, regardless of his parentage.

"Yes," she said.

"Yes," William agreed. "I love Josh." He took Amelia's hand in his. "We'll have Abe arrange the adoption as soon as we're married. But right now, you'd better come with me, Dr. Sheldon. We have a wedding to attend."

Epilogue

"Did you know that during the Middle Ages, people believed birds picked their mates on Valentine's Day? That's the origin of the connection between romance and this date."

Amelia started to laugh. "You've been teaching school too long, Ella," she announced. "I've delivered more babies than I can count, and this is the first time a mother's ever given me a lesson during labor."

Ella grimaced as a contraction swept over her. "It's better than thinking about the pain." She bit her lip, then screamed.

The door was flung open so violently that it slammed against the back wall. "Don't leave me, Ella," Ben cried as he burst into the room. His hair stood on end, mute testimony to the number of times he had run his fingers through it, and his spectacles perched precariously on the edge of his nose.

Amelia glared at Ben from her station at the foot of the bed. She had known he would be frantic during Ella's confinement, but he was proving worse than she had expected, interrupting each time Ella moaned. Though some women might be comforted by their husbands' concern, Ben's worries had the opposite effect, increasing the strain on Ella.

"Everything's normal, Ben," Amelia repeated for the twentieth time. "Now, leave us alone. Go play poker with William or do something constructive like filing the new patients' charts. We don't need you here."

"I'm a doctor."

Amelia smiled, remembering how Ben refused to handle maternity cases. "You're a fine doctor, but today you're an expectant father, and that means you don't belong in this room."

Amelia ushered Ben out of the room as Ella bit her pillow to muffle her scream. "Come on, Ella," she said when the door was closed. "The baby's almost here. Push now. Hard."

Only minutes later, Amelia placed a red-faced infant in Ella's arms.

"You can go back in now, Ben." Amelia walked into the parlor where Ben and William were playing cribbage. Judging from William's disgusted expression, Ben was doing little more than moving his pegs. "You have a tired but happy wife and a healthy baby girl."

Ben jumped to his feet. "They're alive? They're both alive?"

Amelia nodded. With a burst of exuberance, Ben swept her into his arms and kissed her soundly. "Thank you, Amelia."

William tapped Ben's arm. "Watch it, old man."

As Ben dropped his arms, Amelia laughed. "You can't be jealous of him, William. He's my partner." Just the week before, Ben had announced that he was making Amelia an equal partner, and they had signed the papers that morning.

"I can be jealous of any man who kisses you," William countered. "But, under the circumstances, I'll excuse Ben." He clapped the older man on the shoulder. "Congratulations!"

Amelia linked her arm through William's. "Let's go home and celebrate."

The brief winter sun had already set, and a light snow was falling. When they reached Main Street, William started to turn left. Amelia steered him to the right, toward their house.

"Don't we need to get Josh from your sister and Abe?" The boy spent days with Belinda while Amelia was on her rounds and William was at the mine.

Amelia shook her head. "He's going to spend the night with them. Belinda agreed it would be good practice. Besides, I wanted you to myself tonight."

William grinned as he opened their front door. "I like the sound of that."

Amelia led William into the parlor and handed him a bottle of champagne. "Today's a special occasion," she said.

William poured two glasses, handing one to Amelia. "Congratulations to Ben's new partner." He touched his glass to hers. "I know how much that means to you, Amelia, and I'm very proud of you. My wife, the doctor.'' He shook his head in amazement.

Amelia took a sip of the bubbly liquid. ''That's not the only thing we're celebrating.''

''You're right.'' William clinked their glasses again. Without hesitation, he said, ''To Ben and Ella's daughter.''

Amelia took another sip. ''There's more, but you're getting closer.''

This time William had to think for a moment. ''To Belinda's pregnancy,'' he said at last.

Amelia smiled. Belinda and Abe had been overjoyed when Amelia had confirmed her sister's pregnancy, and Amelia had found the news did not hurt as much as usual. Having Josh had proven an unmixed blessing. In less than six months, he had become such an integral part of her life that Amelia could not imagine being without him.

''There's more to celebrate,'' she said, ''but you're very close now.'' She smiled at William, knowing her next announcement would surprise him as much as it had her. When he raised his hands in a classic gesture of surrender, she said, ''Darling, Belinda's not the only Sheldon woman who's pregnant.''

Her words met silence as William stared at her, his eyes reflecting his confusion. ''What are you saying?''

''I'm pregnant.'' Amelia saw first disbelief, then hope cross his face. ''We're going to have a baby in late September.''

''Baby . . . September . . . but . . .'' William struggled for words. ''I thought you couldn't have children.''

Amelia's laugh filled the room. ''I guess those Philadelphia doctors made a mistake,'' she said, ''because I'm very definitely pregnant.''

She had never seen such happiness on William's face. His gray eyes sparkled, and for the first time she learned what inner radiance meant. William exuded it, as every fiber of his being seemed to glow with happiness. Not even in their moments of closest intimacy had he shown such unguarded joy.

''I can't believe it.'' With a look of wonder, he put his glass down, then placed his hand on her stomach. "Do you know how happy this makes me?"

Amelia laid her hand on top of his, protecting the new life they had created. "I know how important having a son is to you. I can't guarantee a boy, but—"

William placed his fingers on her lips to silence her. "Listen to me, sweetheart. I told you the truth when I said that adopting a child would satisfy my longing to be a father. Josh is all I need." He smiled again. "This is about you, Amelia. I'm happy for you. Happy? I'm thrilled."

William traced the contours of her lips, sending shivers of delight to each nerve ending. And while his fingers worked magic on her senses, his words set her heart aflame.

"I know how you've dreamed of experiencing every part of motherhood, and I would have given anything on earth except our life together to make that dream come true," William continued. "Darling, you've given me the finest gift a man could want. You've shown me that together we can make dreams come true."

Amelia thought her heart would burst with joy, for William's words were the sweetest she had ever heard, proof of the love he had promised her under the midnight sun.

"Oh, William, I love you!"

"Then, Mrs. Gunning," he said as he swept her into his arms and started walking toward the stairway, "may I suggest you show me how much?"

"I thought you'd never ask."

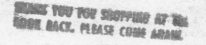

NORAH HESS

After her father's accidental death, it is up to young Fancy Cranson to keep her small family together. But to survive in the pristine woodlands of the Pacific Northwest, she has to use her brains or her body. With no other choice, Fancy vows she'll work herself to the bone before selling herself to any timberman—even one as handsome, virile, and arrogant as Chance Dawson.

From the moment Chance Dawson lays eyes on Fancy, he wants to claim her for himself. But the mighty woodsman has felled forests less stubborn than the beautiful orphan. To win her hand he has to trade his roughhewn ways for tender caresses, and brazen curses for soft words of desire. Only then will he be able to share with her a love that unites them in passionate splendor.

_3783-1 $5.99 US/$6.99 CAN

WINTER LOVE
NORAH HESS

"Norah Hess overwhelms you with characters who seem to be breathing right next to you!"
—*Romantic Times*

Winter Love. As fresh and enchanting as a new snowfall, Laura has always adored Fletcher Thomas. Yet she fears she will never win the trapper's heart—until one passion-filled night in his father's barn. Lost in his heated caresses, the innocent beauty succumbs to a desire as strong and unpredictable as a Michigan blizzard. But Laura barely clears her head of Fletch's musky scent and the sweet smell of hay before circumstances separate them and threaten to end their winter love.

__3864-1 $5.99 US/$7.99 CAN

Lacey
NORAH HESS

Norah Hess's historical romances are "delightful, tender and heartwarming reads from a special storyteller!"

—Romantic Times

Stranded on the Western frontier, Lacey Stewart suddenly has to depend on the kindness of strangers. And no one shows her more generosity than the rancher who offers to marry her. But shortly after Trey Saunders and Lacey are pronounced husband and wife, he is off to a cattle drive—and another woman's bed. Shocked to discover that the dashing groom wants her to be a pawn in a vicious game of revenge, the young firebrand refuses to obey her vows. Only when Trey proves that he loves, honors, and cherishes his blushing bride will Lacey forsake all others and unite with him in wedded bliss.

___3941-9 $5.99 US/$7.99 CAN

Hunted by the fiend who killed his illustrious cousin Crazy Horse, Black Wolf fears for the lives of his people, even as a flash flood forces him to accept the aid of gentle, golden-haired Madeline Penrod. Pursued by the madman who murdered her father to gain her hand in marriage, Maddy has no choice but to take refuge from the storm in an isolated hillside cave. But the breathtakingly virile Sioux warrior who shares her hideaway makes the nights far from lonely.

___4414-5 $5.99 US/$6.99 CAN

Dorchester Publishing Co., Inc.
P.O. Box 6640
Wayne, PA 19087-8640

Bestselling Author of *Hand & Heart of a Soldier*

With a name that belies his true nature, Joshua Angell was
born for deception. So when sophisticated and proper Ava
Moreland first sees the sexy drifter in a desolate Missouri
jail, she knows he is the one to save her sister from a ruined
reputation and a fatherless child. But she will need Angell to
fool New York society into thinking he is the ideal
husband—and only Ava can teach him how. But what start
as simple lessons in etiquette and speech soon become
smoldering lessons in love. And as the beautiful socialite's
feelings for Angell deepen, so does her passion—and finally
she knows she will never be satisfied until she, and no other,
claims him as her very own...untamed angel.

___4274-6 $4.99 US/$5.99 CAN

Dorchester Publishing Co., Inc.
P.O. Box 6640
Wayne, PA 19087-8640

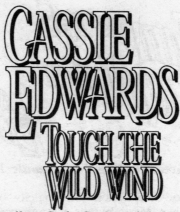

CASSIE EDWARDS
TOUCH THE WILD WIND

Alone and penniless, Sasha Seymour has thrown in her lot with a rough bunch, and she is bound for an even rougher destination—the Australian Outback, where she and her jackaroos hope to carve a sheep station from the vast, untamed wilderness. All that stands between her and the primitive forces of man and nature is the raw strength and courage of her partner—Ashton York. In his tawny arms she finds a haven from the raging storm, and in the tender fury of his kisses, a paradise of love.

____52211-X $5.50 US/$6.50 CAN

Flames of Rapture

Lark Eden

"Great reading!"—*Romantic Times*

When Lyric Solei flees the bustling city for her summer retreat in Salem, Massachusetts, it is a chance for the lovely young psychic to escape the pain so often associated with her special sight. Investigating a mysterious seaside house whose ancient secrets have long beckoned to her, Lyric stumbles upon David Langston, the house's virile new owner, whose strong arms offer her an irresistible temptation. And it is there that Lyric discovers a dusty red coat, which from the time she first lays her gifted hands on it unravels to her its tragic history—and lets her relive the timeless passion that brought it into being.

_52078-8 $4.99 US/$6.99 CAN

SONYA BIRMINGHAM

Song of the Lark

When the beautiful wisp of a mountain girl walks through his front door, Stephen Wentworth knows there is some kind of mistake. The flame-haired beauty in trousers is not the nanny he envisions for his mute son Tad. But one glance from Jubilee Jones's emerald eyes, and the widower's icy heart melts and his blood warms. Can her mountain magic soften Stephen's hardened heart, or will their love be lost in the breeze, like the song of the lark?

___4393-9 $5.50 US/$6.50 CAN